PRAISE FOR *CHILDR*

"In Marlin Barton's superb new nove[l] ... find common cause in an attempt to _____ ____ ances- tor, Rafe Anderson, and the mysterious _____ two of his newborn children, but what makes *Children of Dust* most memorable is Barton's refusal to simplify and judge. His characters are never caricatures, and they reveal that the greatest mysteries of all lie within the human heart. Marlin Barton is one of our most underrated writers, and I hope this novel gains him the attention he's long deserved."

—Ron Rash, author of *Serena* and *In the Valley*

"*Children of Dust* is a brutal and beautifully written tale of family secrets, the complications of race, and a past forever connected to the present through blood ties. Marlin Barton brilliantly transforms the tropes of the traditional Southern novel—the horror of the lost war, positionality of women, miscegenation, rigid social codes—exploring the interiority of the people who lived it and the effects of their choices on the gener- ations who came after. Though most of the novel takes place in the late nineteenth century, the present, in an ironic twist, keeps interrupting the tale of the past with ever growing urgency because for all of its focus on the past, the story is really about the present moment. The novel asks a quintessential question of Southern history: 'How can you kill (or deny) your own children?' Barton's haunting novel, which in many ways says what Faulkner could not about Southern families, answers this question with honesty, nuisance and grace."

—Jacqueline Allen Trimble, author of *American Happiness*, winner of the
Balcones Poetry Prize

"Through his complex characterizations, Marlin Barton elucidates Faulkner's adage that 'The past is never dead.' In *Children of Dust*, the past haunts the present, possessing our imaginations and revealing its violence, if not all of its mysteries. This moving literary achievement is a thoughtful reminder of the complexity of race relations and the truths that bind us."

—Anthony Grooms, author of *The Vain Conversation* and *Bombingham*,
winner of the Lillian Smith Prize

"The serenity of Southern rivers often hides a deceptively strong current, and such is the truth of Marlin Barton's novel, *Children of Dust*. Strong currents pull at the reader from the opening passages, where a new baby brings the conflicts of race, class, family ties—and possible infanticide—to the forefront. Barton's lyrical writing and his unwavering honesty draw the reader back in time and place to actions taken that bear fruit through the generations. This is a universal story, but also one very personal to Barton. That connection gives the author power and a hard won understanding of the characters. This is a rich, compelling story told with assurance and an unflinching eye. *Children of Dust* is a story for the times we live in."

–Carolyn Haines, *USA Today* bestselling author of the Sarah Booth Delaney mystery series

"I just finished Marlin Barton's intense and beautifully written novel *Children of Dust* and am full of admiration for both the book and its author. It's about many things at once—history, forgiveness, love and endurance—and while it's never didactic, there are lessons in these pages for all of us. This is a deeply moving tale by a richly gifted writer."

–Steve Yarbrough, author of *The Unmade World* and *The Realm of Last Chances*

"Marlin Barton's *Children of Dust* is so fully engaging that you plan your day around when you can continue reading. Courageous and beautifully written, the novel exposes unhealed wounds and unanswered questions that remain more than a century-and-a-half after the American Civil War. Barton brings to life a host of diverse characters whose distinctive voices dramatize the inequities of race, gender, class, and age. Viscerally real men, women, and children from the nineteenth century form a cloud of witnesses that testifies to two characters of the twenty-first century, and all of them, past and present, remain forever alive for the reader who shares their painfully felt, life-altering connection."

–Allen Wier, author of *Tehano* and *Late Night, Early Morning*

CHILDREN OF DUST

Marlin Barton

Regal House Publishing

Published by
Regal House Publishing, LLC
Raleigh, NC 27612
All rights reserved

ISBN -13 (paperback): 9781646030798
ISBN -13 (epub): 9781646031047
Library of Congress Control Number: 2020951632

Interior by Lafayette & Greene
Cover design by C. B. Royal and Lafayette & Greene
Cover images © by rck_953/Shutterstock

Regal House Publishing, LLC
https://regalhousepublishing.com

Printed in the United States of America

For my cousin, Blakely C. Barton,
whose stories of our shared family history
inform much of this book

and

for my wife, Rhonda,
who sustained me all the way through

He searches the dark windows along the front of the house and wonders if anyone is watching him, this white boy on a yellow bike who carries the same last name, Anderson, as the people who live inside, but don't own, the house. The wind cuts through his clothes, but Seth stands still, his legs straddling the crossbar of his bicycle, his cold hands gripping the curved handlebars. The day feels as gray and as old somehow as the unpainted house before him, some of its boards cracked by rot. His father has told him that original hand-hewn logs cut by freed slaves lie beneath the boards.

A Black woman steps into the dogtrot, that large passageway through the very middle of the house. He can easily see the overgrown backyard and the small cabin at the edge of the woods beyond. The woman pays him no mind, if she's even seen him, and begins to climb the steps that lead upward to the loft. She moves slowly, carries nothing, her weight her only hindrance. Then she disappears into dark space. There are no windows upstairs that he can see, not across the front, but on each end there are two, and none at all across the back. He knows this because his grandfather told him how, when a boy, he once sneaked up there, found the cases of old rifles, and took aim at first one then another of the children playing below him at the side of the yard. Before he realized who had a hold of him, his aunt, Bunyan, grabbed the gun away, the rifle still loaded and ready, just like all the others lined in their crates.

He tries to imagine now this woman with such an odd first name, tries to imagine his grandfather as a boy and the children playing in the yard below him, even tries to imagine the man who built this house, his grandfather's grandfather who left those rifles for a boy to find. They all move like shadows in his mind, shadows with voices he can almost hear and that move toward him and maybe frighten him a little, as if he owes them for something more than his very existence.

The Black woman now stares at him. She stands in the middle of the front porch, beneath the rusted tin roof, perfectly framed by the dogtrot behind her, a passageway he wishes he could walk through, but she's there, much more real than any shadow in his mind. He's not sure what to make of her expression. It isn't nice; it isn't mean. It simply says, *Yes, I'm here.*

He turns from her, sits back on his bicycle seat, and pushes against the pedals, trying to find balance in roadside dirt once rutted by wagon wheels.

ONE

The room was already hot from the fire and the flame of the coal-oil lamp, but Melinda's face and body burned with a heat of her own, hers and that of the child, who was still inside her and not wanting to come. The pains were hard, awful in their intensity, reaching so deep into her they seemed to tear at her core in a manner that went far beyond physical—and they shouldn't have been coming for *this* long, all day and into the night, not after nine other births. Annie Mae Posey, her housekeeper and a midwife, kept wiping Melinda's face and stomach with a damp cloth, her touch gentle, softer than the touch that had brought Melinda this child.

She screamed again, then asked, with the words coming between breaths, "You put—those scissors—under—the bed?"

"They for later," Annie Mae said. "They only cut the pains after the baby come. But you don't believe in that nohow."

Melinda shook her head, too tired to say how desperate for relief she was, hurting so much she needed to believe, for once, the strange mixture of Choctaw and Negro superstitions Annie Mae carried with her, as unusual a mixture as her brown and copper-colored skin now cast in firelight, shadow, and sweat.

"They finally beginning to ease again, ain't they?" Annie Mae said. "I can see it in your face."

Melinda nodded. The pains were leaving, and with them another chance for the baby's coming, which was no relief at all.

She wondered now if Rafe was anywhere inside the house still, or was he so used to the birth of his children that he didn't need to hear their first cries, even when he knew that sometimes cries, and never a single word, were all that would ever pass their lips?

But she let go of the wondering for the moment, knew that her oldest daughter, Bunyan, was just outside the door, trying to imagine the mystery within, worried, excited, waiting, ready to help care for another child, probably hoping for the day when she would have her first. Melinda remembered her saying, at twelve, "Mama, I saw my flowers," and knew who had taught her that expression.

"I'm gon' go get you some more of that tread sash tea," Annie Mae said, "help keep your body warm, help the baby come."

She let herself go limp against the damp pillow and the mattress's center, where she could feel beneath her the outlines of both herself and her husband imprinted deep into the ticking; so it was hard for her to move or raise up, as if the contour and union of their arms and legs held her down. "My body's already got plenty of heat in it," she said.

"Then maybe we gon' have to make your pains come even stronger."

"No, I'm not going to drink that other mess again. And how can they come any stronger?"

"We hadn't used it yet, not this time. Not last time neither. Might be the thing."

"You've already got it boiled?"

Annie Mae nodded.

She remembered the dirty, acrid taste of the dirt dauber tea and watched Annie Mae walk toward the door. "You're going to make me drink it." The words weren't a question.

"It's what's got to be done," she said and began to open the door.

"Look and see if Rafe's here in the house. I want to know."

Annie Mae mumbled then and Melinda could make out only the one strange word, *buckra*. She knew it meant a white man, and never sounded like it could signify anything good. She'd asked once, but Annie Mae wouldn't tell her, not even if it was Choctaw or African.

She heard Bunyan's voice beyond the door, and Annie Mae telling her, "No, child. Not yet." Then the door closed and the room closed around her as if her being alone somehow drew the walls in on her, squeezing her and the baby who would not be moved.

By the time Annie Mae returned with the tea in one hand, a bucket in the other, the pains had begun again, but she asked, through the gathering pain, "Is he in the house?"

Annie Mae shook her head. "He right outside, and not the first man to stay out the house when a baby come."

"Outside where? In your old cabin?"

"No."

"He's not with Eliza*beth*?" The pains cut off her voice at the end of the girl's name, made it catch in her throat.

"No, now go ahead, drink this," Annie Mae said, leaning in close. She helped Melinda into position, placed the bucket in her lap. The tea tasted thick, grimy with pepper, which filled her nose and the first hard sneeze came then. Soon enough the taste of bile rose in her throat, and finally, after more swallows, the retching and vomiting of the tea and whatever was left in her stomach. The contractions came hard with each retch and emptying, the pains so deep again, so private, that no outcry could truly express them, but she screamed, couldn't help herself. Annie Mae at last put the bucket aside and was ready, waiting, but still no crowning.

After the pains eventually began to slack, Melinda said what they both knew at this point. "The baby's turned wrong."

Annie Mae nodded slowly, with acceptance it seemed, and without fear. "I ain't one to turn them."

"I know."

"But we'll get that child out of you and into this world. It'll be all right."

Melinda looked away, and the walls still seemed too close.

Annie Mae sat down heavily on the foot of the bed, slipped each shoe off with a toe of the other foot, then, with some effort, swung her legs onto the bed and faced Melinda. "When they start up again, we'll be ready. You put your feet up against mine and bear down. This gon' be all about feet, ours and the baby's."

She lay back deep into the bed again and wondered if she still had bearing-down strength, or any strength at all. She well knew babies, and mothers, died in birth, sometimes both. So far the children of hers who'd died had died *after* birth, days, months, years—Anne Mary, the one girl, and three boys, gone.

The soles of Annie Mae's feet were warm, rough against her own, and so wide, as if they helped Annie Mae walk a larger path than what Melinda could make for herself. When the pains came again, Annie Mae held out her hands and Melinda took them, trusted them, squeezed so tightly around the palms she saw Annie Mae wince. The two of them were a mirror image in the angles of their bodies—knees bent, arms straight, backs arched forward. Melinda imagined Bunyan coming through the door, seeing them in such a strange and unladylike position, holding and pushing, sweating and straining. Maybe her oldest daughter would see just what it meant to be female, nothing a son could bear to witness.

Now the contractions came hard, and she pushed hard with the pain, screamed once, and entered into it with mind and body and let the pain guide her and the baby. Entering hurt, she knew, was the only way through it.

"I see a foot," Annie Mae said and shifted herself so she could get at the child. "Now I'm gon' have to push it back in a little. I got to get both feet at the same time. Just one foot won't do."

Melinda felt Annie Mae's fingers enter through the pain, felt them searching, then pulling down, the hurt widening with the baby's body, rippling and ripping through her.

"He coming, but he reaching back. I got to go in and get that arm down over his head."

She felt the deeper probing, waited, then pushed and pushed some more while Annie Mae pulled and the pains widened to a point seemingly larger than herself, kept widening, and finally, at last, the body slid down and out, and she was empty inside, delivered from the worst of the ordeal. When she heard his first cries break the air she felt some uncertain need to hold him. After a moment Annie Mae wrapped the child partially in a clean cotton blanket and placed him low on Melinda's stomach. She felt his soft wet skin against her own, smelled the deep covering scent of birth, and gently touched her fingertips against his head through the matted wisps of auburn hair. The red heat now began the slow ebb from their bodies. Against her own skin she could feel his chest rising and falling with his breaths, his closeness somehow a measure of herself, one in which she found herself lacking, and yet she wished she could claim him for herself only, but that was impossible. Rafe would always claim what was his.

"I'm gon' tie the cord now," Annie Mae said, and leaning over the child with a piece of white string in her copper fingers, she made the knot. Then Melinda saw the shining pair of scissors in her hand. "They good and sharp," Annie Mae said and cut the cord, leaving a small stump protruding from the child's belly. She wiped the blades and then leaned down beside the bed and placed the open scissors underneath. "There. Just because you don't believe don't mean it won't help."

"I'll try to believe," she said. "If you can, maybe I can too."

Melinda helped the child find her breast and nipple, a mechanical action she'd done so many times she didn't have to think about it. She had never been one to use a wet nurse, though Elizabeth, Annie Mae's daughter, was close, probably in her cabin, and able. She would not give Rafe the gift of *that* vision.

"I got to see about the afterbirth," Annie Mae said. "Yours usually turn right a loose."

Melinda then felt a contraction, and Annie Mae gently pulled, careful not to tear. The "life of the mother" some called it, which always puzzled her. Did that mean a woman's life didn't begin until a child came, or was her life something that could now be cast aside, salted and buried?

"It's coming whole," Annie Mae said, continuing at her work. "I take care of it later on, put it near all the others."

"No," Melinda said. "I don't want you to bury it this time."

Annie Mae stopped, as if startled that Melinda would interfere with what was always supposed to be done. "But if the dogs or some other animal gets it, that mean this be the last child." Annie Mae looked at her then, studied her in the fire and lamplight. Annie Mae was older, always seemed to know more than Melinda, but even though she'd delivered so many babies, Annie Mae had only the one daughter.

"This is my tenth," Melinda said and let the number say all she felt.

Annie Mae pursed her lips and the skin around her mouth tightened. "Maybe that's enough then."

But Melinda knew she wouldn't be able to break from the ritual. It didn't matter. Annie Mae understood what she had really said, and why she'd said it. She'd had too many babies, had already decided she wanted no more, but then this one came.

The fire had died down now, but the room was still warm. Melinda felt the continual pull at her nipple. He was strong, healthy. No one needed to tell her that, not Annie Mae or even a doctor.

"Mama," she heard through the door. "Can I come in now?"

"Just another minute," Annie Mae said, and then turned to Melinda. "You bleeding a little too much." Annie Mae took a clean, neatly folded cloth, one side of which, Melinda knew, was thick with spider webs, and placed it carefully between her legs. She pulled away the bloody extra bed linens, wrapped them in a bundle, then helped Melinda cover herself, made her presentable for a daughter maybe still too young to see as much as she thought she might be ready for.

"Bunyan," Melinda called, or attempted to call. She found she was too exhausted to raise her voice. "Tell her she can come in now," she said to Annie Mae, her voice somewhere above a whisper.

When Annie Mae opened the door, though, it wasn't Bunyan who stepped through but Rafe. He wore a dark box coat, and when he came near the bed, she saw that his light complexion was flushed red from the cold, although in the room's dimming light his face appeared bruised, as if he'd been in a fight.

"What is it?" he said, and it took her a moment to understand what he meant.

"A boy." She looked at him to measure his response, found herself waiting out of a kind of habit, to make sure he was pleased. She turned herself away from him.

"You all right?" he finally asked, and the question sounded like nothing more than his part of a ritual for which he cared little.

"Fine," she said, determined to play as small a role as he would allow in the repetition of this scene.

"Lost more blood than she usually do," Annie Mae said. "She wore out. Need rest, and a lot of it."

"Have you picked a name for him?" Rafe said. "I told you that you could choose again this time, just to tell me before anyone else. I know I don't have to explain why."

"Tomorrow, when I do the taking-up ceremony," Annie Mae said, "that when he get his name."

"But I need to know it first," he said, and Melinda saw the bruise on the side of his face darken, his features tighten—the blood and the muscle, his most basic of elements, quickened by Annie Mae's words, although his attention remained on Melinda. "You can choose, but if it's a name I don't care for, you'll have to choose again."

"Give me until morning," Melinda said. Then she dared herself, and added, confident in the child's strength, "If he's still living, I'll have a name ready."

"I've told you I won't abide that kind of talk. Why wouldn't he be alive? He looks plenty healthy there at your breast."

If she weren't in bed with a child, with Annie Mae so close, perhaps she wouldn't have pushed, but she felt some measure of protection. "God counts the children, of any color, mixed children too, and takes away when there's too many. He makes things balance. He could take this one."

"What makes you say that? Do you want him to?"

"Of course I don't want him to. It's experience that makes me say it." She felt her exhaustion spread even further with the thought of all that she'd just said.

"Really? Well, I've had some experience too. In four years of killing from Virginia to Mississippi, God seemed pretty damn indiscriminate."

She shifted the baby away from her breast, covering herself as best she could, the weight of him in her hands and against her body a fullness so much larger than the space he'd taken up inside her all those months. "I'll give you his name in the morning. And if it's not one you favor, I'll have another for you."

"That's all I'm asking," he said. He turned toward Annie Mae. "Then you can do the taking-up ceremony."

Annie Mae remained quiet, picked up a stick of wood from the pile on the hearth, and placed it onto the fire. When she took the heavy poker to the logs, lifting and opening them, the sudden rush of oxygen made the flames rise into a blood-red brightness.

Melinda wanted to ask if he would be sleeping in the room with her that night, not because she didn't already know the answer, but because she wanted to make him say it.

He bent to kiss her on the forehead. She let him, felt the press of his lips and the softness of his short beard against her skin. "I'd like to hold him before I go," he said and reached for the child without waiting for her response. He picked him up carefully, keeping the blanket beneath his body. For a moment she felt robbed of something whose value she couldn't measure, wasn't sure of, but he was Rafe's child, a son for a man who already had more sons, more children, than a husband should. He held the baby directly above her and against his chest, slowly rocking his body backward and forward. Annie Mae looked on as if this scene were simply what it appeared, a mother and father sharing their newborn child, but Melinda knew, as did Annie Mae, their life belied what it appeared.

He placed the child back into her arms. "Bunyan," he called as he stepped away from the bedside, and their daughter came quickly into the room and brushed past her father. Melinda saw her daughter's smile, saw her dark eyes settling on the child as she leaned forward and brushed back, with one hand, chestnut-colored hair that made Melinda think of a finely curried horse's mane. What Melinda didn't see, though, in her sixteen-year-old daughter's face, was the look of excitement she'd expected. It was as if that had been tempered by memory and a knowledge of what could happen, had happened.

"Is he all right, Mama?" she asked.

"He's all right. You don't have to worry about this one."

"What's his name going to be?"

Melinda looked over at Annie Mae, and then she realized Rafe had disappeared from the room. Annie Mae waited now, along with Bunyan.

"Jacob," she said.

Two

Annie Mae didn't wake Melinda in the night and didn't want the baby to wake her; she hoped she could prevent it. She went out to the cabin and brought Betsy to Melinda's room, saying at the door, "You stay quiet. Let that baby nurse. Melinda wore out, got to sleep, get her rest."

"But in the morning she's going to figure somebody nursed her baby," Betsy whispered, "and know it was me. I'm the last person she wants touching her baby."

"I'll be the one to tell her, maybe say I brought the baby out to you." She then gently pushed her daughter into the room and watched her walk slowly toward the crib.

She might have to hear Melinda's anger later, but as tired as Melinda was, as much blood as she'd lost, letting her sleep was more important than any scolding looks she might show Annie Mae. Or maybe Melinda would understand and forgive her, realizing she'd been trying to do her a kind turn.

Melinda did surprise her sometimes, never more than one morning years before when she'd told Annie Mae to call her by her first name, without *Miss* or *Miz* in front of it. "Only when we're alone," she'd said. "Never around Rafe, or even the children." Melinda had talked so quiet, like she was breaking a law, and in some ways she was. Annie Mae had tried to figure why. Maybe it was because she was older than Melinda, and Melinda couldn't get used to being called with respect by an older woman. She wasn't *that* much older, though. More likely it was Annie Mae's skin color, more reddish or copper than black, making her, in Melinda's eyes, something different than Negro, not bound up by all the same laws and ways for a freedman or woman. And though her father had been a slave, Annie Mae hadn't been. Finally she decided that most likely Melinda needed herself a friend, and maybe Melinda getting rid of *Miss* or *Miz* showed a kind of respect Annie Mae needed, and Melinda knew she did. She sometimes wondered, though, had Betsy come to Riverfield with her in the beginning, instead of years later, if she and Melinda would ever have reached such a time of closeness. No, they probably wouldn't have. And it surprised her they could keep any kind of friendship at all after her daughter finally did come, even one that was hidden away from all but the most watchful.

She walked out into the dogtrot now and then made her way up to the sleeping loft. She sometimes wandered the house at night, leaving her pantry-sized room off the kitchen to look out the parlor windows and see the moon in its changes—a truer keeping of time than any numbers on a calendar—or to sit at the piano bench and touch a key so softly that its sound didn't even rise above the ticking of the wall clock. Often she'd look in on the children—the two older boys, William and Henry, on one side of the loft; the two girls, Bunyan and Kate, on the other; and three-year-old Philip sleeping in his small bed near them.

She realized it was little Philip she most wanted to check on. There had been so many lost the last few years: three-month-old James, the boy R.A. and Anne Mary both at three years, R.A. dying of fever soon after she'd first come to Riverfield. The redheaded boy had just burned up from the inside out. Then the loss of the last one, only two days old, had made her especially fearful Philip might be taken, and that was when she'd begun to climb those loft steps so many nights. Of course, they weren't her children, or grandchildren, but when a child played at your feet, hugged your legs, and climbed into your lap, and was a brother or sister to your own daughter's children, how could you not find yourself fearful? Often, when going up the steps, she'd find Melinda coming down. One night, near the bottom of the stairs, Melinda placed her arms around her, held her, and whispered, "Thank you. I know you worry too."

Some nights she'd want to look in on her grandchildren out in Betsy's cabin, but there wasn't the same need somehow. Death had never taken a child of her daughter's; and if she had eased into the cabin on any given night, she knew who might have come in before her, who she might find in her daughter's bed.

The windows at the end of the boys' side of the loft let in very little light, but enough so she could now see thirteen-year-old William on the near side of the bed. Sweet William was so gentle, but he would fight ten-year-old Henry, lying just beyond him, when he had to. Henry could be mean in a way you wouldn't expect from a little boy; he was always ready to start a fight even when he knew he couldn't win. Henry might do himself in one day, she knew. He might make someone kill him. With some children, you could see their whole life run out before them while they still ran barefoot.

On the girls' side, the moonlight shone more brightly through the windows, and she was reminded how much light the nighttime world could make for itself. One of the girls was lightly snoring. She wasn't sure which, though Kate had been sick with a cold and so wouldn't be allowed near the baby until she was well. Annie Mae walked silently over to Philip's bed, leaned over him, and heard his quiet breath.

Then she caught the sound of a whisper and, turning toward the girls, eased nearer their bed.

"Is Mama all right?" It was Kate—her voice husky still—the one most likely to ask about her mother first.

"She fine. Sleeping good," Annie Mae said.

"And the baby?"

"Healthy. Now you go back to sleep. Feel better."

The words to the next question came slowly. "Is Daddy home?" Even inside the whisper she could hear the narrow hope in the girl's voice.

"Go to sleep, child," Annie Mae said and wondered herself where he might be. Night hunting with other men? Gambling or drinking? A little of all three, maybe. Or gone across the river to Demarville on some kind of night business he thought he could keep hidden no matter how much light the nighttime made for itself from the moon and the stars. But not everything stayed hidden, not even dark children a wife had never laid eyes on, children darker than Betsy's.

The cold had crept into her clothes, and the warmth of the down-stairs rooms was welcome when she entered them again. Betsy stood at Melinda's door, waiting.

"He nursed good," she whispered. "And she might have stirred a little, but she kept right on sleeping."

"Good," Annie Mae said and realized Betsy's voice sounded more relaxed now than when she'd walked into Melinda's room. "I'll come get you again before daylight."

Betsy nodded and walked quietly toward the door that opened onto the dogtrot.

Annie Mae slipped into the room and felt the child's forehead. Warm, not too hot. Now she would lie down for a while and sleep some; but she could tell herself what time to wake and knew she could judge the time just as sure as the clock hands would move toward it.

Later, she woke, still plenty tired, and this time she slipped on the burnoose Melinda had given her, pulled the hood over her head, and went again to Betsy's cabin—which had once been hers and Betsy's until Rafe moved her inside to the pantry off the kitchen—and brought her daughter once more toward the house.

"Maybe she's had enough sleep now," Betsy said, after silently following her mother across the yard. "At least enough so she can get up and let her baby nurse."

"No. Now come on. This the last time I'm gon' ask you. She'll sleep right through it." When she reached the porch she turned and saw Betsy still standing at the bottom of the steps, the moonshine bright against her light-colored skin. Annie Mae thought about just how young her daughter remained, despite the two children she'd borne, despite this woman's errand she was on. "Do you want me to bring the child out to you, out into this cold?"

"No," Betsy said and began walking up to the porch. "But it's bound to cry."

"Then hurry, go on in, see can we keep that baby quiet, not wake up Melinda." Betsy entered the house ahead of her. "If she do wake up, just put the baby down and come straight to me. I'll answer to Melinda."

Betsy then stepped into the room. For a moment Annie Mae stood, watching. Satisfied finally, she left her daughter, walked out the door to the dogtrot, and went back to her bed for a final hour of sleep.

At first she couldn't find rest. Then she dreamed of her mother, as she often did when restless, and watched herself on a bed delivering Betsy into her mother's Choctaw, midwife hands. Then, through a kind of bent time, she became her mother, delivering her child's first child into her own hands—Betsy's child lighter skinned even than Betsy.

Her bent dream-time stopped then, but it wasn't her own internal clock that woke her, nor was it any particular sound; it was movement, not across her small room but on her bed, and when wakeness took hold more strongly, she saw Melinda sitting beside her, waiting.

"He's cold." Those were her only words at first. Then, "Feels like he's been cold for hours."

Annie Mae wanted to ask, *Who? What do you mean?* But in the dim light she could see enough of Melinda's face and the way she held her body stiff to make the answer clear. There was no pushing the knowing away. "The baby," she said.

Melinda nodded.

She pushed herself up in bed, still tired, and pulled Melinda to her, one hand on her slender neck, the other across a shoulder. She felt Melinda resist at first then give way and let herself be held like some lost daughter. Her skin and hair smelled sharp from the sweat of such a long childbirth. How could it have happened again, and so quickly? She waited for Melinda's tears but none came. Too empty, she thought, as if the dirt dauber tea had taken everything inside her.

"I'll go see," she whispered. "Maybe he just..." She couldn't finish but felt Melinda nod a second time.

She made her way out of the bed and put on the burnoose that hung on the back of her door. "You want to lie down while I'm gone?" Melinda didn't answer. "Sit here like you are, if you want, or lie down. Either way all right."

"See to him," Melinda said. "Like before."

Annie Mae left her then. She found the child lying in his crib, just as he'd been earlier in the night when she'd felt his warm forehead. Now, though, he was not warm. She lit the lamp, turning it enough to burn brightly. When she turned back to the child and opened his eyes, he saw nothing before him. For a moment she wasn't sure if she should return to Melinda or prepare the child's body for burial. He might need a clean diaper, she realized, and pulled back the small blankets that covered him. She saw then brownish-red smears across his stomach and for a moment could not understand how he'd gotten dirty, his skin stained. With what? She put a finger to her tongue, rubbed clean a spot on his belly, and tasted. Blood. Thin streaks marked his blankets. But why streaks?

After taking off his diaper, she looked for any kind of wound on his body. She found none, and who could have hurt him, anyway? She took the ends of the string she'd used to tie the umbilical cord and pulled at them. They were tight, and she felt sure the bleeding hadn't been caused by any fault of her own. A relief, but one she decided was selfish.

She'd have to clean the child's body and later search him close in better light, in good daylight. Something had caused the bleeding. She kept studying the smears of blood, puzzled still, kept thinking there ought to be spots of blood, not smears.

Then she knew.

She looked around and saw, beside the bed, a few small drops of blood on the floor. She wiped at them with her fingers, then rubbed her hands together and watched as the blood disappeared into her copper touch. But there hadn't been enough blood from the baby to drip like this, she thought. This was probably birth blood from the bed linen she'd taken off before Bunyan came into the room. Still, she wasn't sure.

The fire burned low, and she looked down at the hearth and on either side of the logs, and there, beside an andiron, she saw a small strip of white, ash-dusted cloth that had not burned. For a moment she remembered again those stories her mother had told about babies who'd died only hours after birth, and how tribal doctors had blamed witchcraft to protect themselves from blame and retribution. They'd point at some old woman, or young girl, and say the one word: *witch*. Betsy must have found the child dead and panicked. Maybe she thought she could wipe off whatever blood there was with the child's blanket, then burn it. Annie Mae picked up the poker, pushed the piece of cloth into the burning coals, and watched it become smoke and vanish.

Now she had to work quickly. Melinda was waiting, needing her. She took a clean diaper and went to the water pitcher and basin that sat on a small table. The pitcher was still half filled, and she poured enough water to wet the cloth. The child—*Jacob*, she kept telling herself, *his name's Jacob, remember his name*—was difficult to handle, his body stiffening, but she moved him from one position to another with her left hand, wiping him clean with her right until his skin looked as pure as any newborn's. She dressed him in a dry diaper and wrapped him in one of the last blankets. Betsy couldn't see to get him all the way clean, she thought. Couldn't light the lamp to see, too scared she was gon' wake Melinda, and so she left the little bit of blood she didn't know about or didn't want to know about. Then Annie Mae wondered if Betsy had gotten blood on herself.

She thought about moving the child and his crib into the parlor but didn't want Melinda to see him there, not yet. That time would come later, if Rafe would allow it. Instead she moved him out of the bedroom and placed him in front of a window in the adjoining room that Rafe used as an office. The early morning light wasn't strong but it was enough to illuminate the child's face, and she told herself he looked peaceful and believed it because no infant only hours old carried enough knowing of the world to make him anything other than peaceful.

The wet, smeared diapers and blanket still had to be taken care of. She didn't want to burn them. Instead she carried the small bundle, wadded up carefully, and placed it on the back porch where she always piled clothes ready for washing in the iron pot at the back of the yard. The bloody linens from the birth were already piled there.

When Annie Mae returned to her, Melinda rose from where she lay on the bed, sat at the edge, and placed her feet on the floor as if she had to make herself ready to hear whatever Annie Mae might say.

"I had to change his diaper, clean him up a little. Then I moved him into the room next to yours." She sat down near Melinda and moved slowly closer until their bodies touched, and she knew Melinda could feel a gathering warmth between them. "He looked peaceful," she added, "the way a sleeping baby should."

"We won't say his name." Melinda spoke quietly. "Like last time. The way I learned from you."

Annie Mae nodded, understanding. She'd been taught by her mother the Choctaw belief that the names of dead children should never be spoken, and her mother, who had not once uttered the names of Annie Mae's two long-dead brothers, nor her mother's dead brother, hadn't explained why but let Annie Mae learn for herself, over time, that silence was a way to honor, not to forget. So she was proud now that Melinda wouldn't speak her child's name, though she knew the problem it would cause.

"Do you want me to go ahead and wake up the children? Tell them? They be getting up soon, anyway. Don't want Bunyan to come looking for the baby, find him by herself."

"Let them sleep as long as they will," Melinda said weakly, as though she perhaps wanted to protect them. Or it could be that she feared they would too soon fall into play and routine—the boys, at least—too used to death now to reflect her sorrow. Melinda shifted away from the edge of the bed and Annie Mae wasn't certain if she was about to rise or lie back down. "If he gets home in time enough, I'll need to tell Rafe first. He doesn't need to hear it from any of the children."

"Or from me? That what you really thinking?"

"I have to be the one to tell him," Melinda said.

"You need to eat something. Got to get you some strength. Let me take you back to bed, see if you can sleep, and then I'll have you some breakfast and you can eat what of it you will. If the children come down, I'll just have to tell them," she said, then added, "Mr. Rafe too." She'd never allowed herself to drop the *mister*, not even when she and Melinda were alone. There was something too frightening in the idea of speaking his name so plainly, but she would not let herself think *mister*, would not give him that respect. And she did not use the word when she talked to Betsy about him.

She helped Melinda back to her room and into bed, pulled the covers to her neck, and gently stroked her forehead. "Just sleep for a while."

"But when I wake up, I'll have to live it all over again."

Annie Mae didn't try to answer such a plainspoken truth.

Instead of heading toward the kitchen, she walked out of the dogtrot and down the back porch steps. When she reached her daughter's door she didn't knock and didn't expect to find Rafe inside. He wasn't. Betsy stood at her fireplace nursing Lakeview, her youngest, and little George lay on a pallet on the floor. Betsy didn't seem surprised that she'd entered the cabin so suddenly. In fact, her daughter looked as if she'd been waiting.

"When you finish nursing that girl child, close up the front of your dress and let me have a look at it," she said.

Betsy lifted her gaze from Lakeview's small body. "Why?" she said and met Annie Mae's eyes for what might have been the first time since Annie Mae had come to ask her to nurse Melinda's newborn.

"To see if there's blood on it."

"I didn't," Betsy began and then lowered her child's body, held her carefully cradled in her arms still, and took two steps toward the rough-made crib and placed Lakeview inside it. "I don't know what happened," she said finally, quietly, as if she were trying not to bear witness to something she couldn't have imagined beforehand. "It was awful."

"What? You know something. Tell me what happened." She went to her daughter then, and Betsy reached for her the way all mothers inwardly hope, in weak moments, their children will always reach for them, maybe all the more when a mother and daughter have suffered years apart. Now Betsy's bare, full breast and milk-wet nipple no longer seemed a sign of womanhood but one of a naked helplessness.

"I nursed him just like you told me to. He was fine," she said in that proper voice Annie Mae still could not get used to, one she knew was so different from her own way of talking.

"Both times? You nursed him both times?"

Betsy pulled away now, covered herself—the front of her dress not stained with blood—and looked down at George crawling on his pallet, then back up. "No, just the first time. He was dead when I went back."

"Did you drop him?"

"No. I swear. I held him good."

"So when you went back in, how did you know he had blood on him? It was too dark to see."

"I felt it, knew what it was."

"You not making sense. How did you know?"

"I just did. It was slick. Didn't smell like pee. But it wasn't that much, not enough for him to have bled to death." Betsy moved away from her, closer to the fire's heat. Lakeview made a few muffled cries, and George reached toward his mother's feet.

"How come it is you didn't come tell me what had happened?"

"I don't know. Too scared. I thought I'd had him cleaned good, thought Miss Melinda would just find him like she found the last one."

"You should of told me. I cleaned him up, after you. And now I got to get him ready to bury, see if we can bury him proper or not. If Rafe let us this time."

Seeing to the burial wasn't something Annie Mae wanted to fall on her, but she'd buried the last one, dug the grave herself that was without a marker still, and it might well be this one would have no marker either.

Maybe it wasn't only the gift of helping children into the world that had been passed down through her mother's blood and hands. Her mother's mother had been the only woman in their tribe chosen as a bone-picker, one who cleaned the bones of the dead and then placed them in a hamper and carried them to the bone house with the wailing family walking behind. She'd even cleaned the bones of her own dead son. Maybe Annie Mae held in her hands an ability with the dead too. Hadn't she already this morning cleaned a child's hardening limbs? But that *wasn't* for burial. What she'd done this morning had been for her daughter's sake only, not for the dead and mourning.

"Was there anything wrong with that baby?" she said now. "Anything that didn't seem right about him?"

Betsy looked at her hands a moment, then dropped them to her sides. "I felt something," she said, "when I was first nursing him."

"What?"

"Something in my fingers."

"You not making sense again. What was it? His cord stump? Something with his cord? You pull at it?"

"I don't know. Whatever it was, I left it alone. He kept right on nursing. Then I put him down, covered him up again so he'd stay warm."

"You cut that child with something? Them scissors? Tell me!"

"I didn't hurt that baby. Rafe would kill me for such a thing. Maybe he hemorrhaged after I put him down."

"You take his breath when he *didn't* bleed to death? That what you done?"

"No. How can you think that?"

Annie Mae heard the door then, knew who it was without having to look, thought *buckra*, and as the door swung open, she felt something close between her and her daughter, as if whatever knowing Betsy held was wrapped so tightly in her fist it couldn't be pulled free.

THREE

Rafe stared out the window but saw nothing before him, not the woods behind the house nor Betsy's cabin, and his mind felt as empty as his vision. He finally made himself concentrate on the closed cabin door he'd left standing open not half an hour earlier. Staring at it slowly made the door real. It was the small weight he held in his arms that didn't feel real, just as his wife's refusal didn't feel real. But why hadn't it? She'd refused him before, had not told him the previous dead child's name, and only moments ago refused once again to name for him this dead son he held.

Rafe gently laid the body back where he knew Annie Mae had placed it, probably hoping he would see the child there before anyone prepared him for it. The child's arms and legs held themselves stone still at his sides, his face turned straight ahead, as if he lay at full attention. Maybe it never occurred to Melinda or Annie Mae he needed preparing, and he could almost understand that, but just because you'd seen more dead bodies than you could ever count, and at all peculiar angles of repose, didn't mean the sight of your own dead child would not leave you visionless for one empty moment, no matter what others might think.

He hadn't raised his voice to Melinda, had not damned her, or struck her—the one thing he'd never done, though she had once told him she'd prefer it over any other punishment or shame he might lay upon her. No, once he understood she wouldn't tell him his child's name, he'd walked out, slammed the door behind him, and come in here to see the still body, to make himself face, once again, what had been visited upon a child of his. Always his and Melinda's, not either of Betsy's, or Virginia's, the darkest of his children. Maybe God did make things balance. But he pushed the thought from his mind. Nothing in the world ever balanced, and God's hand hadn't touched the dead infant he looked on now and who did not look back at him. Its eyes had been closed, touched only by some human hand, probably Annie Mae's. He couldn't recall their color, if he had noticed it—and he didn't want to open the child's dead vision, didn't want to see the same lost stare and the vision it would bring of those fallen in the aftermath of every skirmish and battle in which he'd fought.

Before he turned away, he touched the boy's porcelain cheek and then put his hand to his own warm face, feeling the coldness of his son's body in his rough fingertips.

"Daddy," he heard then, and despite the huskiness, he recognized which daughter approached him. He hadn't known she was sick.

"Don't come in here, Kate," he said and moved his body enough to better block her view of the child. "You don't want to see this."

She continued toward him, coughed once into her delicate hand, and then stopped. "I've seen it before," she said. "The last one, I mean, in the parlor where he was laid out, before…" Her voice trailed off as if fading with the memory she didn't want to recall.

"Before I made Annie Mae take him out of there."

"Yes, sir," she said, still trying to look beyond him, or at least, for the moment, not look into his eyes.

"Well, you won't see this one in there." He met her gaze then, her pale brown eyes that reminded him of her mother. And like her mother's eyes, they always appeared to accuse him, though Kate seemed unaware this was so, which made her all the more difficult to face. In fact, she was the only one who had such a strong effect on him, and he was mostly puzzled as to why. "Do you know this child's name?" he finally asked.

"No, Daddy," she answered and did not look away.

"Your sister know? Have you two talked? I want to know my own child's name."

"If she knows, she didn't tell me." She held her stare a moment longer, then looked toward the top of the window and at the growing light that colored its panes.

"How'd you know the child was in here?"

"I heard Mama crying, then heard your footsteps, and when I looked in and saw you standing there holding him, I knew what I was afraid of had happened."

He only nodded, realizing she had not mentioned the sound of the slamming door. She seemed to be waiting for him now, to see what he might do. A level of what might be called fear, of a different kind from a moment before, registered on her face. He could raise his voice, order her from the room, and almost did. Instead, he gentled his words as much as he knew how. "I'm sorry this happened, sorry for all of us. I don't have an answer for it, but I want one."

He then walked to her, touched her shoulder, and without another word left her alone in the room with the brother she would never know, except, perhaps, his name.

The barn sat beyond Betsy's cabin, and the back of it opened onto a fenced horse pasture where his chestnut stallion, Wheeler, grazed in warm weather, along with a mare, Mollie B., and a roan-colored gelding named Benjamin. They were in their stalls now, along with the two mules, Ida and Ned, plain names to match their station in life. He'd fed them all earlier, before Annie Mae and Betsy told him about the child. He hoped Samuel would realize they'd been fed and wouldn't feed them again when he came. But he would probably see Samuel first anyway.

He walked to the one empty stall where he stored lumber and tools, chose the best pieces of pine he had on hand, and pulled out the sawhorses. It wouldn't be fancy, just squared at both ends, but it would hold what it had to. He'd made the last one too, but he'd made Annie Mae dig the grave, punishment for her small silence. What would he do with her now? It was the Choctaw in her that gave her such strange ideas, the same Choctaw blood that in Betsy had made his blood rise when he first saw her.

He measured the pieces of pine and marked with the end of a nail where he'd need to make his cuts. He soon had the longer pieces done, then sawed the squares for both ends. He wouldn't use hinges. Once he placed the body inside, he would simply nail the lid shut, sealing the child into darkness that would hold its own place under the ground until the pine finally rotted.

As he began to nail the pieces, he realized the sound of hammer against each square nail head would be nothing less than a call to his sons, who would have to see what work Samuel or their father might be engaged in. No boy could resist the sound of a hammer, and he was glad his sons were no exception.

Henry arrived first. He stood there just inside the barn doors watching with dark eyes that peeked out from under hair grown over long and that his mother should have already cut. He wore no coat, which meant he'd slipped out of the house on his own. Rafe would not send the boy back inside. He could learn for himself how to dress for the cold, but for now Henry would most likely tough it out, never admit he needed the warmth of a fire.

"What you making, Papa?" he asked, no longer able to stand quietly.

Rafe was about to answer when William walked in. "It looks like

Father's making a coffin," he said, his words spoken simply, as if all events and undertakings were of equal weight and had to be accepted for what they were.

"Why?" Henry said, not looking at his brother, whom he ignored, but at his father.

"Because Mother's baby died," William said, his voice still calm.

"Again?"

William walked closer to the two of them, hands in coat pockets, his light complexion flushed red with cold that somehow made the small, crescent-shaped birthmark on his neck more pronounced. "He didn't die *again*. You can only die once. The last one died and now this one died."

Henry turned to his brother in a sudden manner that suggested he was about to turn on him. "I know that. Nobody can die twice. I'm not stupid."

"Didn't say you were."

Rafe looked up from his work again, recognizing that Henry was about to move past words. "Boys, don't be waking snakes."

"Yes, sir," they both said, their attention drawn away from each other and converging on their father.

On another day, under different circumstances, he might have held his own tongue and let them go at it. Boys and brothers had to fight, and Henry was a fighter. Rafe could see it in his every movement, his strong will residing in each small limb, even down into fingers that seemed always curled into tight fists. The only time he saw Henry gentle himself was with Philip, some bond there Rafe did not fully understand, one that went deeper even than what Kate and Bunyan naturally showed for the youngest child they could play mother to. Maybe Henry's bond with Philip had more to do with Henry feeling superior to a younger brother he didn't yet see as a threat. And yet there *was* gentleness there. More than once he'd seen Henry leading Philip by the hand.

"Don't be so sure," Rafe said now.

"Of what?" William asked and moved closer to his father.

"I've seen men die twice."

Henry looked at him wide-eyed; William, too, appeared skeptical, but no thirteen-year-old was ever ready to discount mystery if it was stated boldly enough.

"In the war?" Henry said, clearly hoping for an explanation that wasn't beyond his understanding.

Rafe slowly nodded at both of them, the hammer hanging still in his lowered right hand, his left holding on to the unfinished coffin. "That's right. I saw men rise up after lying three days in the field of the dead. Then didn't take another last breath until we threw dirt of top of them."

"Three days," William said, as if drawing some conclusion he didn't know how to speak.

"Like Jesus," Henry said.

"No, not like Jesus, just like men who didn't know they'd died until we filled their mouths with dirt."

Henry stood still in hard thought. "Will the baby take one more breath?" he asked as though trying to understand the connection between a field of dead soldiers and his mother's child.

"He already did," William said and Rafe, for a moment, was unable to raise the tool in his right hand so struck was he that his oldest son could answer for him in the same way he would have answered.

"Where's your brother?" Rafe asked.

"With the girls," Henry said, seemingly disappointed at having to give such a reply.

"Henry, you're not going to let Kate and Bunyan turn him into a gal-boy are you?"

"No, sir," Henry said, and Rafe saw his small fists tighten.

"Maybe my oldest son can make sure that doesn't happen."

William looked up from the hammer in his father's hand. "Yes, sir," he said, and Rafe knew he'd gotten his son's attention.

Samuel appeared in the barn then, and Rafe was surprised he hadn't heard Samuel's approach. Perhaps he'd been too attentive to his sons. To remain unaware of another man's advance was to invite one's own demise, and this wasn't the first time Samuel had come upon him in such a fashion, though Rafe had been careful on each occasion not to acknowledge the surprise.

"Was wondering when you'd get here."

"Yes, sir," Samuel said, though not admitting to any lateness because no matter Rafe's implication, they both knew Samuel wasn't late.

Still, he pushed the suggestion further. "I've already done the feeding."

"Yes, sir." Samuel finally looked away from Rafe in a narrow show of respect that was almost too little for Rafe to let pass.

"Boys, y'all might run along now."

"Yes, sir," they both said, quickly and firmly, and walked past Samuel nodding hello as they did but perhaps sensing somehow that this wasn't a time to talk with Samuel as they normally would have. Then, after a few more steps, William stopped and, turning back toward Rafe, stood a moment, hesitant. "Will there be a funeral this time?"

Rafe knew it had taken some gumption for the boy to ask the question. "That would be up to your mother. I'm not going to have a funeral and a proper burial in a graveyard if there's no name to put on a marker."

"Yes, sir," William said and turned away, leaving Rafe unsure if he'd allowed William some level of impudence he shouldn't have.

He focused on Samuel now. "I suppose you know the baby died." Samuel nodded slightly. "You must have been in the house already."

"No, sir, not the house."

"Where then?" Rafe asked but had already guessed the answer.

"Betsy, she give me some coffee."

"She usually do that?"

Samuel tightened his arms over the sides of his worn coat. "When it cold."

"You go in her cabin?"

"Yes, sir. Sometime." He paused a moment, maybe a moment too long. "Sometime not."

Rafe drove in the last nail, except for the four he'd use to secure the lid. "I thought maybe you were still young enough not to let the cold bother you." Samuel didn't answer. He merely looked at Rafe and then up toward the loft, as if he might be trying to remember how much hay was stored in its space. "Don't be going in there no more. Drink her coffee outside, you hear? If she brings you any."

"Yes, sir."

"After you clean these stalls, I want you to take the shovel to Annie Mae. Tell her I said she'd know what it's for. Then you can split some wood."

"I'm sorry," Samuel said and looked down at his feet in a way that seemed practiced but still unnatural to him.

Rafe felt confused, as if Samuel had just spoken some riddle he could not puzzle out. "Sorry for what?"

"Miss Melinda's baby."

"Oh," he said, still with a sense of confusion. "It ain't your fault. What you got to feel sorry about?"

"Nothing, I reckon." He walked over to the shovel where it leaned between Wheeler and Benjamin's stall doors. Wheeler, who'd remained unusually quiet, now lowered and raised his head at Samuel's approach, blowing out a breath, as if to remind them both he was present and should be attended to, suggesting somehow with short, dismissive jerks of his head that nothing he'd heard or witnessed was of any great importance. Rafe recalled then, as he laid down his hammer, the calm weariness with which his various mounts during the war had carried him through the fields of soldiers who'd fallen and waited to die again.

When he entered their room for the second time that morning, he found Melinda still in bed and Annie Mae trying to feed her from a tray. "A little more," she said, holding a fork full of fried egg.

Melinda, who sat up against the headboard, shook her head. "I've eaten enough."

"But you so empty."

Melinda looked at Rafe then, and Annie Mae must have followed her gaze because she turned on the bed enough for Rafe to see the side of her face and the corner of her watchful eye.

"Samuel's going to be looking for you in a little while, Annie Mae," he said. "Soon as he finishes in the barn."

"He know where to find me," she said and, because she didn't ask why he'd be looking for her, Rafe wondered if she had already guessed at the reason. Clearly she wasn't going to give him the satisfaction of asking.

"He'll have a shovel for you."

She turned back toward Melinda, the fork still in her hand, but Melinda remained motionless, her mouth closed.

"That's enough," he said. "Take the food. Leave us alone." Annie Mae rose, placed the fork on the plate, and picked up the teakwood tray. Her movements were slow, maybe too deliberate. She didn't speak, except for a brief whisper to Melinda. "Where's the child now?" he asked.

Annie Mae stood facing Rafe. "Must be in your office still."

"Good. Don't be going in there and don't carry him to the parlor. No one will be coming for a viewing. He'll be buried before dark, long before."

She looked past him, toward the door. He let her pass, and something in her silence and her carriage spoke with a familial authority, reminding him in a way he didn't often consider that she was grandmother to two of his children, that their blood was immixed in Lakeview and George, two children who appeared as hardy as mix-bred calves that could survive sickness in winter when purity might mean death.

Melinda, still sitting up, looked pale, ashen even. Was there some weakness in her that his blood couldn't overcome? Five of their children had lived, five hadn't, these last two dying so quickly. What was to account for that? His other children were all healthy, and the very darkest of them—Fannie and Walter, Virginia's children, almost as dark as their mother—both thrived. He'd seen them last night, felt them squirm in his lap, laughing, while their mother sulked across the room. And every morning he saw Lakeview and George, they were already awake, one playing, the other still nursing.

Maybe mixed blood created balance. Melinda had said something about balance herself. Five and five. There was balance, though he knew Melinda had meant something else, something beyond the two of them—an implication, or accusation, that he'd upset the scale that measured the life in their home. George was born, and a child with no name died. Lakeview came, and now another nameless child was taken. Did God's careless hand create *that* balance? He didn't think so.

And some of the five had lived longer than merely hours or a day. There was R.A., dead of fever at three years and James dead at three months, both after dark Fannie came from Virginia's womb. And Anne Mary, made over in her mother's image even more than Kate, also dead at three years, right after Virginia's Walter came—Walter as dark as his sister but with hair already showing red curls rather than black kinks.

"You've made a coffin?" Melinda asked now. Her body appeared taut, stiff.

"If you want to use that word." He turned toward the fire and stoked it.

"Why wouldn't I?" She spoke softly but there was a firmness he heard in the shape of her words that echoed her body's posture.

"Because it looks more like a box than a coffin, one you might use to ship something on a steamer."

"I see."

He started to tell her she didn't see anything, that it didn't have to be this way. He could go to Demarville, purchase a finely made coffin, one built to size that did more than simply hold; it would offer *containment*, comfort even, in its padded insides and polished wood. But he didn't really believe this and remained quiet for the moment. Besides, such an offer wouldn't have drawn the child's name from her.

She still did not sink into the bed or burrow down into the covers. He wondered what held her up. Whatever it was, a part of him wanted to make her cower again and knew he could, just as surely as he'd stoked the flames at the hearth until they threw heat into the room.

"Did you see to the child in the night?" It was a question he hadn't asked of her earlier, but now, after having time to think, he wanted to know more.

"Yes," she said. "I got up. He wasn't crying, but I held him, tried to get him to nurse. He wasn't ready. I put him down and barely made it back to the bed."

"And he was all right then?"

"Yes, all right." She spoke his words back to him as if she were too reduced to offer her own.

"What about later?" he said, looking down at her, studying her face and body, seeing finally some odd disproportion that took a moment for him to comprehend—the full breasts against her thinness, suggesting weakness but strength enough; strength to do what? he wondered.

"*She* came in."

She could only mean one person, but he asked anyway.

"Something woke me, and I saw her there, letting the child nurse."

"Did you speak to her?"

She closed her eyes, turning away as if shamed. "No," she said, her voice sounding more fragile.

"Why not?"

Still she wouldn't look at him, and he wondered if she was ashamed of what she hadn't done, or perhaps of something she had.

She looked far away, not through a window but at what might be some distant memory or a blank place in her mind, if she could find one. "I knew Annie Mae must have brought her in. So I let her." She looked at him now, saw him, he felt, in a way she hadn't earlier. "I was too weary to shout at her." She took a slow breath. "So I trusted Annie Mae."

"Did you ever get up again, check on him?"

"Only when I found him dead."

"What about Betsy? You see her again?"

"No," she said and would not look at him when she spoke.

"Is there anything else you can tell me? Anything else you did?"

Now she let go of herself, let her shoulders and head settle forward, found her way deeper beneath the quilts, kept lowering her thin body.

He stepped from the dogtrot and onto the back porch, noticing again the pile of blood-soaked linens at the edge. Annie Mae needed to get those washed, soon. They were nothing he wanted to keep looking at. Then he heard voices and knew what he would see before he looked up. There stood Samuel at Betsy's door, a cup to his lips, the shovel leaning near the door; and there was Betsy, turning and looking at where he stood on the porch.

Rafe didn't use the steps but made the small jump to the ground and walked in a forward lean, the two quiet now, still, not daring to move or look away or at each other, the cup Samuel held raised partway between them, its steam rising into the air, heat made visible in front of their faces.

Rafe timed his last step forward with the drawing back of his right hand across his body. He swung, first his knuckles and then the back of his fingers striking the tin cup. A dull ring sounded and the cup spun into the air above their heads, the coffee cast into a black arc. "You've had your goddamn coffee. I believe I gave you some work to do."

"Yes, sir," Samuel said and looked down. "I didn't go inside. She brung it out."

"Did I ask you?"

"No, sir."

Betsy didn't speak, but he recognized her anger, the quietness of it. He knew it could not equal his, and so it was of no concern to him.

"Take the shovel to the back door. Tell Annie Mae to dig the grave beside the other one. Do it now."

"Yes, sir." Samuel walked to the shovel, and Rafe listened for any word beneath his breath but heard none.

"Four feet will be deep enough," he said to Samuel's back. "Tell her."

"Yes, sir, I tell her." He continued toward the house as though on a simple daily errand, but Rafe knew whose grave Samuel wanted to dig.

He heard Lakeview's irritated crying from inside the cabin. "Go in and see to her," he said.

"She probably needs changing."

Betsy entered the house and he followed, placed his hand to the small of her back, and pushed her toward the crib. She slowed enough so there was a physical tension between them, a resistance expressed. The first time he'd placed his hand against her back, it had been bare. There had been a different kind of tension between them then, or maybe not so different.

He picked George up from the blanket on the floor. "Papa," the boy said with a smile, his brown eyes widening with pleasure. Rafe sat down at the table of rough lumber, his straight-back chair fashioned from white oak splits. He held the boy, let him settle into his lap. Betsy changed Lakeview on her bed, placed her back in the crib, and took the chair across from him.

"I don't want you inviting him in again."

"I won't and didn't this time. Just brought him coffee with a little molasses in it."

"Guess you know how he likes it."

She didn't respond, and he did not expect her to. She was young but smart enough to know when to let things be with him. Her silence was where her strength showed itself. It had taken a while for him to see that in her. She wasn't so unsure of herself as she sometimes appeared.

"Miss Melinda saw you nurse the child." He spoke over the top of George's head, then leaned the boy back against his chest.

She didn't show any surprise or fear. "Mama said Miss Melinda needed rest. I didn't want to, but I did what she told me."

"Did anything seem wrong with the child? Was he weak, not breathing right?"

She moved a hand to the edge of the table, gripped it, but kept looking his way. "He was fine. Nursed good. Then I put him down."

He was quiet a moment, and so was she. The baby made small noises in her own little language.

"Did you know Miss Melinda saw you?"

"I thought she was asleep. She didn't make a sound."

He stood then, walked his son back over to the blanket on the floor, and let the boy climb down. Betsy watched him, perhaps wondering what he might ask next. He moved toward her until his legs were pressed against the chair and the side of her body. She looked up at him with what appeared to be anticipation, and he folded his arms tightly across his chest. "What happened?"

"I don't know," she said. "Sometimes babies die."

"But more die here. Why is that?"

"Only two. The others was children, not babies."

"At three months, James was still a baby."

"But not a newborn is what I meant."

"No," he said. He lowered himself to her eye level, leaned in close enough to smell some sweet scent on her skin, and watched her pull away from him. "You think Miss Melinda hurt that child, did something to him?" She didn't look away but remained silent, appearing to give his question hard thought, almost as if she were coming back to it because the question had already occurred to her.

"I don't reckon so," she said finally. "She doesn't seem like somebody who'd do such a thing as that. And she loves her other children." He saw her look first toward George, then at Lakeview lying in her crib, and finally back at him. "I can see why she might have, though, or why some women might. Babies can be a trial for some, or one too many can."

He closed his eyes then and held them shut, as if he might have just heard some truth confirmed, one he was not ready to accept, not for Melinda or for himself.

FOUR

The top of the ground was frozen, but she'd broken through, and while Annie Mae dug the narrow hole, she thought not of death but of birth—how a child emerged wet and wanting into the world, the way the Choctaw, as her mother had told her, emerged from under Nanih Waiya, a great mound that marked the site of her people's creation. They'd come forth from a hole under the mound, gathered around each tall side, and waited to dry before they went and found their place in the world.

She turned now and saw Bunyan and Philip approach and stand near the side of the small hole, and she wondered what they waited for.

"Is Daddy making you dig this one too?"

She didn't reply but kept digging. Bunyan had to already know the answer. Philip stepped closer, curious, as if this hole might be for him, and he wanted to make sense out of it. Annie Mae dropped a shovelful of dirt near his feet, and he picked up a clod of it and held it to his nose.

"Don't be eating that," she said. "Some women with a baby on the way, *they* might eat a little. Say it taste cheese-like, even put a little salt on it."

Philip looked at her as if nothing made sense to him now, not dirt eating or why she might be digging a hole at the edge of the horse pasture. "I don't want to eat none," he said and dropped the clod back at his feet. Annie Mae noticed that half the buttons on one of his shoes weren't fastened all the way up. Bunyan was usually more careful than that.

"Kate told me she saw the baby," Bunyan said, "but I don't want to."

"That best, child. You don't need to see him."

Bunyan pulled her hair away from her mouth where a wind had blown it. "Where is he now?"

"Gone from where I left him." She had finally looked back in the room, despite the fact that Rafe had told her not to. She'd wanted to look at him closely. "Your daddy may have done put him in the box he made."

Annie Mae kept digging, needing to bend down farther and farther to reach the deepening bottom. The hole was not large enough for her to step into and still have room to work. Soon she would have to get down on her knees at the edge and put her back and shoulders into each thrust with no help from her feet and legs. The work would then feel most like what it was—punishment for her small silence. If only Rafe knew what larger silence she kept, what she'd already washed out of the diaper and linens that now soaked in the iron wash pot over a fire.

She stopped, wiped cold sweat from her face, and looked up the rise and toward the back of the barn. Here came Henry, William not far behind, then Kate, like some funeral procession with the grown-ups left out. It was unusual to see them all gathered together, unless they sat at the long dining table ready to eat. Most times they were spread here and there, the girls meandering through the house or one of them gone to the store their daddy owned, hoping to find him there but usually not; the two older boys tended to travel farther—into the woods, down to the creek, watching trains come at the depot, sometimes together, most times not.

Henry came up behind Philip, took his hand, and pulled him away from Bunyan.

"Annie Mae," William said from behind her, "I can dig for you."

"No, honey, you can't," she said and finally got down on her knees, the hard crust of ground cutting through her dress. The cold would soon be wicking its way into her bones.

"I can dig better than William. Let me," Henry said and stared up at his brother.

She knew William wouldn't say anything back at Henry, and he didn't. It would take more than that. "No, child, I got to do this. I'll have it done directly."

Kate coughed twice, each visible in the cold air but not as deep as a few days ago. "Papa should have Samuel do it, not you."

Annie Mae stopped and looked at the small gathering around her, these white children she knelt before. They stood still, quiet. Something was rising in them, though. She felt it. They watched her with such serious faces, as if they were studying hard on what to do, how to help her—when they ought to be with their mother, she thought, or at least so ought Kate and Bunyan. Philip slipped down into the hole, picked up loose clods in each hand, and threw them onto the mound of dirt she'd made. Henry came quickly after him, but instead of lifting his brother out, he too took handfuls of dirt and scooped them up, the two brothers so crowded they could hardly reach down.

"You two boys got to let me work," Annie Mae said, though the sight of them helping moved her.

"Henry, get Philip out of there." Bunyan already sounded so much like a mother. "Y'all going to get Annie Mae in trouble."

"Shut up," Henry said.

"I'm not going to tell you again. Get Philip out."

Henry threw a handful of dirt at Bunyan's shoes. And when William reached down, Annie Mae knew that what she'd felt rising was about to turn into something else. William grabbed Henry under both arms, probably harder than he needed to, and dragged him out. Henry squirmed and kicked. As soon as his feet found solid ground, Annie Mae called out, "Stop that," but Henry was already drawing back. He punched William in the stomach, then head-butted him. William shoved.

"You little son of a bitch," William said, and Henry hit the ground, back first, then head. Annie Mae struggled to her feet, dropping the shovel across the hole, but Bunyan was already at Henry, holding him down. As she squatted, Annie Mae noticed how wide Bunyan's hips had become.

"If you don't stop, I'll spank you myself," Bunyan said.

"Go ahead and let him up." William stood over the both of them, but Bunyan held him still, waiting, Annie Mae knew, for some of the fight to leave him.

"Back away, William," Bunyan said but kept all her attention on Henry. She knew how quick he was.

Annie Mae went over to William, placed a hand on his shoulder, and gently pulled him back a few steps. "Don't you be talking so ugly. You even cussed your mama. You know that, don't you? I can't have that."

"No, ma'am. I'm sorry."

She turned his face toward her and smiled at him. He was the only one of them who called her *ma'am*. "All right then," she said.

Annie Mae picked up her shovel and, slowly sinking again to her knees, saw Henry come to stand at the end of the hole again. Still some fight left in him. She could see it. Then she imagined a grave marker where he stood, though she knew good and well one would never stand at this grave. The marker she imagined was cut at an angle across the top for a life cut short. She shook her head and Henry watched, his face a question, as if she knew something about him he did not know and never would.

"There's Papa," Kate said in a low voice that barely marked the air in front of her.

Annie Mae, despite herself, turned just enough to see him standing on top of the little rise on which the barn sat. She realized he'd watched it all and didn't seem to mind that he'd allowed a fight on a day of sorrow. He then walked into the barn, disappearing inside its shadowed insides.

"So is Mama by herself?" Kate asked.

Though she knew it wasn't really a question that needed answering, Annie Mae did answer. "You know she is, and she shouldn't be, Kate."

In a moment the sound of hammering began, and Annie Mae and the children stopped to listen. It rang out of the open barn doors. She counted. First one nail, then another. Finally a third and a fourth. Then the quiet that signified something finished.

Soon Annie Mae would have to begin cooking noon dinner. Bunyan, before she'd brought Philip outside, had fixed all the children breakfast, biscuits and eggs, while Annie Mae tended to the more grievous chore. She'd left the shovel beside the grave, its handle leaning at a low angle against the mound of dirt, ready, waiting for a second use. She hoped she wouldn't be the one to lift it again, not this day. One thing she'd wanted to do, now she couldn't. The child was sealed up, and she could not look at him again, could not check his body in better light—or maybe she just hadn't wanted to find the opportunity—but now, at least, no one else could either.

She placed more wood in the cook stove, then decided she'd have to go in and see to Melinda. Once the fire caught up good, she closed the stove door, and then saw Melinda, who had slipped in and was sitting at the small table as if she'd been watching her through tired eyes for some time, though it couldn't have been long.

"Didn't mean to startle you."

"You didn't," Annie Mae said.

Melinda pulled the blue robe tighter around her body, re-tied the sash with slow movements. "I heard more hammering a while ago." She was quiet a moment. "He isn't buried yet?"

Annie Mae sat down across from her, felt the rising heat of the stove at her back. "I don't think so."

"He had you dig."

Annie Mae nodded. "Down in the horse pasture, beside where the other one is."

"I'm sorry. He should have done it himself. Or if I had just told him."

"No." Annie Mae leaned toward her and took her hand, which was warmer to the touch than she'd expected.

"We could still have a church burial," Melinda said.

"It's dug now. He don't need telling. You got to keep something for yourself."

Annie Mae let go of her hand, and she waited to see what Melinda might tell her. Before she'd walked down into the pasture with the shovel, Betsy had stopped her in front of the cabin, said Rafe told her Melinda had been awake, had *seen* her nurse the baby. How much more had she seen? Annie Mae could only sit now and wait for the silence to fill with whatever Melinda might say.

"Bunyan and Kate came in to see me."

"They should have already done been in."

Melinda shook her head, put a hand to the bottom of her throat. "Children don't know how to handle death."

They've had the times to learn, Annie Mae thought, but she knew a mother had to make allowances, had to forgive, sometimes without ever even realizing she'd offered forgiveness, and the children never knowing they'd accepted it—so much remained unspoken between a mother and her children, choices made before conscious thought.

"I know you were trying to help me," Melinda said. "With the baby, I mean."

Annie Mae tightened her grip on the chair seat and pushed herself backward. Whatever was coming, now was the time. She kept quiet, afraid she might say more than she should, or needed to. She couldn't show her fear.

"She didn't wake me. I know she didn't want to come in, that you pushed her. I saw that. And you knew even if I didn't see her, I'd figure out the baby had nursed."

Annie Mae placed her forearms on the table and tried her best to keep herself and her voice steady. "I hoped you wouldn't be mad. You needed sleep. I figured your rest meant more than you scolding me later."

Melinda rubbed her eyes with the tips of her fingers and spoke through her hands. "I've never scolded you. You know that."

"But you might of been mad."

Melinda dropped her hands from her face and held them in front of her, as if unsure where to place them, the tips of her fingers now touching.

"You sleep again later, after you heard us?" Annie Mae asked, tense again, waiting, growing more tense.

Melinda's sober expression remained unchanged, but Annie Mae watched as Melinda's eyes met hers, seemed to search her face, maybe looking for answers herself.

"I slept some, off and on, maybe more than I realize, but it wasn't restful. Sometimes you wake just as tired as if you hadn't slept at all."

The kitchen was warmer now, but Annie Mae was hardly aware, her sense of comfort no greater, not in the least. "I checked the baby after Betsy nursed him. He was fine."

"I saw you," Melinda said, just that, and then, after what seemed like a long hesitation, added, "I know."

Annie Mae studied Melinda, tried to understand those last words she'd just spoken, but Melinda remained unreadable, as she sometimes did, and Annie Mae suspected, as she'd done before, that what she was seeing, or *not* seeing, was Melinda's deepest strength, a learned hard-ness just beneath her surface. Maybe Henry wasn't only his father's son. Maybe there was some of Melinda in him too.

"Before you come to me," Annie Mae said, "I was going to have Betsy nurse the baby again." She didn't like telling the lie, but there was reason enough for it. Now she waited again, kept watching.

Melinda closed her eyes, held them closed, then slowly opened them as if from a half-remembered dream. "Have you taken care of the sheets and linens?"

Annie Mae felt herself turn rigid with the question and what it could mean. "They washed clean," she said. Then she heard herself keep talking. "I'll hang them to dry in here after everyone eats. They'd be froze on the line if I hung them outside."

Melinda nodded, and whether it was with approval, accusation, or simple acknowledgment, Annie Mae could not have said.

At half past noon the children gathered for the meal of fried chicken, potatoes, green beans, crackling bread, and canned tomatoes Annie Mae had cooked. Henry and William were past their earlier row, it appeared, a truce established between them. Kate and Bunyan sat on either side of Philip, but Rafe was missing. When she'd asked Samuel out on the back porch where Rafe was, Samuel had said, "Don't know. Just gone.

Know where I'd like for him to go." She'd looked around, then said, "Best watch yourself." Samuel ignored her, took the unlit match from his mouth and touched the head against his tongue, something she'd seen him do before, and she decided he liked the taste of fire before the flame.

Now Annie Mae stood behind Kate and Bunyan, a tray of food in her hands ready to take to Melinda. "I want y'all to keep a close eye on your mama. You hear? Help her."

"We will," Bunyan said.

"We would've gone in sooner and seen to her," Kate began, "but I heard Papa in there with her this morning."

Annie Mae didn't let this pass. "He wasn't in there *all* morning."

"No, I reckon not," Kate answered and looked down at her plate.

Keeping a careful hold on the tray, Annie Mae pushed open the door and crossed the dogtrot toward Melinda's room. Not long past noon and this day felt so long already.

Annie Mae was surprised when she heard her daughter at the kitchen door. She knew Betsy rarely set foot inside the house on her own accord, and when she did it was only to the kitchen when she knew Melinda had gone out and the children, all except for Phillip, were in school, which hadn't started back yet since Christmas. Annie Mae had just finished hanging the linens across the room and had to carefully make her way through the lines of saturated white sheets and towels and blankets between herself and her daughter. The cold came rushing in when she opened the door to the back porch, and she saw right away that Betsy had no notion of entering.

"You talk to her yet?" Betsy kept her coat pulled so tight around her the seams at the shoulders looked like they might tear. "She say anything?"

Annie Mae saw the fear in her daughter's eyes and heard the urgency in her voice. "I can't be standing here holding the door open."

"Just tell me if she's said something."

Now she heard demand, and Annie Mae stepped out and pulled the door behind her. "Slow down. It hard to tell. Said she saw you nurse. Way she talked, she might of seen more. Either me or you cleaning up. I don't know."

Betsy kept rocking on her feet, looking down at them, then at her mother. "So what did she *say?*"

Now she gave in to the demand. "Said, 'I saw you,' meaning me, not you. Then said, 'I know.'"

"Lord."

Annie Mae knew there was no prayer in the word. Betsy wasn't one for church. "Wanted to know if I'd got the sheets and blankets washed, like she knew there was more of them than ought to be."

"But she didn't say anything about seeing me later on?"

"No, not about you," Annie Mae said. Betsy looked at her more calmly now, nodded, and let out a white breath into the air between them. "Told her I was going to have you come nurse again but that she come to me first, told me about the baby being dead. She didn't say nothing to that."

"So after I nursed the first time, she might not have seen me again?" Betsy placed her hands in her coat pockets. "Maybe just saw you."

Annie Mae heard the word *you* as if she'd been pointed at, and she looked at her daughter who now seemed some distance from her, as if she stood just beyond the porch. She felt the cold creep into her and realized how exposed she was without her coat or burnoose while Betsy kept her coat pulled tight, her own heat keeping her warm enough. Maybe she was beyond reach somehow, beyond the porch and the protection of the roof overhead, but was she still close enough to be forgiven for whatever she might have done? She'd used the word *awful*, though, had said, "It was awful." If she'd done something wrong, would she have used such a word as that on herself?

"And she trusts you," Betsy said now.

Annie Mae nodded. "Never have gave her reason not to."

The final two words, *till now*, she kept to herself as she turned from her daughter. She closed the door behind her once again and faced the rows of washed linens hanging like some maze she would have to find her way through without help.

FIVE

She'd eaten only a portion of the meal Annie Mae had brought her earlier. The canned tomatoes remained and looked an unnatural shade of red, too dark somehow, and the cracklings had been too hard for chewing. Now the fire began to burn low and the cold found its way into the bed with Melinda as if it were some new companion she had to accommodate. She looked out the window and saw through the imperfect panes with their slight waves inside the glass that the day wouldn't warm with sun. She hadn't expected it to, but she realized that only now.

The door opened, and Melinda prepared herself for her husband, though she guessed it was probably Annie Mae. Instead, Kate entered, alone this time. Without a hint of a word she came and sat down on the edge of the bed. Her silence, Melinda realized, wasn't a consideration but an awkwardness she wanted to help her daughter through. Kate surprised her, though. "Your fire," she said. "Let me build it up." Normally Bunyan would have been the one to notice and do the chore without being asked. Four logs lay on the hearth, and Kate added each one and used the poker to help them catch the flame. Then she sat back down. "I can tell you're cold," she said. "Do you have a chill?"

"No chill, not like you mean, just cold."

Kate seemed to think about this a moment, as if trying to make a decision. Then she pulled back the covers enough to slip into them and edged close to her mother, as a small child might, but heat radiated off her young woman's body and Melinda welcomed it, just as she welcomed her daughter's arms. She was concerned that some of the heat might be fever, but she didn't worry about catching Kate's cold. She would or she wouldn't. Melinda wasn't about to turn away a gift such as this.

"I'm sorry, Mama," she said quietly.

Melinda squeezed her. "Sorry for what?" she whispered. When Kate didn't answer, Melinda felt the side of her daughter's face and found tears there. "For the baby?" Kate nodded her head, but Melinda knew there was more. "For not coming to me on your own earlier?" She nodded again, and Melinda felt more tears warm her fingertips. "Sweet girl. Don't worry. I'm glad you're here now."

"I wish I could do something for you, Mama."

"Maybe in a little while. Stay here for now. You can tell me something, though." Melinda hesitated a moment, but she had to know. "Did your daddy ask you the baby's name?"

Kate wiped at her eyes, pulled herself up higher onto a pillow. "He asked."

"Did you tell him?"

"No. I didn't know it then."

"What about now?"

"Bunny told me."

For one moment, brief as a flame's rise and fall, that pet name made the day disappear, took Melinda back to a time when Kate was a small child, before Annie Mae, before her other children had been taken with fever and sickness, before Annie Mae's daughter Elizabeth. Kate couldn't pronounce *Bunyan*, couldn't make the two sounds fit her small mouth. They'd come out *Bunny*, and so Kate had renamed her sister, turning the sounds into something she could say and point to, after she'd been taught, when one of the small animals appeared at the edge of the woods around the house, maybe finding somewhere in her child's mind a kinship between her sister and rabbits in the yard, both of them perhaps holding a beauty and a wonder for her.

With age, though, the name had disappeared, as so many things had—children, the semblance of a marriage, and even the name *Rafe* had become something else, too, that word Melinda would not say aloud but that Annie Mae sometimes mumbled: *buckra*.

"What made you say Bunny?" Melinda asked now.

Kate didn't answer at first, as if she were trying to understand it herself and then found she couldn't. "I don't know. It just came out. That's strange, isn't it?"

"Maybe," she said. "Or maybe today's a good day to remember you've got a big sister."

Kate seemed to think about this and then accepted it as an answer. "Are you getting warmer?" she asked finally.

"Yes."

Kate began to cough, shallow at first, then deeper. She turned away. "I don't want to make you sick."

"You won't. And if you do, I'll survive a cold. Besides, it would be more than an equal trade."

"What trade?"

Melinda didn't try to answer, to say *for your time with me*. A daughter didn't have to understand everything a mother felt, even when it was the value of that daughter's love and devotion.

Kate reached out and smoothed the quilt over them, its bright and perfect design freed from the folds they'd made with their turning bodies when Kate had settled in. They lay there for some time, quietly.

Then Melinda spoke. "There is something you can do for me, something you can bring me."

"What?"

"The Bible," Melinda said.

"You mean the big one?" Kate asked. "Already? Isn't it too soon?"

"A pen and ink too," Melinda said, wondering if her daughter might be right. Maybe it was too soon.

"If you want it, I'll go and get it for you."

Melinda nodded and Kate slipped carefully from beneath the covers. She would have to cross the dogtrot and retrieve it from the small table in the parlor. The pen and ink she could find in her father's office.

It didn't take her long, with only a little cold air following her in from the dogtrot when she returned. Melinda had already propped herself up against the headboard, and Kate helped her settle the large, decorative Bible in her lap. She opened it to one of the early pages for listing birth, marriage, and death dates, while Kate went for her father's pen and ink.

Melinda ran her finger down the page of names, each in her own careful hand, the letters ornamental, but not too much so. Below Philip's name she read *Male child, November 18-19, 1881*. She'd known the lack of a name might puzzle anyone who ever read the entry, but the dates would be explanation enough. She thought the name to herself now: *Robert Hendricks Anderson*. She saw it spelled out in her mind's eye, the letters clearly formed, as if she *had* written them, the name only she, her daughters, and Annie Mae knew.

Kate returned and handed her the ink-readied pen. Melinda held it carefully and then began to write what she understood would be the only record of her tenth child's existence—*Male child, December 30-31, 1883*—the scratch of the pen against the page sounding so ephemeral somehow, but the ink remained and dried into the thick paper. She wondered whose eyes might one day read what she had just written, what some distant progeny might make of it, if this family survived that long. Less than ten letters could not spell out all the meaning within them, and the numbers in the date wouldn't truly mark the time, they would be lost to it, she felt, but what did that matter in this moment? She knew their meaning, and so did Kate and Bunyan, though their knowledge wasn't as complete as hers and Annie Mae's, especially Annie Mae's.

She handed the pen back to Kate, let the ink dry a bit longer, then closed the Bible. "Take it back to the parlor," she said, "but try not to let your daddy see you with it." She doubted he had ever opened it to read the listing of his children, not when the list, for him, was so incomplete; but she didn't want him to open it now, didn't want him to see the manner in which she'd listed the last two children. Not today.

She slept, unsure how long, and when she woke completely and opened her eyes it was to the dark-eyed stare of Henry at the edge of her bed. Each child, it seemed, was making their way to her.

"Can people die twice?" Henry said.

The question surprised her, but only for a moment. She knew a child could ask almost anything, and that most of the time a simple answer was best. "No. No one can die twice. Did someone say they could?"

"Papa."

"Your father says unusual things sometimes. I don't always understand him myself."

Henry seemed to give this some thought. "Did William understand it?"

"He may have," she said.

"William says we're going to bury the baby in a little while. I helped dig the hole."

"I heard."

Henry's look suddenly turned serious, worried. "Who told you?"

"Bunyan did."

Henry's face tightened, and the fingers on each hand curled inward. "She talks a lot."

"There something you're afraid she told me about, something you did?"

He turned toward the fire. "No, ma'am."

"You can be a good boy when you want to be, Henry. You must remember that." At the angle he stood, she noticed how long his hair had grown in the back, how badly it needed cutting. She thought then about the scissors beneath the bed. Annie Mae might as well take them, put them to use in a way that could do someone some good. Or she might have Henry take the scissors to Bunyan. She could cut hair too, and sometimes had for each of the boys. "You must love your sisters, and your older brother, the way you do Philip."

"But they're all bigger, always telling me what to do."

"I know it must seem that way now, but one day you'll all be grown and it won't be like that anymore."

"Then I'll tell them what to do."

She started to respond but thought better of it. "Henry, there are some scissors under the bed. Would you look and get them out for me?" His knees struck the floor with small thuds, and his head disappeared below mattress level. After a moment she asked, "Do you see them?"

He didn't answer, and then she felt him beneath the bed, his back pushing up into the ticking.

"I don't see any. Why would they be under the bed?"

She didn't want to explain but wasn't sure what else to offer other than an honest answer. "Annie Mae put them there. She says they help cut down on a mother's pain after a baby comes."

Henry rose above the mattress, again eye to eye with her, and he didn't appear puzzled in the least, which made Henry, not for the first time, something of a mystery to her. "Do they work?" he asked.

"No, I don't think so," she said, "not this time," knowing as she spoke that Henry could not fully comprehend her answer without understanding there was more than one kind of pain.

"But they ain't there. Maybe if they'd been there they would have worked. Who took them?"

"I don't know," she said. "Maybe it doesn't matter." Or maybe it did, she thought. Maybe it mattered very much. "Go tell Bunyan to see if she can find the scissors. Tell her I want her to cut your hair."

"But…" Henry began and then obviously decided not to protest. "Yes, ma'am," he said. He turned and walked out of the room and, as was often his way, carelessly left the door open.

In a little while she heard footsteps in Rafe's office, recognized them as his, and then saw that her door had been closed.

She found him standing in front of the gun cases that lined the long wall separating his office from their room. A fireplace stood in the middle of the wall, mirroring the one in the bedroom beyond. There were more guns upstairs, she knew, rifles locked in wooden crates stacked in a corner of the boys' side of the loft. She didn't like thinking about them. She knew what they could be used for, and they frightened her. When she went up to the loft, it was mostly to the girls' side. Why Rafe would be staring at his guns she couldn't imagine, and she was glad he hadn't been holding one after he suddenly wheeled her way.

"You didn't make a sound," he said, as if this were some offense.

"Then how did you know I was standing here?"

"I felt your presence."

She nodded and was unsure whether to back away or not.

"You should probably sit." He pulled the chair from his desk and held it in an almost gentlemanly fashion, which she didn't trust somehow, but perhaps he didn't realize how he appeared. She walked toward him. It was, after all, more than impulse that had brought her in here. Now she sat.

"Were you looking for something?" she asked.

"No," he said, and she understood he did not want to explain, just as she hadn't wanted to explain the scissors underneath the bed to Henry. They were both quiet. "Inventory," he said finally. "I know they're all there, but I like to make sure each gun is where it's supposed to be."

"You want assurance," she said, surprised by a moment's understanding of him. "You want to know things are as they should be."

He didn't respond aloud, merely turned from her, his turning away comment enough.

Now she pushed herself, asked what she'd come in to ask him. "Is he buried yet?" She sat tense with anticipation of his reaction. She knew the answer, of course. The question was only a way to bring up the subject, to let him know that this time she wanted to see the burial.

"No, he's not," Rafe said, offering nothing else.

"I thought you might have done it by now. Why have..." she began but found she couldn't ask him such a direct question.

"Why have I waited?" he said and turned toward her again, away from the fire and the rifles and shotguns on either side, which stood in their parallel lines of blued metal and pointed toward the loft above. "Annie Mae had to dig the grave. Then it was noon and time to eat dinner."

She knew from Bunyan that he hadn't been home for dinner but didn't comment.

"Maybe I've been waiting on you," he said. For the briefest moment, she thought perhaps he meant he was waiting for her to feel strong enough to witness her own child's burial, but she quickly dismissed the thought. He hadn't waited before. "To see if you might finally come to your senses this time," he continued. "To see if you'll be *reasonable*."

She wanted to answer him, to speak a reason for her silence that she maybe understood only partially, on some level words couldn't quite reach. "By not saying his name, it's a way for me to keep the child... whole," she said.

"Whole? What could that possibly mean?"

Maybe his building anger made her retreat deep enough into herself to find the word. *Alive*, she wanted to say, but didn't. As long as the child went unnamed to the world, it was as if he were still waiting to be born, still somehow whole inside her, held in some tiny part of her womb. Yet she'd spoken the child's name once before he died, to Bunyan and Annie Mae, but they were female, and that made the difference. Except for Bunyan, who'd told Kate, they would never repeat the name again. It would remain private, *hers*, in her possession. Rafe, nor anyone else, could have it, could have the child. He would be hers always.

She spoke none of this, knew there was no logic to it that Rafe, or anyone else, could understand.

"It's nothing but goddamn defiance of me, and most men would beat you for it," he said and moved toward her, hovering over her close enough for her to smell whiskey, though she knew he was not drunk. "But there's probably not one man in the world who's had to put up with the likes of this, unless it's some damn Choctaw whose woman won't talk to him."

She didn't attempt to explain the custom to him that among the tribe neither the mother nor the father would repeat the name of a dead child. She knew, though, he was partly right. It was a defiance of him, a passive defiance, or, perhaps now, not so passive.

"After what you told me about Betsy," he said, "about her nursing the child, I went to her. She said she nursed him once, and that when she put him down he was fine, which is what you said, that he was *fine*. Well, he's not so fine now, is he?"

She was listening to him. She had to, but she was imagining him in Elizabeth's cabin, the two of them with their children, together, talking, maybe on the bed, discussing *her* child. It was as if they, her husband and his young, Black, Choctaw mistress, were taking away what she'd so far managed to keep for herself—was still trying to keep, despite what she was hearing. How dare they speak of her infant son.

And she would not speak now, would not say that Annie Mae had also entered the room in the night. She would keep from him everything she could.

He leaned against his desk, his back to the window so that the gray light framed him, caught him in a still moment, as if in a blurred, colorless portrait that left him ill defined. "How did you let that child die?" he said.

She began crying, silently, unable to stop herself, though she knew it might encourage his anger. At first he did not move. She didn't look up at his face but could feel his stare, his questioning of her. Then he walked toward the fireplace, and she watched as he placed his hands upon the mantel, keeping his back to her.

"He'll be buried within the hour," he said as if she had just asked, and then he turned and left her alone in the room, the question, Had she let the child die? still holding fast in her mind like the gray light caught in each windowpane.

She wasn't sure how Annie Mae came to her so quickly. Perhaps she'd seen Rafe enter his office and had waited for him to leave, knowing beforehand that the child was soon to be buried.

"Let me help you back to your room," Annie Mae said.

Melinda was already standing, but unable, she knew, to hide the fact that her eyes were reddened, wet still. "Maybe you better help me," she managed to say.

"I'll help you dress, too. This time I'm gon' carry you down there. I'll tell Samuel you said get the buggy hitched."

Melinda nodded, entering her room on Annie Mae's arm, and sat on the edge of the bed. She watched then as Annie Mae opened the cedar wardrobe. "Not a black dress," she said. "That would be too much like a proper church burial, and he might get angry, wouldn't let me stay."

"What then?" Annie Mae said.

"The dark gray one, with the high collar."

It seemed ridiculous somehow, this choosing of a dress, but it had to be done, a choice made.

She watched Annie Mae pull the dress from the wardrobe, and as Melinda began to remove her nightgown, she felt the cold wetness of the material across her breasts but wasn't embarrassed. Without a child to nurse, it couldn't be helped, and it was only a matter of time before she would run dry.

Without a word Annie Mae handed her a small, clean towel from the dresser, the only one left there, and Melinda dried herself, then allowed Annie Mae to help her with the dress. She let her fasten the bodice, which was heavily padded in front and would hold seepage, though she hadn't thought of that when she made the choice.

Annie Mae placed a pair of shoes by Melinda's feet and laid a heavy coat on the bed beside her. Finally she went to her with hairpins in her hand. "Turn and let me fix your hair," she said. Melinda obeyed and Annie Mae's careful hands gathered her hair into a bun and pinned it in place. "I'll go quick now and find Samuel."

Melinda nodded, thankful that Annie Mae would be beside her. She leaned over the bed, slipped on her shoes, and listened to see if she could hear anyone else in the house. The loft directly above her, the boys' side, was quiet, but she could hear footsteps and movement on the girls'. Still sitting, she pulled on the coat and then looked in the mirror on the dresser. Her light brown eyes appeared dark now, deep and shadowed, her face thin and tired. A woman's labor, of any kind, was always too hard, took too much of a toll. She might not be wearing black, she thought, but her face wore her grief heavy as a garment.

She heard the girls come down the loft steps and Annie Mae speak to them. "Y'all go on down to the grave."

In a moment Annie Mae entered the room again. "He'll have the buggy ready in a few minutes," she said and went and stood by the window. "You stay where you are till he come. Rest yourself."

They were both silent, waiting as if this were a formal funeral service they were about to attend, and for a moment, that was how it felt. Then Melinda heard the buggy stop and saw Annie Mae look out the window.

She let Annie Mae take her arm as they descended the porch steps, and then she used Samuel's arm for balance as she climbed into the buggy seat. The cold air still felt as hard and brittle as it had earlier when she'd crossed the dogtrot to Annie Mae's small room and sat quietly on her narrow bed, waiting for her to awake, for this awful day to begin.

Annie Mae took up the reins, released the brake, and coaxed Benjamin forward. They rounded the house, Samuel already ahead of them so he could open the gate to the horse pasture. Melinda wouldn't allow herself to look toward Elizabeth's cabin but stared straight ahead at the barn. Then as they entered the pasture while Samuel held the gate open, she saw Bunyan and Kate halfway down the little rise, and beyond them stood the boys—William, Philip at Henry's side, all of them at the mound of dirt, their father with the small box in his arms. She watched him place the homemade coffin beside the hole and then slide down into the grave, only the very upper part of his body showing above ground.

They were closer now, alongside the girls who walked faster and looked up at her in the buggy, their faces drawn, serious, battling the cold perhaps. Then she saw Rafe pick up the box and lower it into the hole, his whole body mostly disappearing for a moment. He seemed to take his time, and when he rose and straightened again, he appeared cut in half, the upper half of his body separated from the bottom, a kind of illusion from this distance and angle, the hollowed earth creating the deception.

By the time Annie Mae stopped near the mound of dirt, Rafe had managed to climb out of the grave and was dusting partly frozen soil from his hands. He stood at what Melinda took to be the head of the grave, the end nearest the fence; but with the simple boxed shape of the coffin, how could Rafe, or any of them, know at which end the head lay? Kate and Bunyan stood on one side of the grave, Kate wearing a dark blue dress and a black coat, Bunyan in deep brown with a long coat similar to Kate's. The boys stood on the other side, dressed as they had been—Henry without a coat of any kind, but his hair had been cut. Annie Mae set the brake and remained in the buggy.

Rafe slowly looked around at each of them, his eyes squinting against the wind, his hair blown back. "Nothing will be said by anyone. That seems the precedent set." He kept his gaze on Melinda and she didn't turn from him. "He'll lie next to his brother, and if there's a next world, how they will acknowledge each other I don't know. Or maybe *they* know their names."

Melinda heard Annie Mae whisper under her breath but could make out no word. She continued watching her husband, trying to imagine what he might do or say next.

"If anyone wants to say a silent prayer, I can't stop you, but I don't want to see lips moving. Pray to yourself. See what that will gain you."

She heard crying then. It was Kate, and she saw Rafe look Kate's way and away from her again. Melinda knew he could never face her for long, that Kate held some odd dominion over him that Melinda did not understand but envied, and she also knew that her younger daughter didn't suspect she held this power over her father. Such was the limited awareness of youth, or perhaps merely the innocent.

All remained quiet now, and the wind died for the moment. Melinda tried to begin her own silent prayer, but she could not concentrate on any world beyond or on any being larger than herself. She was too filled with questions, ones she couldn't ask others and didn't know how to answer on her own, or didn't want to. What she kept thinking about, going over and over in her mind, was what had happened in the night. Yes, she'd seen Elizabeth enter and nurse the child, and she'd seen Annie Mae come in soon after and check him. She'd probably slept some then, despite the anger she'd felt at Elizabeth's appearance. Exhaustion did not leave much for anger to feed upon. She had awakened on and off several times to the quiet and the night, then to dark movement, to Elizabeth again, except Elizabeth wasn't nursing the child but handling him, trying to clean him, from what Melinda could see in the shadows created by the firelight. Yet it wasn't the way one would clean a child after removing a soiled diaper. The girl's movements were larger; she held the child too high, and with only one hand, while she appeared to wipe him down with the other, not his backside but his stomach. And Melinda had lain there, not moving or speaking a word. Had she felt fear, or some old suspicion of Elizabeth rise within, back to the last child who lay buried without a marker? But then she'd seen Elizabeth place another diaper on him and set him down gently in the crib as if he were fine, clean now, comfortable. Yet something had held Melinda back, kept her from speaking. She'd realized a kind of relief spread through her, one greater, somehow, than it should have been. From what exactly did she find herself relieved—from worry? Or something beyond, maybe, relieved of another child's existence. Then she'd thought *balance*, and could not deny thinking it. What was it she'd done, or rather *not* done? Rafe had already asked that, and she'd kept asking herself the same. Then Elizabeth had walked toward the fire, leaned down, and thrown something into it. At first the flame had lowered and smoke had boiled up and out enough for Melinda to smell it. Finally the fire had risen and cast a brighter light in which she'd watched Elizabeth back away from the hearth and mantel and look toward the bed. Melinda had closed her eyes then, waited, and heard Elizabeth quietly leave the room. She waited longer even, maybe to see if Annie Mae would again enter the room. And finally Melinda—after lying there how much longer?—had gotten up, gone to the child, and put her fingers to his cheek and found it cold. She touched his chest beneath the blanket and found it cold too, not cool, but *cold* and understood it had been that way for quite some time. She removed her hand and stood there, not sure what to do, what exactly to think or even feel. She realized she had already failed her child. She had not driven Elizabeth from the room when she first laid eyes upon her earlier in the night. Because she hadn't, maybe that meant she'd wanted Elizabeth there? Had her own suspicion about what had happened to the last unnamed child grown into something more assured? And now she had only herself to judge since she'd allowed Elizabeth's presence. Or had it even been Elizabeth's work? The girl had laid the child down so gently. Maybe some larger presence had been at work, creating balance.

She walked slowly, absently, toward the fire and then saw a scrap of white cloth lying just beyond the coals. Here was confirmation in its burned edges. She stared at it a moment, considered reaching for it or pushing it into the fire, but instead left it alone, a small proof, a hint, for anyone who might notice, that something out of the ordinary had happened. She would let chance judge her too, leaving herself open to fate.

Rafe moved toward her now, stopping beside the buggy. She saw the children watching them. "Annie Mae," he said, "walk back with the children. Tell Samuel to fill the grave."

She nodded and placed a hand on Melinda's knee, and Melinda felt her fingers tighten.

Once Annie Mae climbed down, Rafe took her seat and turned the buggy. The cold wind rose again. As they started up the rise, he turned to her. "Did you kill that baby?" he asked.

The question did not startle her. Perhaps she'd been waiting for it. She answered slowly, carefully. "No more than you did."

By that evening she realized he had left. She was not surprised, and had no idea, of course, how long he'd be gone from the house. She never did. His absence was a relief, though his question, and her answer, remained with her. Did he understand that what she'd said to him was an accusation, and how much blame did they share?

The next day she kept to her bed, held there by grief and guilt and the exhaustion each filled her with and that she could not fight. Annie Mae brought her meals, little of which she ate. Bunyan and Kate made their appearances, once bringing Philip, their worry clearly growing when she remained in bed a second day. Then William came, and Henry with him, though Henry seemed merely impatient with her, and while that told her he missed her, needed her, she found no solace in such an understanding, felt only his judgment against her.

Finally, late in the second evening, she felt driven from her bed. Perhaps it was because of a hunger she couldn't ignore or a need to escape herself and her thoughts, or maybe she sensed something at hand in a way she could not have explained. She slowly rose, puzzled by her own actions, and put on a robe and found slippers at the foot of her bed. She walked out of the bedroom and then into the dogtrot. The cold air coursing through it pushed her into the other side of the house, and once she closed the door behind her she heard a child's voice she didn't recognize coming from the kitchen. She could not decide what child it might be, and then, when she entered the doorway and saw him, realized she *had* known it was George and could not believe Elizabeth stood just beyond him, her eyes widening in either fear or defiance. Already Annie Mae was opening the door that led outside, saying, "Come on and go. Take the child."

"Stay," Melinda said, her strength rising, her voice a command that she knew couldn't be ignored. "Tell me what you're doing in here. Is it not enough that you live within my sight?" Elizabeth looked away from her, toward her mother and the open door. "Don't you dare walk out."

"I came to talk to my mother." Elizabeth spoke quietly, without meeting Melinda's eyes. Annie Mae had taken George by the hand, led him toward the door, and stood watching, rendered silent, it appeared.

"About what?" Melinda said. Elizabeth shook her head, as if it were a question she did not know how to answer, the words it would take beyond her. "Maybe you want to know where my husband is. That it? Your mother doesn't know, and neither do I. You best get used to wondering. That's the life of a concubine. I see this boy here. He doesn't belong in the same house as my children." The words coming from her now were unplanned, simply rising from inside her, born out of anger and spilling forth. "Where's your youngest? You're nursing her. Don't you need to see to the child? Is she healthy, or do you have poison in your breasts? Is that what my child took from you? Poison?"

Elizabeth held her mouth closed, her lips pressed tightly. Her eyes seemed to search the room, looking for escape. Annie Mae opened the door wider now and pushed George through. "Go," she told her daughter in a more powerful demand than Melinda had spoken, and her daughter obeyed, grabbing George by the hand and letting the screen slam shut behind them.

Annie Mae turned to Melinda, looking as if she were about to speak some kind of apology, which Melinda did not want to hear. She merely held up her hand to stop Annie Mae's words and turned quickly from her, back toward the cold coursing its way through the dogtrot's passageway.

June 1974

It is blistering hot. Waves of heat rise off the asphalt of the narrow
county road they've just walked across. Seth Anderson stands in front
of the cement block store. His cousin, John, who's fourteen, two years
older than Seth, wants to go inside. He says they have an ice cream
machine that makes soft ice cream and big cones to put it in. Seth looks
again at the sign above the door: Anderson's Grocery. He's fearful, of
what he isn't sure.

His grandfather's store sits directly across the road behind them. It is
cement block also, but it's larger, with a green roof. The sign above the
awnings simply spells out his grandfather's initials and last name: C. H.
Anderson. And there are two gas pumps. He and John have just put air
in their bicycle tires with the hose at the side of his grandfather's store.
They've been riding for the past hour.

Seth wipes sweat from his face. His cousin opens the screen door, but
it's so dark inside Seth can't see anything clearly. John walks in and holds
the door for Seth, who takes it so that it won't slam, but he doesn't follow. Maybe he's hesitant to enter because he doesn't want to be disloyal
to his grandfather, does not want to buy, or "trade" as his grandfather
would say, from another store. Or maybe it's because this family is Black
and yet shares his last name, which still seems odd to him somehow, no
matter how many months he's lived here and been aware of this other
family. His father has told him that former slaves sometimes took the
names of their masters, but he's never said this to explain why these two
signs face each other and spell out their family name.

"Who that with you at the door?" he hears a woman say to John. Her
voice sounds deep, large. He wonders if this is the same woman he saw
in the dogtrot of the old house months ago. His eyes begin to adjust
more to the darkness inside and he sees that it is.

"That's Mr. Anderson's grandson," John says.

The woman laughs quietly. "I know who he is. Tell him to come on
in." Then she says, looking at Seth, "Come on and get you some ice
cream."

Seth feels caught. He can't move. He's too unsure of himself, feels
as if there is something here that's just beyond his understanding. He

knows he can't keep holding the screen open and has to decide. He finally eases it shut.

He hears quiet laughter again through the screen. "Honey, you can come in anytime."

Seth stands in the sun, sweating, embarrassed. He looks toward the windows of his grandfather's store and wonders if his grandfather sees him and what he might think.

After several long minutes, John comes out licking at the sides of an ice cream cone, and Seth wishes he had one. There are no cars in sight, and they begin to cross the road. Then Seth hears the screen open behind them and he turns to look. A boy about John's age, maybe a year older, stands in the doorway. His hair is dark but with a reddish tint that also colors his dark skin. "Bye, cousins," he calls out and laughs in a way that's different from the woman. Seth isn't sure if he's being made fun of or not, but without thinking about why, he waves, maybe only because he doesn't want to be impolite, not a second time.

The boy disappears into the store, letting the screen fly, but catches it with his backside or maybe his foot before it slams too hard.

"Who was that?" Seth asks.

John keeps walking. "I think his name's Charles. He visits every summer."

"He knows we're cousins?"

"I guess so," John says and takes a bite from the top of the swirl of ice cream.

Seth is puzzled how the boy could know, but he doesn't say anything. John seems more interested in his ice cream than in answering questions.

Seth doesn't know if he and John are second or third cousins, or some kind of *removed*, which he doesn't understand at all. He does know the way the lines run, that his great-grandfather was named Philip, and John's great-grandmother was named Bunyan, and that they were brother and sister. Seth's father has told him this many times so that he'll know their family history. The way his father says these names always makes Seth think his father remembers these people, but Seth knows they died before his father was born, when Seth's grandfather was still a boy, even.

What Seth wants to say to John now is that it sounded like the boy was calling each of them cousin for some other reason, that he meant more than just what he said, but Seth doesn't know how to say this, or ask about it.

He picks up his bike beside the air hose, and John stands his bike up with his one free hand. They roll them to the front of the store while John works at his ice cream.

Seth sees his grandfather under the front door awning with his keys in one hand and a bank bag in the other. He's wearing his small-brimmed dress hat with the dark band. "You boys having fun riding?"

"Yes, sir," Seth says.

"I'm headed to Demarville, to the bank. Seth, you be here when I get back. Your grandmama will have noon dinner ready by then. I'll ride us home."

"Yes, sir," he says again. "I'll be here."

John takes a loud bite out of the cone, then another, and melted ice cream covers the ends of his fingers.

"Seth," his grandfather says, "if you want some ice cream too, go ahead inside and get some out the box. But get a small cup. Don't want to ruin your appetite."

"Yes, sir, but I'm not hungry right now."

His grandfather nods, as with approval, then turns and walks to the other side of the store and into the shade of a tree where his truck sits waiting.

Seth mounts his bike, pedals out into the road, and John follows. When Seth takes one more look toward Anderson's Grocery, he sees the boy, Charles, standing in front by himself. He looks at Seth and John, and as best as Seth can tell, it seems like he wishes he had a bike too, and that he and John would ask him to ride along. He waves at them, and Seth knows he's not making fun. He looks lonesome, like he's wishing for something greater than a bike. Seth waves back.

In the days ahead, he will think of the boy from time to time, and he wonders if he'll see him out in front of the store again, or maybe around the old house with the dogtrot, but he won't. It will be years before he sees him again, and before he does he will first hear his voice on the phone, full of questions, and by then Seth will know some of the answers but not all. He will have his own set of questions too, and they will both remember this day and all that went unspoken between them.

Six

Rafe had not been home for two nights passing. He'd made no plan to stay away, but since he had already taken his customary back corner room at the hotel in Demarville the night of the birth, he returned to it, buying on the Square what clothes and articles he needed to keep himself presentable. He knew the time away would create no problem. It never did. His mercantile business in Riverfield mostly ran itself day to day with Alfred behind the counter. The man had been with him now for more than ten years. And, it being winter, the twelve hundred acres across the road from the Teclaw Place weren't under cultivation. There was very little work, even for Brantley, the farm manager and riding boss, who'd once been overseer on the very same land. He trusted each man and knew they'd dare not cheat him. In fact, years earlier both men had ridden with him, followed his lead when it was most necessary, and performed admirably what became terrible work.

All of New Year's Day Rafe had spent playing poker in a game at the hotel, and though he hadn't lost, he had not won to his satisfaction, hadn't ruled the cards as he sometimes did, and accepted that. He bore none of the men in the game any ill will.

He'd boarded Wheeler at the livery stable behind the hotel and now, early in the evening, rode him toward Virginia's house. Despite having just been there a few nights before, he didn't question his impulse to return. He generally trusted his instincts, in business, in poker, or with women, though women did not have to be managed as business did, or a hand of cards. With women you did what you wanted, and the only instinct that mattered was desire. You took from them what you needed, and they could respond as they chose. It was a hard way. He understood that, but women he'd found were his only respite from a part of himself that he understood little though knew existed; he had known of this dark part of himself even before he'd almost beaten a cousin to death at age fifteen and then run away from his family's North Carolina home. During the war this corruption, as he sometimes thought of it, had only grown larger inside him, as had his desire for women. With their beauty, their bodies, their gifts of mercy, they became a kind of counterweight to the worst of himself, and yet often he allowed them to bring out his worst. He understood that too.

As he neared his destination the streets became narrower and fewer and fewer of the houses painted, until finally all were of weather-darkened wood in a dark world. Some of the denizens who happened to be outside acknowledged him from their porches as he passed, and he sometimes returned their nods. A white man passing alone on a horse was not uncommon on these streets and at this time of evening, and neither was a mount with fine saddle tied to a porch post.

He knew Virginia would be home by now, released from the family she worked for and trying to tend to her own, which consisted of just the two children, his own. There would be no others by him. He rode Wheeler into the small, clean-swept yard and tied him to the iron hook he'd mounted in the post at the corner of the porch. With the heel of his boot he broke the ice that had hardened across the top of the water bucket she kept there.

The door was not locked, and he entered without the call of her name. Fannie, five, jumped up from her mother's chair like a spring-loaded toy, ran to him, and hugged his leg; Walter, two years younger, rose from the floor almost as quickly and wrapped his arms around Rafe's other leg.

"What you got for us, Papa?" Fannie asked, and then buried her face in the crook of her arm as if she'd just remembered she wasn't supposed to ask such a question.

"Look and see," he said and saw Virginia emerge from the back room and into the kitchen. Her face bore neither surprise nor welcome, but that was to be expected.

Each child dug into this coat pockets and found the pieces of hard, store-bought candy they anticipated, Walter a peppermint stick and Fannie two round lemon drops, both children clearly satisfied.

"Thank you, Papa," Walter said. The boy smelled of ginger for some reason. He sat back down on the floor, a handful of clay marbles spread around him. Fannie still clung tightly to him with one arm. She always needed the most attention, maybe even more than her mother had. He picked her up at her waist and spun her around once, then twice, before sitting her down back in her mother's chair while she laughed, squealing the way both Kate and Bunyan used to, though he did not often have thoughts of one set of children while with another, and it surprised him now that he did.

"I brought you something too," he said to Virginia, setting his sight on her and walking into the kitchen. She stood at the table slicing a cured ham and only looked at him, her expression unchanged. He reached into his inside coat pocket and took out the bills he'd won in the poker game, laid them on the table's edge.

"Jackstraws," she said as if she'd just answered a question.

"I told you, I've heard enough of that."

"No doll for Christmas, just Jackstraws, and that days late. And clay marbles, not even glass."

"I imagine this money here is good enough for you."

"I'll take it. I bet that new baby will get better presents than clay marbles."

Rafe waited a moment, found he had to gather himself. "I already got him something," he said and hoped she could hear the warning in his voice.

"What?"

"A box."

"Box of what?" she said slowly and laid the knife down on the table, perhaps sensing his answer might be something unexpected. She studied him with light brown eyes that were such a contrast to her dark face and hair that it always seemed to him some other person lived inside her, someone other than who he thought he saw at a distance or at first glance. "You got white eyes," he'd once told her. "You just seeing what you want to see," she had said. "I'm nothing but black. What you thought you wanted."

"I gave him a pine box to put himself in," he said now, a simple riddle for her to solve. He waited.

It took only a moment. "Oh," she said and looked as if she were about to say something more but stopped herself. She placed her fingers on the knife handle but didn't pick it up yet. "How many days ago you bury him?"

"Two," he said.

"Where 'bouts?" she asked quietly.

"The horse pasture." He knew she would understand what that meant. He'd never had to explain himself to her, which is one reason he'd kept returning to her well beyond his norm. Then the two children had come and kept him returning, and she continued to give now in ways that were always unexpected.

"He only lived the one day?" she said, her way, he imagined, of asking what happened without having to ask outright. She sliced into the ham with a sure stroke.

"Not even that long."

He took a chair at the table and told her all he knew, including Betsy's nursing the child in the night. She cut her eyes at the mention of Betsy's name, but he kept talking, explaining that Melinda had seen Betsy holding the infant, that it had to have made her angry in a way only a woman can be angry. He finally realized at some point he was expressing his suspicions and that Virginia realized it before he did.

"So that's two now, one after the other," she said, again asking what was really a question of him, wanting to know what he thought. She sat down at the table with him.

"Yes, two, at least."

There was a silence then, he not wanting to break it with a direct accusation of his wife but still wanting to know what Virginia would say. To understand one woman, he knew he had to hear from another, and despite their history and the anger in her that sometimes showed itself, he could give credence to what Virginia told him, and maybe that was because of their history. She knew he was not coming back to her in the way she wanted, but still there were these children, *their* children, a connection he would not deny, though at times she had accused him of denying it.

"You want to think your wife did something to this last one, and the one before. Want to think she punishing you."

"I don't *want* to think anything. The mind speaks. It's not like you can stop it. Anyone who tries is a fool."

"Lot of fools in the world," she said and picked up a piece of ham, held it in front of her mouth as if she might take a bite of it. A callous gesture, and he wanted to swat it all away, already seeing the ham scattered across the floor. She put the piece down.

"I'm not a fool," he said. "Never have been."

"No," she said, "you not. But maybe you looking wrong, and too worried about looking a fool."

"So where do I look?"

"At that yellow girl."

"She's not yellow and you damn well know it."

"Don't have to look yellow to be yellow."

He pushed away from the table and thought about standing, leaving. "She's a light copper if she's anything, if you want to talk color."

"She mixed in a way you like. And her children, they can pass, least the one I seen can. Guess that why you give them your name to go by and won't let mine have it. Mine too dark to carry your last name."

He looked at the plate of ham again. "That matter's settled. I will not discuss it again."

"Your wife won't name your children, and you won't name mine."

"It ain't the same," he said. "And that ain't what I came here to talk about."

She sighed and looked away from him, then looked back with what appeared to him a familiar and tired acceptance, which she always seemed to find and which he valued, and maybe demanded. "I don't know what that girl Betsy might of done," Virginia said, "if she done anything. Maybe all this just in your mind. You think everybody like you."

"How's that? Like me how? And I didn't say anything about Betsy doing anybody harm."

"You think everybody hard as you. Got inside them what you got."

He considered this, weighing the truth of it. She didn't have to explain further. "Maybe you're too hard toward Betsy."

"Probably am. Tell me a woman who wouldn't be. When you went to her, me and your wife, we must of felt the same. And you still take from your wife what you want. You got her that dead baby. You take from me too, just in a different way."

"I give to these children, and to you. The money tonight is something extra. What I bring every month is generous."

She nodded. "You bring money and I listen, tell you what I think even if I know you don't want to hear it. That's how this works."

"That's why this works," he said.

"Hear this, then. There's something going on in your house."

"I know that."

He waited, thinking she might say more. Maybe he'd heard enough. Betsy had said one thing, pointing suspicion toward Melinda even if she'd tried to make it sound otherwise; now Virginia had done the same toward Betsy, which should not have surprised him, and hadn't really. And Melinda had had the audacity to throw his suspicions back in *his* face at the graveside as if those suspicions had been caught in a hard gust of wind. But men went to other women, sometimes had children with them. It did not make them guilty of a child's death.

Virginia finished cutting the ham, the blade of the knife shiny with grease. He stood and walked into the front room. Walter and Fannie were both scooting across the floor, chasing after clay marbles rolling in all directions in some game of their own making. They were quick, agile, their dark hands grabbing here, there. For a moment he remembered from three days ago the opposite of what he was seeing here—the stiff limbs of his dead child as he lay on the desk in front of his office window. Now Walter stopped, raised up on his knees, and held out in his open palm one half of a broken clay marble as if it were some offering Rafe should accept.

The Black Fork River lay discernible beneath the moonlight. He stood on the bank, Wheeler's reins in his hand, and waited for the approaching lantern-lit ferry, the yellow globes creating their small, insular worlds of light. The smell of muddy water filled the cold air. Demarville lay a little over a mile behind him. He'd paid his hotel bill and now would ride home nine more miles along the mostly tree-lined road, trusting Wheeler to navigate the darkest patches beneath thick pines.

When the ferry docked, he paid the fare and walked the horse onto the wide deck, its shoes sounding against the wooden planks. Another man, a traveling preacher who'd already tried to engage him in conversation, boarded behind him but didn't try to speak again or close the distance between them. Rafe had made clear he did not care to be preached to. Toward the end of the war a religious revival had spread through the ranks, and he'd showed with fists on more than one occasion what he thought of a movement of Christian soldiers. One could not go to God covered in the blood of other men, only his own, if then.

The night had grown colder, and more so even as the wind picked up over the middle of the river. The preacher had told him God would offer protection from the dropping temperature and from the dangers of nighttime travel, but the chill inside Rafe told him there was no protection from the cold or from anything else. He'd seen a man frozen to death, and nothing had protected his child who now lay in the frozen ground.

He could have waited to bury the child—not for a day without cold, but for a doctor to pass some kind of judgment on the child's demise. He'd been questioning himself about this for days. Why hadn't he brought over a doctor from town, or taken the child in? Maybe to keep his own business close in hand. It was not his nature to go to others. He handled his own troubles. And yet he'd just gone to Virginia. What did that say about him? Maybe there was some other reason he'd buried the child so quickly, some reason of which he was unaware, or would not allow himself to recognize.

At the landing, Rafe mounted Wheeler and made sure he got ahead of the preacher. He did not want to travel with the man, and yet as he urged Wheeler up the riverbank, he felt himself pulled forward by some other concern that he would not have anticipated and could not quite name, a sense of foreboding, a worry about his children perhaps, or if not them, then maybe Melinda, if that were possible.

He knew Wheeler was rested, and though Rafe didn't push him into a run, he dug his heels into the horse's sides until Wheeler reached a steady and even trot. The dark miles passed—some alongside open fields, some with the moonlight shining through bare oak and maple limbs, then blocked by pines—this road not too unlike the one during the war where he'd ambushed a Union messenger and killed him in the night with a knife before sneaking back into the camp he was not supposed to have left.

Finally he entered Riverfield and passed the gristmill and post office and the few stores, including his own, all quiet. Then he approached his house, some of its windows lamplit still. Instead of taking Wheeler directly to his stall, he tied him to a porch post and then walked just inside the dogtrot. Before he decided which side of the house he would enter, Melinda came hurrying out of the living room door, slammed it behind her, and marched across the dogtrot toward the bedroom side. When he spoke she recoiled as if he were some ghost appearing out of the dark, and she surprised him almost as much when she did not answer him but opened the door before her, walked through, and also slammed it behind her.

He thought he might have heard voices out behind the house, but he followed after Melinda. She still had not entered the bedroom but was in the hall that paralleled the dogtrot, and he could see her only in shadow, unable to recognize her features, and when she spoke it was in a voice he did not know.

"I will not have that girl in my house, not ever again. You keep her and those bastard children out. Whether you're here or not, you keep them from this house."

He did not approach her but kept distance and darkness between them. "Where was she?"

"In the kitchen."

"With both children?"

"No, just the older one," she said, still not moving, her body a stationary shadow cast without benefit of light.

"What were they doing?"

"How do I know? Annie Mae was trying to shoo them out when I walked in."

"I'll see to this. Where are the children?"

"You mean ours?"

"Yes."

"Upstairs. I'm sure."

"All right," he said.

Melinda walked toward their bedroom door, then must have turned back around to speak. "Are you home? For a night?" Her voice still held an edge like a sharpened blade.

"That's enough. No more of this. I'll attend to what needs attending. What you're asking is fair enough, but don't ask me any more questions."

He heard her quick footsteps enter the bedroom and then a silence as if she'd disappeared into some other dark room beyond theirs. He turned, suddenly more tired than he'd realized, and headed toward the kitchen, where he found Annie Mae sitting at the small table, slumped forward as if she too were tired beyond normal measure.

"What happened?" he said.

She looked at him with an expression akin to fright, not in the moment but one recently passed. "Betsy come in with little George."

"For what?"

"Wanting to know where you was."

"And how would you know that?"

"That what I told her. Then she want to know if I think you holed up with that other woman and her—" He held up his opened hand and cut her off. "Then Miss Melinda come in. She mad like I never seen her. Said all kind of things."

He did not need or want to hear more. He wished he were still at the hotel but understood well enough what his absence had wrought. For a moment he stood undecided. "Fix me some supper," he said. "I'll be back for it directly."

She nodded and slowly rose from the table, relieved, it appeared, at having a chore given to her, or perhaps he was the one who found relief by making a demand of someone.

Wheeler had to be taken care of first. He shouldn't have left him this long. Any animal that served so well ought to be tended to. Once outside he patted and stroked the horse's neck by way of apology and led him to the barn for water, feed, and a rubdown. Seeing to Betsy would be another matter entirely, but he would make clear to her what he wanted.

She must have seen the light in the barn from her cabin and guessed that he'd returned, or maybe she had been going out the back door to the kitchen earlier and heard him call to Melinda in the dogtrot. Whatever the case, she was waiting for him when he entered. She'd built up her fire and wore a white nightgown he'd bought her. She sat on the edge of her bed at an angle, and he could see her hair hung loose down to her waist, so dark and with such a sheen that the fire and lamplight caught in its slight waves, capped them, it appeared, with heat. In contrast, her light skin looked cool, flushed with the cold air that filled the cabin when he opened the door. She was just such an exhibition of differences herself, sometimes strong, sure of herself, even defiant, other times so much like a girl still, hesitant, wanting assurance, petulant when he did not let her have her way. When she acted a girl, she was more likely to obey his commands, and yet the girl in her made him uncomfortable, reminding him at odd moments of either Bunyan or Kate. When this happened, he would walk away from her and might not return until the next day, leaving her with questions and doubts, he was sure, but he could do nothing about them and didn't try. He wondered what part of her he would encounter now as he drew closer to her.

"I'm sorry," she said without turning his way, which he wanted to take as reticence and not a defiance that contradicted her words. Lakeview, he saw, was in her crib near the fire, and George appeared to be asleep on his pallet beneath her. Rafe sat down beside Betsy so that she faced him, but she looked down and slightly away. "I shouldn't have gone in the house," she said.

"No, you shouldn't have. You're not to do that again."

She nodded and was quiet for a time. He waited. "You were gone for so long," she said finally.

"And what is your point? You knew you weren't going to find me in there."

"No."

"Then why?" he asked, though he knew the answer. She was desperate for word of him even if it was only her mother's speculation. "So what did she say to you?"

"Miss Melinda?"

"No, your mother."

Betsy looked as if she were about to confess some minor crime and hoped for mercy. "She said you'd come back when you wanted. That there was nothing I could do about it. Said you might be with that Virginia woman, but might not be."

"I have obligations there. You know that. I take care of them." He touched her knee, letting his hand rest upon it. "I stayed at the hotel. Same room I always stay in." He could see the words brought her relief. "But I did see her, and my two children. I left her money, that's all. Not that I should have to explain any of this to you. It is my business, not yours," he said, and yet he found in this instance he didn't mind explaining. He felt some tenderness toward her. Maybe the beauty of her sitting there, her soft expression, the full waves of her loosened hair lit by fire, her skin warming at the ends of his fingers when he touched her neck, maybe all these awakened whatever tenderness he possessed, despite Virginia's words of warning.

She closed her eyes and bent her head downward in a humbled posture as he continued to rub the nape of her neck. She let her body relax, was completely vulnerable to him, surrendered, and he felt the beginnings of desire rise and grow stronger.

"So what did Miss Melinda say to you?"

She straightened, looking at him with what he saw as hurt. "Called me a concubine. Said George didn't belong in the same house with her children. Told me I was poisonous, that her baby took pure poison out of my breasts."

He didn't speak at first, didn't damn Melinda. What else could Melinda have said? He took Betsy's hand. "Tell me again that you will never enter the house."

"I won't," she said.

"And if Miss Melinda ever comes to your door or approaches you in the yard or anywhere else, you tell me."

She moved closer against him, close enough so that he smelled the vanilla on her skin and inhaled it. "I will," she said. "Whatever you say."

He held her like a child and then realized he could not continue to hold her in such a placating manner for long without having to walk away. He began with the button at the top of her nightgown, then, slowly, and with one hand, opened each button down the length of the front. He finally pushed her back onto the bed, pulled her gown away, and felt the slightest dampness where the material had covered her breasts. He saw her nipples firm in the cabin's cool air and got up to turn down the lamp. When he returned she had found her way beneath the bed's quilts and pulled them back for him to enter. He undressed quickly, knew she could see his arousal in the firelight, and slipped into the bed, closed in on her warmth, and after kissing her neck and mouth waited no longer to enter her. He moved with and against her, slowly pushing her body toward the head of the bed and heard from her what always sounded like lamentations. As his urgency increased he slowed, pulled backward, and lowered his head between her breasts. She turned slightly one way, then another, but he lifted his upper body, held himself at arm's length on either side of her, then pushed forward and soon the only sound he was aware of was the slapping noise he made against her open thighs. He finally reached the moment that sometimes he could not reach, but that when he did, as now, always erased time and memory for him—however briefly—took him out of himself and separated him from every awful thing he had ever done or imagined.

Afterward, as he lay against her in the trough-like indentation of the mattress, his exhaustion beginning to pass, he reached to cradle her head in his arm, to feel again her soft, thick hair, of which he knew she was overly proud, and she turned away just enough to create a kind of distance despite the touching of their bodies. He didn't reach for her again or question her as he knew she must want but simply lay silent as long as the silence would last.

"You wouldn't take my breasts." She spoke the words quietly toward the fire. He barely heard them, then wished he hadn't.

He closed his eyes, waited. "You're nursing," he said.

"You done it before."

"It isn't manly. I won't do it again, not while you're nursing," he said.

He knew the answer didn't satisfy her. She didn't act as if she'd heard him. She didn't move or speak. He guessed it was Melinda's words about poison that kept sounding inside her head, and his refusal just now had only echoed them, damning Betsy further, though that had not been his intent. He simply hadn't wanted what she'd offered, and if his explanation had not been enough for her, it was for him. Women studied on things too much, found meanings that were not there, though Virginia, he knew, would argue differently.

He soon rose from the bed, turned up the lamp just slightly, and dressed. As he tucked in his shirt, he happened to see what he hadn't noticed earlier—two coffee cups on a table by the door. Betsy still lay in the bed, and he turned, stared at her. "You had him in here?"

"Who?" she said.

"You know good and well who."

She looked up at him, appeared perplexed, but he couldn't be sure. She might well have left the cups there for him to find. "Those are from the other day," she answered after glancing at the table. "I took some coffee out to him."

"I thought I told you not to do that anymore."

"You said don't have him in here again. I didn't."

He remembered more clearly now and realized she was right, but still he was angry, and he approached the very edge of the bed, stared harder at her, and tried to decide if Samuel had been in here or not.

"He told me something, something I didn't know," she said quickly, perhaps to ward off whatever she expected him to say or do, or maybe she hoped to please him somehow, show her love and loyalty.

"What?" he asked with genuine curiosity if not complete trust.

"It was about his daddy. He said his daddy was one of the ones that got shot down, killed at the river."

This gave him considerable pause. No one outside of the men who'd ridden with him had ever spoken to him of the event, and only a few of the riders had. Once it was over Alfred and Brantley hadn't uttered a single word about the subject in his presence, and he doubted they'd spoken of it to anyone else. He didn't realize Betsy had known about the episode but quickly understood that it must be something the Negroes still talked about, and Betsy or Annie Mae would have heard, being closer to their color.

"I never heard Samuel ever mention a father," he said, "figured he didn't know who his daddy was."

"Hardly did. He said he was just one of his daddy's yard children."

"Why are you telling me this?"

"Thought you ought to know," she said.

He nodded, tried to consider her motives. "Don't speak of this again, not to anyone."

"I won't," she said. "I'm only telling you."

He finished dressing and pulled on his coat. He knew she wanted some further reaction from him, thanks or gratitude, or even some confession as to what exactly had happened, but he had no intention of giving it to her and walked out without another word, the sights and sounds of that day all returning as he exited the cabin and entered into the cold shock of the outdoors.

Annie Mae had left a plate for him on top of the stove. He ate quietly there in the kitchen, knew Annie Mae was in her small room, but was certain she would have the good judgment to leave him to himself this particular night.

He then crossed the dogtrot and headed to his own bed for the first time since Melinda had gone into labor. He walked into the dark room lit only by dying coals in the fireplace and began to undress down to his long underwear. If Melinda was awake, she pretended otherwise, and he was glad of it. He crawled into his side of the bed—closest to the door—and found comfort enough there, but as weary as he was, sleep did not come as he'd hoped it might. The day had been filled with what amounted to one fray after another, and his mind and body remained ready for the next, it seemed. It was the way he lived, had always lived. How could one change that? Any man who waited for the next fight or moment of contention would always find it. He knew that and was sometimes, as now, exhausted by it.

Melinda's breathing remained steady. Perhaps she was asleep. He focused on the silence of her calm though he knew, even if asleep, she was anything but, her dreams bound to be stealing any true rest. He tried to bring his own breathing into agreement with hers and managed to do so, the evenness of their long breaths a comforting sound there in the cold dark.

He didn't want to think of it now, but his suspicion (or was it conviction?) about what Melinda did or might have done to the child, or children, grew larger in his mind. What kind of woman was he lying next to, and how many husbands would lie with such a woman? Yet he found he could. He had known all along that he *would* come back to this bed, as he always had. He'd known her since she was a girl of fourteen, had married her when she was twenty-one, and knew his hardness drew her to him, that it spoke to her in some way. They were bound by the private history of a man and wife, and maybe they were bound by more than that now, through a deeper kinship he was only just recognizing. Perhaps she had simply done what she was compelled to do and had not questioned it, acted without thought, almost with a kind of innocence he wasn't sure how to define but knew contained no forethought. He'd often done the same, though he'd never thought of himself as innocent. He had no fear of her, certainly, and, in this quiet moment, no disgust for her. But how was that possible? He wondered what he would have done if he were her. Would he have behaved any differently? He remembered the lone Union messenger on the road that one night, how he'd come out of the trees and the dark and attacked the man when he could have easily let him pass without consequence. He'd not thought one way or another, only acted by his own set of instincts, the same way he'd attacked and almost killed his cousin at fifteen.

His side of the bed began to warm. He listened, and his breathing was still even with hers—balanced, he thought, in length and tone, without effort on his part, an accomplishment that felt natural enough.

He knew she suffered him, and he was sorry for that. It could not be helped. She was a good mother to their children and did her best as wife to a man like him. Her failure, or failures, if one could call them such a thing, had to be measured against that, against him. Virginia had said, "You think everyone like you." Maybe he knew one woman who was, or was much closer than he'd ever considered.

Sleep was coming now. He could feel it, and he no longer had to wonder why he hadn't brought a doctor to examine the child. It was their business, his and Melinda's. Whatever she'd done to the infant, he would have no one else suspect or malign her.

SEVEN

The first time she saw him, at fourteen, was a day when everyone had the sun grins. It was February, and Melinda had come into Riverfield with her father who farmed, trapped, and bought furs from other trappers, then shipped them downriver to Mobile. *Sun grins* was a phrase he sometimes used in winter, and she was never sure if it meant when the sun was so bright it made you squint and grimace, or if it meant everyone was so glad to see the sun after so many gray, cold days that it made them grin with pleasure.

Rafe had not been grinning. He stood on the porch of the Stagecoach Inn, a stranger to all, and stared at her as she and her father passed in their wagon. They stopped in front of Mr. Lassiter's store, and she went inside with her father, who needed feed and wanted to go ahead and purchase new plow lines for spring. She had come for such staples as flour and coffee. Her mother had been dead for not quite a year, and, because she was an only child, the household had become her responsibility. Her father was patient with her as she learned her new role, much more patient than her mother had ever been with either of them, truth be told. She'd often wished he'd been less forgiving, even if that had sometimes meant less forgiving of her, too.

She stood looking at a bolt of red cloth, and when she turned she saw Rafe at the counter, waiting, but also watching her intently. She guessed his age at seventeen, guessed he was traveling with family, and that just maybe he found her attractive, though she was far less sure of this last notion. She learned soon enough she was wrong only about the second guess.

"I'm looking for Mr. Lassiter," she heard him say in a voice that sounded more man than boy. It lacked a boy's hesitation.

The clerk behind the counter, whom she knew only as Joseph, eyed this stranger, then asked, "Who might you be?"

"Not that it's your concern, but it's a fair enough question," he said, and she noticed the way her father looked over at him, not dismissively but with a wariness. "I'm distant kin of his. When will he be in?"

"Maybe by lunch."

"Then I'll come back," he said and turned abruptly from the counter.

She didn't realize she was staring until her father caught her eye with a wave of his hand, and she saw his look of mild disapproval.

Rafe walked toward the door, then came her way, this boy with a name she'd not yet heard and who did not sound like a boy, and whose hair needed cutting and clothes mending. He stopped. "Rafe Anderson," he said. "I intend on establishing myself here." He did not wait for her to speak but walked on out the door, some force of him remaining, pressing itself against her in a way she'd never experienced.

She looked again at her father whose eyes were closed as if he did not want to see what would eventually lie in the young man's wake.

On Sunday she and her father again made the four-mile trip into town, though the ford at McConnico Creek was almost impassable in their buggy. She had hoped to see Rafe in church, and when she didn't, she realized through some sudden instinct that she might never see him there, despite it being the customary place where all gathered, socialized, and learned news.

It was weeks before she saw him again, and again it was in the store, this time behind the counter.

"Where's Joseph?" she managed to ask.

"I wouldn't know," Rafe answered with a bluntness that made her curious but kept her from asking further questions.

He looked considerably cleaned up. His dark red hair was cut short, though still long enough to part along the side. His face was smoothly shaved, and his clothes appeared brand new, the shirt a bright green, the cuffs buttoned at his wrists. She noticed his fingers splayed against the counter, and his hands looked strong and muscular.

Her father was in the post office, and she knew they might be alone for a few minutes more.

"You know mine, but I don't know your name," he said.

"Melinda Jane Hendricks." She didn't know why she said her middle name, only knew that it sounded too formal. For months he would call her Melinda Jane until she finally told him she went only by her first name.

She then braved a question she already knew the answer to—from her father—but it was a way, she hoped, of learning something more about him. "Did you travel here with family?"

"No," he said, his gaze upon her intent, expectant somehow. She felt as if she should *do* something, perform for him in some way, though she knew it was a silly idea. "I came only with a slave named March. An uncle in North Carolina, on my mother's side, gave him to me," he added. "He helped me get here."

"Have you sold him?" She knew Rafe could have no work for him without land or a house of his own.

"No. I wouldn't want to do that. He took the name of my mother's people, Whitney. Maybe a name means something. I've loaned him out to Mr. Lassiter for my room and board."

"You're kin to Mr. Lassiter?"

"On my father's side."

"And you're from North Carolina?"

He suddenly appeared hesitant to answer, even suspicious of her. "Near Durham," he finally said. Then her father walked in, and before she could recover herself, step away from the counter, or speak to him, Rafe spoke with a kind of boldness which should not have surprised her but did. "Sir, I'd like permission to call on your daughter after church on Sunday."

Her father took a moment to answer with words that sounded carefully measured. "Not yet. She's not at an age that I deem appropriate." He looked as if he were about to say more but thought better of it, as though any other words would weaken his position. She understood on some level that *not yet* meant something inevitable had been set in motion. For the moment, though, and maybe a good while beyond, she would have to wait.

That first meeting had been long years ago, and now, in church on Sunday, Kate sat on one side of her, William on the other, the rest of the children filling the pew, Philip between Bunyan and Kate, Henry fidgeting, never able to keep still. Somewhere above them Annie Mae sat in the balcony with the Negroes. Elizabeth never attended, nor Rafe. She always imagined they used this time, and if she had any prayer this day it was that the two of them were not together in her home. After her exchange with him when he finally returned from town the other evening, surely Rafe wouldn't bring Elizabeth into her house, and, please Lord, not into her bed.

It wasn't, of course, an actual prayer she prayed with folded hands, or in Christ's name, but perhaps it was as close to a prayer as she could come. For a long time she'd struggled to hold on to her belief the way she had held on after her mother's death and found comfort through it. But belief was easier for the young, and the well married, she imagined. Loss and hard years had made her faith fade, and she hadn't found the strength to retrieve it, not in the way she would have liked, with a fullness that could sustain her. Maybe she was no better than Rafe, her presence in this pew more truly an absence, not physical but spiritual, an abomination in God's eyes. She sometimes asked him questions. If God had her children, her lost children, did he see them, know their names? She knew she should not ask such things, certainly not inside the church, but she did, though always to herself, never even to Annie Mae.

The preacher, Reverend Lamar, called for "O Worship the King" as the closing hymn. She stood and the children all followed, Henry last. She sang, trying to catch Henry's eye so that he would take up the hymn, but she couldn't. What caught was her voice on the words "children of dust," and she choked, swallowed, then became as silent as Henry, unable to continue.

At the close of the final verse, Reverend Lamar made his way to the church door and then spoke the benediction. She knew she would have to speak to him as she passed and that he would see she'd given birth. But when he took her hand in his, the skin of his fingers and palms as dry as parchment, he looked at her gravely with washed-out blue eyes that held one's attention in their oddity, just as if they were bold and piercing, and neither asked after the baby's health, nor offered congratulations. "May God be with you in your time of trouble," he said. "It is not ours to question."

"Yes, Reverend," she answered. "Thank you."

He nodded and a light wind caught at the wisps of his gray hair. She kept moving, trusted that each child followed behind. Bunyan would make sure. She wondered how he knew already. Perhaps one of the children had said something to another child or parent and word had spread. Then another thought captured her and grew quickly in her mind. Maybe Elizabeth had told it among the Negroes, and then they'd spread the story to the white families they worked for, pretending to have it teased out of them by the mistress of the house while they meant to tell it all along. How often news traveled that way. Gossip knew no race. Or it knew every race. And just how had Elizabeth told it? What dark suggestion had she whispered, intimated?

Once in the churchyard she stopped, letting the children mix with others their age. A light-haired boy, the oldest son of Rafe's storekeeper, approached Kate and Bunyan. It was a cold but bright day, the sky a hard-frozen blue. Then she saw them, the sun grins on her children's faces. Pleasure or grimace? She wished her father could see them and tell her the answer. But he was gone now too. Pleasure, she told herself. It had to be pleasure, for her children's sake, and she made herself believe it so. Maybe God was even there in their faces.

She spotted Annie Mae walking away from a group of Negroes. She'd been waiting for her, knowing the balcony did not empty until the rest of the church did. Annie Mae drew near, the sun bright on her face, but with no suggestion of a smile or grin of any kind. Melinda understood why. "I'll sit at the table for dinner today," she said flatly.

Annie Mae shielded the sun from her face. "I guessed you might since you got out for church. Be good for the children to finally see you there."

Melinda wondered if this was meant as a reproach, but if not, she felt she deserved one. "I've been in my room long enough. And after we eat, I'd like for you to change the linens." She paused. "I want to know I have a clean bed."

Annie Mae nodded, then appeared to look around for the children. Melinda saw all three boys walking together away from the churchyard and toward home, Henry on one side of Philip holding his hand, William on the other. It was rare to see all three boys this way, and she was glad for it.

"Was it you or Bunyan that gave Henry a haircut?" she asked then.

"It was Bunyan. Kate come in and told her you wanted it done."

Melinda began walking toward home and motioned for the girls to follow now that the storekeeper's boy had walked away from them. "Where were the scissors?" she asked.

Annie Mae stopped walking a moment, then turned and faced Melinda. "They was in the kitchen, in the drawer where they stay."

"How'd they get there when they'd been under the bed?" She saw the question turned Annie Mae much more serious, and she gave Annie Mae her own questioning look.

"I asked Bunyan that. Told her I'd put them under the bed for to help you with the pains. She laughed, but that didn't bother me none. Told me she wondered why she'd found them there. They was just under the edge. She figured after I cut the cord, I must of mislaid them. Said she put them away where they belonged, just like she would do. If Kate been the one to see them, they might be under the bed still."

In the past she might have wondered if Annie Mae was trying to make her smile, but that wasn't possible now, it seemed, not after all the ugly things she'd said to Annie Mae's daughter while they stood in the kitchen.

She decided she might still ask Bunyan if the scissors had looked clean, or stained with something, though she wouldn't use the word blood. Melinda was mostly certain Elizabeth hadn't reached beneath the bed that night. She would have seen her. And the girl might not have even known the scissors were there. No, she was satisfied Elizabeth had done nothing with them, but that didn't make her any less guilty. The girl's hand had acted in some way—even if it hadn't held scissors.

She watched Annie Mae turn now and continue walking, and Melinda's speculation turned in her direction. She didn't have to wonder what a mother might do for a daughter. That she already knew. If the scissors *had* needed moving, and Annie Mae had known, she would have moved them and cleaned them long before Bunyan carried them to the kitchen. Annie Mae had done *something*, though. Melinda more than sensed it.

They walked, Annie Mae a half-step ahead, the boys farther on, the girls behind. They passed the store and the Stagecoach Inn, then turned past the Teclaw house with its columns made of tree trunks, the bark stripped away but with stubs of limbs near the top, a peculiarity that made the house unique beyond its steep-pitched roof and the large number of chimneys that grew out of its sharp angles.

Melinda then saw smoke rising from her own chimneys and thought about the piece of white cloth she'd left from when Elizabeth had thrown the linens into the fire. It was gone now. Bunyan or Kate could have picked it up or nudged it into the coals with a toe, giving it no thought, but she suspected Annie Mae had thrown it into the fire after she'd gone to see to the dead child. Annie Mae had taken quite some time, claimed the baby needed changing. Maybe she'd done more than change a diaper, had done whatever she needed to protect her daughter. Melinda couldn't remember seeing the scrap of cloth when she'd first returned to her bedroom, but she hadn't thought about it then, only saw later that it was gone.

The boys were now climbing the steps to the loft and would soon be out of their church clothes. Melinda followed Annie Mae onto the porch and into the dogtrot, out of the sun's bright reach. They stood in shadow, both silent for the moment, as if they didn't want to separate and weren't sure what to say to each other and hadn't, really, since that night in the kitchen. Some curtain or partition Melinda didn't want to acknowledge felt drawn between them.

"I'll soon have dinner ready," Annie Mae said finally.

Melinda nodded, finding she couldn't speak.

Annie Mae waited a moment, her face darker now, obscured by the shade of the dogtrot or a deeper shade of something internal. She turned away, then headed to the kitchen, and Melinda wondered for the first time if Annie Mae had already known the child was dead before Melinda went to her cot and woke her, wanting and needing the comfort of sorrow shared.

Rafe wasn't home for noon dinner, or at least he was nowhere inside the house. Melinda listened to the voices of the children at the table and watched their faces as they ate. They were still flushed red from the cold but looked healthy and vibrant.

"Henry," Bunyan said, "don't eat with your elbows on the table."

"How I eat is my business." He leaned forward and placed each elbow more firmly on either side of his plate.

Bunyan looked like she might respond, but Melinda shook her head at her daughter and felt as if she might be taking her place again among her children. Henry couldn't be scolded for every little thing.

"I don't have mine on the table," Philip said.

"That's because you have good manners." Bunyan patted Philip's head and smoothed his hair.

Henry glared at his younger brother, and Melinda saw what had to be the look of a boy who felt betrayed.

William was quiet, his eyes darting Henry's way from time to time. She worried for him. He was truly well-mannered, more her child than his father's, and he fought Rafe in his own way, Melinda knew, so as to keep himself from cowering. She'd seen and heard him question his father's rule in such subtle ways that Rafe would appear unsure if he should be angry or not, and maybe only she could see how unsettled Rafe would become. At times she found it almost humorous and would want to applaud her son. She knew at such moments he had occasionally caught the hint of her smile, and in response she'd seen the quick flash of light in William's eyes when his head was momentarily turned from his father.

She worried for Henry too, who was too much his father's son. She was afraid she would lose him in all the ways a boy is lost to his mother as he becomes a man. And Philip, she had no sense yet of which way he would turn, toward or away from his father. When she would see his hand in Henry's, following behind him, she feared she knew, and yet to see Henry's tenderness for Philip gave her a hope for her middle son she would rather not let go of.

"I think Richard likes you, Bunyan," Kate announced with no prompt of any kind as she laid her napkin down without folding it.

Melinda remembered that was the name of Alfred's son. He sometimes came into the store while his father worked. She saw William look Bunyan's way and noticed he tried not to smile. Then she looked at Henry hard enough to keep him from teasing his sister.

"He's just friendly," Bunyan said. "That's all."

"Well, I wish he was as friendly to me as he is to you." Kate was smiling, not teasing. "You know he mostly runs that little farm his family has."

"Then maybe you should marry him and go live there," Bunyan said, her soft face suddenly hardened.

"Maybe I would, but he hasn't asked me."

"That's enough," Melinda said quietly. "He seems like a nice boy. Let's not worry over him."

Because Melinda understood them better, or differently, or perhaps because she knew what Kate and Bunyan would face as young women and was better prepared from experience to help them, she found she worried less for her daughters than for the boys, though she knew that probably ran counter to what most mothers felt. Both Kate and Bunyan had loving natures, and she prayed each would find a man who would know how to appreciate that. Yes, for this she found she could pray with a depth that approached what she'd once been able to achieve. Bunyan gave her a little more concern than Kate, perhaps because Bunyan was older and would not return to school again after the end of the spring— she was closer to having to find her way as a woman. She saw what a good mother Bunyan would be, and yet she sensed some fear in her daughter she wasn't sure what to make of. Melinda wondered if the fault was hers. She'd protected her too much. Maybe she shouldn't have excluded her from this last birth. Girls younger than her took part. But maybe the fear Bunyan felt was deeper than that of only birth. She'd spoken so briefly with the storekeeper's son, who was handsome in a way that at least Kate seemed to admire, but Bunyan must too.

Henry stood up from the table. "May I be excused?" he said.

Melinda looked and saw his plate was empty, and yet his question seemed greater than simple, rote table manners. "For now," she said, and wanted to add, *but not for always*. William laughed.

Late in the afternoon, she sought out Bunyan, first looking in the kitchen and finding Annie Mae, who answered for the girl's whereabouts but said nothing more. Melinda returned to her room, put on the heavy dark coat she'd worn to church, and found Bunyan inside the barn in front of Benjamin's stall, stroking the white blaze on his face.

"He's beautiful, isn't he?" Melinda said.

"He is. I brought him some sugar cubes from the kitchen."

"Did you bring any for Ida and Ned?"

"I always feed them theirs first. You know, like the Bible verse says, 'The last shall be first.'"

"What about Wheeler?" Melinda asked, mostly in jest.

"I try not to go near him."

"Just as well. It's not like your father would ever allow anyone else to ride him."

Wheeler blew out a breath as if he understood, as always, that he was being talked about, or maybe to say he wanted the last of what Bunyan held in her hand. Melinda and Bunyan both laughed quietly, and the small bit of laughter felt like a shared gift to Melinda. "Wheeler's more than just beautiful," she said.

"He's a match for Daddy, isn't he?"

"I'd say so. That's why your father takes such pride in him, I think."

She watched her daughter move to Mollie B.'s stall and turn back toward her with a look of surprise. "He must be out riding Mollie. I didn't realize she was gone."

"Must be," Melinda said. "He takes her out sometimes."

Bunyan looked at the sugar cubes in her hand. "I guess it wouldn't be fair not to give him something." She approached Wheeler who stuck his head farther through the open top half of the stall door, and she reached her hand out at some distance and let him take the last three cubes.

Bunyan walked toward her now, and when Melinda happened to look down, she saw them both standing in sawdust that littered the hard-packed dirt floor. Bunyan noticed too. "From the coffin," she said, and then seemed worried that she'd spoken the words aloud.

"I know."

"How do you stand it, Mama?" she asked, as if she'd found courage enough since the subject had been broached.

"Maybe sometimes I don't. But you can only take to the bed for so long." She put her arm around her daughter's shoulders and pulled her close. "And I have other children who still need me. Maybe even my oldest."

Bunyan nodded, hugging her with both arms. "I should be the one comforting you," she said, her face tucked for the moment against Melinda's shoulder.

"You already do."

"Were you out here looking for me, or were you going to visit the grave?" Then, without waiting for an answer, she asked another question. "Does it bother you he's not buried in the church graveyard?"

Melinda didn't answer at first but walked to the rear barn door, opening it only far enough for the two of them to look out into the horse pasture and see the small mound. "It bothers me, but not enough to give up the little part of him I want to keep for myself."

"I know his name too, though. You mean the part of him you want to keep from Daddy."

"I guess you're right about that."

She could see that Bunyan wanted to ask another question. Then it came. "Are all marriages hard?"

Melinda heard the fear in her voice and closed the barn door against the wind, faced her daughter, and watched her brush at her windblown hair with the tips of her fingers. She was struck again by this daughter's beauty that was so much deeper than eyes and hair and skin. "I don't think so," she said. "They don't have to be, but some are. Tell me," she said, having decided this was the time to ask, "if Richard called on you, would you see him, be glad for his attention?"

"I'd see him," she said.

"Good, because I think he'll call. I was younger than you when your father first wanted to call on me."

Her daughter's face seemed to darken. "Back then, was he like he is now?"

"Enough so, but I didn't understand then. No way I could have."

Bunyan looked worried again. "How is a girl supposed to know?"

"She listens to her mother, if she's lucky enough to have a mother who's still alive. I didn't, you know." Bunyan nodded. "But she probably couldn't have stopped me, or maybe I should say she couldn't have stopped your father. No one could."

Melinda decided she'd maybe said enough about the past, and before Bunyan could ask another question, she took her daughter's arm in her own and walked out of the barn with her. Once she closed the door behind them and turned toward the house, she saw the girl Elizabeth in front of her cabin, standing alone and still, staring as if she'd been caught somewhere she wasn't supposed to be. She'd been shaking out a rug, and it hung loose now in her hands, though dust flew from around her, entered the air, and was carried away until it seemed to disappear. Elizabeth held their looks, maybe with defiance, or maybe not. Melinda couldn't be sure, but the girl did look from one to the other of them. There was no further acknowledgment, no nod, no words spoken, except those whispered close to her ear in a warm breath by Bunyan: "I hate her."

Melinda didn't respond to her daughter but kept her eyes on Elizabeth, and despite the brightness of the day, which would soon be tending toward shadow, she saw the dark figure of the girl in her room that night, holding the child, later lifting him and placing him back in his crib, then throwing the linens into the fire. This was what she could remember, but there was more she could imagine, *and* remember, with the last child.

Elizabeth finally entered her cabin with the rug hanging limp in one hand, and shut the door behind her.

"I hate her," Bunyan said again, stronger this time. "Don't you?"

Melinda remained still, taking her daughter's hand in her own. "Sometimes. When I haven't it's only because I remember how young she is, and that she's Annie Mae's daughter." Melinda did not let herself say more, nothing about what she'd seen the night of the birth or the undivided hate she felt now. And she did not ask Bunyan about the scissors she found, if they were stained. She didn't want whatever hate Bunyan carried to grow larger.

She let go of her daughter's hand, and they began walking slowly toward the house, past the girl's cabin, but her mind went back to that other night, the only night of the other child's life, the boy she'd named Robert Hendricks. Rafe had been home and wouldn't allow the child's crib to be placed in their bedroom, so Annie Mae moved it into Rafe's office and gun room. The birth had been an easy one, and in the early evening, after Melinda had nursed him, Annie Mae put the child down in what would be the temporary nursery. Sometime near midnight Melinda heard him cry and went to her child to let him nurse again. Then she laid him in his crib, covered him, and made sure he was warm. In the morning, Annie Mae would do the taking-up ceremony and the child would be given its name. Late in the night, or early morning, rather, Melinda awoke to the sound of footsteps and the closing of the door to the dogtrot. She knew it would have been Annie Mae checking on the baby, or maybe Bunyan. In the morning she found him cold, and later, when she asked, Bunyan told her she'd not come down from the loft, and Annie Mae said she had checked on the infant after one o'clock, or maybe a little later. She'd not been sure exactly. Melinda had helped Annie Mae dress the child for burial, and there was no sign of any harm. She knew sometimes infants died in their cribs for no reason doctors or anyone else could understand. But she kept remembering the sound of steps and the door in the night, though at times doubted her memory, and wondered if it had only been the sound of the house settling, or if her imagination had become memory that was less than fact. Then, a week or so beyond the child's death, she saw Elizabeth outside her cabin carrying her first-born child, a boy, Rafe's boy, she was fairly certain, only months old, and imagined, then suspected with an ambivalent conviction, that the girl had come up these back steps she and Bunyan now ascended together and had crept into the nursery with a jealousy so deep that it took the child's breath.

She'd known jealousy herself. As a girl of fifteen, when her father allowed her to attend dances in Riverfield, always with him present, she would see Rafe dance with older girls, usually one of them gaining most of his attention for the night. The next dance it would be another, but he'd dance with her, too, at least once, sometimes twice, and she thrilled at his sure movements and strength, disheartened almost to sickness when he'd walk away from her and toward another.

Then one October night, when she was sixteen, and they moved in step together through the sound of fiddle and guitar, and in lantern light and cool air, he said, "Not yet, but soon."

It hadn't been soon enough for her, but he did finally begin to call, and her father allowed it. She supposed he knew that it would happen. At first Rafe would simply sit on the porch with her on Sunday afternoons. Later there were walks, and later still, buggy rides and picnics. Then she would not see or hear a word from him for weeks or a month at a time. She knew there were other girls, girls she knew at school and church, and while she did not blame them, she'd find herself angry and upset. Her father would say nothing while she stewed and imagined who he might be with and what they might be doing. She heard from others that he went with town girls, too, in Demarville and Valhia. When he kissed her, touched and held her, she could sense his experience and knew that on the Lassiter place he was surrounded by girls of a different kind, dark skinned and so poor they were probably willing for anything they might be offered, a bit of cloth, a fifty-cent piece—or maybe they admired him too. She sometimes wondered if he had given them anything beyond reward for their services—though *services* would not have been a word she'd known then—maybe children with nappy red hair.

Finally, he spent more and more time with her, as if he had made a decision. But then a distraction came, something so large and daunting she knew she could not really fathom it, not beyond what it meant for her. It was war, and she understood it would take him from her. Before he left, on a warm, late-spring night, he both took and left something for her, each a matter of blood. What he took left only a smear of red, and then for three months her monthly was gone. She wrote but did not name for him in a single word of what she carried. Finally one night in her bed there was pain and blood again, and what she carried was lost, a loss she kept secret. That night she burned her own linens and then re-made and crept back into her childhood bed, which felt oddly foreign.

He answered her letters only occasionally, but he made clear his plans for when he returned, *if* he returned, he said, which he did after escorting a retreating President Davis as far south as Georgia.

So she married him, and within a matter of months she saw in his demeanor and treatment of her and anyone near that he'd brought the war back home with him, then realized it had been in him long before he left, his very nature always at battle with anything and anyone beyond himself.

EIGHT

Annie Mae had seen, through the kitchen window, her daughter shaking the rug in front of her cabin and knew Melinda and Bunyan might walk out of the barn at any moment. When she saw them emerge, she feared what could happen. Bunyan said something to her mother, whispered it looked like, and most likely had kept Melinda calm. Annie Mae felt grateful to Bunyan for that. Then Betsy showed enough good sense to go back inside her house, and maybe an ugly scene like the one in the kitchen had been avoided; but as Bunyan and Melinda walked toward the house, Annie Mae was filled with dread, not for what Melinda would say to her, but with the sense that something would happen in the days and weeks ahead that could not be got past.

She felt she knew why Melinda had asked about the scissors, knew maybe what Melinda suspected, but whatever Betsy'd done, *if* she'd done something, it hadn't been with scissors. Melinda's questions worried her, though, and made her more fearful for her daughter than she already was.

Annie Mae heard the door to the dogtrot open, and in a moment Bunyan walked into the kitchen alone. She looked worried, distracted, and was quiet. Annie Mae didn't speak either but watched Bunyan sit down at the small table. She continued to put dishes away and waited to see if the girl could say what was on her mind. The only sounds in the room were Annie Mae's steps on the floorboards and the thick clink of plates as she stacked them.

"Sometimes I forget Betsy's your daughter," Bunyan said finally. Annie Mae felt as if a hand had reached through her and squeezed her inside. She realized they were about to have a talk like they'd never had before and was surprised Bunyan might be forward enough. Annie Mae stood still, her backside braced against the sideboard. "Or maybe it's not that I forget," Bunyan said, not looking directly at her. "Maybe I try not to remember."

Annie Mae found herself wanting to apologize, maybe for her daughter, maybe for herself, yet couldn't. She hadn't brought Betsy here for Rafe's use, hadn't foreseen George and Lakeview. She'd only helped deliver them when they came, their births more worrisome for her than joyful. It was Bunyan's father Bunyan needed to blame, but a girl her age couldn't be expected to separate out such things, not when most grown women couldn't, not in a situation like this one. Yet Melinda *had* with Annie Mae, at least until now when it looked like a truer and deeper blame could be laid at her daughter Betsy's feet.

"When she came here," Annie Mae said, "I just wanted my daughter with me. That was all."

Bunyan looked at her, tentatively, as a child might, and Annie Mae saw her, for a moment, as the girl of nine she'd been when Annie Mae first arrived. She remembered how Bunyan had begun to follow her around the house and yard and let herself be held. This was after Melinda had lost R.A.—the first of the children to die—and Melinda had taken to the bed for a month, ignoring her other children. Now here Bunyan sat, trying to understand grown-ups, even trying to talk like one.

"It was better when you both lived in the cabin."

"I know, honey. But I didn't have much choice when I moved in here to my little room, and didn't really know what would happen."

"But you didn't *have* to. You weren't a slave. Y'all could have lived somewhere else, or moved away."

Annie Mae tried to tell herself that Bunyan didn't know how much those words would hurt. "No, I never was a slave," she said, but didn't add, as she could have, that at times she'd been forced to pass herself off as a slave when it was better to have been Negro than Choctaw. "Would you really have wanted me to move off, leave all you children?"

Bunyan seemed to think for a moment, and then shook her head as if she felt ashamed for what she'd said.

"How much do you think the other children understand?" Annie Mae asked, and it was something she'd long wanted to know.

Bunyan didn't hesitate as Annie Mae thought she might. Her dark eyes held the knowing, and maybe Annie Mae had already seen that they did. "Kate knows, but she pretends she doesn't. I mean pretends to herself." Annie Mae nodded, surprised a little that Bunyan understood such a thing. "And William knows, but he never talks about it." Bunyan looked out the back window for a moment, or maybe she was imagining each of her brothers and sister in turn. "Who can tell what Henry thinks? If anyone his age *could* know, it would be him, not that he'd understand everything."

"I guess I had it figured about the same as you," Annie Mae said, and realized what she said was true. "Kate the one I wasn't sure about."

Bunyan placed a hand at her mouth as if she wanted to stifle a question, then removed it, laying her hand on the table. "When do you think Mama first knew?"

Annie Mae walked over and sat down at the table. At first she didn't know if she dared, but she sat close enough to pat Bunyan on the knee and left her hand there the way she used to do when Bunyan was a child. "I couldn't say. Something like that, a woman just start to know. Could be she started knowing about the time I did, before Betsy's first baby come. Something told her before Betsy even started to show."

Bunyan looked away and back at her, and Bunyan's eyes seemed to hold more knowing that she wouldn't tell. Annie Mae remained quiet, wondering about Bunyan's own notions and how much she might have guessed about Betsy. Sometimes it seemed as if children could come closer to the truth than they knew. Something spoke through them, or for them, especially if they were right in between a child and a grown-up. It was hard to know, hard to judge the level of someone else's knowing.

But what about her own? What had Annie Mae known, and how far back? She'd been asking herself these questions for days now. Maybe she was like Kate, who knew but wouldn't let herself know. Hadn't Melinda asked her if she'd checked on the last child—the other boy, in the night— and wanted to know when, what time exactly, as if Melinda knew *someone* had come in when they, Annie Mae and Melinda, were asleep, or were supposed to be asleep? Maybe Betsy had been up in the night and come into the house on her own, without being pushed or made to nurse a child whose death approached. Whenever some quiet moment came her way these last days, one answer made her feel a terrible *unquiet* inside. She didn't know what to do with such a thought that doubled her worry and fear. Twice now a sudden loss since Betsy had come.

"Your mother's been through too much," she said. "I'm sorry for that."

Bunyan pulled away, looking down at the tabletop. "It's not your fault."

"But you blame me anyway?"

Bunyan looked as if she'd been asked some question at school that was too complicated to answer, too far beyond her, and Annie Mae wanted to help her past it.

"Or maybe do you blame your daddy?" she asked and then wished she hadn't, but the words had come too fast. How could she ask such a question of a daughter?

Bunyan stood up from the table in a quick movement. "I know who's to blame and who's not," she said. "And I know who my father is. We all do."

Just before Bunyan walked away, Annie Mae saw her flash of anger turn to tears, and as much as she wanted to, she knew she could not go after her.

When she'd first come to Riverfield, traveled up through the pine forests of South Alabama, where she'd lived most of her life, Annie Mae hoped Betsy would eventually follow, hoped it wouldn't take years, but it hadn't been that simple. Betsy's father was a white man who owned property and had come home early from the war, wounded in the leg that was then missing from the knee down. Though he was married, with children of his own, Betsy was light-skinned enough that he claimed her, after a fashion, and in a manner that was not unknown. He had his sister and brother-in-law, who were childless, take Betsy in, the act seen as charity among the community, no matter the rumors, or open secret, of the child's paternity.

The couple soon moved to Mobile, a city with so many half-claimed, mixed race and Creole children that one more would not stand out. Annie Mae was taken from the woods where she worked at collecting turpentine and, years earlier, had escaped continued attempts at Indian removal by passing as a slave, and she served as the couple's maid in the large brick house, her midwife skills unneeded. The wife, though, made her life difficult. Maybe Annie Mae was a constant reminder of what the woman could not give her husband, or it may have been a fear of what her husband might give Annie Mae, who still had a younger woman's figure then. And playing at mother to a child with the real mother there in the very same house may have finally proved too much. The wife eventually accused her of stealing, claimed her an unfaithful servant, and sent her away. Betsy's blood father had known Rafe from the war, and arrangements for Annie Mae were made, which she accepted. Life had not been simple then, nor was it now.

Betsy, when old enough, finally left her complicated origins behind and joined Annie Mae, only to make these new complications for herself and her mother. Congress between races might be a natural enough fact, Annie Mae well knew, but its complications went beyond those of ordinary adultery. Yet the consequences, if children could be called such a thing, were as innocent as anything that ever came into the world. All she had to do was hold Lakeview and wide-eyed George to know that much. They were her flesh and blood, but they were Rafe's too, and sometimes maybe, like Bunyan, she tried not to remember that.

Annie Mae looked out into the yard again, and in the last of the day's light she saw Samuel approach the house, trailed by a partly crippled fyce dog that had been following him off and on for several days, and behind them came Henry, sometimes taking quick steps to keep pace. It was not an unusual sight to see him following like that. She had Samuel's supper ready for him to carry home in a syrup bucket, which he brought back every morning and left on the back porch beside the kitchen door.

Annie Mae pulled on her coat and carried his supper out to him. She found him sitting on the edge of the porch and sat down beside him as she often did, despite the cold. She placed the bucket between them and he thanked her. The dog nosed Samuel's feet and sat on its haunches, probably smelling the food and hoping for a supper of its own.

Henry walked up and petted the dog. "Reckon how come dogs like to follow you, Samuel?"

"Don't know, really. Just do." Samuel spoke with unconcealed irritation, as if he were tired of Henry being so close underfoot.

"Some people, they got a way about them animals like," Annie Mae said, but she suspected her answer wasn't enough for Henry, that he already had his own idea and was ready to tell it. He didn't often look for answers from grown-ups, only times to tell them what he thought.

"Dogs are colorblind," he announced, and when neither she nor Samuel responded, he added, "They don't see colors. Just see black and white. And they must see white as black and black as white. That's what I think." Annie Mae looked over at Samuel, he at her. "That's why dogs like niggers so much," Henry said and looked up at them, pleased with himself, ready to hear their agreement.

Samuel shook his head and turned away, and Annie Mae whispered, "Hush now," to him. Then, to Henry, "Best go inside and get warm."

Henry didn't move at first. It seemed as if he were waiting for them to at least nod their agreement. Then he trudged up the steps, the dog sniffing at his heels but not daring to walk onto the porch.

"George and Lakeview got them some kind of brother there," Samuel said and stood, stamping his feet as a way of warming himself, it appeared. Annie Mae hugged her body with both arms and was about to get up herself, but Samuel kept her down with what he spoke next. "So you think she killed this one too?" he said.

His words, quiet as they were, took away any urge to move, even for warmth, no matter the cold that filled her body. "Who?" she asked.

He looked at her as if surprised by the question. "Miss Melinda."

"Why you think that?"

"Just make sense," he said. "Why she want more children with a man she know been having yard children?"

Annie Mae stood quickly now, pointing a finger into his face. "Don't be calling them such a name as that. They my daughter's children, my grandchildren."

"I'm sorry. Didn't mean nothing by that. I know they your grandchildren," he said, "but they got his last name."

"Miss Melinda don't know that," Annie Mae said.

"Maybe not yet. These last two of hers went fast. She figure he can have his nigger babies but not her babies."

"They not niggers."

He nodded. "I mean how she think."

"And who been thinking for you?"

He'd produced a matchstick from some pocket and placed it in his mouth. "What you mean?" he said and rolled the match with his tongue from one corner of his mouth to the other.

"Who put such notions in your head?"

"Nobody did," he said and turned sideways to her, though he was still able to see her from the corner of his eye.

"You been talking to Betsy about this?"

He faced her again, the head of the match barely protruding from his dark mouth. "Some, and she think the same as me."

Annie Mae felt the cold in her bones again. "I bet she does."

"What you mean by that?" he said.

"Loose talk don't do anybody no good. Sometime babies die. Putting a bad word on somebody don't make anything true, and sometime the one doing the talking the one to get in trouble. Maybe you need to remember that. Betsy too."

Samuel nodded. "People can say one thing or another, or nothing, but what's true is true."

"Just don't be thinking you the one who always know what true. You start talking like you just did, you gon' make trouble like you can't even see."

Samuel looked as if he might respond but instead picked up the syrup bucket off the porch. "Thank you for supper," he said and walked away slowly, the fyce picking up right behind him—like trouble following on crooked legs.

By the middle of the next morning the weather had warmed considerably and the sun was out, the air still. Annie Mae carried clothes to the wash pot and checked the fire beneath it. Samuel was splitting wood by the pile at the far edge of the yard. Beyond him, just inside the woods, Annie Mae saw a flash of movement between the trunks, then another, and another, both smaller and slower than the one in the lead. At first she thought it was the three boys playing some kind of game, then realized the first one she saw was too small to be William, and William, she knew, considered himself too old now to be playing games with Henry and Philip.

All three figures suddenly burst out of the woods with high-pitched yells—Indian whoops, she imagined—and ran right between Samuel and the stump he used for a chopping block, the axe still raised over his shoulder. She saw then that it was Henry, Philip, and George, the sight of her grandchild with Henry and Philip like some flesh and blood apparition, nothing she'd ever seen before, or ever expected to see, but probably should have. They ran by her, and Henry grabbed at the bundle of clothes she held, pulled a shirt from her, and flung it into the air, Philip and George close behind, grinning, faces flushed with cold and delight. She was struck not just at George being with them, but how much George and Philip favored, their movements, their coloring, the shape of their small faces.

"You boys, stop!" she yelled now at their backs. George and Philip obeyed immediately. Henry ran a few more steps, looked back over his shoulder, then turned around.

She walked toward George and Philip, the clothes still in her arms, and the two boys, side by side, waited for her, their grins disappearing. Henry seemed resigned and walked slowly toward his two brothers. Annie Mae, closest to George, looked down at him over the top of the clothes. "What you think you doing just now?"

"Playing," he said in a small voice, looking up at her. He didn't cower, nor did he look at her with defiance the way Henry would.

"Playing what?"

"Indians."

She knew whose idea the game was and that George didn't yet know he did not have to *play* at being an Indian. She would have to tell him something of his Choctaw blood, to make a beginning at it that he could understand, or maybe go ahead and fill him with the mystery of his people's creation and let his young mind explore that opening from under Nanih Waiya.

"So where's your mother?" she said, still not regarding either Henry or Philip, her first worry her grandchild.

"In the house. She let me come out."

"Why don't you ask him where his father is?" she heard from behind her and recognized Rafe's voice. Maybe he had come from the barn or Betsy's cabin. She wasn't sure. She turned his way, wondering what he had in mind. He reached down with both hands and picked George up effortlessly, and the boy laughed until Rafe got him settled into his arms. "Henry," he said, "go and pick up that shirt you threw down, and I mean right now."

"Yes, sir."

Annie Mae watched Henry walk over to the blue shirt where it hugged the chill ground. He kept looking up at his father, not so much out of fear, it seemed, as curiosity, a struggle to understand what he was seeing even as he picked up the shirt and carried it to his father.

"Don't hand it to me," he said. "Can't you see I've got my hands full? Besides, I ain't the one who washes the clothes. Give it to Annie Mae, and tell me what you were doing."

He first gave her the shirt back, pushing it into the bundle of clothes she held firm. Then he faced his father again. William, she noticed, had walked out onto the back porch, and Bunyan stood just behind him, their appearance more than mere audience to this small spectacle. They lent it a weight somehow that Annie Mae had only just begun to feel, their eyes riveted on their father and the child he held.

"We was playing Indians," Henry said.

"So I heard. You're just lucky you didn't get yourself scalped when you ran under Samuel's axe, or get your head cut off completely. Did you think about what I would have had to do to Samuel if he'd managed to kill you?"

"No, sir."

Annie Mae looked back at Samuel for a moment, who remained motionless, hard-faced.

"And just why did you throw my shirt to the ground?"

"We was attacking."

Rafe shifted George in his arms, placed a hand across the child's small back, and let the boy lean over his shoulder. "Always best to attack from horseback, and since you don't have a horse, don't let me see you charging Samuel and Annie Mae again. I'll tan your hide good. You hear me?"

"Yes, sir," Henry said.

"You can play games with your little brothers—and this boy I'm holding is your brother—but don't be leading them into trouble."

Henry nodded and said, "Yes, sir," again, giving no indication that he understood what he'd just heard. Annie Mae, though, felt as if Rafe had suddenly spoken a word of Choctaw whose meaning he had no way of knowing, or as if he had said aloud the name of some dead Choctaw child to its mother; and yet what he'd spoken was not insulting or hurtful, not for her or for George. Bunyan, she saw, had already walked back into the house and slammed the door behind her with enough force it seemed to break the door's hardware. William stood alone, still and quiet—acceptance, for him, a thing already in the past.

Head down, Henry now began to walk toward the woods, either weighted with shame at his scolding or with a burden whose meaning he'd just this moment come one step closer to understanding. Philip looked up at his father, who hung on to George as he carefully surveyed the reactions of all those around him, which was maybe Rafe's own simple acknowledgment of what he'd just announced: brothers. Shared blood. All Rafe's children. As Annie Mae turned toward the fire and wash pot, the thud of the axe and the sound of splitting wood rent the air.

After washing the clothes and getting them hung outside to dry, since it was not cold enough for them to freeze, Annie Mae went to the cabin. When she opened the door, she found Betsy changing Lakeview's diaper. George sat by the fire but ran to her, wanting to be picked up, probably needing assurance that she wasn't still upset with him. She squatted down and hugged him to her. "Everything all right," she said, though she knew it wasn't. She handed him a biscuit she'd brought from the kitchen, and he bit into it hungrily.

Betsy put Lakeview down between two bed pillows and moved to the edge of the bed. She seemed to eye her mother carefully, trying to take her measure.

"Did you hear any of it?" Annie Mae said.

"Some. I came to the door, cracked it open a little."

"What about Rafe? Did he say anything to you?"

"No."

Annie Mae sat down on the bed beside Betsy. Sometimes she could see in her daughter the girl she'd been—bright eyes, mischievous smile, suddenly capable of shyness—but there were those in-between years when Betsy had become a young woman, and she'd missed seeing the turn every child makes. Maybe because she had missed that change there was a part of her daughter she could never know, just as the white woman who had played at raising Betsy could never have known all of her either, even though Betsy had learned to talk like her, to talk proper, to talk white. Betsy would always be part mystery, and maybe those missing years were not the reason but only an explanation Annie Mae wanted, or needed, to believe. The truth might be that Betsy was unknowable, that there was no cause or accounting for it. She suspected Rafe felt it too and that unknowing was part of what drew him to her. Maybe they were alike in that way and so recognized each other. But there was another thought that had also come to her lately, one she had to face now. Maybe her not being there for her daughter's turning away from girlhood and into a young woman had made Betsy who she was. She'd been shaped by absence, and it might be that absence accounted for whoever her daughter had become, and for her actions. If that was so, then how much of the blame for all that had happened belonged to Annie Mae? Maybe all of it. She'd led her daughter into the dark of Melinda's room in more ways than one; she had led her there all the way from the turpentine woods of South Alabama by a shaping hand that had not shaped as it should have.

"So why didn't you come outside," she finally asked, "if you was already at the door?"

"Didn't seem anything for me to say or do."

"Looking after your child not something for you to be doing?" Annie Mae looked at Betsy and waited for some kind of answer from her daughter but didn't expect anything that might satisfy.

"His daddy was out there, and they didn't need me."

"So how George come to be outdoors?"

"He's old enough to play outside, and he wasn't by himself. He was with his brothers. His daddy was around the barn, and I heard Samuel out chopping wood. Besides, I kept a look through the window."

"So you knew he was playing with Henry and Philip and you let him?"

"Children are going to play together."

"What if Miss Melinda had seen them? Or maybe she did."

"I can't keep him locked up in this house," Betsy said. She stood up with impatience, it appeared, and looked down at her mother.

Betsy was right, Annie Mae knew, but she wouldn't turn away from her daughter's dark, answering eyes. "Samuel told me some things. Wanted to know did I think she killed this one too. Scared me the way he talked." Lakeview began to cry but Annie Mae kept her gaze on Betsy who did not yet look away. "I was afraid of who he meant. You hear me? Said *she*. I thought he meant *you*. Then come to find out he meant Miss Melinda, that you two been talking. You and Samuel best watch what you say and who you say it to."

Betsy picked up Lakeview and held her gently, and the child stopped crying. "She could have hurt those babies. She's got reason."

"We not talking about hurting babies. We talking about more than that. And why you and Samuel talking about *babies*, more than just the one?"

Betsy placed Lakeview in the crib and then faced Annie Mae again, her eyes seemingly untroubled and her body as calm as the baby now appeared. "'Cause the last one died too."

"Like you know something about that one?"

"I know they both died in the night."

"When everyone asleep," Annie Mae said. "Or supposed to be. But I wasn't, and somebody else wasn't. I know because I heard them. I'd just looked in on the child."

"But you didn't get up again," Betsy said, tucking a length of hair behind her ear.

"How do you know?"

"'Cause you would have seen them, or seen her, Miss Melinda. Could be you heard Rafe or one of the children. You don't know when that baby breathed its last. Might have been before you were awake or after you went back to sleep."

"Or maybe somebody came in the house," Annie Mae said and let her words settle between them.

Betsy walked toward the fireplace and turned her back to it. "It *wasn't* me. Why do you want to think it was? 'Cept for the kitchen, when I went in to see you, I don't go inside that house. You're the one made me go, pushed me in the room with this last child. I didn't want to, and wouldn't have ever been in there at all if it wasn't for you."

Betsy had spoken the truth, and Annie Mae had no answer for it, only more questions whose answers she knew still would not satisfy, and if they did they might only appall, she feared, and make her question herself all the more deeply.

NINE

When Rafe entered Betsy's cabin, still carrying George in his arms after scolding Henry, he wondered how much Betsy had heard him say, if she realized just exactly what he'd said for all to hear. It hadn't been anything he'd planned, was no grand announcement, but the words "your brothers" were plain enough, and it was time to say them. Betsy's pleased expression when he handed George to her told him that she'd both heard and understood.

Now, though, inside his house, there were no pleased looks. Bunyan had not come near him, and he hadn't seen Kate either. If Melinda had heard, she hadn't let on, but her demeanor toward him could be no worse than it already was. He'd seen William about to head up to the loft, and the boy had spoken but wore a worried look.

Rafe pushed back from the desk in his office and called loudly, "William, go tell Samuel to saddle Wheeler and Benjamin." He knew his voice could carry through the loft floor. "You and I are going to take a ride."

The sound of William's steps above were his only answer, but it wasn't like the boy to raise his voice.

He gave both William and Samuel time for their tasks, then pulled on his coat which hung on the back of the chair. He looked into the bedroom but Melinda was not there. She had slipped out without his noticing, probably in soft-soled slippers, and was maybe in the loft herself, on the girls' side. Yes, everyone take a side, he thought. Maybe that was what this ride was about, a need to have his oldest son beside him, sided with him, or maybe he was simply restless and wanted a riding companion.

Both horses were tied to the fence by the barn, and William stood waiting. "I saddled them myself," he said when Rafe drew near. "Didn't need Samuel."

Defiance or independence? Rafe wondered. Then he decided that for a boy William's age they were the same thing. "Good," he said and made a point to check the girth on each saddle. He first poked Wheeler in the stomach, then managed to cinch the girth tighter. He did the same with

Benjamin. William turned away, into the light wind that was just cold enough and hard enough to force tears. "These two will blow up on you, hold their breath and keep their stomachs swelled out. Got to watch that. Don't want your saddle to slide off."

"Yes, sir, I know," William said, still facing the wind.

"Next time, don't wait too long to pull tight after you poke them. But don't poke Wheeler too hard."

The boy finally turned toward him, nodded.

"No need to feel bad when I show you something, William. No one else around right now to hear. It's just me and you."

"Yes, sir."

Rafe untied Wheeler, stepped into a stirrup, and pulled himself up. "So you *want* to take a ride with your father?"

William hesitated a moment, finally said, "I do."

Rafe saw a light, and not tears, in the boy's eyes, and Rafe realized he'd briefly held his breath when he asked his son the question. There hadn't been anything sly about the breath-holding, either, only worry that he hadn't expected or gauged very well—although maybe he'd wanted to hide that from his son. It was rare he felt a *need* for any of his children, and he wasn't sure what to make of it.

William mounted with more ease than Rafe would have thought him capable, and soon they were past the house with Rafe just in the lead, William beside him but a step back. Once they approached the Stagecoach Inn, Rafe turned them away from town.

"We headed to the farm?" William asked.

"I want to find out from Brantley if anything needs my attention and see things for myself. Sometimes it's best to just show up, surprise people."

Rafe had set up Brantley, his riding boss, in a small but well-built house on a hill that overlooked a large part of the property. Because he'd been an overseer before the war, Brantley knew well the Negroes who'd stayed on the place to work shares. He'd always been fair enough with them and knew the day laborers too, who to hire when they were needed.

"Don't you trust Mr. Brantley?"

"Much as I can trust any man," Rafe said, and it was true. After the trouble, when Brantley and Alfred at the store had served him so well, he'd given Alfred a raise and Brantley his own small part of the shares. "You have to live among them," Rafe had told him. "When a hard hand is needed, let me know and I'll be the one to do it." But he knew Brantley was capable, too.

He kept Wheeler at a steady pace, and William rode abreast of him. They forded a small creek and the road began to rise until they topped a ridge. Beside them were hardwoods, pines, and cedars, but beyond the ridgeline, where the land stretched out into gently rolling hills to the left and right, lay open farmland where mostly cotton was grown. Shadows darkened the road in places, and they rode in silence for some time, as if the shadows had created the quiet between them.

William then broke the quiet. "Can I ask you a question, Father?"

Rafe had always demanded respect from his children, but the way William so often said "Father" struck Rafe even as too formal, yet he had never said anything to the boy about it. "Go ahead," he said.

"Earlier, when you got onto Henry, why didn't you whip him?"

Rafe thought a moment, slowed Wheeler slightly, and decided this was merely William's way of bringing up what had happened that morning, and what he'd asked wasn't the question he really wanted answered. "I suppose I should have," he said. "In fact, there's no doubt of that." He realized he was still searching for a reason to offer. "You might say I had other things on my mind." He'd see if the boy wanted to push any further.

"Don't you usually?" William dared a glance at him. "Have other things on your mind, I mean."

"That's true enough. A man has responsibilities. Work, family." He waited, then added, "And some men have more than one family. You know that already, I realize, and it's truer than you think for a lot of men."

"Why do some have more than one?"

The question was fair, and was asked in such an even-handed manner and tone, which he knew was William's way, but how to answer him? "You can ask about the right and wrong of it, but right and wrong don't really enter into the question as far as I'm concerned. A man needs what he needs to survive, and some need more of whatever that is than others."

The wind gusted across the ridge and through the bare winter limbs. William tucked his head against it until it let up. "Why do some need more?" he said. "And what exactly do they need?" He spoke quietly, without any hint of challenge that Rafe could hear.

"Depends on what a man's seen and done. I've seen, and done, hard things, some might say terrible, in the war and after it, before it too. When I was a little older than you, I nearly beat a cousin to death. Didn't plan to do it, didn't really *want* to do it, but I did." Rafe was silent a moment, heard only the hoof falls of each horse now that the wind had died, and found himself surprised he'd told his son about the cousin. "I carry what I've done with me, but maybe I carry it different from other men. It's just knowledge of myself, not guilt, and that sets me apart." What he wanted to add, to truly answer the boy's question, was that being with a woman he found himself wanting was the only peace he got, and if William had been older maybe he would have spoken the thought. "Could be what I carry is too much for any one woman," he said and was the most he would offer. "I don't know. But I *will* take what I need in this world. It's the only way I know how to live. I am the man I am. Be damned if I'll apologize for it." He knew William had to be thinking, *But what about my mother?* He could not answer that and wouldn't try. "As for Henry," he said, "I may have to whip him when we get home."

"Don't do it because I said something. I didn't mean to get him in trouble again."

Rafe considered a moment. "I'll have to give that some thought. We'll see."

They soon turned off the ridge and down a road that led toward Brantley's house and beyond, where the land was dotted with small shacks that stood in addition to the old slave quarters. All were occupied, some by Negroes who had stayed after the war, some by Negroes who'd left, just to prove to themselves they *could* leave, and then had come back.

Standing behind Brantley's house, like some out-of-place statuary, was the one remaining chimney of Mr. Lassiter's home. It had been large, two-story, with plain, square columns across the front, not a white mansion but big enough. Mr. Lassiter had bought the house and place sight unseen and left North Carolina after his wife died. Now he was buried in the Methodist cemetery plot where these last two children Melinda bore would have been buried, and Rafe had inherited the store and land, the house already burned to the ground by federal troops in the last year of the war.

Rafe dismounted in front of Brantley's and called out his name. William followed suit but remained quiet, and in a few moments Brantley came stepping out onto the porch, pulling on a coat, a worn bowler already covering his head. Rafe rarely wore a hat and knew it was considered odd. Brantley spit tobacco juice over the edge of the porch, far enough away as to show no disrespect.

"Hadn't seen you in a while," Rafe said, "or heard any word from you. You been all right?"

"Laid up sick. Quinsy. Last time doctor said my tonsils needed to come out. Not ready for that yet. Been up and around last day or two." He spit again. "How you, William?"

The boy nodded. "Fine, sir."

"You're talking like some sick old man," Rafe said.

"I ain't that yet."

Rafe walked up onto the porch. "Any trouble among them?"

Brantley shook his head. "Old Fluke died. They got him buried."

"Sorry to hear that. He was about wore out, though. Didn't come in with enough for a bale back in the fall."

"No, he didn't." Then, as if trying to remember something else he could report, Brantley said, "Your nigger's been up here."

"Which one?" he asked, knowing Brantley had to mean either Annie Mae or Samuel as the rest of them all lived and worked on this property.

"The one works around your house, and up at the store sometime."

"Samuel. Anything strange about that?"

"Probably not, but I ain't ever seen him up here much, and he's come three or four times lately. It's a long walk."

"Maybe he's got a woman up here, one worth walking for."

"Could be. Long walk in the cold, though. And all I've seen is him standing around the fire in the middle of the Quarters with the rest of them. Couldn't tell you what they were talking about. You know how they are. Get all quiet when they see me. But I ain't seen him with no woman."

Rafe nodded and looked down at William who still held Benjamin by the reins, one hand in his coat pocket, patiently listening, studying the both of them up on the porch, it appeared. Rafe was struck by the boy's air of maturity, the sense of intelligence in his eyes. He felt pride and wondered if Brantley noticed his son's bearing.

"I've told you I ain't never liked that Samuel," Brantley said. "And my judgment of them is one reason you hired me."

"I know that, and I know I can handle Samuel." Rafe saw movement at a window, as though a draft of air had pushed at a curtain, but he knew it was more than that. "You got company?"

Brantley looked toward the same window and didn't answer for a moment. "Housekeeper," he said finally.

"I see." Rafe glanced at William and wondered if the boy understood. His best guess was that he did.

"She helped to see to me while I was laid up." He moved closer to Rafe, turned toward him so that his back was to William, and spoke in a quiet voice. "She saw Samuel up here before I did, being out among them, you know. She told me something."

"What?" Rafe asked and looked to see if William was trying to listen. The boy walked Benjamin farther from the porch and stared down the hill as if he knew what was expected of him.

"I know you was kind of close with that nigger of yours named March. She said it was Samuel's daddy, Shack, for sure killed March, right before all the trouble. Said he knew March had gotten wind of things that were about to happen, knew he'd warn you."

"Samuel's daddy was Shack?" Rafe made sure not to show how taken aback he was at not knowing such a fact. When Rafe had first arrived in Riverfield, March had arrived with him. After Rafe had beaten his cousin and run away to escape his father's punishment, he'd gone into Pittsboro after a week of hiding and traveling and run into his mother's youngest brother, who'd once been in jail and was never spoken of. The uncle gave him money and March, who was ten years older than Rafe. He was the only slave Rafe had ever owned, and maybe the fact that March carried his mother's maiden name made him feel some deeper connection than he might have otherwise. And the idea they might be related by blood was something he'd thought about more than once, though never spoke of. In the two years they traveled together through North and South Carolina, Georgia, and across Alabama, they'd had to depend on one another for their lives. More than once men had come upon them and tried to steal March away from a boy they reckoned was not worthy of the property he owned or up to the task of holding on to him when confronted by determined men. Those men had been mistaken and lucky to have lived to reflect upon their mistake.

Though it had been over twelve years now, and they had never talked about the event, Brantley did not have to explain what he'd said. A large gathering of Freedmen, angered by their treatment from white men who were regaining power, decided they would arm themselves down near the Black Fork and advance on Riverfield like some dark, righteous army, or at least that's how Rafe decided they must have thought of themselves. It had been Rebecca, March's wife, who'd come to tell Rafe about the uprising. She said she'd heard the shot and found March dead in the road a half mile from their house, that she knew what he'd known and where he was headed. She'd now have to flee the countryside, she'd told him, and he had helped her do that.

"Your housekeeper seem to think Samuel knows his daddy killed March?"

"That boy probably didn't even know who March was, and if he did he was too young to have any reason to remember him. Don't think he even knew his daddy, not really. You know how it is among them."

Rafe nodded. He recalled what Betsy had told him about Samuel and his father. Probably Samuel had at least seen his daddy, Rafe thought, or had him pointed out. And somebody, when he got old enough, must have told him what had happened to his father. Some men might have wondered why Samuel would want to work for him now, but Rafe did not. Your father's enemy was your enemy, no matter how many years passed or how little you may have known him, and some men know to keep their enemies close. Rafe knew, too, how easily Samuel could point to him and blame Rafe for the death of his father, even if Rafe himself had not been the one to put a bullet through the man's stomach or head.

"Don't worry about Samuel," Rafe said. "He's probably coming up here because he's got his sights set on some woman he ain't got at yet."

"Just thought it was something worth telling you."

"It was. As for Old Fluke, find somebody to take on his plot of ground, and see to his mule till you do. Don't rely on anybody else."

"All right," Brantley said.

"Whoever you find, make sure they know to trade at my store only."

Brantley edged to the end of the porch, looked beyond William and out over the place, then spit dark juice expertly onto the ground. "They'll know that already, but I'll make sure."

Rafe turned toward the curtain he'd seen move earlier. It remained still, but no matter its thickness, he knew so surely that a figure stood just behind it he could see her, someone who'd carried more knowledge than he had, and maybe still did. None of them are going to tell it all, Rafe thought. And why would they when all they could ever really own was something you didn't know?

When he reached the bottom of the steps, William was already mounted and waiting for him. Then Rafe climbed onto Wheeler, and the boy nodded a respectful enough goodbye to Brantley.

They kept the horses at a good and steady pace, but by the time they made the end of the ridge and were about to begin the slow descent, it was nearly good dark and getting colder. William hadn't tried to ask about what he and Brantley had discussed, though Rafe knew the boy must be wondering. William finally did venture a question. "I was named for Mr. Lassiter, wasn't I?" It was again a question that maybe William hoped would lead somewhere, thinking that whatever he and Brantley had talked about must have something to do with the Lassiter Place, which is how people still referred to it, particularly the Negroes who worked it.

Rafe kept them moving. "Your first name, yes," he said.

"Why was I named after him?"

"He died not long before you were born and didn't have children. I wanted some part of him to live on. He was a good man, and a name means a lot. I owed him something."

And this was true. When Lassiter took him in, the man had not written to Rafe's father. He'd understood a need to break all ties and knew enough of Rafe's father to leave well enough alone. After the war, when he'd already moved into Demarville, Mr. Lassiter had been one of the first men in the countryside to farm his place on shares. He'd managed to keep the land where his old house lay in ashes and heaps of bricks, with the single chimney still standing. He'd given Rafe one-third ownership in the store, and let him plant three hundred acres in cotton, had staked him what he needed to put the crop in.

Rafe thought William might ask now what he'd meant by owing Mr. Lassiter. But William asked a different question. "Who was March?" He kept his eyes directly on the darkening road. Rafe realized just how sharp his son's hearing was and how little the boy missed. It was a brave question too. William knew he was not supposed to have overheard any of the conversation on the porch once Brantley turned his back to him.

Before Rafe could begin to answer, he detected both the figure and the sound of a rider approaching ahead of them. Out of old habit he reached inside his coat and placed his hand on the Colt Navy revolver he always carried in a holster on his belt. Soon the rider drew close enough for Rafe to see it was Samuel on a mule, and he withdrew his hand from inside his coat. Samuel, he saw, noticed the movement and had to know what it meant. For a moment he thought the mule might be Ida or Ned, and though he realized it wasn't, he asked Samuel anyway, let the question serve as a warning.

"No, sir," he said. "I wouldn't be riding one of your mules." He wore a wide-brimmed hat and pulled it lower on his forehead, which appeared more a nervous gesture than his trying to keep off the cold wind.

"I know it ain't your mule," Rafe said. "So whose is it and where are you headed?"

William kept Benjamin still and aligned with Wheeler so that the two of them were mostly blocking the road, but Wheeler was anxious to move and Rafe had to keep him in check.

"It's Fluke's mule. He died, so when I left from up there last night, I borrowed him. I'm taking him back now."

Rafe tightened the reins on Wheeler again. "You're telling me that you're riding all the way up there just so you can turn around and walk all the way back? That's mighty responsible of you. Downright conscientious."

Samuel didn't respond, only sat there waiting, it appeared, for this encounter to pass. Finally he said, "Yes, sir," as if in answer to one of a hundred inconsequential questions Rafe might have asked.

"Did Brantley say you could borrow the mule?"

Samuel looked away, hesitating, as if he might be weighing the chances of getting away with a lie. "No, sir. He didn't."

"So that *is* my mule you're riding. I own everything used to farm my property. And why you been going up there?"

"I reckon you could say there's a girl got my attentions." Samuel spoke the words easily enough to make them sound believable. And maybe they were true, but more than likely there was something more he wasn't telling.

"All right, Samuel. You can pass on. But when you get up there, stop and tell Brantley you're bringing Fluke's mule back. And if you don't, I'll know."

"Yes, sir," Samuel said and nudged the mule with his heels.

Rafe stepped Wheeler aside and saw that William mirrored his movement with Benjamin. Samuel passed between them, dark and quiet in the growing darkness, a figure hunched forward toward some curious purpose.

They dismounted in front of the house and Rafe let William lead the horses to the barn and care for them, which he hoped was a clear gesture of trust that William recognized.

He started up the front steps and crossed the porch quietly, aware that his boots were often a loud announcement of his arrival. Perhaps his family needed and deserved a moment to prepare themselves for him. Maybe he shouldn't begrudge them that, he thought, but nonetheless he continued to step quietly.

A dim light touched the living room window inside the dogtrot, and he looked through its panes and saw that the source of the light came from the parlor beyond. Maybe Melinda was in there reading or one of his daughters crocheting. Bunyan had taught Kate. He could not fathom its usefulness, and yet he loved the look on Bunyan's face as she worked with the needles. There was a calmness there he admired, found beautiful, and perhaps envied. Kate's expression with the work was more pained, as though her fingers and mind were not suited to the task, yet knew some level of skill was expected of her.

When he entered the room, he did find Bunyan and Kate but neither of them was at work with needle and yarn. They sat next to each other on the small red sofa with the ornate mahogany back their mother had ordered from Mobile. Both sat up straight, looking at him, expectant, anxious even. Kate held the large Bible closed in her lap, and Bunyan's jaw was set in squared anger.

"You've been reading the Bible together?" Rafe said, though their appearance told him this wasn't so, despite the book's presence, his suspicion making him ask a question that might have seemed absurd to anyone looking on.

"Yes, sir," Kate said, but Bunyan spoke in sharp contrast, her words riding over the top of her sister's. "We've been reading the list of all your children."

Kate shot Bunyan a surprised and angry look, as though she'd been betrayed on a level past what she ever would have expected and could not believe her sister's tone.

"Is that so?"

"Yes, sir," Bunyan said.

"All of my children, you say. And how many would that be?"

She still met his stare. "Depends on how you count," she said, and a slight shake within her voice and in her hands where they gripped her knees now betrayed her fear, though her anger was still evident, a hard energy within her that she couldn't quite contain. "If you count the ones who've died, or..." She looked away, the words she wanted to summon not coming yet, but finally she pushed, it seemed, as if she'd found someplace within herself that wasn't girl or daughter but grown woman. "Or the others. Your other children."

"Open the book, Kate," he said. She didn't respond, did not look at him, her hands still across the ornate cover. "Open it, I said."

"Yes, sir." She finally moved her hands, opening the Bible to the page of names.

"Bunyan, you can get a pen and ink and list the others. Shall I give you their names? Kate, turn the book my way. Let me see if there's enough room for them." He glanced toward the page of names as if he were really looking, and his eye caught the words *Male child* followed by dates. He saw the same just above, earlier dates following. He debated whether or not to force this contest of words and names with his daughter any further, but then found himself saying, "There are four others. Two of them have names you probably know. The other two maybe I'll keep to myself. Seems to be the way of things you women prefer, though I'll tell you, one is a boy, one a girl. Put that down." Bunyan remained motionless, looking at him, or through him, as if she could see the other, darker children playing in the dusty street in front of their mother's house. "If you were a son," he said, "I would strike you. But don't push me this way again. Do you hear?"

"Yes," she said and then slowly added the word he waited for—"sir," a signifying that she was indeed still his daughter.

He turned, walked out of the parlor and into the living room, and was certain he saw beyond the dining table and at the kitchen door the disappearance of Annie Mae's shadow. They are always listening, he thought.

"What I showed you," Kate said, her voice a sharp whisper that penetrated the distance between them and Rafe, "was only for *you* to see."

"Why show me what Mama wrote?"

"Because…"

Rafe stood still, waited past the silence that fell, and if he had thought about it afterward, would have realized that what he really waited for was Kate's understanding of either herself or her mother.

"Maybe because it was brave of her to write what she wrote."

"Hardly," Bunyan said.

The exchange that followed between them, in lowered tones, no longer concerned Rafe, and he walked out into the bracing air that divided his house.

When he looked toward the barn, he saw a lantern was still lit, and he walked toward it, deciding he would rather have the company of his horses than anyone inside the house. He found William in the stall with Benjamin, currying him in short strokes. "Longer strokes are better," he said and saw that he'd startled William. He hadn't realized, this time, that his approach had been so quiet.

"Yes, sir," William said.

Rafe entered the stall, breathing in the familiar smells of hay, sweet feed, and manure. "Have you done Wheeler yet?"

"I did him first."

"Let me," Rafe said and reached toward William.

William handed him the curry comb, and he saw the look of disappointment on the boy's face as if he felt he'd failed at such a simple task. Rafe took hold of the comb, unable to explain that he merely needed to put hands on the horse, more for his own sake than Benjamin's. But there was no way to express such a thing without sounding odd or compromised in some way. How to say that you need to absorb the power and beauty of something larger than yourself?

As he stroked the horse's flank, William slipped past him, and after a moment, when Rafe turned to speak, William had disappeared, and whatever failure the boy had felt now entered Rafe.

He finished with Benjamin and walked over to Wheeler's stall, briefly touching the animal's face with a bare hand. He then turned down the lantern and blew out the flame. After closing the barn door, he walked past Betsy's cabin, no need of her pulling at him this night. When he heard her door open a crack, he kept walking, would not turn her way.

Just before he entered the house, he removed his belt and holstered pistol, and with his first step inside he heard their voices, Melinda's and William's, though he could not distinguish their words. He walked toward the bedroom and saw William standing just inside it, his mother sitting up in the bed. Their talk had already ceased when Rafe fully entered the room. When he looked toward William, he saw what he took for dread in the boy's expression.

"So you were telling your mother something," Rafe said, "the day's news maybe?"

William swallowed. "Just that we'd ridden out to the farm."

"Nothing about the ruckus Henry caused this morning with his brothers?" Rafe dangled the loose belt from his left hand, held the pistol and holster in his right.

"No, sir." William looked away from both Rafe and his mother as he spoke and toward the darkened window as if it held something beyond their own reflections.

"He said it was a cold ride," Melinda said. "I hope he doesn't take ill." She and William then looked at each other for a moment, as though her words carried some further meaning they both understood. Rafe couldn't be sure, but the fact that Melinda asked nothing about Henry's ruckus seemed to have its own meaning. Normally she wanted to know whatever her children had been up to, particularly if it was Henry causing trouble.

But whether or not Melinda knew of Henry playing Indians with Philip and George was not what really mattered. The question now was William, and why the boy still would not look at him. It seemed as if, without even moving, William had taken a step toward his mother's side.

September 1996

Seth doesn't recognize the voice on the phone, but he does recognize the name, Charles Anderson, and even before the conversation truly begins, he feels as if they are about to continue a conversation they never really began, or if they did, it started with the one word spoken long ago: *cousins*.

"Is it all right that I've called?" Charles asks. "I've wanted to talk to you for quite some time. Do you mind?"

Seth hears the hesitancy in his voice, maybe even fear, and pictures him as he looked then, about fifteen years old, standing alone in front of his grandmother's store, waving as John and Seth rode away on bicycles down the road between the two store signs that mirrored the name Anderson.

"It's fine," he says and finds that he means it, is curious. No, more than simply curious, something deeper lies within him, a desire to know the past from the other side, the one that went unspoken of for so long.

"I talked to your father a while back. Was in Riverfield and went by to see him. Maybe he mentioned it."

Seth settles onto a kitchen chair, yet feels unsettled, unsure what to say or where this conversation might lead. "He did tell me."

"Your father didn't seem to mind my stopping. You know, I first talked to him years ago, on the phone. Maybe he never told you about that time. He wouldn't give me your phone number, not then. Maybe I wouldn't have called, anyway. I might have been too afraid, not knowing how you would react. Maybe our being close in age had something to do with it. Could be I didn't want to be rejected by someone of my own generation."

He remembers what his father told him about that call. Seth was in college then, majoring in history. He had not yet started graduate school and was hearing, for the first time, family history that he had not guessed at, or if he ever had, he'd dismissed it, or let go of it so quickly it barely registered, either because of the overwhelming concern for self of all teenagers, or because he didn't want to process the idea and the reality that he had Black cousins. After all, it had nothing to do with his life, or so he would have thought then.

Charles had been doing research on family history and wanted to confirm that George Anderson, the son of Betsy Posey Dishmond, was half-brother to Philip Anderson, who was Seth's great-grandfather. His father had told Charles yes, they were, that they were very close, and that George had even worked for Philip in his store business. Charles then revealed that three Anderson brothers had left Ireland for England and finally made their way to the United States in 1821. So he hadn't really needed confirmation at all. He'd already traced their shared family tree back several generations.

"My father did tell me about your call," Seth says. "When I came home for a weekend."

"Did you already know the history? Had he already told you?"

Seth finds the truth hard to admit, but something he feels between them compels honesty. "No," he says, "he hadn't."

"Did you ever guess at it?" Charles asks.

"I'm not sure. I don't think so." Seth realizes his answers are short, as if he's holding back purposefully, though this isn't his intention.

There is a long, quiet pause. How could you not have guessed at it? Charles's silence seems to ask. Was our existence so unimportant to you?

"But you knew my grandmother and my aunt who lives behind the store now?"

"I knew your grandmother when I saw her." And he had first seen her standing in the dogtrot of the old house while he straddled his bicycle. "I don't think we ever spoke, not really. She never came in our store, not that I remember."

"And you never came in ours," Charles says. It isn't a question.

"No, I didn't."

"Though you almost did. Do you remember that? Remember me?"

"I do," Seth says. "That day has stayed with me."

"Do you know why you didn't come in?"

"It's hard to say. It's like I knew there was something complicated at work, but I didn't know what. I can't explain it."

"So do you know my place in the family?" Charles asks.

Seth adjusts himself in the kitchen chair, tries to find a more comfortable position. "George Anderson was your grandfather."

"That's right."

"And you live in Bay Minette?" Seth asks.

"All my life. I teach high school biology. I'm married with two children. How about you?"

"Single, though I'm with someone. I think we might be headed to-ward marriage." Seth wonders why he's divulged something this person-al. "My father may have told you, I work at the State Archives here in Montgomery."

"A history major?"

"A master's."

"Your father says you've written and published articles. Have you done any research on Rafe Anderson?"

"I know his Civil War record. Not that there's much information on him specifically. I've read the history of the two regiments he fought with, and I know he was wounded at the Battle of Seven Pines." He realizes as he finishes speaking that Charles may have no interest in the war history of a man who fought to preserve slavery.

"He was a violent man," Charles says.

Seth looks out the window of his apartment. He lives in one of the older sections of town. It is a beautiful, early spring day, the bright sea-son at odds somehow with the subject of their conversation. History so often seems to carry within it the dark weight of winter. "He was that," Seth says. "Violent, I mean."

"Of course, if you go back deep enough, you always discover ugly things."

"I've found that to be true," Seth says.

"There's ugly in this family—our family, I mean."

Seth wants to be careful here. He doesn't know what it is exactly that Charles might know, doesn't know if Charles could have any knowledge of what Seth's grandfather always referred to as "the nigger uprising." Or maybe Charles has other knowledge of which Seth knows little or nothing. Seth remembers an older cousin, a daughter of Bunyan, now dead, who would never answer a single question about family history. "Too many skeletons," she always said.

"You know Rafe had a third family?" Charles says. "Two children with a woman named Virginia Henry, a former slave. Did your father tell you that?"

"He did, years ago, after your call. He hadn't known about that until you told him."

"There was bad blood between her and Betsy."

"I can see why there would have been," Seth says.

"It's more complicated than you might think."

"It always is." Seth leans forward now, places his elbows on the table as if he's bracing himself for something he doesn't want to hear.

"I'm not sure how much more I should say right now. Maybe this is enough for the moment. One can only handle so much history at a time."

"Maybe so."

"So we should talk again?" Charles asks.

"We should, I think. Yes."

"Tell me, when you go home to see your father and grandmother, do you ever go see my Aunt Rose? You know she still lives behind our old store building."

Seth is hesitant to answer again, but he knows he must. "No, but I sometimes run into her in the post office."

"Have you ever talked to her about family history?"

He feels his body tighten just as a boy's does when he's about to be scolded or punished in some way. "No, I haven't. She usually tells me to say hello to my father and grandmother, or maybe tells me some memory she has of my grandfather."

"Do you think your father has ever talked to her about our history?"

"I don't know. He might not have. But maybe I'm wrong."

Charles is silent again, and Seth senses the quiet reproach that seems filled more with disappointment than anger but is still palpable enough for Seth to feel he and his father carry a shared and culpable guilt, and maybe not only for their silence but for something passed down to them they don't know how to define or even name.

TEN

The children were back in school finally. A teacher had been found, to replace the one who'd left at Christmas. She'd moved all the way from Selma. Melinda noticed the house was quieter now during the day. Philip spent much of his time with Annie Mae in the kitchen, and when he went outside, Annie Mae was always with him. Melinda felt she knew the reason why. Annie Mae didn't want Philip near George.

Bunyan had told her what had happened with the three children playing together and what she'd said to her father in the parlor with Kate. Melinda doubted that Bunyan had fully understood at the moment *why* she'd told her what happened. Mostly Bunyan was angry at her father, Melinda knew, for claiming aloud that the boy was his own, and for counting out his other children for her, but that wasn't all.

Melinda had been sitting on the bed with Bunyan, upstairs on the girls' side of the loft, talking with her while all the other children were scattered elsewhere. "Kate says it seems like you're mad with me, too, Bunyan. Are you?" Melinda asked.

Bunyan rose and walked toward Philip's small bed, which they would soon have to move to the boys' side. Philip was too old to stay with his sisters any longer, but Bunyan would be hesitant to let him go, just as she was hesitant now to answer the question she'd been asked.

"If you are, it's all right," Melinda said. "I don't know how to truly stand up to him. Maybe you've learned how, or you're starting to, and you're mad because I haven't."

Bunyan walked back toward her and sat on the bed again. She looked relieved, as if she'd had something explained to her that she didn't realize she already knew. "I'm sorry," she said. "Maybe I was mad with you."

"There's only so much a wife can do with a man like your father. It may be a daughter can do more."

"Kate does better with him than either of us," Bunyan said.

Now it was Melinda's turn to realize something she'd somehow already known. "She does seem to have a way with him. Not always, but sometimes."

"She's not as mad at him as I am. Maybe because she didn't see what happened out in the yard. I already knew, but to hear him claim the boy the way he did, it was too much to bear." Bunyan looked toward the window at the far end of the room and then back at her mother. "And you didn't see or hear anything outside that morning, either? Didn't see Daddy pick up the boy?"

"No, though I think William maybe wanted to tell me about it the other night, but he didn't. I just knew something was wrong. Kate would only tell me you were upset, but I could already see that, and she wouldn't tell me why."

"How long have you known, Mama?"

"About his other children?"

"Yes."

"As soon as the girl began to show, and I already knew there were probably others. He'd spent too many nights in town for there not to be. It's something wives have to live with, some wives. It's nothing to be talked about."

"But we're talking about it," Bunyan said.

"Yes, but only because you wanted to, and I can't deny you. It's nothing I would *ever* have brought up with you." Bunyan nodded her understanding. "Let me ask you something," Melinda said. "Are you afraid of your father?"

"I don't think he'd ever hurt me," Bunyan said after a moment.

"No, he wouldn't. Not the way I think you mean."

"It's almost like he doesn't care enough to hurt me."

Melinda found herself so surprised at what her daughter said that she knew no words to say. All she knew to do was reach for her and pull her close. She pushed Bunyan's hair out of the way and kissed her neck. Melinda smelled the scent of vanilla extract on her daughter's skin and wondered if Bunyan had begun to wear it like perfume, one more awkward step toward growing up, though a deeper maturity clearly ran far beyond her outward awkwardness.

It was early afternoon, and Melinda walked away from the house and toward the barn. She wondered if Annie Mae was watching her from the kitchen window. It might be Annie Mae was worried Melinda was heading to Elizabeth's cabin. She wasn't—though the errand she was on had everything to do with the girl. For the moment she was only hunting Samuel.

She found him walking up from the horse pasture and toward the barn, posthole diggers in one hand and a small roll of barbed wire in the other. When he saw her standing in the open barn doors, he quickened his pace, though for her it wasn't necessary. He was probably puzzled about why she was waiting for him and hadn't sent Annie Mae to ask for whatever it was that she wanted. It wouldn't hurt to leave the both of them guessing about what she was up to, Melinda decided. Word would get around soon enough.

"Samuel," she said, "I want you to hitch Mollie B. up to the buggy for me."

He stopped beside her, briefly studying the roll of wire in his hand. "Yes, ma'am," he said, now looking toward her.

"Are the roads down in Dawes Quarter in decent enough shape for traveling?"

He held her gaze longer than he probably ever had with a white woman. Maybe she shouldn't have given this much away yet, but he couldn't know exactly what she had in mind. Then again, what difference could it really make? He'd know where she'd gone by nightfall.

"They passable," he said while looking down once again at the wire he held.

"Good."

"Is they something I could do for you back up in there?"

She didn't expect such a question, knew he would never have asked it of Rafe, but she found she wasn't bothered by it. He'd asked out of curiosity, of course, wanted to know why a white woman would go there, but maybe there was concern too, some desire to help. Samuel was hard to read, though. She knew this from Rafe, and she'd seen it herself, his quick mind at work, his letting you see it at work and knowing you had. She'd never known another Negro to be so defiant without speaking a word.

"No," she said, "but thank you. I can handle this myself. If you'll go ahead, I'll wait here for you to hitch up Mollie."

"Yes, ma'am," he said and entered the barn.

She stepped just inside the doorway and looked back out across the horse pasture. Without Samuel approaching her to hold her attention, she couldn't help but find within her vision the small mound of dirt near the fence line. She remembered the sound of Rafe's hammer that morning and the question he'd asked her at the graveside later in the day. *Did you kill that child?* Each felt like blows to her now. And who else might wonder to himself the same question Rafe had asked? There were always rumors about women with one child after another who lost one, then two, then three. But she could maybe defend herself against such blows and questions by driving Mollie B. into the dark confines of Dawes Quarter and letting the Negroes there think they knew what she had in mind when perhaps she could actually make herself as hard to read as Samuel.

Once he had the buggy ready, she climbed into the seat and took the reins. "Thank you," she said and drove out of the open front doors and past Elizabeth's cabin. She knew the two of them would be talking as soon as she was out of sight.

She kept Mollie B. at a steady gait and soon left her house and the nearby Episcopal church behind her. Then she passed the schoolhouse. The children were all inside and hopefully would not see her pass. If any of them did it would be Henry, the most likely to be staring out a window and not paying attention.

The wind wasn't very strong, and she'd dressed warmly enough. After half a mile she turned Mollie B. onto a narrow road that ran mostly north, passing one shack after another, the only sign of life in them the smoke from their chimneys, though she knew she wasn't passing unnoticed. Then she saw a handful of Negro children around a fire in front of one house whose two windows on either side of the door were so dark that the house appeared to have shut its eyes and gone to sleep. Yet she knew even then someone from inside was keeping eyes on the children at their fire and on this white woman passing. The children watched her in silent curiosity.

She now turned Mollie B. onto the road that would take her back into Dawes Quarter, a place she'd never been. To her knowledge, the only times whites entered this place it was men with torches and guns, their destination predetermined by either the real or imagined offenses of some Negro man whose fears were not deep enough to hide him from a wrath that burned as bright as white men's torches.

Her own destination was predetermined too, but she would have to have help finding it. She drove Mollie B. on and after rounding a second curve saw the back of a tall Negro woman walking ahead. As she drew nearer the woman turned, probably surprised to hear the quick wheels of a buggy instead of the slow, heavy plodding of a wagon. She was young, still in her twenties, and carried a child in her belly.

Melinda pulled alongside her and stopped. The girl was already still, and Melinda could see that she recognized whose wife this was holding the reins tight and keeping in check a horse the girl or her man could never imagine owning. "I need you to tell me where someone lives."

"Yes, ma'am," the girl said. "Who it be?"

"Leathy." Melinda let the name do its work and saw the girl's eyes widen for the briefest of moments. "I've got business with her."

"Yes, ma'am. She on up the road about a quarter mile. Got a big cedar in front her house. She on the right-hand side the road."

"Thank you," Melinda said.

The girl nodded, smiled. "She help lots of folks. Done told me I got me a boy coming, my first. Said it gon' be healthy."

"That's a comfort, I know."

"Yes, ma'am." The girl placed a hand on her stomach as if she might be comforting both herself and the boy she imagined curled within her. If it proved to be a girl, or was sickly, what would she think then? When a second child came, would her mistrust and fear grow in her belly too? Melinda gave a slight shake of the reins and pulled away. She hoped the girl would not end up questioning her beliefs. The young needed whatever faith they could find. God or hoodoo or some unexplainable combination of both, what did it matter?

Not many of them did question Leathy, she knew. But it wasn't only Negroes who believed. Leathy was well-known among whites too, and even though her name was mentioned always in jest, Melinda suspected what the laughter and jokes sometimes hid—just as Black maids and cooks carried deep within a pocket some token or notion sack filled with who-knew-what powder or charm out of Dawes Quarter and handed it to a white mistress with whispered instructions in a bedroom or kitchen empty of husbands and children.

She found the house and pulled the buggy into the small yard and set the brake. Nothing about the dwelling looked unusual or different, and, notwithstanding the air of mystery or secrecy that surrounded the woman, the scent of wood smoke in the breeze held nothing foreign or unnamable. Melinda climbed down from the buggy seat and walked up onto the porch. She made herself knock loudly enough to be heard. Now was not the time to be timid.

Leathy answered the door and showed no surprise in her broad, brown face at who stood on her porch. Perhaps Leathy had already seen her through the window. Melinda recognized her easily, having seen her at Rafe's store and in the street before it as Leathy went about her business. The one place Melinda had never seen her was the churchyard, either before or after church. Maybe Reverend Lamar had told her she wasn't welcome, the balcony insufficient to obscure her presence from those who would judge her—and be fearful of some brief nod of familiarity.

"Come on out the cold, Miss Melinda." Leathy stepped back from the door, and Melinda walked inside and nodded and made herself smile so as not to show the nervousness she felt.

Leathy shut the door behind her, and Melinda's eyes had to adjust to the darkness of the room. A coal-oil lamp burned low and because of the overcast day the windows held little light. Leathy seemed suddenly aware of the darkness and turned the lamp higher. Melinda saw more clearly then the shelves that lined the walls. Colored jars of various sizes and shapes sat in neat alignment. Below them were cloth sacks, some small enough to fit in one hand, others larger. Most appeared filled to one degree or another, a few empty. On the tallest set of shelves handfuls of dried plants and roots were piled and stacked by likeness. Melinda couldn't have called the names of any of them, and what Leathy called them was probably different from anything found in a book.

"We can sit here," Leathy said and motioned to a small table in the middle of the room. Two chairs with twine-woven seats and ladder backs sat on either side.

"Thank you," Melinda said. "I hope I'm not keeping you from something." She sat and took a long, quiet breath.

"No, ma'am. Peoples come by. I expect that. But don't you worry. If anybody come now, I send them on their way." Leathy sat down on the other side of the table. The iron potbellied stove behind her ticked and would soon need sticks of wood added to it. "I reckon there's something maybe I can help you with. I'll see to what I can."

Melinda had thought about what she would say, knew Leathy might expect a certain proper tone from her, one she would need to deliver on so that what she said would be given weight and taken with seriousness beyond what she really intended. She looked into Leathy's face and saw expectancy there, some level of what appeared to be true concern. "You could say someone has done me injury, a great injury."

Leathy shook her head as if in disbelief, but Melinda doubted the disbelief, knew this woman had heard far too much not to trust the worst of what people did and said.

"I needs to ask you a question, one I wouldn't regular ask a nice white lady like yourself."

"You may ask. I knew you would have certain questions."

"Was it hurt to your body?"

"No, not to my body."

"Your heart, then? That what it was?"

"Yes," Melinda said and knew now was the time to say what she had to, and once the words were said a course would be set in motion, she hoped, one she couldn't completely control, like Mollie B. at the end of a set of reins. "But not just my heart, a body too." She waited and saw the confusion in Leathy's eyes. "Not *my* body," she said then.

Leathy shook her head, again a practiced measure of disbelief, but beyond that maybe something genuine, some shared knowledge of grief. "It was a child's body, wasn't it?"

This was not second sight, Melinda knew. Leathy would have heard word about the loss of her child. Perhaps she even knew where the infant was buried and why a horse pasture and not a churchyard.

"It was a child," she said, realizing there was no need to say *my* child.

"Lord have mercy," Leathy said.

Melinda could see the next question in her mind, but Leathy held back, did not ask *Who? Who did this injury?* Not yet. Maybe she wouldn't. But Melinda needed her to ask. She remained quiet, waited.

Leathy took her time, looking past Melinda and into her own thoughts, it seemed. "They be certain things I can give you for to take use of. They help keep you safe, protect you and your children from any other hurt might come along later." Now Leathy seemed to be studying Melinda as she spoke, trying to decide if Melinda could believe or did believe. "Things I got here on my shelves, they got powers when they mix together through my hands."

Melinda nodded and remained silent, felt what was maybe a kind of power rising within herself.

"Whoever it be what done this hurt, they be male or female?"

"Female."

"All right then. Let me ask this. Do she be old or young?"

"Young," Melinda said and realized that maybe it wouldn't be necessary for Leathy to ask *who*.

"She live close or far?"

"Close," Melinda said. "Very close."

Leathy bowed her head and when she looked up again her face looked grave. "See, I got to know certain things to know what all you be needing. Not all powders and charms work the same on everybody. What work on a old man or for him don't work on a young woman. And what work on a woman with children and a woman who ain't got none ain't the same neither. Do this woman got children?"

"Two," Melinda said, doubting all she'd just heard but thankful Leathy had her curiosities and had asked and said as much with her questions as if she'd spoken Elizabeth's name aloud.

Leathy stood slowly and went to her shelves. Her broad body obscured Melinda's ability to see, but Leathy seemed to be picking and choosing carefully, placing items in the crook of her left arm. She walked to a different wall and lifted a root from the tallest shelf and slipped it into a brown cloth sack. Then she turned and looked meaningfully at Melinda, as if what this particular sack now held was of some consequence and concern.

She placed on the table one blue bottle of medium size, four white sacks with drawstrings, and the one larger brown sack. She sat down and pushed the blue bottle toward Melinda. "This here a root powder. I grind it myself. This protect you and your children. What you do is spill just a little in front the doors to your house, all the ones what lead inside. Since it winter and your windows all be closed, don't have to worry with them. Then spill just a little in front the doors of the rooms you all sleep in, just for good measure. And don't sweep the house for one full week, the porches neither. Got to wait seven days."

Melinda reached for the bottle, held it with both hands, and lifted it for a moment before setting it back down, as if its weight were some small clue to the mystery of its abilities.

"That not all. Put just a pinch of it in your coffee or tea. It need to pass through your body too. Just the one time. For your children too. It a little bitter, but a pinch all you need."

"All right," she said. "I can do that."

"Now these here sacks, you leave what in them drawed up tight, and drop them under each side the house this girl live in. They make like walls all around her she don't know there, keep her from doing you any more harm. If she try, won't do her no good. And even if she do find one, if the moon done been full, it be too late. Moon be full in two more nights."

Melinda nodded and pulled all four sacks toward her, feeling a softness inside them; but one that was thicker, more dense, than mere powder; and in all, toward the necks where the drawstrings closed, her fingertips detected pieces of something thin and hard, like sticks or small bones that may have given shape to a bird's wings. Later she would have to look, her own curiosity as strong as Leathy's had been earlier, more powerful now than her disbelief in what Leathy practiced.

"This one here," Leathy said, as she pushed the larger sack across the table, "it the same root I make that powder from, but it still the raw root. It clean, though, washed good. Using it different, and you might not want to use it at all. Fact, I reckon a lady like yourself wouldn't want to take it up, but I'm gon' let you have it. You can decide. I don't need to know what you does with it. But if you uses it a certain way, it bring ruination to the one what done you harm." Leathy stopped speaking and appeared to study Melinda again, as if she might divine what Melinda would be willing to do. "Thing is, you got to chew the small end, and after you done chewed it good, well, you got to spit it out against the sides of the girl's house, down low. Then throw the root in the dirt up under the house. That's what'll make it take."

Melinda met her gaze and did not look away. She let the seriousness of her expression speak and answer Leathy's question, though if there was ruination she knew it would not come through a chewed root or spittle on cabin walls, not in any direct manner. Whatever befell Elizabeth would come from Melinda's presence here in this small house and at this table, from the eyes that saw her pass and learned where she'd stopped and entered. Talk and pointed fingers would be directed at the girl. Why else would a white woman come to Dawes Quarter seeking Leathy if not to put hoodoo on someone, and who would Mr. Rafe's wife want cursed more than the girl who'd born his outside children? But Leathy would need to tell just once what she now knew. If she would speak the girl's name, and name the injury, the murder of a child, or *hint* at it strong-ly, that would be curse enough. The girl would be shunned once word spread, and Melinda would have defended herself. But what if Leathy remained quiet? She had to know that keeping silent about what was said to her by all who came seeking help or revenge amounted to Leathy's own survival. Still, Leathy was known to wield her position and power among her people. Knowledge of roots and powders was one thing, but knowledge of people's desires and actions, of even their crimes, was another, something more powerful, and frightening.

"Can I ask you something now?" Melinda said.

"Anything you wants. I'll answer best I can."

"What if the one all this is for doesn't believe in it herself? Say she goes around telling people you don't have any powers like you claim, not a single one. Will it still work on her?"

Leathy leaned back in her chair, lowered her head slowly, and let her eyes close. She nodded as if she understood much more than just the question. Her face then seemed to darken despite the constant flame from the coal-oil lamp, as if the darkness came from within. "When you throws that chewed root up under her house, throws it way up under there," she said, and Melinda felt no need to ask or say anything further.

That night, Rafe was at home, and stayed home, reading the paper in the parlor and then sleeping next to her in their bed smelling faintly of leather and tobacco. So she remained in bed all night, though little sleep came to her.

By the following afternoon, a Saturday, she noticed Annie Mae was more quiet than usual with her, even with Henry, whose talk somehow always demanded response. At the supper table, Melinda sat between Kate and Bunyan, the three boys across from them, with Rafe absent from the head of the table, which was so common it bore no comment. When Annie Mae brought in the food, she put each dish down carefully, as though any one of them might break, and her glances around the table and room seemed furtive.

"Annie Mae, do you feel all right?" Kate asked.

She looked the girl's way. "I feel fine," she said, and then she added, "Maybe tired a little," as if she knew she needed to explain herself somehow. She stepped back from the table then and paused a moment before turning toward the kitchen. Melinda saw that Annie Mae's attention lingered on her, and she felt Annie Mae was watching her from a place where she might gain some vantage point of understanding, as if Melinda had said or done something most odd.

"What's wrong with her?" Kate whispered when Annie Mae disappeared into the kitchen.

"You want me to spy on her?" Henry spoke in a voice nowhere near a whisper.

"You'll do no such thing," Bunyan said. "You make enough trouble for yourself. You don't need to go making trouble for anybody else."

Melinda couldn't help but wonder then how much trouble she herself might have made, but she pushed the question from her mind.

And when she awoke that night, alone, she still did not let herself consider for too long what her next actions might mean. She lit the lamp and added wood from the hearth onto the fire. Then she went to one of her dresser drawers and pulled out the cloth sacks and the bottle

Leathy had sold her. She'd placed three dollars on the table and Leathy had merely nodded. Melinda would learn only with time how valuable the items really were. But she could look now, see what the small sacks held. She drew one open, hesitantly, as if there might be something to fear, and shook the contents onto the top of her dresser. A few blue feathers fell onto a small amount of dirt mixed with a yellow powder, and an assortment of thin bones crossed themselves. Some were just large enough to have been squirrel bones, others maybe had belonged to a bird. The feathers held a blue jay's coloring, and that seemed appropriate enough. Blue was a peaceful color, but jays carried more meanness than most birds.

She carefully palmed the contents back into the sack and drew its strings tight. What she had to do next felt like a ridiculous act, but it was something she would have to do. She took the large root from the sack, rubbed the smaller end with her fingers, feeling for any remaining grit or dirt, then touched it to her tongue. It tasted faintly like a turnip, she noted, as she bit into the firm pulp. The taste of it grew stronger as she chewed, developing into something unnamable that filled her mouth with a mixture of sourness and a sweet sharpness that made her purse her lips tightly, as if it otherwise couldn't be contained, would *have* to be expelled. There was really no choice but to make everything she did follow custom, or at least appear so. She had no intention of spitting against the walls of Elizabeth's cabin, but when her mouth filled and she finally spat into the clean nighttime slop jar and noticed how dark the color was, she guessed, rightly she discovered later, that the spittle would stain the log walls, would leave them marked, just as it now had perhaps stained her tongue, left her marked, at least temporarily. She did not plan on throwing the root far under the house. She would leave it in plain sight where maybe Samuel, not Elizabeth or Annie Mae, would find it and recognize it for what it was.

Before she slipped out of the house and crept down to Elizabeth's cabin with the sacks and root in her hands, she decided she would sprinkle the powder in front of her bedroom door, and before each door that opened into the house, just as Leathy had instructed. She began with her room door and sprinkled it heavier than was called for, wanting to make sure it was seen by Annie Mae, who would be bound to tell Elizabeth, and Elizabeth would almost without doubt tell Samuel, who might then spread word all around and would not leave out what he'd seen of the dark stains on Elizabeth's cabin walls.

As she worked spreading the powder she felt that curious level of power rise within her again, as if she truly believed in hoodoo, and she did not let that feeling stop her. Instead, maybe to the contrary, she surprised herself with the determination that filled her like the heaviness of the dirt in those sacks, just as she would find herself surprised in the morning when she discovered that the front of each doorway was already swept clean.

ELEVEN

Annie Mae knew she was bound to hear Samuel's knock at any moment. He came to her for coffee each morning now and not to Betsy as he'd been doing. Rafe had put a stop to that. The coffee was hot, maybe too hot. She'd been up for hours, her worry even greater than the day before.

Samuel arrived late, not too much so, but later than normal. She had the door open before he knocked, which seemed to catch him by surprise. None of the children had come down yet.

"Thought you would of done been here," she said.

"Had to come all the way from the Lassiter Place."

"Walking?"

He closed the door behind him. "Yeah," he said. "Can't use Fluke's old mule no more."

She handed him a cup of coffee, and he leaned against the pie safe, which still held a few pieces of the two custard pies she'd made three days ago.

"What you been going up there so much for?"

"I got my reasons."

She'd already sat the coffee pot back on the stove. Now she turned toward him again. "Sound like maybe I ought to know them reasons." She stared at him hard, as if she hoped her vision could gain some control of him when she seemed to have control over little else. Even sweeping a fine powder into a dustpan had been difficult enough.

"I been talking to some of the older folks up there."

"You mean *old* folks, or just folks older than you, which ain't old at all?"

"Some of both, I reckon."

"'Bout what?" she said, afraid she might know the answer, Samuel already gossiping about Melinda and dead babies.

"The uprising," he said, which she didn't expect him to say, though maybe she should have given what Betsy had told her about Samuel's father and what all Samuel figured probably lived in other people's memories.

"That before I come here."

"And that why I ain't asked you about it."

"You must be too young to remember it," she said and waved a hand dismissively.

"I was old enough. Just didn't no grown-ups talk about it around us children. And now my mama dead three years. Can't ask her."

"So what you know about it?"

"I know my daddy was killed in it." He looked as if he might say more but stopped himself.

"But you didn't know your daddy."

He was about to take a drink of his coffee but lowered the cup. "Hard to be knowing somebody when they dead."

"I mean before that."

"Quit pretending you know all about me," Samuel said.

"I know enough. Know what Betsy told me. So now you tell me what you done learned."

"'Bout the uprising?"

Annie Mae nodded, and Samuel moved closer to the stove for warmth and sipped his coffee, patient with her, she imagined, because she was older, maybe the same age as his mother when she died, and able to forgive her hard tone with him for that reason only.

He told her then what she could have guessed even before she moved here. And there were pieces of information she had gathered for herself from conversations overheard and sometimes whispered to her directly. In fact, it was in whispered talk where she'd first heard the word *buckra* and knew without being told it meant a white man beyond mean. So Samuel told her now, in his own low whispers, about the lynchings that had taken place, where simply to be seen voting or walking home from a Freedman's meeting could mean a beating that would leave a man scarred or permanently lame. He told her how quickly Freedmen saw all the ways they were cheated out of their shares on the cotton they grew. "And so my daddy led them," he said, "twenty-five men, all with guns."

"But you could of heard every bit of that anywhere, and probably heard it all a long time ago, when you got old enough to know how to ask. What you got to go up to the Lassiter Place for? You not making sense."

"'Cause you know who the Lassiter Place belong to."

"That don't answer," Annie Mae said. "Why you going up there

talking about all that when you knows it already? Maybe you just trying
to stir up something old, wanting to make trouble. Get the young ones
who don't even remember it all riled up. Or is there something else you
doing up there?"

"Maybe they some other talk going on. People be asking me what I
know."

"'Bout what?"

"Miss Melinda, and that baby."

"And who starting that talk?" she said and moved close to him,
smelling her coffee on his breath. "I'll tell you—you, that's who. I done
told you already don't be talking about things you only *think* you know
about."

"It ain't my fault folks think she killed them last two babies."

Annie Mae backed away from him a few steps but kept her eyes
locked on his. "And you helping them right along believe it. What you
got against Miss Melinda?"

"I ain't got nothing against her. What I care about her killing two
white babies, especially ones what belong to Mr. Rafe? She always been
nice enough to me. I don't reckon *she* the one I got my mind set on."

Annie Mae already knew it was Rafe who'd gotten word of the uprising and led the white men against them. Now she understood more. "So
you think it Mr. Rafe killed your daddy?"

"If it wasn't him, might as well a been."

"You figure since Mr. Rafe ain't put her out the house, you gon' put
the bad mouth on Miss Melinda, make people think she killed them
babies. Hurt Mr. Rafe that way? Make people think Mr. Rafe got a crazy
wife he can't control? Make *him* look bad?"

Samuel didn't respond at first but occupied himself with taking sips
of his coffee. "What you care about Miss Melinda after what she done
the other day? You know she didn't go see Leathy just for no regular
sit-down visit."

Annie Mae knew he was right, and the powder she'd already swept up
this morning had made it all the clearer. So much didn't seem to make
sense, not the notions in Samuel's head or Melinda believing in hoodoo.

For a moment she was undecided but then found herself telling
Samuel what she'd swept up from in front of the doorways, wanting to
judge Samuel's reaction, to see what he made of it. Or maybe she felt
desperate enough that she had to tell the first person she *could* tell.

"She must a wanted you to see it," Samuel said. "Maybe you should of left it alone, pretend like you didn't."

She understood Samuel's point, knew he was right, but some part of her had felt too great a need to erase what she'd found, just as she'd cleaned up the child and the bloody linens she'd discovered so early that morning after Betsy had gone in and nursed the baby. She knew also the powder was supposed to mean protection, and though she didn't really believe, if her daughter was without protection, at least beyond what protection Annie Mae could offer, she didn't want Melinda to have it, not after what Melinda had gone and done.

Annie Mae heard voices that sounded like Bunyan fussing at Henry as they came in from the dogtrot. Samuel held out his empty cup to her. "Reckon I better get to work before Henry come in here and want to give me some of his wisdom. Believe I heard enough of that." He turned and walked out the door to the back porch just as the children entered, and Annie Mae realized she didn't yet have breakfast ready.

Bunyan seemed to recognize things weren't as they were supposed to be and looked at her with concern. "I'll help cook," she said, and Annie Mae was grateful. The eggs wouldn't take long, and there were leftover biscuits that hopefully weren't too hardened by the dry kitchen air.

Melinda came and sat at the dining table just as the children were finishing, and Annie Mae brought her plate, said a quiet good morning.

"Annie Mae's been lazy," Henry said.

This time it was William who scolded his brother. "The only lazy person here is the one who won't do his schoolwork."

"Schoolwork don't amount to nothing," Henry said.

"That's enough." Melinda spoke with more force than normal and the room quieted.

Each child finished his or her last bite and Kate helped clear the table. Then Annie Mae was left with washing the dishes, but she knew she could stay in the kitchen only so long. She would have to go out to where Melinda sat alone and ask if she needed anything. When she finally did, Melinda was already looking up at the kitchen door as if waiting on Annie Mae to appear, her pale expression unreadable, foreign somehow. Now there was this yellow dust between them, dust that Annie Mae had gotten rid of—and clearly Melinda had already seen it was gone—but that still existed nonetheless, its residue coating everything, it seemed.

"Were you up early?" Melinda said.

"Yes, but was moving slow, I reckon. Was a little late with breakfast."

Melinda nodded absentmindedly, as if she were really listening only to what was unsaid between them. Annie Mae let the silent conversation unfold as it would, then had to speak. "Miss Melinda, you want more coffee?"

Something made Melinda look directly at her now, as if Melinda were finally and fully present, and Annie Mae heard the word she'd just spoken, the one she hadn't used in years when the two of them knew they were alone: *Miss*, that word of forced respect. They both held each other's gaze with a recognition of what the word meant, a recognition that couldn't be denied.

"No," Melinda said finally. "No coffee. I've had enough."

Annie Mae took a step back into the kitchen doorway and turned toward the work that awaited her with a kind of tiredness she'd experienced too much of lately, and yet this time the tiredness surpassed anything she'd felt before.

In a little while, after she'd taken up the empty plate Melinda had left, she heard a light tap at the window and saw Samuel there motioning for her to come out onto the porch. She pulled on her handed-down burnoose and stepped out the door. Samuel's face had an expectant look about it, as though he couldn't wait to tell her something he knew.

"What?" she said.

He had one hand placed in a coat pocket, the other angled inside its unbuttoned folds, as if he were hiding something. "Don't know whether to tell you or show you," he said.

"Come on with it."

"After what you told me, decided I might go take a look around Betsy's cabin."

"And?" she said, still not sure of what she might hear or see.

"They purple on her outside walls. She done been rooted." Samuel pulled his right hand out from within his coat, and she saw the foot-long piece of tapered root with small marks on the narrow end. "Found this right up under the edge of the cabin."

Annie Mae felt disbelief at first, a wanting in her to doubt that Melinda had gone this far. And what did Melinda believe? A woman like her couldn't really give credence to hoodoo, could she? And Annie Mae herself, while she believed in all she did as a midwife, both the physical and the practical, and also the ritual, she didn't really believe anything beyond what she could do with her own hands, which had never touched hoodoo. She had only wanted to stay away from it, disbelieve it by her absence from its practice. But what was stronger, disbelief or belief? As her mother had told her, when a tribal doctor lost a child in birth, he could point to a woman and say *witch*, and the blame was no longer turned his way. Now it seemed Melinda was wanting to use belief to point blame at Annie Mae's own child.

Samuel pulled the other hand from his pocket. She saw the small cloth sack. "Found one of these on every side of her house. When I seen the first one, knew the others be there too."

Annie Mae's ruminations stopped, and the tiredness she'd felt earlier began to leave her. What entered in its place she wasn't sure of at first, but there was strength in it, a power that could be believed, and she realized finally that both her hands were clenched into fists.

"You can't say nothing about this," she said. "Can't tell nobody. If you do, think about who it hurt, my daughter."

She saw his mind at work already, though, saw the expectancy still in his face, his calculating of how wide the hurt could reach, how little he cared but for what he needed for his own end, which was silent and cold revenge on a white man. She saw his thoughts just as clearly as if she had second sight. He could hurt Melinda or Betsy. Didn't matter to him. Both were Rafe's women.

"You give me those," she said and took the sack and the root from him. "Now go get me them other sacks, all three of them. You hear me?" Then she said again, "Don't you tell nobody about this," but she knew her words held no power, that word would spread, first all through the Lassiter Place, and finally beyond, to white ears, until word came home to the man who had his own word, buckra, and while a white man might not care too much what Negroes thought, he would care what whites thought and said about his own wife and where she went and how she behaved in public for all to see; and how much damage would spread to her daughter Annie Mae could only guess at. It would depend on what people wanted to believe.

She burned the root and the sack in the kitchen stove and threw in the others once Samuel returned and handed them to her at the door. What was left then were the stains on the cabin walls, and she walked down to Betsy's house late in the morning to see if lye soap would take them off. If not, she'd have to take further measures.

But there was Betsy to see to first. This time the door opened for Annie Mae before she could knock. Betsy stood in the doorway, her hair bound in a long, single, perfect braid that had probably taken some time to achieve and now lay angled across her breasts. Annie Mae saw the tightness in her lips and high cheeks. "Samuel done told you what he found?" Annie Mae asked.

Betsy nodded and stepped back to allow her mother in.

"Figured he had," she said as she closed the door behind her. George came to her and she handed him a biscuit she'd brought. Lakeview lay in her crib and appeared to be asleep, her mouth partly open, her soft lips formed into the shape of a kiss. "So you worried about being hoo-dooed?"

Betsy made her way to a chair by the fireplace and waited for Annie Mae to follow and sit near her. "No, not really bothered by that," she said. "I was raised not to believe in superstition."

Annie Mae wondered sometimes if her daughter knew the hurt she caused when she spoke about being brought up by another woman, someone white and well-to-do. She let the words pass, deciding not to remind her of what that woman had put her through.

"It's Miss Melinda got you worried," Annie Mae said.

"I was already some worried when you told me who she'd gone to see, but I couldn't really make much sense out of why she'd go to a hoodoo woman, no matter what you told me. And now she's done this. What exactly is she trying to do?"

Annie Mae found herself struck once again by how much Betsy sounded like a white woman when she spoke. The fact that she couldn't understand the ways a white woman might act told her again how Betsy lived such a between existence, never all of one thing, not Black, not Choctaw, not white, but all of them at the same time. Annie Mae had felt this way from time to time herself, but Betsy had that third blood mixed in, and that made the difference in her child and made Betsy a mystery to her.

"What she trying to do?" Annie Mae said. "To answer that, you got to know she think you killed her babies." Annie Mae realized she'd used the word *think* without trying. She'd not said *know* when the three of them—herself, Betsy, and Melinda—had to understand the truth, even if only one of them knew exactly what had happened. Or maybe Betsy somehow didn't quite know what she'd done to hurt the baby or hadn't done it intentionally. Or *hadn't* done anything at all. Annie Mae had tried to hold on to that notion, but there was the earlier child that could not be forgotten. How could two babies die one after the other and it not be on purpose when Betsy was in the house the one time and could have been the other?

She watched her daughter now, looked for some sign that might tell—a turning away, a frown, a hand over her face, an inward stare—but she saw nothing but the same worried look she'd seen at the door, and maybe that was tell enough. Annie Mae could not bring herself to ask again the question whose answer she did not want to hear spoken aloud and knew it wouldn't be anyway. "She want to hurt you, that why she done what all she done. Make it look like you hurt them babies. She trying to point the finger any way she can."

"But she's the one," Betsy began as she stared toward her fireplace.

"You can tell that lie to Samuel, and I can't stop you doing it but don't tell it to me."

Betsy turned her way. "I didn't kill that child," she said, and she looked at Annie Mae as if she'd told the truth, though she also seemed to accept that her mother would think what she wanted. But couldn't that look on her daughter's face be a lie too? A part of Annie Mae wanted to abandon herself to whatever fate awaited her daughter. And yet she knew she couldn't allow herself to forsake her child, and that meant staying where she was as long as Betsy stayed—and with two children, Betsy would not leave. Odd that only now did it occur to Annie Mae that somewhere deep inside her mind she'd already contemplated leaving this house and her daughter, maybe while sweeping up yellow dust, but had rejected the notion. All she could do with any good conscience was quietly fight what came.

"Get you some soap and water in a bucket," Annie Mae said, "and a wash rag. We need to get them stains off the sides this house. You gon' do the scrubbing."

Betsy didn't protest but gathered the things Annie Mae told her to, and Annie Mae followed her outside. She noticed that her daughter went first to the side of the cabin facing the house, which is where she would have told her to start. Betsy wet the rag and rubbed lye soap onto it, then scrubbed at the purple stain that had splotched and drained against the weathered logs. The stain faded a little at first but then held its color stubbornly.

"Keep at it," Annie Mae said. "We don't want nobody else see this, especially Rafe. It bad enough Samuel done seen it."

"How come?" Betsy said as she continued to scrub, then stopped and looked at her mother. "Why say that about Samuel?"

"Don't you see? He do anything to hurt or shame Rafe, through you or Miss Melinda either one. And Rafe don't want his wife going down into Dawes Quarter and messing with no hoodoo. All the white folks be laughing at him behind his back once word gets out."

"I'll tell Samuel not to say anything."

"You can try, but I don't believe he be able to help himself. And he too headstrong to listen to nobody."

Betsy turned back to the logs and kept changing hands, scrubbing with first one, then the other when one hand and arm grew too tired. Finally she stopped, took a deep breath. "It's just not going to come out."

"All right," Annie Mae said. "I can see that. I was gon' wait and do this tonight if I had to, but Rafe ain't here, so we gon' do it now."

"What?"

"Just wait here," Annie Mae said.

She walked into the barn and to the stall where Rafe kept his tools and found a metal rasp. Then she walked back quickly and handed it to her daughter.

"What am I going to do with this?"

"Scrape them stains out, but watch how you hold it. Them teeth will cut you."

Betsy was hesitant, but she finally held the rasp at each end and began to scrape against the curve of the logs. Purple shavings fell, littering the ground with their color. Annie Mae knew she would have to scoop up these signs and bury them. But then a question came to her, one she felt she should have realized already. Wouldn't it be better to let Rafe see these stains, find out what Melinda had done, and let her suffer the consequences? That would make her think twice about trying to cause more harm. Still, Annie Mae wanted these signs erased from all eyes that might see. Who would see, though? The children for one, and children can't help but talk, and anyone Samuel might tell, they might want to come see for themselves and pretend to pay a call on Betsy.

But the shavings, they could be proof enough for Rafe, and he could see the rasp marks on the logs if Betsy pointed them out to him. Annie Mae squatted, then put her knees against the cold ground as she'd done when digging the last grave in the horse pasture, and began collecting the shavings.

"What are you doing?" Betsy asked and stopped her work.

"You gon' show these to Rafe, tell him what's been done. We gon' have to let him get on to Miss Melinda."

Betsy nodded, clearly understanding the sense of what Annie Mae had said, and did not seem bothered by the idea in the least, which showed Annie Mae again how far apart she and her daughter really were.

Annie Mae, still looking up at Betsy, saw that the girl's fingers were indeed scraped and bleeding from the rasp. She reached for her daughter's free hand, as if across time to when Betsy was the small child she'd once been, and Annie Mae wiped the blood from the knuckles and fingers into her own hands until her daughter's were mostly clean, and then picked up the small pile of stained shavings she'd put down. The red and purple against her copper skin looked strange to her, like colors she'd never seen before, and she thought of Melinda then, how she'd pulled that last child bloody and free, finally, and delivered Melinda from her pain. Now here she knelt with her daughter's blood against her skin and wood shavings full of Melinda's spittle, and it felt like two lives in her hands, one of which she'd have to drop.

That evening, before good dark, which was slowly coming later on clock time, she heard two children's voices on the back porch or just beyond it. When she came through the door, she saw Henry walking off as if he'd been ordered away, his back and shoulders squared, his steps purposeful. George stood still, directly in front of Melinda, who sat at the top of the steps in a heavy coat.

"So do you know my name?" she asked.

"You Miss Melinda." George looked afraid, but maybe proud of himself, too, for knowing the answer. He remained fixed in place, unable to move, it seemed.

"And what's *your* name?" Melinda asked in a voice that wasn't pleasant in the way most women, and mothers, would ask a question of a child who stood wide-eyed before them.

"George," he said.

Annie Mae looked on, unsure what to do or say.

"What's your *whole* name?" Melinda asked. "Do you know?"

Annie Mae closed her eyes, not wanting to hear the answer her grandson might deliver.

"George Anderson," he said.

Melinda nodded slowly. "That's my name too. Did you know that?"

George looked confused, as if he had little idea what was expected of him from this woman he'd only seen from a distance until this moment.

"And how did you come by that name?" Melinda asked.

Now George seemed more confused. "I don't know," he said. "I reckon from where you got yours."

Melinda looked up at Annie Mae, clearly having heard and sensed her there for some time. "He's a smart boy, isn't he?" she said and waited a moment, it seemed, to see if Annie Mae would respond. "That might become a burden to him at some point," she added, and Annie Mae heard some vague hint of a threat she couldn't have fully explained. She felt then a need to remove the boy from Melinda's presence, quickly, before Melinda could utter another word.

"Come on, George. Time for you to go inside your house," she said and made her way past Melinda who remained as motionless as some permanent obstacle.

She was finally able to sleep that night but recognized his footsteps through the kitchen—his were always heavier than William's—and wondered if the sound was what had woken her or if he'd called out to her in some way other than with her name. Then he filled her doorway, the bare outline of a figure. She sat up on the edge of her bed but didn't move to light a lamp or a candle. The darkness seemed fitting for what might transpire.

"What's this craziness going on?" he asked, and before Annie Mae could decide how to answer, he kept on. "Betsy told me. You said for her to show me those pieces of log and to explain them." It hadn't occurred to Annie Mae that her daughter would bring her into it, but now she wasn't very surprised that Betsy had. "Why'd you tell her to do that?"

"Figured you would want to know, that you best hear it from her and not somebody else."

"So you're on my side now?"

"Ain't never been against you, Mr. Rafe. It's your house I work in."

"That part's right enough, I guess." He was quiet a moment. "So she went to see Leathy like some nigger would do?"

"Looks like it," Annie Mae said before he could say, or ask, more.

"A white woman in Dawes Quarter. And all of you knew about it, including Samuel, and decided *together* to keep your mouths shut, not tell me. That right?"

She knew he didn't want any correcting or long explanation. "We didn't hardly see you, and it wasn't our place." Annie Mae let those last words sink in, knew he couldn't argue them. His silence after she spoke said as much.

"Couldn't say anything till now, that is. Lord. No telling what people saying about her." He paused again and shifted in the doorway but remained an unrecognizable figure. "Well, I won't stand for it. You hear me? No white man can."

Won't stand for what? Annie Mae wondered. What he thought Melinda did to that dead child or just what all people had been saying she did? What was worse in Rafe's eyes?

She became aware finally of the coldness of the floor against her feet, and more quickly realized she could answer that last question well enough. Maybe the real question, though, was did he *know* yet what people had already been saying about Melinda since the last child's death, starting with every Negro on the Lassiter Place—all because of what Samuel had told them?

Twelve

It was before daylight when he approached her cabin, pulled there maybe by the same need he'd felt the night before and that he hadn't had answered when Betsy showed him the stained wood shavings and told him that Melinda had gone down into Dawes Quarter to see Leathy. So he was returning now to her in the way maybe they both needed. He knew her need could be almost as great as his, though the why of it could not be the same.

The cabin was dark, quiet, as he'd expected. The moon was down and the stars had disappeared. So the cabin was the vaguest of outlines, discernible to him only because he knew it so well, knew the path and his relationship to the cabin with each step, as if he'd once counted his steps and knew when to reach his hand out for the door latch, how high to reach for it in the night or early morning's greater darkness.

Then he saw some askew angle that did not seem to belong to the shape he knew and that he couldn't account for. But four steps closer and he saw. The door was ajar. Betsy could have gone to the privy, but the shadow that was the door swung hard, wider, and a dark shape shot forward with a rush of sound made somehow by movement only— not the slamming of the door against the cabin wall, or even footsteps against the ground, just a body moving through cold air, or maybe the suck of breath and then more hard breaths from a man believing he might be breathing his last. Rafe watched the vision quickly disappear into nothing but darkness, the rush of sound quiet until it was replaced by footfalls through leaf-littered woods that crashed and began to diminish before Rafe could decide whether to give chase or not.

But he had already decided more quickly than he realized, his brain moving faster than the shape he knew had to be Samuel. It was Betsy he wanted to see before going after Samuel, before even trying to understand how Samuel had guessed at his approach (though later he would wonder if it was the sound of his booted footsteps, a clearing of his throat of which he was unaware, or if Samuel had been fortunate enough to have seen the whiteness of his face through a window). He wanted only to catch Betsy in her nakedness or half-nakedness, her hair disheveled, maybe her body covered by a sheet, or her hand obscuring where Samuel had been and left his traces.

"Don't," she said from the doorway. Her voice was like the darkness speaking, and though it surprised it didn't startle. "You can't find him in this dark. Come on in to me."

Rafe moved toward the door, which stood open. "You let him in, and *let* him?" When he stepped over the threshold, light appeared and pooled on the table she had retreated behind.

She stood unmoving, looking at him, her eyes not wide or filled with fear of him. "He came in on me," she said. "I didn't *let* him in."

"So do your best to convince me he hasn't been where I think he has."

She waited, seemed to be thinking of proof she might offer. "Look at me," she said and raised her arms from her sides, lowered them again. He saw the heavy gown she wore, and the yellow robe he'd given her was tied tight at her waist; but how much did that mean when Samuel could have been there for hours taking his pleasure, and his retribution?

"He's been here all night, and I damn well know it."

She shook her head and looked toward the fireplace, as if she might find some answer for him there. He saw George on his pallet then, near the hearth, the boy's eyes lighted by the lamp flame, open and observant, watching the way grown-ups behaved in a world beyond his own understanding. Lakeview made sucking sounds in her crib, hidden within the folds of a white blanket.

"He came in, slipped in, not thirty minutes ago. Woke me quiet," she said, "then sat on my bed, pulled the covers down, put his hand on my back. I told him no."

"You shoved him out of the bed?" He walked toward her and she sat down slowly in a chair, and despite the fact that he stood over her, he felt no advantage.

"No, didn't seem any call for that. I stayed calm. That's best with men."

Just as she remained calm with him now, he realized. That gave her a gain against him, not unlike Virginia might achieve. "But calm wasn't enough, was it? Or did you just give in?"

The lamp fired the waves of her hair and made a dark light around her face. She closed her eyes, opened them again. "He started to undress himself. I could tell he'd been drinking."

"But you wanted him."

It took her a moment to respond, and that told him he was not wrong. But he waited, watched her face, saw the shape of her parted lips as she began to speak. "I knew what he really wanted. It wasn't me, not exactly. Could say it was you." She paused, let him hear that. "I stayed his hand, pushed at his legs when he wanted to climb on in."

"Did he force you?"

"Might have thought about it, but he didn't. I got up then, was already wearing this gown. Put my robe on over it, told him to get up."

"Did you see him?"

"See what?" she said, clearly confused by his question.

"You know what I mean."

She looked away, then back, maybe had tried to hide the intimation of a smile. He wasn't sure, then decided no, she hadn't. She would never act amused at him in such a way. "Not like you're thinking," she said, her voice and face serious. "He was in his state, but never got that far undressed."

Rafe knew she had no way of knowing it, and maybe he didn't fully understand himself, but her answer might have just saved Samuel's sorry life. It did not, however, save between them the moment he had come for. That had passed, his earlier desire lost to the night's ending.

He was not surprised to find Melinda still in bed when he returned to the house. He built up the fire in the room and didn't try to be particularly quiet while he went about it. After dropping the poker on the brick hearth, he decided she had to be awake by now though she still pretended not. "I know good and well you don't believe in hoodoo," he said, his anger rising again, nearing the level it had reached at Betsy's cabin. She finally opened her eyes and turned herself more in his direction but didn't speak, her silence maybe a way of antagonizing him. "I still want to know what you called yourself doing. It makes no sense to me," he said, his voice rising further. "I realize my claiming the boy in front of our children must have been hurtful to you, but enough to send you to Dawes Quarter to a hoodoo woman? Lord. You have to be the talk among the Negroes. Why would you want that?"

She seemed unsure what to say, undecided about how to evade his questions, except with silence. He considered pushing her again, intimidating her to a greater degree. "If you went to Leathy because you wanted to curse Betsy for having those children, why wouldn't you have done it before now? There must be some other reason you went."

"She deserves to be cursed for all the harm she's done."

"You're still not answering my question. And what harm has she done compared to what you've done? She's only brought healthy children *into* this world."

"Believe what you'd like."

"One has to believe the truth," he said. "No matter how hard it is."

"We can agree on that, at least."

Rafe heard the dogtrot door open and footsteps approach. He expected to see Annie Mae at first, but he realized the footsteps were too soft for Annie Mae. The bedroom door, which was slightly ajar, now opened wider and Kate appeared somewhat timidly from around it. She looked from one to the other of them. "I don't feel good," she said, but, to Rafe's ears, not very convincingly.

"What's wrong?" Melinda asked.

Kate kept looking at each of them, and Rafe saw that she was taking their measure. She'd heard their arguing, he surmised, along with the other children, and needed to see how things stood between them in the beginning of the day's light, her need for such a thing always greater than her brothers' and sister's. She looked at only him now, her gaze steady and penetrating, and he realized that Kate's having heard their arguing bothered him more than the other children's hearing, and that her presence actually made him feel some small level of regret, though he could not allow regret to hold sway over him.

"Come on in the room," Melinda said. Then she looked at Rafe and added, "Could you leave us alone for a few minutes?"

"All right," he said, and it dawned on him that Kate did hurt, though it was not her stomach but the periodic suffering some women had to endure more acutely than others. This was not the first time Kate had come to her mother for such comfort, which Melinda always gave.

Rafe walked out without another word and closed the door behind him. He found himself trying to take his own measure of this woman who, he was certain, had taken from him their last two children.

He did not push Wheeler. There was no need for hurry since he hadn't any real business in town. He would take his usual room, maybe pass some time with cards if players were present, then take an early supper. He rode the ferry alone, and once in town, left Wheeler at the livery stable, telling the owner he'd be back for his horse at exactly a quarter to six and to have him saddled.

When he mounted Wheeler that evening, there was still light, which he was glad for. Early darkness had always bothered him, the shortness of December and January days somehow reminding him that everyone's days were brief and time always limited. By the time he made it to Virginia's house he felt the temperature begin to drop. Her windows were lit, and he knew her stove would be warm. What he was uncertain of was the kind of reception he might receive. He hadn't seen her in some weeks, perhaps the longest period of time he'd ever gone without seeing her and the children.

He knocked before entering but didn't wait for her to open the door. She sat at the kitchen table near the stove, and though she did not turn her face toward him, she must have seen him from the corner of her eye because just as Fannie and Walter let out sharp cries at the sight of their father, Virginia reached an arm toward each of them and kept them in their chairs.

Rafe approached the table. "No hugs from my children?" he said. Both squirmed under their mother's halting hand.

"Papa," Walter said, and Fannie held her arms out.

Virginia turned to him finally and her hard look stopped him for a moment, but he reached for Fannie and lifted her from her chair, and she put her arms around his neck. Then, once he had her settled tightly, he placed a free hand on top of Walter's head, and the boy smiled up at him.

"They ain't done eating yet," Virginia said.

"I can see that. Far be it from me to interrupt a meal."

Virginia mumbled something he couldn't quite hear.

After placing Fannie back in her seat, Rafe took a chair at the table.

"Did you bring us something, Papa?" Walter asked.

Rafe looked at him, noticing for the first time, and with a kind of shock, the resemblance between Walter and George—something so completely similar around the mouth and the eyes both, the thin slightly downturned lips and the same arch of the brows. He had never seen any of his own features in either child and had never thought to look for them, his sureness that they were both his never a doubt in his mind—so he'd not ever felt the need to look. He wondered if the two could know each other at some point, be brothers through more than Rafe's own blood. He supposed they could if he wanted them to, and the same for the sisters, Fannie and Lakeview, though he would probably have to bear

Virginia's wrath to accomplish it. But if he desired it strongly enough her wrath would not matter, nor Betsy's.

He became aware again of Virginia, that she was speaking. "So did you? she said.

"Did I what?"

"Bring them anything."

He saw she had already intuited the answer despite the fact that he'd never failed to bring them some little trinket or candy before. "No, not this time," he said.

She didn't respond, merely watched the children finish their meals. Her own was only half eaten. Finally she said, "Y'all go put on your coats, go play outside a few minutes."

After quick glances toward Rafe, then back at their mother, they said, "Yes, ma'am" and slid from their chairs, and in a few moments they were gone out the door.

Now she looked at him. "You must of come here for some other reason than your children." He realized she was right. There was no use in denying it. But before he could say anything, she added, "That all I care about, though, that them children see you, know they daddy. Guess you see them other two plenty."

"I suppose I do."

"These two here, they come first."

"No," he said, leaning in toward her, "there were others before Fannie and Walter, lest you forget."

"Your white children don't count. Of course you got white children. All white men do by the time they your age. I don't worry about them."

"Then just worry about your own."

"That what I'm doing. Next time, you bring them something. Don't have to be big, but it best not break."

"I'll see to them. I did bring you money, which is for you *and* the children." He reached into his coat pocket and laid the bills on the table. "There would be more, but the cards fell wrong at the last hand."

She stared at him now. "Fell wrong? This the longest you ever stayed away, and you don't bring no more than what on this table because you lost playing cards?"

"There'll be more. You know that."

She looked away from him and toward the door, toward the sounds of her children's voices beyond it. "I don't know what I know," she said.

"Except I know that Betsy, she don't even have to work. I work, and don't mind it, but she don't."

"Nothing here," he said and motioned around the house, "has anything to do with her."

"My children not *nothing.*"

He was dumbfounded at first, unable to comprehend that she'd spoken so illogically. He decided, finally, that she still held more ill will toward Betsy than he'd realized, which he knew was due to his own faulty thinking, or perhaps lack of thinking. "You know I didn't mean that, not for a second. What's gotten into you?"

She looked back at him, nodded her head slowly, and, for a moment, kept her eyes on the table, her way of expressing apology, or at least acknowledging she was wrong. He realized she'd never actually spoken any kind of apology to him and knew himself well enough that he'd never really warranted one.

He noticed her slender right arm resting on the table and was moved to lay his hand upon her wrist, but before he placed the tips of his fingers against her burnished skin she pulled away, holding her arms close to her body as if they afforded her protection.

"So what you here for? I know something be on your mind," she said.

He wasn't sure how to begin and showed her a hesitancy he didn't intend. "My wife," he said finally, and he saw in her eyes that these were the words she was expecting; words she had known were coming when he'd first come through the door.

"She been to see Leathy," Virginia said, and as soon as her words settled on the air, he realized they did not surprise him. Of course she would know already, but how? Sometimes it seemed she had powers and a presence larger than anything Leathy could lay claim to.

She must have seen, or guessed at, the question in his mind. "Just 'cause I ain't lived in Riverfield since after the uprising don't mean I don't know people there, don't mean I don't never cross that river and go home. I do, more than you know. You ain't the only one who gets about."

He knew what she said was bound to be true, but he'd never thought of her crossing the Black Fork. It was as if that river kept his life separate from hers, was a dividing line for him, and it hadn't occurred to him that it wasn't a dividing line for her as well, marking the early years of her life apart from the years she'd lived since bearing his children and even before. Once her sister, Rebecca, March's wife, had had to flee after March was killed and Rebecca had warned Rafe about what was coming, Virginia hadn't anything to keep her in Riverfield. Their father had been sold and taken away well before the war and their mother had died. Virginia had never been in any danger the way Rebecca had; she'd simply chosen to leave. And once Rafe had begun to take up with her from time to time, he felt some relief that she removed herself from Riverfield, discretion something he still cared about at that time, not that he'd planned for what went on between them to last for years or to lead to children, though it had. Unlike some others, she'd never held it against him that he'd led white men against Negroes seeking vengeance. She had known of his friendship with March and his aid to her sister.

Virginia's ability to see him as he was and understand him was not something he'd thought he could ever leave behind, until he first saw Betsy. But even now he *hadn't* left it behind, not completely, his need for her still stronger than he wanted to admit to himself—the same need she saw and knew he wanted to hide but couldn't. It gave her a power over him he never intended or could reconcile for himself.

"So why would she have gone to Leathy, embarrass herself like that?"

"You mean embarrass you."

"Whatever a man's wife does out in front of people, it's a comment on him."

She rested both arms on the top of the table again and leaned forward so that her arms held some of her weight, her body relaxed now, a look of confidence returning. "Your wife, she ain't trying to hurt you. And I don't suspect she care much about herself and what people be thinking of her, either one."

"Then what's she trying to do?" Rafe said.

"What you asking that for? It so plain you got to know already. She went to hurt that Betsy."

"But why hoodoo, something she doesn't even believe in? And why now?"

Virginia shook her head in such a dismissive way, as if she couldn't believe how little he understood, but instead of making him angry, as it might have on any other day under different circumstances, he felt again his need of her.

"She think the girl killed her child, and probably figure she killed the one before that, too. That just what she told Leathy, I bet. And she know a white woman going to Dawes Quarter to see a hoodoo woman look right desperate, enough to make folks wonder and speculate on.

Then when she mark them walls, she be pointing a finger right at that girl."

"But it wasn't Betsy who killed the child. We both know who did it. Maybe Melinda's only trying to make someone else look guilty. And how do you know about the stains on Betsy's cabin, anyway? Annie Mae got rid of them."

Virginia was quiet a moment, her head turned at an angle, and he realized she was listening for the sound of her, their, children. He heard Fannie's voice then, calling Walter's name, and other children's voices filling the air the way they do when some made-up game is taking its course.

She turned back to him, satisfied her children were near. "*You* think it Melinda. I done told you already what I think. And as for them stains, somebody be spreading the word on them, and that ain't all."

"Who's spreading word?"

"You think a minute and you'll know." He had an inkling but waited for her. "Samuel," she said. "He making sure everybody know who put hoodoo on that girl."

Now need gave way to anger, but he kept himself under control, feeling his body tighten within, but he did not move or speak out. Virginia saw it in his face, though; looking in his eyes, she doubtless saw them harden and narrow. "And what else is he saying?"

"What you think, that your wife killed them last two babies."

He was standing before he realized he'd moved, so close to the stovepipe he could feel its heat, an incandescence equal to his own. "I cannot have that. And won't. I met him in the road going up to the Lassiter Place, riding my own damn mule, and knew he was up to no good. The son of a bitch. Then this morning I ran him out of Betsy's cabin. He'd been after her." He didn't bother to explain that it had been his mere approach that had run Samuel out of the cabin.

Virginia remained seated, as if she felt the need to keep the table between them, her arms crossed against her body. "What difference it make what he do or be saying? You think he telling the truth."

He knew without doubt, even in his angered state, that she realized the difference. She was trying to make some point, forcing him to understand how he would align himself. He couldn't be halfway. He was either for his wife, would serve her, offer what was within him to give—love, support, protection, and sanctuary—or he was against her. Perhaps he'd already made that choice, but now he had to make it more completely, to act on it. But what of such public shaming against a husband, among Negroes, no less? How does a husband, he thought, balance protection against impudence?

Virginia stood and walked away from the table. He wasn't sure why. Maybe because he hadn't answered her question. But it hadn't really been a question at all. She was in the front room now, and he realized the children had come inside, though somehow he hadn't heard the door close or their voices until Fannie said, "Because it got too dark out, Mama."

She helped them take off their coats, and he paid no further attention, simply sat back down at the table for the moment, though in a way he was already on the road home, drawn there by concerns that had to be dealt with. So many questions and thoughts about Melinda, the dead children, Betsy, and especially Samuel's treachery went through his mind.

Finally she stood before him at the table again, stared down at him. "What you just sitting in here for? You not gon' pay no mind to your children, too mad with your wife and hired help to take up some time with them?" He rose suddenly and saw from her expression that she realized where all of his anger was pointed, but she rose to it. "All you worrying about across the river. You here now, and they two children here too, the ones you ain't seen in weeks." She grabbed at his wrist and pulled him toward the front room before he jerked his arm free. He scowled at her, but he saw them as she intended, sitting on the floor in front of the fireplace, each looking up at him with fear and worry marking their faces, like stains. Fannie's quiet tears had started, the sound of raised voices and her own confusion enough cause for them. In Walter he saw something beyond fear, a look of disappointment maybe, or disillusion, words the boy couldn't know, could only feel and know the meaning of from within.

Virginia was speaking again, but he didn't listen. He heard only the name *Betsy* come from her mouth. Enough. He'd had enough this night and turned from his children, away from Virginia, and without any word of his own directed at her, or the back of his hand, he walked out, leaving the door open to the cold air, then mounted Wheeler and rode away into the separating darkness.

He decided to wait until morning after all, so he spent the night in his hotel room. By the time the sun reached nine o'clock, he neared his store and saw Alfred sweeping the porch. The man wore a white apron, a narrow-brimmed hat, and a worn Chesterfield coat. When he looked up he saw Rafe and did not wave but seemed to make a motion asking him to come near.

Rafe approached and dismounted, tying Wheeler at a post. "Things all right?"

"I reckon. No business right now, except for my boy Richard inside getting a few things." He was quiet for just a moment and continued holding his broom still. "I think my son wants to speak to you."

"What's he want?" Rafe stepped up onto the porch and came close to Alfred, who didn't seem to want to speak further. "Call him on out here, then, if you can't tell me what he wants."

"I best let him talk for himself." Alfred walked over to the window, tapped at it with his knuckles, and motioned for his son to come out.

In just a moment the door opened and the boy walked onto the porch—though not so much a boy as the last time Rafe had made notice of him. He'd filled out some, and his face had taken on the more angular shape of his father's, so much so that it looked as if it had been carefully measured and squared. "Morning, Mr. Anderson," he said. He looked down at the porch, then back up at Rafe with a kind of determination that Rafe couldn't help but recognize. "I wanted to ask you something."

"All right, go on ahead."

"Yes, sir," he said, which didn't seem in direct answer to anything. Then the boy managed to gather himself. "I've been sitting with your daughter at church the last few Sundays. Would it be all right if I called on her this Sunday afternoon?"

Rafe looked over at Alfred, who seemed a little nervous himself about what his son was asking. Then he looked back at the boy. "Which one?"

"Sir?"

"I got two daughters. Which is it?"

"Bunyan, sir."

Rafe nodded. "I reckon she's old enough, especially if her behavior of late is any indication. They're all difficult, boy. You best remember that."

At first Richard didn't seem to know how to respond. Finally he said, "Thank you, sir," and the relief he clearly felt was still present too in Alfred's face when Rafe looked his way again.

"Wouldn't you agree?" Rafe said.

Now the father seemed as hesitant as his son had been at first. "Well," he said after some pause, "my two daughters have sometime been a trial to me."

"I can imagine." Rafe turned to the boy. "All right. You can go on back inside and get what things you need."

"Yes, sir," he said and walked through the door again, his steps too stiff somehow, as if he were trying to hold himself back from displaying too casual a bearing.

"He's a good boy," Alfred said after his son was out of earshot. "Works hard. On his way to being a man."

"I don't doubt it at all," Rafe said. "I meant what I said. It's fine for him to call on Bunyan."

"Thank you."

"No thanks needed. I know I've always been able to count on you, all the way down to raising a son right."

Alfred simply nodded and began to make short strokes with his broom again.

Rafe went and mounted Wheeler and held him to a slow walk, but he could feel the bridled power waiting to be called upon. And just before his thoughts turned once more to Samuel, he felt the unexpected intrusion of a memory called up by place and circumstance. He even looked back at the store building, and the cold morning of his first day in Riverfield came back in full. He'd walked into the store and asked for Mr. Lassiter, then laid eyes on Melinda and knew he would pursue her, though the word "pursue" probably did not come near to describing what he had in mind for her. Weeks later, when he was the one installed behind the counter, he asked permission to call, which her father denied, though Rafe could see the denial would not hold, that her father already recognized the inevitability of what was before him and his daughter. Then he was finally given allowance and ultimately took what wasn't allowed. So Melinda became his, was still his—and what lay between them, whatever loss and guilt and betrayals were theirs and not to be undermined, certainly not by Samuel.

He rode on home, past his house and Betsy's cabin, then dismounted and led Wheeler into the barn. He knew he'd have to put out feed in the troughs for Benjamin and Mollie B., and Ida and Ned. Then he noticed Benjamin wasn't in his stall and wondered if maybe William had ridden him to school, though he'd never done such a thing before. Rafe had a strange sense of something being wrong. But he took his time caring for and feeding Wheeler. Then he looked out the back door of the barn, checked the horse pasture, and saw that it was empty. At least the fence looked fully repaired.

He closed the heavy door, scooped buckets of feed, and went to Mollie B.'s stall first. Then Ida's. When he moved toward Ned's, he was surprised not to see him waiting, his head at the opening above the half-door, anxious for his own feed, irritated at being last. Rafe began to lift the bucket as he neared, then saw that Ned was lying on the ground. He knew the animal was dead even before he saw the blood or the curious piece of scribbled slate lying crosswise on Ned's flank. He lowered and let go of the bucket, opened the stall door for a better look, and took in the large gash down the neck and the darkened matted hair. He touched Ned behind an ear and felt warmth still, but very little. Then he saw the other stab wounds, three of them near the gash. Blood was pooled across dirt and hay like syrup poured by a far too generous hand. He felt shock at what he saw and was surprised by it. The number of dead horses and mules he'd seen during the war hadn't been countable. Here was just one, but it was his and it had served, done all that had ever been asked of him, his stubborn nature forgiven because you could not fault a mule for being a mule. He picked up the puzzling slate then, a child's school slate, studied it as if there were some lesson to be learned, and read the letters scrawled across it: *Here your mule.*

As any man would, he felt anger at the words, but there was something within him that went past anger and into what he thought might be a deeper understanding of his enemy, an understanding that brought with it a cold, pervading calm he knew would serve him in due time. He placed the slate in the trough and walked out of the stall, turned and shut the half-door, and noticed his own bloody boot prints that followed him.

As he approached Betsy's cabin he knew she would emerge, but she didn't, not at first. Then he heard her door open, and he looked. He saw her standing alone in a loose dress of dark brown, her hair unplaited but gathered in her left hand and held at the front of her shoulder, a gesture he'd seen before, as if touching the beauty of her hair soothed and reassured her.

"You not…" she called out but didn't finish. He could see her forlorn look, and that look told him what no answer in words from her would.

"You don't know, do you? You haven't seen him."

"Who? Samuel?"

"Of course Samuel."

"Not since he ran. He's done something else?"

A part of him wanted to say nothing, to keep his own counsel, but he needed to see her reaction. "Just killed my mule and looks like stole my horse."

She closed her eyes with what looked like a dread that weighted them enough to keep them closed. She finally opened them again, as though the vision behind them wasn't anything she wanted to see. "Come in the house," she said.

"No. It will have to be later."

"When?"

"I don't know." He spoke the words harder than he'd intended. Beyond his current anger, he felt an irritation, still, at Virginia from the night before, and any demand from a woman was more than he wanted to hear, especially now. He turned and kept walking.

He ascended the porch steps and went first to the back door of the kitchen. He found Annie Mae near the stove and Philip on the floor, playing with a set of blocks he had cut for the boy. Instead of entering the room, he simply said through the open door he held on to, "You heard any word of Samuel?"

His question was a kind of test, and she seemed to take notice of the way he'd worded it. "No, sir," she said. "He ain't come this morning, not that I seen."

Rafe nodded, closing the door abruptly. He knew Annie Mae would learn from Betsy what had happened, and he trusted Annie Mae to keep Philip away from the dead mule. He walked into the dogtrot and into his and Melinda's side of the house, hoping she was there and not in the living room or parlor.

He found her standing in a dark blue dress in front of the open wardrobe and decided she might have been looking at herself in the mirror that hung inside. She didn't acknowledge him at first, but then she finally turned his way when he pulled their bedroom door closed. "I'm not looking to argue," he said.

"Good." She appeared apprehensive. Perhaps his closing the door made her so, or the look from the barn he probably still wore. "I saw you ride in on Wheeler a little while ago," she said. "Didn't expect you in the house so soon."

He knew what she meant by this—that he hadn't gone to Betsy. He didn't tell her what had distracted him from Betsy. He always held inside himself any violence he'd witnessed, or done, especially when it came to telling Melinda. He took his coat off and sat at the edge of the bed. She turned and faced him but did not move from the front of the wardrobe.

She looked as if she might want to ask him something, but she didn't speak. "Can you sit beside me?" he said. He held his hand out toward her, and while she didn't take it, actually appeared puzzled by it, she did sit down on the bed, clearly intending the space she made between them.

At first they were both quiet. "Alfred's son is showing interest in Bunyan," he said eventually. He hadn't known this was what he would say. They were simply the first words that came to him, and he wondered, for a moment, why.

"I know about Richard." Melinda said the words flatly and didn't elaborate.

He realized he expected her to say more, or hoped she would, though the subject really didn't bear any discussion. A boy was interested in their daughter. It was a simple enough fact.

"He wants to call on her."

"All right," she said.

Now her short answers irritated him, but he withheld his displeasure. "He asked me up at the store about calling on her. Made me think of you, when we first met." He looked at her, and she seemed to be staring at the angled mirror on the open wardrobe door, though he didn't imagine she could see herself. Maybe she was able to see him this way—askew, her way of placing him at a greater distance. "Then later, in the store, if you remember, I asked your father about calling on you."

"And was denied."

"I guess you wished he had stopped us."

She looked at him oddly, as if to say, How am I supposed to answer, how to untangle and make sense of all that has happened between us? What would be the point of trying? "He knew you would not be stopped," she said.

"And that's what attracted you to me."

She looked away again, away from him and any possible reflected image of him. "Why do you take everything you want?"

"It's the only way I know how to exist," he said, which was true and there was no explaining it. "But I've given to you too. Children, a home. And though you've taken from me, I will still offer what I can to you."

"And what's that?"

He wanted to say protection—from anyone who would do her harm, who would say bad things about her—protection, indeed, he wanted to add, from her own foolishness, but he didn't. And though she was still turned from him, he could see the tightness in her neck and in the line of her jaw, her rigid posture. He lifted his hand and touched the side of her face, feeling with his fingers the knotted muscle that told him her teeth were clenched. She leaned farther away from him. He could have taken her chin into his grip, made her look at him, but that wasn't his desire. He didn't want roughness. He wanted to offer her something beyond it, something he was seldom able to give and didn't really know how to name, though some might call it tenderness. He could have told her what Samuel was doing, what Samuel had just done, and what he was prepared to do to Samuel, but he didn't. Maybe his not telling her was a kind of protection too. And wasn't there some level of tenderness in that?

He lowered his hand and placed it gently upon her knee.

"No, Rafe," she said, slowly.

He nodded and then realized she hadn't seen his silent acknowledgment. "There will have to come a time," he said, "but it's not something I want at the moment. We haven't, though, been man and wife together in some long while."

"No, and you must understand why," she said. He felt her dread at the idea and didn't know what to do about it other than to be the man he was and care for her the only way he knew how.

In the middle of the afternoon, before going to see to the dead weight of Ned's body, he heard the children come in from school and begin to climb the stairs outside. The two sets of pounding feet had to be Henry and William, with Henry probably trying to race past William to be first. He then realized what this sound confirmed, that William had walked home with the others and had, of course, not been riding Benjamin. The horse was gone, and Rafe imagined Samuel's feet in the stirrups of one of the finer saddles.

He rose from his desk with anger now, walked outside, and tried his best to temper himself when he saw Kate and Bunyan about to ascend the stairs side by side. They stopped and waited for him.

"Bunyan," he said, "let me talk with you a minute." He saw a mild look of concern on Kate's face, a deeper one on Bunyan's. Both stood very still, absolutely together, perhaps in a way that only sisters can manage. "Kate, Bunyan will be on up in a moment."

"Yes, sir," she said and nothing more. Her face was reddened a bit from the cold but in a way that looked healthy, beautiful even. He felt pride in that. She walked up then, her steps so much lighter than her brothers'.

He turned to Bunyan, saw her darker features, the concern still in her face, and was struck by how much of Melinda he found in her. She certainly did not appear pleased to see him, which he expected. He hoped what he had to say might change that, though it occurred to him she would rather hear it from her mother, and that Melinda could very well be disappointed in not being the one to tell her.

"Yes, sir?" she said, the subservience of her words belied by her tone.

"I understand Alfred's son Richard has been sitting with you in church."

She lifted the two books she was carrying and hugged them against her chest, tightly. "Yes, sir. He has." He watched her search his face, trying to decide, probably, if what she saw in him was approval or disapproval.

"He asked me at the store earlier if he could call on you on Sunday."

Her dark eyes widened for a moment, with pleasure, he thought, but then they slowly narrowed, as if with caution, and he did not know why. He wondered if she felt a need to show caution toward him, or if there was something about Richard's calling that provoked such a unique reaction. Most girls would have been so pleased.

"I told him that would be acceptable, that he had my permission. He appears a fine enough young man."

"Yes, sir. He is. Thank you."

"So you would like to see him?" he asked, still perplexed at her reaction, though perhaps the anger he felt toward Samuel was overriding and clouding his perceptions of her.

She raised her books a little higher. "Yes, sir."

It occurred to him now that maybe her words were so guarded because she didn't want to give him the satisfaction of her happiness.

They stood there in silence and discomfort. "May I go on up now?" she said finally.

"Yes," he said. "You may. Whatever you wish."

She looked at him as if she'd heard some small and unexpected level of hurt in his voice and couldn't take in the fact of it, did not know it could exist, and so backed away from it, and while taking the steps with less fury than her brothers, she went up them just as quickly.

He was left alone then, standing in the cold, wondering why lately every time he saw and talked to his daughter it felt less like a conversation and more like an encounter with someone who might be either friend *or* foe and he couldn't decide which.

THIRTEEN

Melinda was sitting in the parlor, trying to read the weekly *Riverfield Progress*, which mostly carried social news that interested her less and less and lately not at all, but she read it anyway and couldn't have said why. Philip sat on the floor playing at her feet. William and Henry entered the downstairs now—she knew it was them by the force of the door opening and closing—and were heading toward the kitchen, she was certain, for leftover biscuits. "Philip," she heard Henry call, but Philip was already up off the floor and quickly making his way toward his brother, as if the world had just come alive for him. "He's coming," she said and wondered if the boys heard her. Annie Mae had probably just gotten down the pan of biscuits, unless she'd slipped out to see Elizabeth.

In a few moments Bunyan and Kate appeared, Bunyan entering the parlor first and sitting beside Melinda, which surprised her. Kate took the cushioned chair near the front window and looked toward the both of them, smiling and waiting, it appeared, for what her mother was about to hear.

"Daddy just told me," Bunyan said.

This truly did surprise her, and she didn't have to ask what Bunyan meant. Her only question was why Rafe had suddenly done something most other fathers might have. But instead of a moment of closeness between a father and daughter, maybe it was simply to rob Melinda of her own moment with Bunyan. Or perhaps he'd done it for some other reason, out of some deeper need.

She placed a hand over her daughter's and felt the slenderness of her long fingers. "I knew it was only a matter of time before Richard couldn't bear not to see more of the pretty girl he's been sitting with at church." She watched Bunyan blush, the color in her high cheeks so at odds with her skin tone.

"Look at her turning red," Kate said.

"No teasing your sister."

"I didn't mean to, Bunyan."

She saw the look between her daughters then, felt the comfort in it, and wished for a moment that she hadn't been an only child; she knew, however, that she was lucky to have daughters who could love each other. Not all did.

"What if," Bunyan began and stopped. Melinda saw a look on her face that approached something akin to fear. "What if I don't know what to say to him?"

"Then just listen. He'll talk, though he'll be nervous too. And *really* listen, and whatever he talks about, ask him questions. Ask him about running his family's farm, if he wants his own farm someday."

"Call me in," Kate said. "*I'll* talk to him. Or there's always Henry. I'll send Henry in and he'll talk Richard's ear off, and the boy won't ever come back."

Melinda saw the hint of a smile at the corners of Bunyan's mouth, but still there was a kind of worry that didn't allow the smile to fully form.

The boys' voices were coming close now. "Don't," she heard William say and, the tone of warning so strong, she knew he must be talking to Henry. William walked in, shaking his head, looked at Melinda, and then walked past the small sofa where she and Bunyan sat. She could feel him near her now, standing right behind, as if ready to offer protection from what he couldn't stop.

Henry advanced into the room, followed by Philip, Henry's small, quiet shadow that always made his presence seem larger.

"How was school today for you boys?" Melinda said, which was what she usually asked when they came home, though now the question only served to prolong hearing whatever was going to come from Henry.

The boy stood in the middle of the room and looked at each of them as if he'd stepped onto his own small stage. "Miss Lofton paddled me today," he announced.

Melinda was surprised he would confess to being disciplined instead of trying to keep it from her. Subterfuge came to him so naturally. "And why did she do that?"

"'Cause I hit Richard's little brother, punched him in his dumb face."

"Why did you do that, Henry?" she asked, wondering if it was some-how related to Richard's wanting to call on Bunyan, if there had been talk about it in Alfred's home that the child had repeated.

"He won't tell us," Kate said, looking toward her sister. "But I think William knows. He was out in the schoolyard when it happened."

Melinda waited for William to speak. When he didn't she turned toward him, twisting her body awkwardly, and he first looked down at the floor, then back at her. "He's going to tell you, though I told him to keep his mouth shut about all of this."

"Why, Henry?" she said after facing again her middle surviving son.

Henry placed his hands on his hips, took a deep breath, and appeared as boldly positioned as any statue. "Because he said you been down to see some crazy nigger hoodoo woman in Dawes Quarter. Said that makes you just as crazy. Did you do that, Mama? Did you put hoodoo on somebody like some crazy woman would do?"

She knew it was not only Henry who awaited an answer. She could feel all of her children watching her and wondered if the silence in the kitchen meant Annie Mae's absence or anticipation. If she was inside, it would have been impossible for her not to have heard Henry.

"First, Henry, you children are not to use the word nigger. You know that. If you do it again, I'll whip you. Now, I went down into Dawes Quarter to see someone about a certain matter. But I don't believe in hoodoo, no intelligent person does, and I did not place any kind of curse on anyone. That is all you need to know." She looked around the room, at each surprised face, Kate's showing the most puzzlement. "So don't ask me any other questions about what is my adult business."

"I'll punch him again if I have to."

"William," Melinda said, "what is this child's name?"

"Lucas."

"You will *not* punch Lucas. You will not punch anyone unless they punch you first, no matter what they may say about me. If you do, I'll whip you. Do you understand?"

Henry's stance remained rigid. "Yes, ma'am," he said, but his words were spoken defiantly, and he marched out of the parlor. Philip was hesitant, not sure if he should follow.

Melinda saw Henry stop beyond the threshold, then look toward the kitchen. "You think my mama's crazy?" She knew Annie Mae had to be standing in the kitchen doorway or even near the dining table.

"No, child, I don't." Her voice was not loud, but it carried far enough, as far as Annie Mae intended, Melinda guessed. "Your mama's a smart woman. I know that better than most."

Henry continued his march and slammed the door to the dogtrot behind him, slammed it so hard that if Rafe was still in his office she knew he would investigate, and knew, too, what that would mean for Henry. What his investigation might mean for her she wasn't as certain.

Now Philip started toward the parlor door, but Bunyan stood quickly and took him by the arm. "You stay right here," she said. "You belong to us too."

"I know," Philip said, but it was easy enough to see where his concern lay.

"Mama?" Kate said from her chair then, just the one simple, much delayed word. The light through the near window framed her in a bright haze that seemed to illuminate only her confusion at everything she'd heard, her utterance encompassing all that Melinda could not answer for Kate or any of her children. Melinda merely shook her head, and Kate didn't speak further.

Bunyan sat down again and pulled Philip toward her so that he stood between her legs in the folds of her dress with his back to her. "Mama," she said, "do you think what Henry did could keep Richard from coming to see me?"

Melinda saw William lean over the sofa and look down at his sister with disgust, as if to say, Is that your only worry here? But he held his tongue. "I don't know, Bunyan, but I doubt it. Little boys fight. Parents and older brothers know that. It's no war."

"Maybe Richard heard something that will change his mind," Bunyan said.

Melinda felt her daughter's gaze search her face and understood the remark was directed at her. She chose to ignore it. "I think he cares too much for you to let anything get in his way."

She hoped she was right, hoped that none of the actions she'd taken would end up hurting her daughter or any other child of hers—but Henry had already been hurt, she realized, and she was touched that he had wanted to defend her. For Henry, that punch had been born out of love, or as close to love as he could ever come. But maybe she was wrong. Maybe it had come out of pride only and once again he'd shown that he was his father's son so much more than Philip or William.

"Kate, why don't you and Bunyan take Philip up to your room while you see to your homework?" she said, needing to be alone. She was afraid Philip might protest, but he didn't. Kate and Bunyan both stood and looked at her as if they wanted to say something but didn't know what it should be. The silence in the space between them felt like some argument had just ended, though no voice had been raised, no accusation spoken aloud.

The girls quietly walked out, Philip following behind Kate and in front of Bunyan, refusing either's hand—his own small defiance, perhaps.

William came around from behind the sofa and stood before her. "Do you need me, Mother?"

Such concern, she saw, that overrode whatever questions he had or confusion he held. "No, William. Not right now," she said.

He continued to stand in front of her as if he were afraid to leave, perhaps for her sake, or for his own. "I saw you go by the school in the buggy one morning not long ago. Is that when you went down there?"

"Yes," she said. "It is." He seemed to contemplate her answer, to consider the time elapsed between then and now, as if some unspoken-of change had been at least partially accounted for. "It's all right if you go now, William."

He nodded and left the room, his steps slow, as if he were still heavily in contemplation.

Melinda sat for some time and tried to read more of the paper, but the printed words seemed to hold no discernible meaning. Finally she put the paper down and left the parlor. She saw then what she did not expect, Annie Mae sitting quietly at the dining table in a chair turned away from the table and toward the parlor door. Clearly she'd been waiting for Melinda, maybe biding her time so that she might decide what or how much she wanted to say. Melinda stood still for a moment in the middle of the room and then silently approached the table, took the chair next to Annie Mae, and turned it so that they both sat facing outward, the front windows offering a view that looked out on the empty road where some future they couldn't know would eventually pass, maybe a future that carried their own blood in its passing figures.

In the room's continuing quiet, Melinda heard again the sound of Annie Mae telling Henry his mother wasn't crazy. "A smart woman," she'd said. "I know that better than most." Melinda had no doubt the words were meant for her much more than for Henry, and she knew their meaning. They both did. What was the point of feigning otherwise?

"So do you want me to leave?" Annie Mae said very calmly. "I know it's my daughter you're really after, but I reckon you might want us both gone."

Melinda waited a moment before answering, then had to trust that the right words would come. "Maybe it's more that I'm trying to protect myself and shield my children."

Annie Mae still did not look at her but only toward the windows, as if they were both speaking to a future that lay beyond them, though their words would be lost to it. "She done all the harm she gon' do. And that powder wasn't gon' help nobody one way or another."

"Then why sweep it up?" Melinda asked.

"Maybe for the same reason you put it down and done all the other. It just what us both had to do."

Melinda considered what Annie Mae had said, then tried to decide how best to respond. "While I might want Elizabeth gone, as you say, I don't want you gone. Do you *want* to go?"

Annie Mae finally looked toward her, with either pity or compassion. Melinda wasn't sure which, maybe some mixture of the two as densely compounded as the color of Annie Mae's broad face and deep-set eyes. Perhaps there was anger in those eyes, too. There had to be, didn't there? "I can't go," she said. "Not with my daughter still here. I got to protect my child any way I can."

"And you already have," Melinda said. "Haven't you?"

"I reckon so. Wouldn't you of done the same?"

Melinda wondered what Annie Mae saw in *her* pallid face now. Understanding, maybe even compassion? Was that still possible? "I might have," she said.

"Well, there it is," Annie Mae said. "Not much more to say."

Both remained quiet then. Melinda saw a lone figure pass on the road but could not make out who it was, and lacking recognition, she had no way of judging his, or her, destination, which, at the moment, felt like something she wanted to know, wanted to have some answer to what was before her.

Rafe didn't speak to Melinda about Henry's behavior. He might have been down at the barn when it occurred or in Elizabeth's cabin. If that's where Rafe was, she wasn't sorry. She didn't want to have to face him and what he might have to say. The next morning, though, he was in his office and became all too aware of who came through the door and into his house.

Melinda heard Reverend Lamar before she saw him, or rather she heard his horse neigh as he approached the front porch. The children were already off to school, and crossing the dogtrot toward the living room, she entered and closed the door behind her. Then she stood and waited until she heard his footsteps stop and knew he was about to knock.

When she opened the door, he nodded gravely as though he were in such serious thought he couldn't manage to speak.

"How are you this morning?" she said in as even a voice as possible. She feared she knew why he was here.

"Very well," he said and entered the house. "I hope I'm not intruding, but I need to speak to you about something and would prefer to do it with the man of the house present."

By *prefer* she knew he meant he would do it no other way, but she wouldn't make it easy for him. "My husband was in his office earlier but may have gone down to the barn. I'm not sure. He may have even ridden off to see to some business."

He didn't move or look away from her. It struck her as odd that his skin appeared so thin and fragile and yet was stretched across such a hard face. It was as though his aging body's decay was equaled by a callous growth within.

"We can sit here," she said and motioned to two chairs and a divan near the living room's front windows.

"Yes," he said, "but would you look for your husband first? I'll stand while I wait."

"Very well," she said, echoing his own stiff words, and moved past him toward the door. Once she opened it, she saw Rafe come out of the other side of the house. He seemed well aware they had a visitor, and his demeanor told her that he'd already seen who it was.

He entered and gave her his own quick, hard look but did not speak to her. "Reverend," he said but didn't extend a hand and neither did the preacher. Anyone observing would have thought them foes, and Melinda supposed that in some ways they were, despite having spent a minimum amount of time in each other's presence. "To what do we owe this call?" Rafe asked.

"May we sit first?" Reverend Lamar said.

"Why don't you and my wife sit? I believe I'll stand, if that's acceptable to you."

The preacher merely nodded and took a seat in the Boston rocker Melinda had kept from her father's house. She sat at the end of the divan nearest him, and Rafe stood by one of the windows.

"I've heard some talk that's worrisome to me, if the talk is true. I thought it best to come here and discuss the matter. I'm always concerned when someone in my congregation may have acted in a less than Christian way."

Rafe took a step toward the preacher, looking as if he might come even closer but didn't. "Since there's only one member of your congregation present, you must be speaking of my wife. So tell me your concern. Though I must say that my wife and children have always been *my* concern, and I'm not certain they should be anyone else's."

"A preacher cares for all in his charge, but I understand and respect your point."

Melinda watched as Lamar moved restlessly in his chair but not forward and backward as one normally would in a rocking chair. He kept moving from side to side, shifting his slight weight uncomfortably while having to look up at Rafe at a sharp enough angle to cause himself distress. Melinda could not help but admire her husband's ability to control a situation to his own advantage.

"Speak your concern," Rafe said.

"I have heard from more than one person that Miss Melinda"—he looked her way a moment, focused on her those oddly washed-out blue eyes—"has gone and visited Leathy, a known practitioner of hoodoo, and that she may have left with various artifacts, shall we say, of the woman's craft. And maybe *craft* is the right word too, or very close to it, if I'm not borrowing too much from the language of children's stories and fairy tales."

"So by *craft* you're saying, what, you think Leathy practices witchcraft? Is that it?" Rafe asked. "You think she's some kind of witch?"

"That would be one way of putting it, I suppose. Some might use that word. The Bible does, actually, in Deuteronomy. 'There shall not be found among you any one that maketh his son or daughter to pass through fire, or that useth divination, or an observer of times, or an enchanter, or a witch. For all that do these things are an abomination unto the Lord.'"

"Do you imagine Leathy maybe rides a broom at night?" Rafe said and then moved a step closer to the man. "Maybe boils cats in her wash pot, turns people into toads? Of course this time of year you don't see toads. Maybe in winter she turns them into skunks."

Melinda found she could not look at Reverend Lamar. She felt too much horror at what Rafe was doing. Yet she felt relief, too, as though she were able to step back from the two men into some safe remove that Rafe had provided for her by his mocking.

Reverend Lamar stood but backed away from Rafe. "Hoodoo is not a godly practice. And whether one calls Leathy a witch or not matters little. No one should go to her, especially someone who is a believer."

Rafe remained stationary, but Melinda realized he was keeping himself between Lamar and the door. "A believer in what?"

"Christ, of course. The Bible also says in Leviticus, 'Do not turn to mediums or necromancers; do not seek them out, and so make yourselves unclean by them.'" Lamar stood straighter now. He seemed to have regained some sense of fortitude, as if this errand he'd committed to was worth his effort, maybe done out of some true concern. Even the misguided could be genuine.

"So you think my wife doesn't believe in God, is unclean, that she dabbles in evil conjure ways? Seems to me if you believe in one you might have to believe in the possibility of the other. But maybe now I'm going too deep into theology when we should keep to a more practical discussion. Why don't we just ask Melinda?" He turned to her now, and she was unsure what to make of his expression. It did not hold the hardness it did earlier. Maybe he was about to mock her too, or was he still trying to protect her from what he must see as an assault on her, and by extension, as he would think, on himself? "Melinda, do you practice the dark arts and turn people into toads and skunks?"

She had been observing from what felt like a greater and greater distance as the two men kept up their contest. Now here she was suddenly brought into it and realized she must take her place in it, state firmly what she needed to say just as she had with her children. "No," she said. "I don't believe in hoodoo. I didn't go see Leathy because I believe in what she does." This was as close to the truth as she could come, and she knew it might not be enough to satisfy. It certainly hadn't satisfied her children.

"Then why did you go?" Lamar asked as he looked down at her, unaccountably, it appeared, without the condescension she expected.

She wanted to say she had a right to go wherever she chose, though she knew as a woman that this wasn't really true. Instead, she found she didn't have the time to formulate a reply. Rafe began to speak for her.

"I think she's answered enough of your questions, Reverend. I know why my wife went to see Leathy, and that is all that really matters. She had her own good reason that will remain private between us. You'll have to accept my word that she's done nothing wrong, nothing that need be any deep concern of yours or anyone else's in your congregation."

She saw some level of relief in Reverend Lamar's blue eyes, a wanting to trust what he heard, though there was still worry too. "I suppose I'll have to accept your answer," he said.

"I suppose you will."

Lamar didn't respond to Rafe, which may have been his way of dismissing the retort. He now turned toward Melinda, his face softening. "I *am* sorry," he said, hesitating, "for the recent loss of your child. I understand you had a home burial, and I think I can understand your need to keep your son near. I hope there's some comfort in that for you, and for your husband."

What he said was so unexpected, so unlike what he'd told her at the church door some time ago. She was afraid of what Rafe might say or do at hearing his words. "Thank you," she said quickly, hoping to move them past the subject.

Rafe looked like he might advance on Lamar, back him into the corner of the room. "You understand little, Reverend, and there was no comfort at all to *me* in that home burial."

"I'm sorry for that. Maybe I shouldn't have spoken of it."

"That's a safe assumption," Rafe said. "It's not as if you officiated at the graveside."

"I wasn't asked."

"No, you weren't. And the reason for that is also private between my wife and me."

Reverend Lamar turned toward Melinda then, as if looking to her for help, which she didn't know how to offer. "May I pray with you?" he asked finally.

She felt he might very well be trying to use prayer as an escape from the sudden turn of the conversation in which he found himself, and she assented. A large part of her did want to help him, and agreeing to prayer was a simple enough way.

He kneeled down slowly on weak legs, and as he began she heard Rafe's steps toward the door. He did not close it gently, but neither did he slam it with force, which was perhaps as gentle as he could be considering what had just transpired between the two men.

Once Reverend Lamar took his leave, she went and found Rafe in his desk chair. As she approached him he kept his back toward her, and she stopped almost, but not quite, within reach of him. "Thank you for what you did," she said. "I'm sorry he brought up the burial."

He turned to her just enough for her to see him in thin profile. "If a man comes to shame my wife, or worse, shame me in front of my wife, I'll embarrass him first, if he's a man that can't take the beating he deserves."

"I think you did it for more reason than that."

He looked at her for a moment and turned more fully toward her. "Perhaps. Just so you understand that your own actions caused this, and may have already caused problems beyond my having to deal with an old, decrepit preacher, including the stealing of my horse Benjamin, and the killing of one of my mules, which maybe you didn't know about. A man could die for such a thing, and Samuel might."

She saw a hardness creep back into him and didn't question him about what she'd just heard. She understood he might already know far more than he was saying.

All during church on Sunday morning, Bunyan kept looking toward her mother with worry and then finally anger. Richard was not in the pew beside Bunyan, and his parents, Melinda saw, sat in their usual place two rows ahead. Alfred kept his arm behind their youngest son, and his wife, Olive—who must have been named for her complexion—occasionally turned just enough to catch sight of Melinda and then turned away with a noticeable uptilt of her head, as if her hair were so severely pulled back and pinned that with any movement whatsoever it lifted her head unnaturally. Richard wasn't with them.

Afterward, Melinda spoke at the door to Reverend Lamar, who made no mention of his visit but was civil. She then thought of trying to speak to Olive in the churchyard but decided to catch up to Bunyan, who walked far ahead of the other children, even Kate, with whom she would usually confide. Melinda herself walked in advance of Annie Mae, and whether her quicker steps were more for the sake of catching up to her daughter or avoiding Annie Mae, she wasn't sure, but she was aware of an unbalancing pull and push.

Kate slowed and allowed Melinda to walk with her on the road home. "She's upset about Richard."

"I know," Melinda said.

"Just let her walk on by herself. If he shows up this afternoon to call on her, then she'll have been upset for nothing."

At noon Rafe took his place with them while they ate dinner. The table was always quieter when he sat at its head, but today everyone was quieter than usual, to the point where even Rafe noticed.

"Must have been a powerful sermon," he said. "You all seem to be contemplating your sinful ways."

"Not me," Henry said. "I don't have none."

William laughed. "That's right. You are 'he without sin.' You'll be casting stones any minute now."

"And the first one's going to be at you," Henry answered.

Melinda watched Bunyan. Usually she would be the one to respond to Henry, but she kept her eyes on her plate. Then Rafe caught Melinda's gaze and looked Bunyan's way, then back toward Melinda. Obviously he realized there was a problem with their older daughter. Melinda slowly, almost imperceptibly, shook her head as a warning against his making any comment. Thankfully, he refrained.

Later, when she was alone in their bedroom, Rafe entered. "So tell me," he said, "what is wrong with Bunyan?"

She had to answer, so she told him Richard had not been in church as he normally was and that Bunyan was worried he wouldn't call this afternoon.

"Why wouldn't he?" Rafe asked. "Like most young women she's worrying too much about what a boy may or may not do."

Melinda didn't answer. She didn't agree and couldn't so easily dismiss Bunyan's worry, but she realized too late that not answering Rafe was a mistake.

"Unless there's something you know and you're not telling me. Is there some reason he wouldn't come?"

"No," she said, "no reason I can imagine."

Rafe studied her, and she felt exposed beneath his gaze, as if he were all-powerful and could divine her thoughts the moment she had them or tried to hide them. If Richard didn't come, she knew Rafe would push, would find out about Henry's fight with Richard's younger brother, and would hold her responsible, or he might decide that word of her visit to Leathy and her following actions were in and of themselves enough to mark their family as too troubled to enter into. So all she could do now was wait and pray that Richard would show. Her wish for the boy's arrival, she feared, was more for her own sake than for her daughter's.

By late afternoon he still had not come.

They sit facing each other as grown men for the first time. Seth doesn't feel particularly awkward, but he isn't at ease. They've asked the waitress of the chain restaurant, who wears tan slacks and a green apron, to give them some time before they order.

"I'm glad you didn't mind the short notice," Charles says. "Since I was coming through, and by myself, I figured, Why not? I recognized you right away."

Seth isn't sure about this last part. They've seen each other only once, twenty-six years earlier. And though there were any number of people outside walking past the restaurant, Seth was the only white man standing alone and obviously waiting. He could not have been difficult to spot.

"You doubt me," Charles says. "I don't mean I recognized you from when you were a boy. You look a lot like my uncle Blaylock, when he was younger. That would be my father's, and my aunt Rose's, youngest brother." Charles almost laughs. "So I'm talking about a family resemblance."

Seth isn't sure what to say. "Well, we are family," he finally manages.

"Do you remember ever seeing him, Blaylock?"

Actually, Seth does, but he can't recall any resemblance between Blaylock and his own side of the family. "Yes," he says. "Late one afternoon when I was about thirteen, he had his truck parked in front of your family's store. He and a couple of men were looking at something in the truck bed. Then he saw me and my father come out of my grandfather's store and called us over. Said, 'Come take a look at this.' I didn't know who he was, but my father called him by name, and we went and looked."

"What was it?"

"A coyote. It was lying dead on top of some hay. He'd shot it while he'd been out deer hunting. Nobody had ever seen one in that part of the country, not then. They'd just started moving in. So it was a real oddity. They're all over the place now, of course. Anyway, that's why I remember him."

"And I can remember him telling me about the coyote. He even showed me a picture of it. Strange that we saw the same thing, only in different ways. I just wondered why he'd wanted to kill it. I've never been much into hunting, don't care to kill anything."

"Not even when you visited Riverfield?" Seth asks, remembering how he'd hunted as a boy, how everyone there did.

"No, and I mostly went during the summers, not during hunting season."

"So why didn't I ever see you again?" It's a question Seth didn't know he was going to ask. It only just now occurred to him, and he wonders what this says about him, about the importance to him of the family history embodied in the man who sits across the table from him.

Charles laughs this time, and it is a genuine laugh. "Probably because I got a lot more interested in chasing girls than visiting family. I just didn't go there as much. Plus, we didn't exactly travel in the same circles." He isn't laughing now, but his point is made gently enough.

"No, we didn't. Things were pretty segregated then. Still are. You know I went to the private academy in Valhia. All the white kids in Riverfield did then."

"Not that that made it right, but I can understand, I guess."

"If I'd gone to the public school, I would have been the only white person there," Seth says and realizes how he must sound.

"You don't have to justify it to me. When I said I could understand, I meant you were just a kid, doing what the other kids did."

Seth nods, as if to acknowledge Charles's generosity and lack of judgment. "So when did you first get interested in family history?" he asks, partly because he's curious, but maybe it's a way to change the subject, though ultimately, he knows, everything between them leads back to race. Or is there a way to get past that? Can blood mean more than skin? he wonders.

"I was always interested, always listened to the family stories my father and grandmother told, and my aunts and uncles."

"Then we have that in common," Seth says.

Charles leans towards him, looking over the short, unlit candle that sits in a dark globe. "I first knew I had a white great-grandfather when I was twelve. My father told me about him, including that he fought in the Civil War, and he sure wasn't trying to free the slaves. Made me think a lot about who I am, how I've got two sides in me, more really, when you take the Choctaw into account. Some people don't worry about such things. But it affected me in ways I probably didn't fully understand. Somehow I realized, though, that history and identity are complicated things. Then I learned how violent Rafe Anderson was. And remember, this is my father telling me about his *grandfather*, and not his great-great, nothing so removed as that. He was telling me about a man who once beat a cousin of his so bad he thought he'd killed him. Then hid down in a well and ran away that night. In some ways it was hard to know I had his blood in me."

"You know that story too, about the well," Seth says, surprised but realizing he shouldn't be. He understands that the stories he knows must have long existed in the collective memory of this other parallel lineage.

Charles looks away and then directly at him again. "All my life, since I was twelve, I've been able to imagine him down in that well, can feel the dampness, hear his brothers and sisters calling out to him, trying to find him. I can feel his heart pounding in his chest when he snuck back inside the house to get his few things before running off into the dark."

Seth has imagined, many times, every moment Charles has just described, imagined them since the age of ten, imagined this man who loomed so large in life and large enough to exist as myth in Seth's mind, so much so that imagination almost *becomes* memory. And he and Charles share this, the blood and the memory. And now, for a moment, Seth is past it, past skin.

The waitress finally comes, having waited far too long, really, to return and take their order. Charles is ready and orders from the menu. Seth simply names the first thing that comes to mind, a hamburger, cooked medium-well. The waitress turns, businesslike, with her notepad, tucks it into her apron, and is gone.

"So when did you first know of Betsy?" Charles asks.

The question is one they've talked about before, over the phone, and Seth wonders if Charles's real intent is to remind him that he came late to knowledge of this woman because his side of the family held her secret and wouldn't acknowledge her or her children. Maybe his question carries a judgment Charles can't completely let go of.

"What I remember my father telling me is that Betsy was Rafe's housekeeper, after his wife died. But I learned from you that wasn't exactly right."

"No," Charles says. "Betsy's mother was his housekeeper, and Melinda was still living. Guess your father felt the need to couch things as much as he could. Didn't want you to think your great-great grandfather cheated on his wife. So when did he tell you?"

"I was in college, maybe a sophomore. I'd already decided to major in history and had begun to learn that it could be open to interpretation. So I was home for a weekend, and my father and I had just driven by the old dogtrot house and started talking about family history. When he told me about Betsy and the children, I should have realized it wasn't the whole truth, or at least had an inkling. The truth is always there if you look deep enough and are willing to see."

"And now you write history."

"I do," Seth says. "And I've never wanted to change or deny any history I've learned."

"Maybe it's hard for you to think, though, that Rafe truly loved Betsy."

These words surprise Seth, and he realizes the idea has never occurred to him. Rafe Anderson has always struck him as a man who had mistresses because he wanted them, because he wanted to possess them almost as a *thing* is possessed, and the children who came mattered little to him, or not at all.

"You doubt me again," Charles says.

"No, I suppose that could be true."

"It is. She was the love of his life, though I know to say it that way is cliché, maybe makes the relationship sound commonplace. It wasn't. Of course, mixed-race relationships were more common back then than people want to think. They did have children together. The fact that there was more than one says a lot."

"He had other mistresses," Seth says and understands he's just spoken the counterpoint in an argument he doesn't want to have.

"Only the one we know of for sure. Virginia Henry."

"He had children with her too, though." The words are out, and he realizes he's continued the argument. He hopes not too stridently.

"But he ended the relationship with her when he took up with Betsy. And it was only Betsy's children he allowed to take his name. I think that says a lot, too." Charles looks at him, appearing deep in thought, as if there's something in this history Seth can't imagine and that Charles isn't ready to tell. "Plus," he says, "my father knew what he was talking about. He made sure I understood they had a true love for each other. Forgive the way I might sound here, but it's our side of the family that kept this history and passed it down." He holds both hands before him, opens them in a gesture that asks for understanding and intends good will, and one that asks for good will in return.

Seth smiles, nodding. "I'm grateful for all you've told me. I mean that." And he does. It occurs to him, though, that while Charles wants him to acknowledge Betsy's place in their shared history, Charles may not have ever spent a moment considering Rafe's wife, Melinda. But why should he? There's no blood kinship there, just as there is no blood kinship between Betsy and Seth. So maybe they are equal in their absences of thought. Seth realizes, too, that of all the figures in his family's history, it is Melinda he knows least about, and maybe because of this she has never loomed in his imagination the way Rafe has. But he's wondered how she dealt with her life, how she survived her husband's treatment.

"So do you think he didn't love his wife?" Seth asks. "Do you know anything about her?" He hopes the tone of his question doesn't reveal that he is purposely continuing the argument he finds he can't let go of.

Charles looks again as if there's something he doesn't want to tell. He pushes at the glass salt shaker, then slides it back into place as though it's a chess piece. "I know she was jealous of Betsy. She had to be."

"Safe to assume. But is there something you can tell me?" Seth realizes the irony here, that he's asking a man of no blood kin to his great-great grandmother, and who's a different color of skin, to tell him something about this woman that Seth should already know himself, from his own side of the family. He should be the one passing along information, if Charles had any interest.

"She had children who died."

"I know that," Seth says. "They're listed in the old family Bible, in her hand."

"But there are others who wouldn't have been listed. Were never even given names."

"No, they're there. I've seen them. The entries just say 'Male child,' and then the date of their birth and death, which is the same day, or at least no more than two."

Charles looks surprised at this. "I was told they lived several days."

"It doesn't look that way. I'm surprised you know about them."

"She didn't want more children," Charles says.

"How would you know that?"

"Think about it. Once Rafe started having babies with the woman who lived right within sight of her own house, and she had to *see* those children, she put an end to having babies with her husband."

Seth pushes at the silverware before him and fingers the salt shaker, but he doesn't pick it up or even move it. He lets it go and folds his hands together, palm against palm, as if he's trying to contain himself. "What do you mean? She did have babies with him. They just didn't live."

Charles looks beyond him, and Seth wonders if the waitress is approaching at his back. But he senses then that Charles isn't looking at anyone or anything, but is only searching his own mind, or is perhaps weighing his response. "She untied their umbilical cords. They bled to death. I'm sorry, but I have to tell you the truth. It's nothing I ever wanted to talk about over the phone."

Seth doesn't know what to say, or to think, but he finds he can't help but question Charles. "How do you know this?"

"Betsy's mother, Annie Mae, found both of them in their cribs. It happened a few days after each of them was born. Annie Mae helped cover it up. She wanted to protect your great-great grandmother."

Seth feels as if he's already eaten his hamburger and is too full from it, his stomach unsettled. He believes what he's heard. He can't imagine Charles would make up such a story. But why would Charles tell this now? Seth wonders if he's been waiting to tell him, maybe for years. Seth can only speculate as to why. "So what did Annie Mae do?" he asks.

"She cleaned them up, and she and Melinda called it crib death. Now they call it SIDS. No one on your side of the family ever knew."

He looks at Charles carefully but sees no pleasure in his face at the telling of this history. Seth knows that history's truth can't be denied, as Charles said. Maybe Charles had already planned, either consciously or unconsciously, to tell it tonight. Maybe resentments Charles weren't fully aware of were at work within him.

Seth realizes then he has knowledge of their shared family history that Charles has never brought up and very well may not know, and it holds violence and death within it too. How many died he doesn't know, but there was certainly carnage. A part of him wants to tell this history now, wants Charles to know what *his* own blood relation did against men of his same color skin.

But he remains quiet, reluctant to use history as a weapon against his cousin. He merely contemplates what he's learned from Charles, and he can't help but think about what his great-great grandmother did, can't help but see in his mind the bodies of two infants lying covered in their own blood. Yet he can't hold the image. It is too much. What replaces it, though, is another body, that of a coyote lying lifeless on top of hay in the bed of a truck, dead for no reason other than its oddity.

The waitress comes now and sets their food before them, and they begin to eat in silence. Later they will argue over who should pay.

FOURTEEN

The day had been warmer than usual, but now that it was almost midnight, Annie Mae felt the full coldness of the outside air as she walked. It had slowly crept back into her body after the warmth of the cabin on the Lassiter Place. She'd delivered a woman's third child, and the baby girl had come easily, the mother doing fine, not too much bleeding. She quickened her pace now along the road and judged she had another half mile before she'd reach her bed.

Samuel had been on the Lassiter Place again, she'd found out, but he wasn't there still. Brantley had covered the place looking for him over a week ago, and after Samuel had stayed hidden from him, he'd left out, or so she'd been told. Betsy had seemed worried for him. Couldn't she see that all of what Samuel was spreading would hurt her too, and that Samuel didn't care?

A notion came to her now, though. It being a Saturday night, Samuel just might be fool enough to come around the throng of people who'd be gathered in and around the stores and buildings in Riverfield, drinking, fighting, gambling on the porches, carrying on in all sorts of ways white folks wouldn't put up with any other time. It was as if white people had decreed that Saturday night was something separate and apart, and if a man got cut or killed, well that was just the price Black folks would have to pay for carrying on so with each other. No law would enter into it, and maybe that was fine with everybody concerned. Annie Mae always stayed far from it, and so did Betsy as far as she knew.

She heard the crowd before she could see it, a low rumble of voices mixed together into one sound that had a slow-rising force all its own. Then she saw the thing moving at its outer edges, as though it were a creature breathing in and out. Who would think such a small gathering of buildings could come so alive beneath a quarter, or even full, moon?

She skirted the crowd and looked in at the faces illuminated by coal-oil light from windows and a few small fires burning along the edges of the road. A handful of men shot craps on the porch of Rafe's store, but she knew Samuel would keep his distance from there at the very least. A few turned, recognized her, and showed surprise at her being anywhere near such a scene. She circled the crowd twice and then gave up, deciding Samuel was smarter than she thought.

But she should have known better. After she passed the Teclaw house with its odd columns made of tree trunks with the stubs of limbs left at the tops, Samuel appeared out of the shadows.

"Was you looking for me?" He came close enough for her to smell the alcohol on him, but he did not sound drunk.

"Where you been?"

He turned away from her, though there was no need for him to be evasive when it was already too dark for her to see his features and read his face. "Around," he said. "Decided I'm free like any other man. I don't got to work for Mr. Rafe."

"You have to kill his mule and take his horse, like a fool?" Samuel didn't answer, and she kept on. "I know you done took up something else, too, spreading ugly words about people and dead babies, and I know who gon' come after you for it, and for everything else you done."

"Sound like you want him to."

"Whatever happen, you brung it on yourself, in all kind of ways." She shifted her weight, crossed her arms beneath her breasts. "But I don't want no harm to come to you. Or my daughter. I'm asking you to stop talking about her being hoodooed by Miss Melinda. It point a finger at her, like she done something wrong she need punishing for."

"You don't got to worry no more about what *I* say. I done said all I want."

She heard the suggestion that something, or someone else, was afoot. "What it is you ain't telling me? Or what it is you wanting to tell me so bad you followed me from out the crowd?"

Samuel was silent a moment, and she was afraid he might disappear into the dark merely to frustrate her. "They somebody besides me be talking."

"Who?" she said when it became clear he wanted her to push.

"I knowed who she was right off when I seen her out in the crowd, or thought I did. So I ask, and somebody say, 'Yeah, that her.' I ain't seen her since I was young, when she live here."

"Who?" she said again.

"That Henry woman in Demarville Mr. Rafe got them children with."

Now Annie Mae remained silent while she tried to decide what the woman might be saying. She even wondered if maybe she'd laid eyes on her a little while ago. She wouldn't know Virginia Henry and had never seen her before, as far as she knew. Annie Mae only knew of her. "She still amongst them?"

"No. She done left out. I seen her go."

"So what she be saying?"

"You ain't gon' like it, but I figure I need to tell you. That why I come to you. She putting out word it Betsy killed them children, saying it like she know for sure."

"People knows Mr. Rafe throwed her over for Betsy. They shouldn't be believing her."

"Maybe some don't."

"But enough do for it to get around," Annie Mae said, thinking aloud. "She know what she doing."

"I reckon," Samuel said. "Thought I ought to tell you."

She felt she heard something that might pass for concern in his voice and wanted to answer it. "You best be careful, Samuel, and not stay around here, 'specially with a horse ain't yours."

"I'll lay low awhile, then figure what I'm gon' do."

He slowly turned then and disappeared into the dark the way she imagined he might have earlier when he left the gathering and followed her.

Annie Mae heard the sound of the crowd again. In the morning there would be a little trash in the road, a few small remnants of fires, the only visible evidence a crowd had ever gathered, but there would be stories told about fights, who lost his week's pay gambling, what woman went off with what man. And now there would be another story, about her daughter.

When she entered the house, she saw a light burning in the kitchen and wondered who she would find. At least there would probably be a fire going in the stove so the kitchen and her small room would be warm. She suspected it might be Rafe, wanting to glean from her Samuel's whereabouts. She found Bunyan instead, eating a small piece of pie, perhaps trying to pretend she wasn't waiting for her.

Bunyan rose from the chair nearest the stove. "You sit here," she said. "I know you must be cold—since you've been out so long."

She knew Bunyan was really asking where she'd been and answered with her own question. "Did your young gentleman call this evening?"

"No," Bunyan said. She looked away shyly.

Annie Mae knew the boy had come much later than expected last Sunday and knew it had caused some consternation. She'd heard Bunyan tell Kate after he left that the boy's mother had made him do extra chores until his father came along and put a stop to it, took over for the boy so he'd be free to call. Annie Mae could read what that meant well enough, and from the way she'd talked, so had Bunyan.

"He'll come tomorrow, though," she said now. "He walked me home from school yesterday and wants to walk with me next Friday evening." The girl put aside what was left of her pie. She looked around the kitchen, pursed her lips the way her mother sometimes did, and finally turned her dark-eyed gaze back on Annie Mae. "Can you tell me why Mama went to see that woman in Dawes Quarter? She won't say."

"Then maybe it ain't my place to, even if I did know why."

Bunyan leaned toward her, holding her gaze. "But you *do* know. You always know."

As unsettled as she suddenly felt, Annie Mae couldn't help but realize she also felt a kind of relief for Bunyan. She saw the girl's strength in a way she hadn't before, pointed directly at her. Bunyan wasn't merely scolding a younger sibling; she was demanding something from an adult, an adult she looked up to, despite Annie Mae's skin color. Maybe the girl was becoming who she'd need to be so she could do more than just survive in this world. But how to answer her now? She could not say, *Because she thinks my daughter killed her child.*

"Does it have to do with Betsy?"

"Don't see how," Annie Mae said. "You know your mama don't believe in all that. I even heard her tell you she didn't."

"She went for a reason, though. And there must be some part of her that wants to see Betsy cursed by something evil."

Bunyan looked away then, as if she couldn't face Annie Mae after saying such a thing. Annie Mae guessed from Bunyan's tone, the way the word *cursed* came out ugly, that the girl wasn't really repeating her mother's attitude but was stating her own. So odd to hear this almost grown child, who she'd often held, speak in a hard way about Annie Mae's own daughter, her mysterious child whom she could still love but not fathom.

Now Bunyan looked at her again with her eyes almost closed, her face drawn, not in anger it seemed but with a deep puzzlement, maybe even sadness. "How do things get to such a place?" she asked. "What exactly happened in this house?"

The question frightened Annie Mae for a moment, but she realized

Bunyan didn't mean any one thing, not any particular act, but everything, all the complications a family can make for itself. She knew they could both point to the same person, and the word *buckra* came to mind again, but blaming one person wouldn't absolve the rest of them.

"I feel scared somehow," Bunyan said. "But I'm not sure of what? Tell me. You must know."

The fire in the stove needed stoking, and the room was growing colder. Annie Mae had no words of comfort or warmth to offer, or perhaps, at that moment, she didn't want to offer any, not after the way Bunyan had spoken earlier. "It's late. We should go to bed." This was all she could manage, at first, for this child she'd helped tend. Then she added, either for honesty's sake or for spite, "Your mother. That's who you're scared for. And maybe you should be."

Bunyan stared at her, looked as if she were about to speak but couldn't, so she held her tongue out of shock. Annie Mae wondered then if Bunyan had heard the words as a threat, and if maybe she'd meant them as one, against a woman who wanted to harm her light-skinned, darkling child who Melinda refused to call by anything other than her formal name, if even that.

Early in the afternoon Annie Mae sat by the hearth in Betsy's cabin holding Lakeview, the child reaching toward her with tiny fingers needing to touch whatever she saw with her searching brown eyes: buttons, dress cloth, Annie Mae's warm face. She was waiting for George to come back in with a few small sticks of wood for the fire. The boy always wanted to feel he was helping. Betsy had asked her to watch the children while she went to the store where she had her own account, which she never had to pay, as far as Annie Mae could figure. Rafe had told her to always go on Sunday afternoon when the store was closed, that Alfred would be there to accommodate her. Why Rafe wanted it this way, Annie Mae wasn't sure. Maybe it was a way for him to show his power over Betsy.

Lakeview was now asleep against her shoulder, the girl's head at an angle buried into Annie Mae's neck. She could feel the child's breath on her, smell the sweet clean scent of her head with its reddish tint of hair. She kissed the child's cheek and held her lips against the soft, light skin, which would turn even lighter beneath the touch of a finger, the imprint of a loving hand. Annie Mae thought then of an old story, one her mother had passed down to her, of the very first child ever born to a Choctaw woman and a white man. He'd come into their country to live, the legend went, and took a young Choctaw wife, and when the child came—her mother had never said if it was a boy or a girl—a council was called to decide if there should be any more marriages between whites and their own kind. They figured that if too many whites came and married into the tribe, their people would be bred out of the world, would no longer be recognizable, their birth out of Nanih Waiya lost to time. The white man was made to leave the country, and it was decided the child had to be killed. So a group of men were chosen to carry out the deed but were slow about it, and the mother hid the child. The men finally came for the infant and, not finding it, said the Great Spirit had taken it away. After several weeks, the mother brought the child back and said the Great Spirit had left it beside her while she slept. The council had already decided that if the child ever returned, it could live; it would be forever under the protection of the Great Spirit and would one day be chief. From that point on, whites and Choctaw were allowed to marry.

But this child Annie Mae held, and shifted now to her other shoulder, hadn't been born in wedlock but out of it, and not only white and Choctaw blood ran through her veins, and George's, but Negro blood too. So how protected could these children be under such origins? Unlike their ancestor from the legend, neither would be able to make much for themselves in this world. And might Melinda mean the two children harm and do what she could against them? Or that Henry woman, what would she do? Maybe Rafe could protect the children in their early years since they carried his name, and with such light skin and the right features, maybe they could pass if they moved away. So a better life might be out there for them. Annie Mae hoped for that, but some fear for them took hold of her, maybe a kind of fear not so different from what Bunyan had talked about. Though she knew it made no sense, she couldn't shake the notion that somehow these two children lived because two of Melinda's children had died. Children always died. You just prayed it wouldn't be yours. But if Melinda's had died at Betsy's hand, were Betsy's children not doomed to a burdensome fate, was Leathy's curse not visited upon them in some way only time would show? The thought made Annie Mae afraid, even as she felt Lakeview's warm breath against her neck and heard George enter with more wood for the fire.

"Be careful," she told him as he crossed in front of her, his little man's body carrying the weight of the two logs Samuel had cut and split.

"Yes, ma'am," he said in his small voice and placed the logs carefully on the fire, then sat down at Annie Mae's feet.

"Don't soak up all the heat. Leave a little for us."

George laughed, knew it was her joke with him. "When Mama be back?" he asked, and she was glad to hear him talk the way he did, realized she was around him enough to have some sway over the boy.

"Soon," she said and felt the anticipation of Betsy's return, knowing she could put off no longer what her daughter needed to know.

When she finally heard Betsy at the door, George ran to it and let her in, closing the door behind her. She held over her shoulder the cloth feed sack she used to carry groceries from the store, and then set it down on the table where they usually sat and ate.

"Thank you for watching them," she said. "I must have kept you from your work."

"That's all right," Annie Mae said. "You know once Sunday dinner be done, I got the rest of the day. Can go do what I want." She remained where she sat with Lakeview in her arms. When she again turned in her daughter's direction, she could see that Betsy must be wondering why she hadn't stood, handed over the girl, and been on her way.

Betsy walked toward her, pulled a straight-back chair near the fire, and sat down without asking for Lakeview. But George slid himself across the floor and settled against his mother's legs. She reached down and rubbed his head, patted his shoulder.

"You seen Samuel?" Annie Mae asked. Betsy didn't answer but kept looking into the fire. "Well, I seen him last night. He told me something." Betsy looked toward her but didn't ask what Samuel had said and revealed no apparent curiosity. "Told me that Henry woman was here last night, out and about among people, saying things about you that ain't no good."

Betsy only nodded. "She's been over here already, before just last night. I've seen her, and know already what she's been saying."

"When you seen her?"

"Maybe a week ago, in front of the post office. I had the children with me. Somebody said, 'There that Virginia Henry,' and looked my way. Then that woman who lives with Mr. Brantley up at the Lassiter Place, she comes up and whispers to me what you were about to, said Virginia been telling people…"

Annie Mae saw her daughter couldn't repeat the words, and her silence seemed like one more confirmation of the truth that neither of them would speak. "The woman what live with Brantley, Leona, she always talking too much and playing both sides."

"I believe what she told me."

"So what did you do?" Annie Mae asked.

"Nothing. There was no need of my approaching Virginia Henry."

Once again Annie Mae heard the proper way Betsy could speak and felt the way it removed her daughter from her. "You tell Rafe what she going around saying?" She wanted a reply, but just as Annie Mae asked the question, she already knew the answer and watched Betsy shake her head. Her daughter could no less say those words to Rafe than she could a few moments ago to her own mother. Betsy was probably counting on Rafe finding out some other way what Virginia had been going around saying. Or maybe Betsy now hoped her mother might set a course for herself, one that took her across the Black Fork. Betsy had a way of letting others do for her, and yet at the same time it somehow always seemed as if Betsy had set things in motion by some word or act of her own.

Annie Mae had to wait until the middle of the week before she felt that she could take the time, and she asked Melinda for the use of the mule, Ida. Melinda had at first been hesitant, maybe because she'd reached a point where she didn't want to help Annie Mae with anything, or it could have been Melinda was afraid she might overstep her bounds with Rafe, making a decision about an animal's use that wasn't hers to make. Finally, perhaps out of a need for defiance of her husband, Melinda had said yes, she could take Ida.

Annie Mae didn't go to town often but knew the landmarks along the road and was able to judge her time. When she reached town, she knew what part to head for but then had to ask to find the house, the same as Melinda had done, she imagined, when she took the buggy and went looking in Dawes Quarter for Leathy.

She'd judged her time well and saw the woman who must be Virginia Henry opening her door—home from whatever white family she worked for. Her two children waited to scurry inside ahead of their mother, they, too, home from wherever it was they had to spend their days.

Annie Mae slowed Ida, then stopped her in the road directly in front of the house. She'd give them time to at least feel like they were home and, since the days were longer and it was still good light, she hoped none of them would look out a window and see her. A white man on horseback rode past, nodding to her in a way he probably thought was polite.

After a few more moments Annie Mae gently dug her heels into Ida's sides, walked her up to the porch, then dismounted and tied the mule to the same iron stob she figured Rafe used.

When she knocked it was the woman who answered. Still, she wanted to be sure. "You Virginia Henry?"

She looked at Annie Mae carefully, as if she were trying to recall from her memory who this woman at her door might be. Then she finally nodded and seemed to look at Annie Mae even harder, maybe divining something from Annie Mae's copper skin as to who she was. Annie Mae knew she and her daughter's origins were sometimes remarked upon, pieces of their story told for others to pass the time with. But no, probably Virginia Henry was only studying this stranger's face, trying to decide how much caution might be needed.

"You don't know of me, but you know of my daughter, Betsy." Annie Mae waited to see how Virginia would react.

But there was no reaction, none that was visible, at least. Finally Virginia opened her door wider. Whether it was so Virginia could step outside onto the porch or so Annie Mae could enter the house wasn't clear at first. Virginia didn't move one way or another. Then she took just enough of a backward step and Annie Mae knew this was all the invitation she would get and edged herself inside.

"Guess I ain't all the way surprised," Virginia said once she closed the door. "And you wrong. I do know of you. The man talks to me about things, and you know who I mean."

There was no reason to put off what she'd come here for, and Annie Mae now saw the way to get to it. "Look like you been doing some talking yourself, but I don't reckon you said it to him."

Virginia moved toward the fireplace, turning her back to the flames that were catching up good from the kindling. "Then you wrong about that too. I tell Rafe what I think. That why he still come here, and for them children." She nodded toward the kitchen where the little boy and girl sat at the table by the stove. Annie Mae couldn't help but look toward them, saw them as slightly older, darker versions of George and Lakeview, and not wanting to consider them beyond that, made herself turn away. They couldn't matter to her, nor this woman.

"I bet I ain't wrong about this then—he don't know you spreading your words about my daughter around the countryside for everybody to hear."

Again, there was no response, which told Annie Mae all she needed.

"You best put a stop to it or I tell him." She moved closer into the middle of the room. "And who gon' believe you anyway? People know you want to put the bad mouth on Betsy 'cause he left you for her."

"I don't know why you even come here. You trying to stop something that done already happen. And people can believe what they want. I just put the truth out there." Virginia was quiet a moment, as if she'd heard some small sound and wanted to figure out what it was, but she kept her eyes on Annie Mae, kept searching her face, and Annie Mae wanted to turn away, afraid somehow of what she might see. "You ain't thought about why you come here, have you?" Virginia said. "Not really. You just come 'cause it your daughter, and coming here the only thing you can do 'cause you know what the truth be too. You know what your daughter done, same as me." Virginia was nodding her head, confirming her own words, and Annie Mae felt the same coldness run through her that she'd felt when she'd been holding Lakeview.

"Maybe I tell Mr. Rafe, anyway," Annie Mae said, "since you think the truth all that. You must of known he gon' hear about what you been saying one way or another, know he gon' be mad about it." Now Annie Mae took her own pause. "Maybe he already mad at you. Maybe *that* why you been talking like you have, putting bad words on my daughter. You figure, why not? What you got to lose? And tell me this, where them two children be when you out roaming round the country on a Saturday night? Don't you think you ought to be home with them like a mother being about her own business?"

"My children be my business." Virginia looked toward the two of them still in the kitchen. "Where they stay when I not with them no worry of yours."

"And my daughter ain't your worry. You remember that."

Virginia only stared straight at her, without acknowledging the warning, or the threat in it.

Anne Mae said nothing further, and they both stood there in a hard silence that seemed to stretch time, and which was broken finally by the small, furtive sound of the children's whispering, which she could not make out, but whatever their words, they were enough to remind Annie Mae that the boy and girl were there. She again didn't let herself look toward them, and it was as if their tiny voices came from a long way off and didn't belong only to them but to other children who'd never learned to speak for themselves but wanted to say, somehow, that they had existed.

FIFTEEN

Samuel could have been long gone, and maybe he had already ridden Benjamin half to death, but if he was still anywhere in the countryside, Rafe knew he would eventually find him. Word of his whereabouts would come from some source. He suspected either Betsy or Annie Mae, or both, knew more than they were telling. He had not yet decided if he would kill Samuel, though he knew that upon confronting him he might not have a choice, depending upon Samuel's actions. It had been the actions of Samuel's father that had brought about his death, and so many others, all those years ago.

March's wife, Rebecca, had come to Rafe as highly wrought as any woman he'd ever seen, white or black. When he first heard her cries out in front of the house, he did not even recognize her voice, despite the truth that he had known her as a woman and had confessed as much to March when March had first taken up with her. He had not wanted anything hidden between them, not after all their traveling together from North Carolina to Alabama, and after all their years of knowing each other.

When he made his way out into the yard and saw who it was, saw the profound grief on Rebecca's face, he knew without any word needed that March was dead, and all he did need at that point was the *how* of it, or the *who*. And so he asked, knew she needed some word from him so that she could break out of her grief for one moment and speak and make sense. "Must have been that Shack," she said. "Real name Shadrack. And if wasn't him, he put somebody up to it."

Rafe led her slowly to the front porch so they could sit at its edge in the not-quite-dark. He didn't know Shack well, but he knew the name and the face, knew Shack had been one of the first to join with the Freedmen's Bureau and began to politic so former field slaves could take office and lord themselves over white men.

Rebecca bent over double after she sat down, then moaned, a sound Rafe had only heard before from dying men, and when Melinda came out onto the porch, Rafe saw her, shook his head *no*, and gently motioned her back inside. He removed his arm from around Rebecca's back and stood before her, both his hands on her shoulders. He smelled some scent on her he did not recognize, something sweet. "Tell me what you need to tell me," he said. "Tell me why if you can."

She looked up at him as if she'd just remembered there was something else she had to say. "March was on his way here, to tell you what they gon' do. He'd done got news of it, and Shack must of known he had, knew who he'd tell. I heard the gunshot not half a mile from the house. Found his body." And so she explained the rest then, all the words that should have been in March's voice about Negroes taking up arms and marching on Riverfield from down on the Black Fork. There had been news, or rumors, of such events the last few years, one over in Mississippi, another up at Cross Plains, enough to keep white men worried, on edge.

"Is March's body still in the road?" he asked when she finished.

"Must be. Like I said, I come straight on here. Didn't want him to die for nothing. Figured I'd do what he was gon' do."

He sat down beside her again, placing a hand upon her. "You think anybody followed you here?"

"If they had, I reckon I'd already be dead too."

Rafe nodded. "With what's about to happen, it'll be too dangerous for you to stay here. You know that, don't you? They'll figure out who came to me."

She let out a long breath, as if she were releasing all of herself, all she had ever been. "Why stay if March gone?"

"There somewhere you can go, where you got family?"

"Aunt in Selma," she managed to say. "She take me in."

"Then that's where you'll have to go. You'll stay here tonight. In this house," he said.

She turned toward him with surprise. "In the house?" she said and lost her voice again to a wordless sound that held both grief and gratitude that Rafe could not help but recognize and feel humbled by—knowing that whatever he did for her would never be payment enough.

"Melinda will see to you tonight, give you clothes to take, put you on the train in the morning. And you'll have money enough till you can get settled. I'll promise you one thing. If it's all right with you, I'll see to it that March is buried in the white cemetery, near where my children are buried, near where I'll be buried one day. Is that all right?"

"Will he have a stone?"

"He will."

She nodded. "All right then."

"We best go inside now. I have a long night ahead of me," he said and felt an old feeling begin to rise within him, one so familiar and that he recognized so completely it was as if some part of himself had awakened from years earlier and from out of lines of men sleeping under thin blankets, wondering if they'd just had their last night's rest on this earth before their eternal sleep was delivered by mounted intruders clad in blue. But there would be no rest at all this night. He had too much ground to cover. He could feel his blood continue to rise, though, knew it would carry him beyond a need for sleep and right into the smoke of deadly fire. He could smell it now as if it had never left his nostrils, and he found he wanted to breathe it deeply.

"Melinda," he called, and she appeared out of the dogtrot. He hadn't realized she was still so close.

"I heard," she said. "I'll do all you need me to." She led Rebecca into the living room and, Rafe assumed, toward the kitchen. They were without a housekeeper for the moment, and Melinda would probably put Rebecca in the room off the kitchen.

He entered the other side of the house, went into his office, and chose his favored cap 'n' ball revolvers, the two Colt Navy guns that had the smoothest, easiest action. He made sure they were fully loaded and took one extra loaded cylinder, then reached down a Sharps carbine and checked its load and picked up extra cartridges. He would return for more firepower before first light. All he needed now was enough for protection while he rode in the night, and if Shack and the others under him thought March's warning lay dead in the road, Rafe most likely would not need what he carried.

He stepped back out into the dogtrot, opened the door opposite him, and called out, "I'll be back before morning. Have some breakfast ready." He then went to the barn, saddled a young, spirited Wheeler, and though it would be the longest ride he would have to make, he didn't want to send anyone for Brantley. He wanted Brantley with him. Then they would go for Alfred and spread the word from there.

Wheeler could not be pushed hard all night, but after they were on the road it was difficult for Rafe not to give him his head once Wheeler felt his familiar rider's urgency. When they started the climb to the crest of the ridge, Rafe began to recall when he and March had first come to Riverfield on this road, arriving in the late afternoon. They'd gone directly past Mr. Lassiter's place and hadn't known it. Once they got to the inn, Rafe arranged for March to sleep in the stable just behind it. At dark he took him an extra blanket.

"Will you be warm enough?" he'd asked.

"We both slept outdoors when it was colder than this," March had said.

"True enough, I reckon." He waited a moment before speaking again. "I'm sorry I'll have to hire you out. I know I've done it before, but Mr. Lassiter won't be hard on you."

March, who was taller and had a larger build than Rafe, settled deeper into the hay and spread the just-large-enough extra blanket over himself. He looked up at Rafe. "If the place big enough, it not the owner you got to worry about. It the riding boss." Rafe sensed what was coming, and he dreaded it. March had not brought it up in months. "'Course, sometime it is the owner. Was just two bad ones you put me under in all our traveling. One didn't neither of us could have knowed about, but the other I warned you."

"I know. I'm still sorry for that. Mr. Lassiter's a good man, and if his riding boss isn't, tell me."

So Rafe had hired him out for some time, and March had had no complaint against Brantley. Then, before Rafe left for the war and Virginia battlefields, he'd hired March to Mr. Lassiter again. By the time Rafe returned, March had stayed on the place and was working shares, but once Rafe began to establish himself with what he received from Mr. Lassiter, he helped March get his own small farm. He had been criticized for it, but he'd never found it difficult to ignore the words of lesser men who weren't worth beating, or killing.

As he topped the ridge now on Wheeler, he was not ashamed of the few times March had scolded him, only thankful no white men had ever heard or seen it happen. But March would never have done that, not so much out of concern for himself but in consideration of Rafe and of Rafe's youth, and the position it would have placed Rafe in and not known how to get himself out of without destroying the unaccountable friendship they'd made. Rafe understood now what March had always understood; he'd needed March in ways that went far beyond what seemed at the time the necessary commerce of hiring out a man that a piece of paper said he owned. And now March had given up his very own life, and Rafe felt a debt he could never satisfy.

When he reached Brantley's, he first asked if Brantley was alone in his house, and when Brantley assured him he was, Rafe explained what was happening. Brantley took it in quickly, said, "We knew this could come, before the war or after. Now here it is." He stepped into a room and came out armed with two pistols and a ten-gauge shotgun. "No rifle?" Rafe asked, and Brantley replied, "Just a smoothbore musket." Rafe realized then that some of the men might not be armed as well as they should be. Brantley also wore a pouch over his shoulder that Rafe knew held more ammunition, including loaded cylinders for the pistols.

The moon was still rising when they made Alfred's. They called out from horseback, and when Alfred came to the door he held a lamp in his hand; his wife stood behind him, her face illuminated by the lamplight but darkening with concern as she listened. "Give me three minutes," he said and closed the door. Soon enough he emerged dressed and armed and headed to his barn. He saddled and mounted quickly, and they moved at a trot to the road in front of Alfred's house and farm. "I know we didn't serve together in the war," Alfred said, "but it looks like we're about to now."

When the road they were on crossed the larger one that led to town, or toward McConnico Creek in the other direction, Rafe stopped them. "We best decide now how we'll proceed," he said, though they all knew there would be no discussion. Rafe told them which directions to ride in. "I trust you to both know the kind of men we need. Tell them we'll meet in front of my store at five-thirty in the morning, and that I want to see faces. They'll have to ride like men or not at all. Anyone in a hood can answer to me."

Brantley and Alfred both nodded. Then Brantley spoke. "We'll need to rest our horses and eat something before everyone gathers."

"The three of us will meet at my house," Rafe said, "and if I'm not there yet, take care of your horses and go ahead and knock at my door. Melinda will be up."

Alfred rode toward McConnico and then was to come back and cover the men closest to Riverfield. Brantley rode with Rafe until they reached the Teclaw house. He sent Brantley toward Demarville, and he rode toward Valhia and would ride a few miles down the Loop Road before he headed back home. He was hoping for as many as thirty men. Some would bring grown sons; others would bring neighbors.

He had to keep Wheeler in check as he rode, and perhaps because of the kind of errand he was on, traveling alone and at night, he remembered, not for the first time, the lone Union messenger on horseback he'd ambushed that night and killed with a long-blade knife when he could just as easily have let him pass. Maybe there was someone dismounted and waiting on him now at the road's edge, some shadowed figure as he'd once been, this one darkened by skin color and not simply by night, or perhaps he and the man he imagined shared a more absolute darkness. He kept a hand on one of his pistols and tried hard to listen for any unexpected sound, and to ignore as best he could that memory of his own actions near the war's end, lest it make him careless now.

At each house the man came to the door as Alfred had, with a lamp in his hand, sometimes a firearm if he hadn't recognized Rafe's voice, and often a wife stood behind. He rode as far as the Oakhill house and even a bit beyond. Then returned the way he'd come and was finally about to make the Loop Road and decided he could wait no longer to do what he was bound to do.

He rode Wheeler into his yard and past his house and to the barn where he quickly took care of Wheeler's needs and then hitched a wagon to Ida and Ned and threw two clean horse blankets into the wagon bed. He then climbed into the seat and set a lantern between his boots. He would have to travel much slower now, but he could still make stops at several houses on the Loop Road before he got to where he judged March's body lay. The closer he came to March, the more danger he would be in, but if the worst happened, Brantley and Alfred could lead without him.

When he finally reached the section of road where he knew, from Rebecca's description, the body must lie, he lit the lantern and began to look for any dark, motionless mass within the moon and lantern's illumination. He knew the body could have been dragged far enough off the road where he couldn't find it, but Rebecca had said it was at the road's edge, and he doubted anyone had returned and moved it. He managed the reins with his dominant hand and kept the lantern lifted with his left. He'd not asked for help at the last house where he'd stopped. Asking for help of a personal nature was not in his nature. He would do this alone, with no words to anyone.

Several times he thought he saw the body but each time it was the trunk of a fallen tree that revealed itself. And then there was no mistaking the twist of large limbs, the shape of a head. He pulled the wagon alongside and then just passed the body, set the brake, and sat the lantern in the bed. He had seen enough dead bodies in his life and had no desire to hold the lantern close over March's face, did not want to see the time-stopped expression, the moment of pain and final realization.

He'd been on many burial details, had lifted and dragged more bodies than he could number, and so March's heft, his dead weight, was no surprise. Rafe's movements, even after the years that had passed, became rote: the positioning of himself behind, the bending down with his knees, the reaching beneath the arms, and then the pulling upward and standing in one fluid motion. He took comfort in the familiarity of it all. Then, with considerable effort, he managed to drag the body into the wagon bed, pulled it forward, head first and toward the back of the seat, stopping in the circle of light cast by the lantern. There it was, could not be avoided, as he'd already known it couldn't; no face of death ever could be. March's eyes were open, not in surprise, but squinted as if he'd been trying to lengthen the distance he could see, vigilant and watchful for danger, or perhaps what he'd last seen was his first glance of the distant unknown that awaited everyone. His mouth was open too, the blood on his lips and chin expressing some final utterance of pain that spoke more clearly than any word might. The angle of his head against the wagon bed indicated nothing akin to sleep but only a body that had been vacated to the most absolute degree.

He covered March with the horse blankets and climbed back into the seat, released the brake, and turned the wagon. He pushed Ida and Ned more than he normally would have, and so the ride was jarring, and he kept the now unlit lantern tight between his feet. March's body would have to ride as best it could on its almost final journey.

When he reached the barn, he stopped the wagon inside it and left March covered with the blankets in the hard bed. If there was any comfort after death, March had already found it, and he would lie on rough lumber for eternity, or at least until the casket rotted and his bones embedded themselves in its rot, the shape of the man still present in the length of his remains.

As he unhitched Ida and Ned, he spotted Alfred and Brantley's horses in the two far stalls that were usually empty. He saw to the mules and then went inside and found the two men at his table already eating, just as Ida and Ned were now eating their feed, and for a moment he recognized that all were in his employ, were at his disposal and for his use as if they were all a kind of livestock, and he accepted that. He knew most men couldn't. Did it mean Ida and Ned were somehow more valuable because he would not be placing them in danger? Then he remembered he would be putting himself in harm's way, and Wheeler, who'd done nothing but serve him well and yet was always his own being, separate and apart and unbroken. The fact that he felt more concern for his horse than for himself, or for Alfred and Brantley, did not strike him as odd or cause him any concern that needed contemplation. This was not the time for contemplation, and if there ever were a time, it was an occupation for lesser men.

He asked Brantley and Alfred how many of the men they'd talked to might actually show up, and then Melinda emerged from the kitchen with a plate for him. He did not imagine she had slept either. Tiredness showed on her face but only as a thin veneer. Both Alfred and Brantley looked up at her with clear admiration of her features, and this did not bother him. It was her due, and perhaps, in some way, his also. He felt any wife of his should be admired.

"Most of them will come, maybe all," Alfred said and Brantley nodded in agreement, though Rafe detected a larger degree of caution in Brantley's slow nod.

Melinda stood behind him now. He could sense her, and she placed a hand upon his shoulder, tightened her slender fingers, and he felt her concern, which she knew better than to speak in the presence of others.

Rafe ate quickly, and when he finished all three rose, the two men walking out before him, perhaps realizing a man and wife would want a moment alone before the ordeal began. But Rafe crossed the dogtrot and went into his office and came out with a leather pouch filled with several more loaded cylinders and ammunition for his carbine. Melinda waited for him just inside the dogtrot door. "During the war I never knew when you were fighting and when you weren't. This time I'll know, and it will be harder knowing."

He put his arms around her small waist and smelled on her the breakfast she'd cooked and the acrid scent of a woman who'd been working in a hot kitchen. He knew she must smell on him the ride he'd been on and the work of gathering the dead, if one could call bringing home a single body *gathering*. "You won't have to wait or worry for long. It won't take a letter from me to let you know I'm still alive. I'll be back soon."

"You always waited so long to write. Such few letters."

"Maybe now isn't the time to scold me for a failure from years ago."

"You're right," she said.

He quickly kissed her, but her lips were too tight with concern, and he felt no response. He was out the door then. He had his business to tend to; she had hers—getting Rebecca on the early train.

A large group of men waited for them in front of his store, some still mounted, having just arrived, others dismounted and standing or sitting on the store's porch, but none of them in any kind of mild repose. He sensed an urgency within them. All showed their faces and nodded as Rafe silently made the count. He saw that Alfred was counting too. Brantley seemed unconcerned with the number, as if he were simply ready to fight with whatever force they had. It was Brantley who'd probably seen the most severe action during the war.

"Twenty-seven, counting us," Rafe said.

Alfred confirmed.

Rafe knew them all. Some he liked and respected, some he didn't. A few owed large bills at his store, but that did not matter now. If the worst happened he would forgive their debt for the sake of their widows. Or if they comported themselves well and lived, maybe a partial forgiveness would be in order, something earned. You had to give a man what he'd earned, though sometimes that could be a beating.

He pulled his watch from his pocket and saw it was only a few minutes past five-thirty. The sun had not showed itself yet but there had been light enough since leaving his barn. "Everyone mount," he said and waited while they did so. Then all eyes were on him. "They're gathering at the river," he said and realized he'd just echoed the hymn but made no remark about it, no attempt at gallows humor. "At the Black Fork on Rattlesnake Bend." He did not speak loudly, aware that a quiet voice could be more commanding and would force them to listen close. "We'll take places along the road out of there, take advantage of the woods and go about our business when I first fire. It will be simple enough, no complicated maneuver."

"How many do you expect?"

He did not recognize the voice, only its youth and nervous expectation, but then two older men, both of whom had fought in the war and bore its wounds—a missing hand and a deep scar across a cheek—parted their horses to either side, and Rafe saw the sandy haired boy named for a father who'd starved to death in a northern prison camp. The boy had to be nearing twenty now, though he looked younger, almost as feminine as the sound of his name, Gene. Rafe felt some sudden dislike for the boy that held no reason behind it until he recognized in the boy's face the memory of a troublesome youth at the war's end who'd followed him around like some lost dog. The boy had finally been shot down in a skirmish with a thieving band of southern marauders, and for some reason Rafe had never been able to forget the boy or the odd angle in which his dead body lay at the end of the brief fight.

"Enough for plenty of killing," he said. "Are you the youngest here?"

Heads turned this way and that, and then Rafe saw men nodding.

"I think so," the boy said with some embarrassment.

"Stay close to me," Rafe said and felt again an anger and mild disgust even as he spoke the words. "Just do as I say."

"Yes, sir," he answered and nudged his horse forward toward where Rafe sat Wheeler.

"We'll ride two abreast. Keep your guns at ready." Rafe then turned Wheeler toward the road. He kept his eyes focused ahead but could feel the boy beside him.

After half a mile the sun had risen and the morning began to warm. They would not have to suffer it very much since it was still April, though the air felt heavy with moisture. There was mostly silence among the men, and the boy remained silent too, unlike the youth at the end of the war who would not be quiet and had kept up a harangue against all they'd just fought for.

Another mile down the road they passed a Negro woman walking who would not look at them but moved off the road as far as she could, as if she feared something she couldn't see but could divine and knew grave trouble was riding past her in the form of hard, ghost-white faces.

After two more miles Rafe could sense the Black Fork, smell the change in the air, and see the wide break in the treetops that always signaled a river up ahead that had to be forded. The road curved and then straightened into a section lined thickly with trees on either side, and the scent of the river came stronger. He stopped Wheeler, extended his left arm with his palm open toward the boy, and waited for the two columns of horses and men to halt. He then turned Wheeler, slowly walked him along the columns, and again spoke quietly, repeating himself as he went so all would hear. "We'll take the right-hand side of the road," he said. "Tie your horses well back in the woods, then line up where I place you."

"Why not both sides?" a man said. "Catch them in a crossfire."

Rafe stopped. It was John McAlpine, who wore a trim beard and whose blue eyes were often remarked upon by women in whispers they thought other men didn't hear. He'd served at Fort Morgan, his only action as a cannoneer when Mobile Bay was taken.

"Do you see any elevation on either side of the road?" Rafe asked, quietly still but in a tone bitten through with impatience.

"No," McAlpine said, bracing himself for what he must have known was coming.

"We'd be caught in our own crossfire, you fool, cut each other down. You want to bury white men today killed by your own bullets?" McAlpine turned and didn't answer. "All right," Rafe said, more loudly now. "Move off the road."

The men approached the tree line and dismounted, and Rafe watched each man and horse disappear into the soft, dappled green of April foliage. Then he entered, finally dismounted, and made sure they tied their horses far enough back. He began to place them so that they had good coverage and could still see a clear view of the road.

"Now we wait," he said after each was settled with weapons ready.

The air grew heavier with heat and moisture, and the morning stretched out and crept along. Rafe's breakfast started to wane, and he knew the other men would soon be growing hungry. He hadn't counted on such a wait; then he slowly grew disgusted with himself as each half hour passed for not anticipating what he didn't expect. He heard low voices begin to speak and did not have to guess at what they were saying, what some of the men would be thinking about him at this point—that his information was incorrect, that he'd led them to the wrong place, did not know what he was doing in the management of them.

He checked Wheeler's tie and went to Brantley, who stood and faced him. "What do you think?" Brantley asked.

"Maybe they know we got word or could be they're waiting for dusk. They *are* there. I have no doubt."

"So what do you want to do?"

Alfred walked toward the two of them, then stood and listened.

"You'll come with me," Rafe said to Brantley. "Alfred, tell everyone to stay put. We'll be back in due time. Any man leaves, he'll wish he hadn't."

"The ones who served," Alfred said, "already know the fighting never starts on time."

Brantley held his shotgun, and Rafe placed his carbine in the crook of his left arm. "We'll edge the road," he said. "They've got to be back in those quarters in the bend."

They threaded themselves through the woods on foot, Brantley walking just behind when the trees and brush were thickest. Mostly the going was not difficult, and after a half mile they came to the edge of the woods where the oaks and pines thinned and the land opened onto a gathering of cabins and another building that served as a church, which a makeshift cross made clear. Men sat on porches in small groups, many more than could live in just these small structures, and all either held their guns across their laps or had them propped against a near wall or post. Mules, and more horses than he would have guessed, all saddled in some manner, were tied everywhere in haphazard fashion. Rafe could see only a few women, one who went out to a well and then back into a cabin and another who handed a man sitting on a porch something to drink. No children played anywhere, as if on this particular day and in this particular world, children did not exist, had never played among these cabins in their innocence and imaginations. And what fate did the men on these porches imagine was ahead of them? Rafe wondered. Some satisfaction for anger and bloodlust, some sense of power they'd never known, a power far beyond what might be achieved by holding an office in a government that pretended to care about them but really only wanted to insult and punish white men who'd defended their own land?

"I count twenty mules and horses," Brantley whispered.

Rafe remained silent, did his own count, and then said, "Nineteen, but I may have missed one."

"They could ride anytime."

"I don't know what they're waiting on," Rafe said. "Maybe on more to show."

"With this much morning gone, I doubt any more will."

"Could be they're close to figuring that out for themselves and so will begin to move."

"Maybe."

"Stay here," Rafe said. "Watch them. If anything changes, come through the woods and let me know. Otherwise, I'll be back with the men, on foot, and we'll get down to the business of why we came."

He pulled back from where he'd been kneeling and slowly stood, crept carefully back the way they'd come, finally moving faster now that he was alone, the stillness and beauty of the woods present to him in a way it hadn't been earlier, a contrast to what was ahead, he knew.

Alfred saw him approach, looked expectant, and when Rafe was near, said, "They're all still here but restless."

"We're about to cure that," Rafe said. "Call the men here."

The boy came to him first and stood close. Rafe had forgotten about him but now felt again burdened with the responsibility of his youth. Others came and kneeled, weapons in hand. One, a man named Wyatt with a large burn mark seared around his left eye that made of it nothing less than an aberrant, jaundiced bull's-eye, crouched and peered up at Rafe. He slowly shook his head as if to question all Rafe was about to order. Rafe almost responded with his own question for this man who'd come to Riverfield after the war with his dead brother's widow, but he knew Wyatt had suffered in the crater at Petersburg and now wanted only to protect the farm he'd inherited from his wife's family. Rafe turned away from the marked eye and described for all what he'd just seen. "This will be harder than taking them on the road," he said. "We'll fire from cover first, shoot them where they sit. Then charge them."

He saw faces tighten with the realization of how close the fighting might be, but he saw a kind of relief, too, with the knowledge of the coming action—no more waiting where the mind had too much time to think, to imagine one's own death and the unimaginable wounds that might precede it.

The wind stirred, delivering a pleasantness across their faces and the scent of dogwood blooms and the river. The day's beauty surrounded them, just as it would when the killing began.

Rafe led them now, the boy right behind, then Alfred and all the other men in quick-moving single file. He soon saw Brantley in his same place, crouched in the same attitude, and then saw what surprised him, Black men coming off their porches, guns in their hands, moving toward their horses and mules not with hurry but with purpose. He took a place beside Brantley again and motioned half the men to one side of them, half to the other, and watched as they kneeled beside trees and behind brush and fallen trunks. He hoped they remembered not to fire until he did and gave them time to choose a man and aim at a head or torso.

The only sound for the moment was the rising din of indeterminate insects making their presence known to one another. Rafe then squeezed the trigger and his carbine echoed sharply through the woods and was echoed again, not by returned waves of its own sound but by the mechanics of forged steel and explosions of powder repeated twenty-six times, or so Rafe imagined if each man had begun his duty. Black men who seemed mere figures, targets, and not yet real, crumpled before them, their bodies in profound interruption, while some simply dropped to the ground for safety, and any number of their mules and horses made what sounded like the most unnatural of screams at a pitch one would have sworn was above their capability but was as real and violent as murder of innocent men.

"Keep your places," Rafe yelled quickly. "Fire again!" Those with re-peating rifles were already continuing their fire with singular, deadly pop-ping as each took aim and squeezed the curved, warm metal of a trigger. Others with smoothbore weapons hurried to reload, and Brantley fired both barrels of his ten-gauge at once in a doubled roar that drowned out even the awful keen the mules expelled through square, gnashing teeth and the bits in their mouths. Then came the sound of Black men cursing and returning fire and one of them shouting orders not to run but to find cover and shoot the white sons of bitches. It was that nigger Shack, Rafe saw, crouching behind a downed horse still struggling. They had to charge them now, he knew, before their confusion gave way to a steeled resistance, and he called out the order and looked to the boy be-side him. "Come on, son. The close work is at hand." Rafe dropped his carbine, pulled one of his Colt Navy pistols, and ran forward through the wisps and smell of hovering smoke and toward open ground, where motionless and twisting bodies lay as if some had found a stillness they could never have imagined and others had entered into a nightmare of pain whose finality they either prayed for or asked deliverance from. The first body he passed looked up at nothing with one eye, the other not closed but its vision obliterated by a ball of lead smaller than any human eye of any shape or color, the socket nothing but shattered bone and bloodshot matter. All this Rafe took in only because of the familiarity of it, memories stored and released in a catalogue of carnage he knew as well as any other man who'd fought and killed until it became a routine one could somehow live with.

He was close now and knew the boy and other men were alongside or just behind him. He looked for Shack again and did not see him, but another black figure, running, appeared in his vision, and Rafe led him as if he were about to shoot a bolting animal, aimed just in front of his head, and fired, a thick red mist exploding the air above him as he fell below it. Another ran toward a porch and up the steps. Just as Rafe was about to fire, he heard again the doubled roar and watched as the body seemed to fling itself against the front wall of the house enacting some mad performance, any passageway to temporary safety denied him by a force at least equal to his desire to survive.

Rafe turned now, circled around so that he could survey the entire undertaking, and saw two white men down, recognized the trim beard on one jerking body and the other motionless, one hand empty of a weapon, the other long missing. Then he watched Alfred take off running toward the back of a cabin and was puzzled at first, but then he saw a flash of blue and a black head making for the woods beyond. Alfred closed on him and stopped and fired into his back just as the man entered the soft, April green and pitched headlong into it, its sanctuary something he would never reach though it closed around him.

Firing continued from all angles and positions. Here in miniature was the chaos of all battles where commanders pretended to move men in orderly fashion but knew once a first shot was fired a battle became its own brainless beast with each man acting and reacting by an instinct that had nothing to do with reason or anything approaching thought. Raise your gun and fire and fire again and *try* to see who you're shooting at, which in the midst of yelling and explosions and smoke and burning woods and houses was never easy. But Rafe now saw a Black man moving toward him out of the sound and chaos, a shotgun in his hands not yet raised, maybe holding only empty shells; he saw the curled gray hair, the length of white beard, and recognized, this time, the one they called Bo Pete for no reason Rafe knew, a customer of his store who always paid his bill on time and had never said an impudent word. Rafe aimed, shot lower than he meant, but hit him in the neck, the white of his beard turning into a blood-soaked rag.

Then came a sound he recognized—hooves against hard-packed ground. Three riders came at him, two with pistols drawn, all approaching full gallop but not there yet. Rafe saw Shack on the left, his thin body and small head. In his periphery he saw the boy, Gene, who stood close, and also saw he was caught, frozen as if standing in the ice of a shallow pond, all of the boy's body rigid with cold fear that had somehow taken this long to expose itself to the elements surrounding them. He shoved the boy, knocked him away and onto the ground, falling with him into the bare dirt that blew up around them in divots from shots fired down by the riders, and rolled with him; finally, still holding his pistol in some instinctive grip, he fired upward at the mounted bastards and watched as two fell, along with one horse, and then a third as another fusillade of fire sounded in the jarring air.

The reverberation of shots slowed, and then finally all became quiet for a moment, and the moment grew larger, stretching time, until Rafe became aware of it again and realized the firing had completely ceased and was unsure how much time had actually passed since the firing of

that first shot. Then only the sound of those pounding hooves belong-
ing to riderless horses came to him and soon faded as the last of the
surviving horses and mules ran into the woods and disappeared. After
this another sound he recognized, the moans of wounded men, which
would have to be addressed by all who were willing.

He walked into the shade of a lone white oak and surveyed the standing men, realizing that all were white, and, like him, taking their bearings,
some still trying to understand that it was over and not yet ready to
trust the fact. John McAlpine remained prone on the ground, but was
still moving, moaning loudly, calling for help. Someone walked toward
him. Another man stood holding his forearm, his sleeve soaked with
blood darkened into the brown, home-dyed material. Three others lay
stretched across the ground beyond any concern.

After he made a complete turn and took in all around him, he heard a
single shotgun blast behind and knew Brantley had begun to address the
wounded enemy in the manner that was necessary. So it was not really
over, not quite. Rafe spotted a dark moving figure beneath a scrub pine
and walked toward it. The large eyes he stared down upon were open
and blinking against the sun, and then the blinking slowed, as if the boy,
twenty at most, were trying to blink Rafe out of existence, as if he could
not be real. Rafe watched the growing stain across the belly and then
purposely cast his own shadow over the face. The boy, who had to feel
relief from the sun's glare, remained silent and now kept his eyes closed
but his heavy lips moved with either the intake of breath or the release
of words without sound that might have still held some private meaning.
Rafe shot him in the forehead.

He then looked up and saw the man Wyatt not ten feet away, staring
at him with his seared eye. Wyatt's intent look held Rafe still, and then
the man turned and began to walk toward the far tree line where the
horses stood well beyond. "Where are you going?" Rafe yelled.

The man did not look back, but said, loudly enough, "Home."

"We did this all the time, damnit. In the war."

"Not in my regiment."

"And those were *white* men," Rafe said, as if his words were an answer.

Three more shots sounded, and then he saw Alfred end the misery of
two of the mules. The boy, Gene, remained on the ground, and Rafe felt
some degree of disgust return. He walked over to him; he did not reach
down a hand but simply said, "Get up, son. You ain't hit. Stand up." The
boy slowly did as he was told and didn't speak. Rafe turned away. He was

done with him, had done what was necessary for the boy, knew he need not concern himself any longer.

He heard crying now, not the moans of men but wails that were entirely feminine. Brantley had opened the door to a cabin and ordered the women and children out and down off the porch. Rafe nodded toward Alfred and he did the same at another cabin, and other men followed suit. Within minutes eight women and twelve children stood gathered in the hard sunlight.

Rafe approached them and their crying did not abate. He spoke over it, knowing they were entitled to their grief and didn't begrudge it. "None of this was any fault of yours. You bear no blame. Go back in your houses and take what you can carry." They did not move but looked at him without comprehension. "Now," he said. "Take what you can."

Slowly they made their way, remaining inside for longer than seemed needed, their figures passing open windows and doorways. And finally they emerged, one by one, some carrying cloth sacks filled to capacity and others with split-oak baskets balanced on their heads, arms free at their sides; it was a sight Rafe never failed to notice and admire, and he wondered if white women, if they had to, could ever learn such a skill. He doubted it. The Black children's arms were full with blankets, frying pans, hoes, whatever they could get their small, thin arms and fingers around.

"You have to go now," he said. "To wherever you can. Do you understand?"

They did not answer but one of them, a tall, lean woman with a clean white cloth tied around her hair began to walk, two small children behind, both girls, perhaps twins, Rafe saw. She placed the basket she was carrying atop her cloth-covered head, found its balance without apparent effort, and continued walking with her head raised and still, her eyes looking forward toward some destination only she knew. The others began to follow, letting her lead. The final woman and small child stopped for a moment beside two downed horses and looked upon near bodies; one of them, Rafe knew, was Shack. Then they too moved on.

"Find shovels first," Rafe said to the men around him. "Then make torches."

Within a half hour the flames from the cabins burned hot and bright into the light and heat of the sun, commingling to such a degree Rafe felt as if some part of the sun's fire had touched this small, blighted piece of earth.

He wondered now, these many years later, as he pondered Samuel's whereabouts, if that woman and child who'd stood over Shack's body might have been Samuel and his mother. It was possible. Maybe Samuel remembered it, or perhaps he didn't. He could have been too young—the memory buried so deep in the folds of a child's brain that the grown man could not retrieve it because he did not know it was even there. Or maybe the woman and child had not looked upon Shack at all but at the other man beside him. Rafe could not know, and it made no real difference. Samuel now had to be dealt with one way or another. The past did not alter that fact.

Just before noon, after looking over the store books, the knowledge he sought came to him in a most unexpected way. He'd decided he would return the books to Alfred and mounted Wheeler, passed Betsy's cabin without looking toward it, and when he emerged from the side of the house and into his front yard, he saw Leathy standing before his porch, completely stationary, as if she had somehow simply appeared there, no motion or travel having been necessary on her part. A foolish idea, he knew, and he chastised himself for believing, even for a moment, as others believed. She might have been standing there for a half hour, waiting.

He guided Wheeler toward her, stopped, and demonstrated his own patience by not speaking a word. She looked up at him with her broad face, nodded as if she understood his silence, respected it, and answered it with her own, which she held long enough for Wheeler to show restlessness.

"He down on the Black Fork," she said finally. "They a cabin there, built over ashes. You know the place."

Rafe did not ask her how she'd come by this knowledge, simply knew it was true, and knew she had her own reason for telling it, which he felt no need to divine.

Sixteen

Sometimes it seemed to Melinda that there was no place left for her in her own home. Annie Mae was almost always in the kitchen, if she wasn't cleaning somewhere in the house, and if Melinda sat at the dining table or in the living room, she could hear Annie Mae working and catch glimpses of her through the door as Annie Mae moved about. The parlor didn't seem far enough away, and Rafe's office and gun room was no place for her. Both sides of the loft were her children's domain. All that was left was her bedroom, which she had to share with Rafe when he was home, and when he wasn't and she took refuge there, it could begin to feel like a cell without bars, and worse, a place of death.

At the moment she had retreated to the parlor but felt ill at ease. She finally walked into the living room, and just as she did Bunyan entered it at the same time from the dogtrot, her expression tense, worried, Melinda saw. She took a step back into the parlor, motioned for Bunyan to follow, then sat and watched as Bunyan hesitated and looked as if she might turn toward the kitchen or walk back out into the dogtrot. But she didn't. She moved toward her mother, and as she did Melinda saw her girl's face emerge, one filled with uncertainty.

Melinda patted the cushion beside her and without a word Bunyan sat. She leaned toward her mother, not merely allowing Melinda to place her arm around her daughter but needing her to. Here was the child she knew, showing herself again. The little girl in her came and went these days, came and went. Eventually she would be gone for good, but that was all right. Long ago Rafe had finally destroyed whatever had been left of the girl in Melinda. She hoped for her daughter's sake that the girl in Bunyan would take leave in a more natural way, that Richard was not like Bunyan's father. Or maybe Rafe's capacity for damage would take Bunyan's girlhood before Richard ever fully saw it. They were both so young still. They deserved to see all of each other, before they grew completely out of themselves and into who they would become.

"Mama." Bunyan's voice was a whisper. "I talked to Annie Mae."

Melinda waited but no more words came. "And?"

"I asked her why you went to see Leathy down in Dawes Quarter."

"I've already talked to you about that." Melinda spoke without scolding, felt no desire to.

"She said she didn't know why you went, but I don't believe her. Did it have to do with Betsy? Did she do something to you? I mean something more than what she's already done with Daddy?"

Melinda would not answer, her silence a protection around her daughter, a wall against knowledge. "No," she said finally, and though she meant, No, I won't tell you, she left her simple reply open for Bunyan to interpret any way she would.

"It's like I don't know the right questions to ask you. Seems like there are things happening that I ought to know about, because I'm old enough."

"No child of any parent, even grown children, knows everything about her parents' lives. We all keep some things private, which you'll do too, maybe with Richard, maybe with someone else."

Bunyan nodded and remained quiet a moment, as if there were things she already wanted to keep private, or maybe she was contemplating the kind of life she would find her way into. Pans rattled in the kitchen, and the door to the stove was swung shut, reminding Melinda who was near. "Annie Mae did tell me one thing." Bunyan's voice was still at a whisper. "She said I should be scared for you. Why would she say that? Is something bad going to happen to you?"

Melinda pulled away from her daughter, turned to look her in the face, and realized what Bunyan saw in her might scare her as much as what Annie Mae had said. Her whole body felt tightened into a hard thing that Rafe would understand the moment he witnessed it, and on some level Bunyan had to understand it too, had to see the hardness that had come into her mother. Bunyan's widened eyes told Melinda that she did. "When she said that, just exactly what did it have to do with?"

"Your going into Dawes Quarter."

"I was not afraid to go in there."

"I don't think that was what she meant. Maybe. I don't know. She made it sound like something terrible would happen to you, like maybe she was worried for you. It was hard to tell."

"You don't have to worry. Nothing bad will happen to me. And if you know anything about your father, you know he won't let anything bad happen to me, not by anyone's hand." Melinda let her daughter consider that, reluctant to explain that Rafe's impulse for protection had less to do with her and more to do with his sense of himself as a man.

"There's something else I need to tell you. It's why I came looking for you. A while ago, you must have been in your bedroom then, I saw Daddy talking to Leathy. She was right out in front of the house. Why would she come here?"

Melinda looked out the front window, as if Leathy might be there still. "I don't know," she said and did not have to feign puzzlement.

"Could she have come looking for you?"

"I doubt it. There's no reason I can think of that she would."

"Maybe Daddy wouldn't let her talk to you."

"Or maybe she came to see him. If she did, we'll never know why."

"No, we won't," Bunyan said, and in her simple response Melinda heard a knowledge of Bunyan's father that surpassed what a mere girl would understand.

"Don't concern yourself with Leathy. You should have more pleasant things on your mind." She saw then some small brightness in her daughter's eyes, watched it grow.

"Richard asked if he could take me for another buggy ride Sunday afternoon."

Melinda was not surprised and was glad Rafe had given them permission. "And you still like going? You feel at ease with him?"

"Yes, ma'am. I think about him all the time. Is that bad? Am I wrong to?"

Melinda wished she could tell her what a daughter's happiness meant to a mother, but the joy of such a moment had to be merely accepted, she knew, not called attention to or named by unneeded talk. "No, that's not bad. It's natural. I want you to go. Just, well, be careful."

She saw her daughter catch her gentle warning and felt Bunyan's embarrassment. Bunyan hugged her then. "Thank you, Mama." She stood up and walked toward the door with lighter steps than when she entered. Melinda watched the movement of her daughter's body, felt the vitality in it, and admired the beauty of her long hair, the way it hung so fully down her back. Then Bunyan was quickly gone, out into the dogtrot, into the brisk air.

Melinda continued to sit, and she felt a weight slowly return to her own body as if Bunyan had taken all the lightness she'd just shared with her. Any chore could be a heavy thing, and she had one facing her now. She rose to it finally, stood, and walked toward the kitchen, toward Annie Mae. When she reached the doorway, she saw Annie Mae's wide back, saw her looking out the window toward her daughter's cabin, knew and understood the concern there, even feeling a kinship with her as a mother, and that was the point; Melinda had come as a mother. "Annie Mae," she said with as much force as she could gather, "this evening you will move your things out of your room and into Elizabeth's cabin. And if you ever frighten my daughter again, tell her she should be scared for me or say anything to cause fear in any of my children, you will be gone from here completely."

Annie Mae was facing her now, taken aback by what she'd just heard, and unable to speak, it appeared. Her mouth hung open as she drew in lost breath. Melinda felt a kind of reversal within herself and realized that in many ways she had always looked to Annie Mae for strength and a gentle hand at her back, the very things a daughter needed from a mother. She was now beyond that, could never return to it, and felt diminished somehow by the fact she had ever needed such support and guidance from Annie Mae, and, at the very same time, knew how much she would miss it, had *already* missed it in these last weeks.

"I didn't mean to say what I did. It just come out. I'm sorry. I ain't been nothing like myself for a time. I wouldn't never *mean* to scare Bunyan, not any of your children."

Melinda considered her words and wanted to believe her. "Be that as it may, I can't just let it pass," she said, "and I won't. Even if what you've just told me is the truth."

Annie Mae looked down at her feet, then ran her hands along the material of her apron, as if she were checking the stitching to see if it held at the seams. Then she looked back at Melinda. "What about Mr. Rafe?"

Melinda immediately understood the question. What would Rafe do without his easy way to Elizabeth? Melinda had not let herself think this far but found she didn't care. Her only question now was if Annie Mae had meant for the question of Rafe to sway her, even scare her, force her to back down, with no concern at all for Melinda and what she might have to face from an angered husband—one with an impediment between himself and what he desired as a man.

"What do you mean by asking me that?"

Annie Mae continued to look at her. Melinda found her face hard to read. She was not staring. There was no glare in her eyes, but there was a steadiness and a strength. "I just know he won't like it."

"So are you worried for yourself or for me?"

She looked away, as if her answer would not matter, as if there were no answer for either of them. "I reckon I'm worried for us both, Miss Melinda."

She heard the address, felt the sting of it, though knew if anyone had been listening it would have been considered a term of due respect. She only wondered now if Annie Mae had used the term to hurt her or if, because of the way things had changed between them, she'd spoken it naturally, in a way that wasn't calculated but was simply a manner of speaking to white people that was so ingrained she did it without thinking. No matter the reason, the word *Miss* voiced something lost between them.

Because there was no Samuel, she had to hitch Mollie B. herself. She knew how, though. Her father had taught her at some point after her mother died, and she hadn't forgotten. It did take her longer than it should have to tighten the leather straps properly, especially the belly-band and loin strap.

She drove past Elizabeth's cabin. She knew the girl probably watched her, and knew Elizabeth was alone. Wheeler hadn't been in his stall. She saw both William and Henry standing on the back porch. Each of them waved without calling to her, and Henry looked up at William and spoke something that William responded to with a firm shake of his head. She realized she could have asked William for help with the buggy, but perhaps she hadn't wanted help.

When she drove past the house and onto the road, Kate was returning home from the direction of the store and was too close to ignore. Melinda slowed Mollie B. and stopped her. "Is your father at the store?" she asked.

"He was." Kate stood close, placed a hand on Mollie B.'s backside, gently patting her. "He left, though. I don't know where he was going. He wouldn't say. Not even when I asked."

Melinda was mildly surprised by this because Kate was about the only one of them Rafe would ever answer to. Maybe wherever Rafe was headed had something to do with who'd come to see him.

"So where are you going?" Kate asked.

She decided she couldn't *not* answer and did not want to deny her daughter as Kate's father just had. "To Dawes Quarter," she said and knew that would be enough for Kate, though it wouldn't have been for Bunyan.

Kate stopped patting the horse, remained quiet, and simply looked at her mother. A soft wind blew her hair into her eyes, and she brushed it away unconsciously. "I don't have to tell anyone."

"That's up to you," Melinda said. "If you do, it's all right. You shouldn't have to tell any kind of lie for your mother. I'd never ask that of you." She lifted the reins. "I won't be gone for very long," she said and prodded Mollie B. forward. Kate stepped away and let her take leave without another word.

She passed the Episcopal church and then the school, wondering if she might find Leathy on the road before the woman reached her house. She turned off the Loop, went past the same shacks as before, and saw various children out in front of them. She realized at least some of them were the same ones who'd seen her before, and they watched her now, whispering among themselves. When she made the turn onto the road that would carry her into the quarter, she saw a lone figure walking far ahead, and, catching up to her, recognized Leathy. She slowed as she came along beside her, and Leathy looked up. She did not seem surprised to find Melinda there. An ability to hide what she really thought, what truly did surprise her, had to be an ability she'd cultivated, a way of signifying that she knew all beforehand.

"We not far from the house," Leathy said. Melinda realized she wouldn't get into the buggy with her, so she did not ask, and she sensed that Leathy would rather talk inside and not on the road, perhaps because if she sat down with her, Leathy would be in a better position to silently seek payment for her time.

"I'll stay with you," Melinda said and tried to keep Mollie B. at as slow a walk as possible. But she reached the house first, set the brake, and waited for Leathy to step onto her porch before she got down.

Once inside, Melinda saw that the shelves were full of more jars and roots than before. She decided that Leathy's work kept her busier than she would have guessed. Leathy asked her to sit and then stirred the coals in the fireplace. Once a flame picked up, she added wood. Finally she sat down across from Melinda. "You wants to know why I was at your house," she said.

"Were you there to see me, and my husband wouldn't let you?"

"No'm. It were him I went to see."

Melinda looked around the room again, felt the growing warmth from the fire, breathed in the musky, fecund scent of the roots and powders on their shelves, and realized it was much stronger than what she remembered from last time, with a bitter smell now that she didn't recall. She wondered what made it, what kind of root it might be from, and what purpose it served. "May I ask you why you came? And I know this isn't the kind of question you would normally want to answer. I'm asking favor, and I know favor has value." She did not doubt that Leathy would understand the meaning of what she said at the last.

Leathy's mouth narrowed, and she half-closed her eyes as if in contemplation; perhaps she was weighing her response. "I know who Mr. Rafe been wanting to find. Samuel been talking too much, saying what ain't true. Maybe he believe it, maybe he don't."

"What's he been saying?"

"The what of it only reason I'm telling you." Leathy leveled her eyes with Melinda's. "He saying you done harm to your children. I know that ain't true. Other things he might be saying I don't like neither, things that don't set with *me*."

Melinda felt the heat of a rising anger at Samuel, though she was not shocked at hearing such news. Then she realized what he might have brought upon himself, and not just for the stealing of a horse or the killing of a mule, and her anger quieted, at least to some degree, with fear for him. "So you told my husband where to find him?"

Leathy didn't speak, only nodded once, slowly, almost imperceptibly.

"Thank you for telling me. I know you didn't have to." She reached into the small purse in her lap, placed a dollar on the table.

"That too much," Leathy said, maybe conflicted about taking the money after all.

"No, it's what I want to pay."

Leathy took the money and held it in her hand beneath the table as if only the sight of it, not the fact, was offensive. "So, was you satisfied after you come here last time? Was it a help to you?"

"It was," she said and stood up beside the table—and did not add a word about the sense of power it had given her. Then, for some reason, a question came to her. "Leathy, has my husband ever come to you?"

The woman remained seated, looked toward the fire and then beyond Melinda. "I can't talk about who come and who don't. Not with no one. That would cost me too much." She continued looking out the window behind Melinda, as if the world of people who came to her were all standing in her yard filled with their worries, concerns, hatreds, and needs, and Melinda wondered just how much it all really cost her to give what people needed.

Once Melinda reached home, she decided she would find William and have him unhitch the buggy and take care of Mollie B. But it wasn't William she first saw upon leaving the barn. The little boy, George, stood at the woodpile beside Elizabeth's cabin, a stick of wood in his hands and his eyes on her as if he'd been caught stealing the split log.

"I didn't mean to startle you," she said when she drew closer and saw his eyes were on her still, much like those of the children she'd seen earlier, as if all white women were some impenetrable mystery, something to observe but never understand. "Do you need me to hand you another stick of wood? If you'll hold your arms out I can maybe put one more stick in, if that's not too much." She wasn't sure why she was talking to the boy, maybe simply to upset his mother, to show Elizabeth she could get near her children if she so chose.

"No'm. I can do it."

"All right." She waited while he struggled, managing to gather up the two logs. She walked next to him then as he carried his burden toward the cabin. The door opened and Elizabeth stepped out, which Melinda expected and realized she'd actually hoped for.

"Go on in the house," she said to the boy but spoke directly toward Melinda. She held the door open for him and partially closed it once he entered. The way Elizabeth stood there told Melinda that the girl already knew.

"Your mother will be moving in with you this evening, if she hasn't already."

Elizabeth nodded noncommittally, her response meaning either she knew or her mother already had, her ambivalent answer full of a quiet aggression Melinda could not help but feel, as Elizabeth surely intended. "It might be a little crowded, but we'll manage," she said.

Melinda hadn't expected a spoken response, but she found she was ready for it. "Maybe if you've less company visiting it won't be an issue."

Elizabeth stared at her a moment but didn't answer. She turned and went through the door she'd been holding slightly ajar, carefully easing it closed behind her so that her anger didn't show when the latch caught. At least this was what Melinda judged.

She continued toward the back of her house, and then Melinda saw William come down the steps. She could see he approached her deliberately, maybe to tell her he would take care of Mollie B. and the buggy if she hadn't already. And maybe he would find some subtle way to ask her where she'd gone.

It was neither. He met her halfway across the yard. "Bunyan has company," he said while fidgeting with his hands in his pockets. "Kate and I left them alone. I hope that was all right."

"Who?" she said.

"Richard. They were in the living room. I think they may have gone into the parlor."

"Unusual for him to be here now."

"Yes, ma'am," he said, and she realized he was not trying to suggest anything with his tone but that his concern for his sister came through naturally. "He asked us if we'd mind his talking to her alone."

"I see. If you will, go and take care of the buggy."

He started to speak but then seemed to think better of it, and she walked on, full of her own concern. As she reached and then climbed the back steps, Richard stepped slowly into the dogtrot, pulling the door to behind him. He did not see her but then must have heard her footfalls against the boards because he turned and saw her, and his ill ease was clear. Maybe her sudden presence made him feel so, or he was already ill at ease with himself. Melinda suspected the latter.

"Richard," she said and he stopped, faced her fully.

"Yes, ma'am?"

"If you'd like to have supper with us, you can stay." He was clearly unsure how to answer, and she saw she would have to help him. "You know, it's customary for a boy to call on a girl when at least one of her parents is home."

"Yes, ma'am. I'm sorry. I didn't mean to be disrespectful." He looked down at his feet, and it was odd to see a boy with such a strong build and large shoulders behave in so submissive a way. She was reminded just how much of a boy he remained, and she wondered if he was that submissive with Bunyan.

"Do you still plan to take Bunyan out for a ride on Sunday?"

He looked up at her now, appeared almost grateful that she'd asked the question. "That's why I came. To tell her I wouldn't be able to."

"You could have let her know that in church on Sunday. Does your family have plans that afternoon, or is some relative coming for a visit?"

He didn't speak. He seemed to search the steps beside him that led to the loft, as if they might allow him escape. "No, ma'am. My mother, she's got things for me to do. And there's work around the place that needs doing, repairs before time to plow and plant."

"What does your mother need from you? Should I talk to her at church, ask her to let you call?" She watched as fear widened his eyes, which confirmed all that she suspected, made her realize the boy was not really to blame, that, however indirectly, she herself was. "Odd that I've never really gotten to know your mother very well when her husband works for mine, and they've known one another for so many years."

"Yes, ma'am. I reckon so. She keeps to herself mostly, though."

Melinda decided to push the boy, forcing him to go ahead and say what he didn't want to but needed to. "Richard, you're not going to call on Bunyan again, are you?"

He looked away from her. "No, ma'am."

"And that's what you really came to tell her. Did you tell her?"

"Yes, ma'am."

She took a step closer to him, and he did not back away. "Well, that took some courage on your part." He didn't respond, didn't know how. "It's hard for a boy to defy his mother, and he probably shouldn't. Not until he's older. But Richard, at some point you may have to."

"Yes, ma'am," he said, and she heard in his voice that he understood, which perhaps meant he would, eventually. For his sake, she hoped so.

"Tell me," she said, "does she have anything against Bunyan?"

"No, ma'am. Not exactly." She again saw fear in his eyes.

"It's me then," she said, maybe more to herself than to him. "She's heard rumors about me she doesn't like, ones she thinks are true." He remained blank-faced, and she sensed the effort it took. "I suspect she doesn't like my husband, either. Probably thinks your father is too loyal to him. And she may be right. Loyalty to a man like my husband can be a dangerous thing." The boy simply continued standing there. She knew she was speaking beyond his full comprehension, that she was only speaking out of her own need, as if saying the words out loud would validate all she thought and understood. "Richard," she said now, "try to forgive her. She doesn't want to see you marry into a troubled family."

He nodded, and she saw relief in his face, then uncertainty about what he should say or do next.

"You can go now, son. Don't worry about Bunyan. I'll see to her."

"Thank you. I'm grateful," he said, and she knew he was. He turned from her and slowly walked toward the front steps.

Melinda took a breath and walked into the house, expecting to find her daughter in tears. Instead she found her in the kitchen with Annie Mae, and both looked at her with reproach.

Seventeen

Rafe had tied Wheeler back in the woods and now sat watching the small, unpainted shack from approximately where he and Brantley had crouched years before. His being here did not feel a coincidence, rather, an orchestration, which is why he hadn't approached as he normally would have. Maybe Leathy hadn't come to him on her own but had been sent, upholding her end of a bargain struck on terms that satisfied both her and Samuel in some mutual way. He could not know. Nor did he have any knowledge of who'd built this shack, how long it had been here, or how Samuel came to claim its use. He did know that Samuel had to have been told this is where the killing took place, or maybe he'd been that little boy with his mother looking down at the dead body of Shadrack and *did* remember at least pieces of the carnage he'd witnessed. If any of this speculation was the case, it might be that not only Samuel was waiting for him, but others, too, a planned revenge carried out in a place sanctified, at least in Samuel's mind, by the blood of his father; the very site of the revenge almost justification enough for the act of it.

He hadn't seen any movement inside or outside the house. There was no horse present—maybe Benjamin was tied in the woods—but there was a thin stream of smoke coming out of the chimney, such contrast to the billowing smoke that had once risen above this clearing in large, dark clouds that might have portended something deadly if it hadn't already happened.

After two hours of waiting and watching—where at one point he'd become so restless he'd considered barging through the door, pistol drawn—he decided that no group of men, Black or otherwise, large or small, could stay cooped up in a shack silent and stationary for this long.

He moved through the woods to a place where he could approach the house from its right side, where there were no windows, only the chimney. He then crept onto the end of the porch, careful to keep muffled the sound of his riding boots against the pine boards. He slowly eased into a chair beside the door without having to pass in front of a window; it was why he'd chosen the right side. He listened but heard no voices, only occasional footsteps, the creak of a bed. Because he was so close now, the waiting wasn't as difficult. He wanted surprise, more for the sake of a mental advantage than a physical one, though one might be as important as the other.

He heard steps again, and then, finally, the twist of the doorknob, and Samuel walked directly past him, oblivious to the fact that a white man sat on his porch. He held an empty bottle at his side and dropped it off the front edge of the pine boards. For a moment it looked like Samuel might follow after it, but he managed to keep his balance. Maybe it was the empty bottle that helped Rafe decide. You could not kill a man who was drunk and alone, not unless he was cursing you or your family. Samuel loosened his pants then, pulled them down in front, and began to urinate off the porch and onto the ground. He reached to scratch the back of his head and his pants fell to his knees, whether by accident or intention Rafe couldn't tell. Maybe it was the insult of having to look at his bare buttocks, or the thought that here was the man who had been after Betsy and, worse, had been spreading word that a white woman who'd never done him harm had been killing her children in their crib; and even if she had, it was not Samuel's business or anyone else's—whatever the cause that drove him, including the stealing of his horse and the killing of his mule. Rafe now rose from his chair. He drew his Colt Navy and stepped up behind Samuel, his movements quieter than the sound of Samuel's full stream of urine against the ground, and clubbed him in the back of his head with the pistol butt, watched him pitch forward, already unconscious but still holding himself in hand, the arc of piss falling with him into his own pool of urine darkening the bare, packed earth. A man who would insult you by showing you his buttocks, even unknowingly, and try to harm your wife, deserved the level of insult in which he now lay.

And Rafe let him lie while he stepped into the small house, saw the unmade bed, the dirty plate on the table next to a mostly full bucket of water, and a loaded pistol on a low shelf. He took the pistol and slipped it into one of the large pockets of his coat, wondering if the loads in the cylinder had been meant for him. The fire was about to go out, and he threw on two sticks of wood from the hearth. A dying fire was something he could not abide.

Rafe looked out the open door, saw Samuel hadn't moved, and decided he was ready to get on with things. He removed the submerged dipper and picked up the bucket of water by its bail, walked out to the porch's edge, and pitched the bucket's contents onto the back of Samuel's head. Samuel began to move, let out a low groan he probably did not even realize he was making, and slowly seemed to gain some sense of himself, though where he lay, how he lay, or why, most likely eluding him at first.

Samuel eventually rolled onto his back and looked up, and Rafe saw that Samuel recognized him and soon realized he was exposed to the cold air in a way no man wanted to endure for long. Rafe had pulled the chair to the edge of the porch, sitting in it with his Colt Navy pointed at Samuel.

"Can I pull my pants up?" Though his words came slowly, Samuel was somehow able to speak in a way that didn't show fear, and Rafe could not help but admire that.

"Touch your pants and I'll blow off what you're wanting to cover up."

Samuel opened his mouth as if he were about to speak but then closed it, deciding perhaps that the words he wanted to speak would either get him killed or maimed. So he waited, unmoving.

"Did you send Leathy to me?"

"What? I got no truck with her. I stay away from such as that. Why I send her to you?" He sounded genuinely puzzled. Liars denied straight out, Rafe knew. Boldness was always their mistake.

"If you try to lie, you'll try my patience. You don't want to do that."

Samuel nodded his response, then said, "I'm cold."

"You don't have to tell me that. I can see it plain enough for myself. I want you to tell me something I give a damn about. Tell me why I'm here, other than your stealing my horse, killing my mule, and going after Betsy."

"What you mean?"

"I hear you asking a question, but you're sounding mighty bold, which to my mind don't add up. We both know the answer I'm looking for. I just want to hear you say it."

Samuel squirmed on the ground. The urine beneath him had to have cooled by now, and no movement of his could bring any comfort or relief. His embarrassment had to be growing larger as he shrank with the cold. Still he remained silent, and Rafe came down off the porch and kicked him in his side as hard as if he were trying to knock over a rotten stump. He then aimed his pistol inches away from Samuel's head.

After twisting and grunting on the ground, Samuel finally seemed to realize the answer Rafe wanted. "Miss Melinda."

"I'm listening. What about her? Keep talking."

Samuel squirmed again. "Things I was saying," he said finally.

"Such as? And look at me when you talk."

Samuel met his gaze, and Rafe remembered other men on the ground here looking up at him, and *not* looking up at him, though their eyes had been open.

"What she might of done to them last two babies," Samuel said.

"*Might* have? I don't believe you been speculating. Not quite how I heard it." Rafe closed his coat up around him, then pointed the pistol back at Samuel.

"No. I said she killed them."

"You believe that?"

"I don't know. Maybe not now."

"Why'd you go around saying it?" Rafe asked. "Who were you trying to do damage to?"

Samuel twisted onto his side but kept his head turned toward Rafe. "I never had nothing against Miss Melinda."

"So me then, by hurting my family. Trying to damage my name. Why? I want to hear you say it."

"You already know."

"Damn you to hell. What did I just say to you? *You* say it."

"'Cause of what happened here."

Rafe started to push harder, wanted to know if Samuel had been here, what he remembered if he had been. Some curiosity made him want to know, though he couldn't have said why. He had no real desire to re-live the event. What did it really matter if that little boy had been Samuel? But something else Samuel had just said registered with him now, something that diverted Rafe's thoughts in a direction his instinct told him was worth pursuing. "When I asked if you believed Miss Melinda had killed the children, you said 'maybe not now.' Why'd you say that?"

Samuel didn't answer with words but with movement as he reached for the waist of his pants with both hands and began to pull them up as he rocked his body from side to side, a kind of delay that was its own indirect answer. Evasion always revealed. Maybe he realized he had something to bargain with now, an answer Rafe didn't already know. "Shoot me if you want. I ain't gon' lay naked no more."

"All right. You can sit up, but stay on the ground, and tell me what I want to know."

Samuel buttoned his urine-soaked pants, sat up, and slid out of the dark spot in which he'd lain. "That woman you got, the one in town."

"The one who ain't none of your business?"

"This the only way I know how to tell you what you want."

Rafe nodded. "Then go ahead, but careful how you say it."

"That Henry woman, she been going 'round telling folks it Betsy."

"Betsy what?" he asked but understood already.

"That Betsy did it, killed your children."

Something about the way Samuel said *your* was jarring, as if Rafe had forgotten that they weren't only Melinda's infant children but also his, and it had taken Samuel to remind him of that. He had known it full well, had felt his blood in them, but the notion and then belief of his that Melinda killed the two children had made them seem more hers as he lived with the fact, as though their lives had been *hers* for the taking, and only hers. There was no stronger claim to anything than killing it. But they *were* his too, or had been, and he'd known this. How could being reminded they were his flesh and blood make him feel he was realizing it for the first time? Was it grief? Could grief come and go like that?

Some other jarring seemed to have taken place too, some notion set loose that worked its way clearer in his mind. Maybe his wanting to think Melinda did it was a way of giving the children over to her and being shed of them himself. You couldn't really grieve the loss of something that had never been yours. Was he even capable of grief? Maybe, but in a way no one else would ever recognize, their perception and understanding of him probably so skewed and off the mark, through no fault of their own, they'd call his grief by some other name: anger, hate, maybe vileness.

He hadn't wanted to believe Virginia when she told him it was Betsy and not Melinda. What did that say about him? And now Virginia hadn't said it just to him but to any others who would listen. Repeating something over and over, though, did not make it true, even if you believed what you were saying.

His mind began to turn to Betsy, to her ability to remain silent, impenetrable, able to hide what she thought; but he saw Samuel was now trying to stand, and he realized all of his thinking had led him to a dangerous place. Any man who let go his watch of the here and now was a fool, and Samuel had almost made him one. He'd done it once before, in the barn with William and Henry present, which had been especially angering.

"Get back down, damnit, before I empty your brain of whatever you're thinking."

But Samuel stood anyway, stupidly defiant, and Rafe fired without aiming, the ground exploding at Samuel's feet, sending upward a spray of dirt but not blood, and Samuel let his body fall backward, braced and ready for the impact with his arms extended behind him, and lay spread across the ground before the sound of the shot and the smell of gunpowder died away.

Rafe stood close over him. "Next time I'll aim, and it won't be any-where near your feet." He saw a hard defiance still in Samuel's eyes and kicked him in his side again. Samuel grunted but did not yelp or even holler, and Rafe imagined he held the pain within, let it turn to deeper hate as it spread through muscle and organs. Again he remembered standing in this same position, a living body prostrate beneath him, a pistol in his hand, his shadow cast over a face. "So were you here? Do you remember?"

Samuel didn't answer at first, finally said, "Just barely." He spoke low, past his pain, his words finding their way around it. "But I was here. I remember gunshots and then the bodies."

"Did you see your father?"

"Before she died, Mama said I did, said she pointed at him. Sometime it seem like I remember, sometime it don't. She wouldn't say much about it. I didn't really ever know him. Never got the chance. What you care?"

Rafe had no ready answer to speak, and so kicked him again, inflicted new pain on top of old, but still only a deep groan from Samuel, one that sounded as if it came from farther within and did not travel through the vibration of vocal chords but took some other path outward, his whole body perhaps speaking through pulsing arteries and charged lines of nerves.

"You best leave here. And I mean today. You hear me? I won't come after you, unless I find out you've made my wife or anyone in my family your concern. Then I'll kill you, drop you the second I lay eyes on you." He wondered why he didn't kill him now, why the impulse didn't go deep enough. Maybe it would feel like he was shooting the child Samuel had once been. "Probably best if I don't ever lay eyes on you again. And if you got design on me, waylay me somewhere, I know two men who'll come for you. Keep that in mind."

Samuel did not speak or respond but simply lay there looking past Rafe's shoulder at a darkening sky that had already taken Rafe's shadow and hidden it from him.

Rafe crossed the Black Fork on the ferry, having felt no need for home at the moment. Benjamin, whom he had found just inside the tree line, trailed behind him on a rope he'd taken from the shack. Maybe he was headed into town because his larger desire was to avoid confronting Betsy for now, and spending a few nights in his readied hotel room would make that easier to accomplish.

That evening he played poker in the game that seemed forever ongoing, forever shuffling the small fortunes of local men. At first he played well, won several hands, but then he found himself even. When he began to lose money, he wondered if he'd displayed some tell that had come upon him without his knowing. He was not normally a man to lose self-awareness. He finally rose from the game and paid what he owed. Then he remembered the last time he'd played and won, remembered what he'd done with the money, where he'd taken it, or most of it. And he became aware now of why he'd come into town. He'd really known all along but hadn't wanted to think about her, which was maybe a way of protecting Virginia from him, at least for a time.

He decided he would send for her, though he knew he ran the risk of her choosing not to obey. He walked to the livery stable behind the hotel, checked on Wheeler, and then asked the stable boy if he knew Virginia Henry, where she lived. When the dark-skinned boy nodded, said, "Yes, sir," Rafe handed him a nickel. "Go get her. Tell her I want to see her. Tonight. Bring her up the back stairs." The boy nodded again as if this last command was one with which he was well familiar.

Within less than an hour he heard a knock at his room door. He rose from the bed, pulled on his boots, and answered. He found the boy standing there. "She say she be here in the morning, not before, and might not come then." The boy went silent and remained stationary, a slight smile playing at his lips like a card he was afraid to turn over.

"If you're waiting on another nickel, you'll be waiting a long time," Rafe said. "And if I discover you never gave her my message, I'll take more than a nickel out of you."

The boy stopped smiling, turned, and walked down the hall. Rafe knew he wasn't lying but wanted to see the boy's impudence fold without having to strike him.

Virginia's knock came the next morning while he was shaving. It was unexpected enough that he nicked his throat and sent a narrow rivulet of blood down his neck and onto his chest. He blotted it away, put on a shirt, but left it unbuttoned when he opened the door. She stood close on the threshold, looking directly at him.

"Thought I'd have to come after you," he said.

"Maybe I don't want you in my house."

He opened the door wide enough to let her in, and she walked to the chair near the dresser but simply placed her hand upon the back of it as if she knew her sitting would give him an advantage.

"Why didn't you come last night?" he said.

"Guess you forgot I got small children. Their names Walter and Fannie. I can't just leave them at home by their own selves."

She clearly wanted anger from him, and he would not give it. "Are they well?" He slowly buttoned his shirt.

"'Course they well. I see to my children." She moved and leaned against the dresser, still facing him. "Now, why you want me here? All I'm gon' do is tell you things you don't want to hear."

"Sounds like you been doing plenty of talking lately. Lot of that going around. People don't know how to mind their own business, or they start thinking my business is theirs. Samuel knows different now. I educated him yesterday. If he forgets the lesson, it'll be the biggest mistake he ever made." He paused, studying her expression to see if she knew all that he did about Samuel, who exactly Samuel was, whose son. Her face remained placid, as unreadable as Betsy's.

"So you figure to teach me something now?" she said. "That why you want me here? So you can beat your nigger woman in a public place?"

"Hush," he said, angry at her words but afraid she'd also seen him wince as she spoke, if his wince had actually been visible.

"'Course, I'm not yours no more."

"You know I've never lifted a hand to you, or any woman, though I can't say it's never been deserved. Beyond that, I've never been the kind of man who puts on public displays. And you're right, you're not mine. I never did own you. It was never like that and you know it." He saw her turn away for a moment, at such a slight angle, but enough to express that she knew he was telling the truth for the both of them and was glad to hear him say it. Odd sometimes how women could be angry and defiant and at the same time wanted to know that you loved them, or had loved them. "You surprised me," he said.

"How that?"

"To know the things you've been going around and saying about Betsy. I didn't think you were vindictive."

"Well, I'm just a woman."

"You're not *just* anything. No woman is, especially you. And you know that too. So don't pretend anything with me."

He sat on the end of the bed, and after a moment where she appeared to weigh her choices, she sat down on the hardback chair she'd held on to earlier. "Maybe I *did* say what I did about that girl 'cause I mad with you, and her too—still. Knew you'd get word, though. Maybe hoped that would get through to you. Make you see what you didn't want to."

"You might be giving yourself more credit than you deserve."

"That might could be, but it don't change what true."

"You can't know for sure Betsy did it."

"That might be too. But I do know you didn't call me here to this room 'cause you thought I was lying. After you talked to that Samuel—and I know who he is, son of the man killed my sister's husband—your gut told you I was right. I tell you what else tell me I'm right. That girl's mother come to my door, told me to stop what I was saying about her daughter. She know I wasn't lying."

"Annie Mae came to you?"

"She did. And you bringing me here close as you gon' come to a apology for doubting me. All you got to do now, for me, is make right not seeing your children for so long. So don't call me to come to you again, and when you do come to me, you bring something nice for Walter and Fannie. And if you thinking you fixing to hand me some money, you keep it. I don't want nothing from you right now. Not till you make right."

"I'll come but not tonight. I know a housekeeper I need to have a conversation with."

"Maybe you ought to talk to your wife. Say the words to her that you can't say to me. I reckon a white woman need them more than a Black woman. Leastways don't no Black woman ever expect to hear a apology. 'Course, maybe your wife don't neither. If she married to you, she ain't like other white women. In fact, she got to be more like a woman with color. Maybe that what drew you to her from the first, and you didn't even know it."

"All right, Virginia. You made your point." He saw that his use of her name surprised her, so much so she didn't speak for a moment.

"You don't usually call my name. But you always known who I am."

"That I have," he said. "How could I not?" The manner in which she sat in the hardback chair, turned at an angle, completely still with the morning sun coming through the window and painting her features with light, made her appear as if she were sitting for a portrait or was perhaps a portrait of herself. "You've always shown me who you are." He meant the words as a compliment, expected her to take them as one and respond to them, but her face remained impassive.

October 2003

It is a Saturday, and Seth, for the first time, has made the drive to South Alabama to see Charles and meet his wife. Seth will spend the night with them, and it has already occurred to him that he has never spent the night in a Black person's home, but he found his way there, both metaphorically and literally, he supposes, with only a little problem—mostly following the directions Charles gave him over the phone. Before he took the exit off the interstate, he passed over Murder Creek and saw again, as he had on his last few trips to the Gulf Coast, that the sign for it was no longer there. He knew the history—how a small camp of early settlers had been murdered on its banks by three men: a Native American, a white man called "Cat," and a slave. Two escaped but the white man was caught and hanged from a tree limb at the scene of the crime. Seth had wondered, when he passed over the bridge, if maybe the sign hadn't been stolen but removed by the state in some passive attempt at obscuring an undesirable history.

Now he sits with Charles in his sunken living room on large, cushioned chairs, and their own shared history already begins to fill the space between them. "Do you want something to drink before we get any deeper into things?" Charles asks, and Seth says no. Charles's wife, Sandra, a tall, slim woman with a complexion only slightly darker than her husband's, had greeted him warmly, visited for a few minutes, and then said she would leave them alone to talk while she went to visit a friend and to shop for their supper.

Seth has begun to take notes on a yellow legal pad as Charles relates the basic facts he knows about Annie Mae Posey and her daughter Elizabeth. Some of this information Seth already knows through occasional phone conversations over the last few years, but of late he's had the desire to get down on paper all he can piece together about their family's past. He has continued to publish articles in small historical journals that focus on Alabama and Southern history, not so much because he's wanted to prove himself a scholar but only when he's come across some incident or moment in time that's truly interested him and wanted to explore more deeply, with the added benefit, he supposes, of making him better understand the subject he loves. And yet he isn't sure if he wants to attempt to publish any of what he's writing down now, though he knows this isn't only a family's history. Contained within it lies a larger story that might speak not just to Southern history but beyond it. But why now? Has it taken him this long to become comfortable with having Black cousins who in some ways know more about his family than he does? He's wondered which has bothered him more, his kinship with another race or their greater knowledge. He's learned one probable truth through his conversations with Charles over these last few years, and that is that Black people have maybe always known more about white people's history than white people themselves. Whites may have written the majority of the history, but it's been Black people who've held the deeper knowledge that dates and bare facts never reveal about the actions of a people who held themselves superior. And yet, *because* the one race held itself superior, the perceptions of the other had to be influenced to some degree by their resentments and bias. How could they not have been? These thoughts and questions run through Seth's mind as he listens to Charles's voice and takes notes and tries not to remind himself there are truths Charles does not know, one of which Seth learned by talking to a practicing midwife about infant deaths, how they can and can't happen.

"So can you give me that date again?" Seth asks.

"Annie Mae was born in 1830. We don't know the month and day, so maybe 1830 is approximate too, but we know it's close. After all, my father knew her. She kept working as a midwife until she was almost eighty."

"What about Elizabeth? You said 1862. What was the exact date?"

"She was born the first week of January. I'll have to look in my papers again for the day, but I know it was early in the month."

Seth writes down the month and year and leaves a space between them.

"So what do you think you'll do with all this information?" Charles asks. "I know you're a historian."

Seth looks down at his yellow pages of notes, then back at Charles. "I just work for the State Archives. I'm no C. Van Woodward." He wonders if Charles knows the name.

"*The Burden of Southern History*. Yes, I know it," Charles says as if he's read Seth's mind, or at least his intentions. "So do you want to write any of this history, our history?"

"I don't know. Maybe."

"Is that why you're here?" Charles leans farther back in his chair. He seems relaxed, or simply wants to appear so.

"I just want to get it all clear in my mind."

"But it's all complicated, isn't it? If you wrote about it, what angle would you take? If *angle* is the right word."

"Maybe I'd look at how common it was for Blacks and whites and Native Americans to intermingle."

"*Intermingle*. That's one way of putting it. But that leaves out a lot of our history. Maybe our history is too dark, so to speak, too personal for you to write about."

Seth feels challenged now, not sure how to continue. "Well, any kind of writing I'd do—scholarly I guess you'd call it—would have to have some distance, or detachment."

Charles rubs at the back of his neck, as if the muscles there are knotted. "Maybe that's the problem with it. Maybe that detachment, as you call it, is actually a kind of lie where real truth is lost. A lie of omission."

Seth nods, knowing his side of the family has told lies of omission for generations. "As I said, all I know for sure is I want to get this information down. I want to know all you know."

Charles smiles, and Seth can't help but wonder if there's some level of self-satisfaction in the smile, at Charles's having more knowledge than Seth does and enjoying the fact. But he knows he shouldn't second-guess and wonders why he's suspicious of Charles. Maybe he can't help but feel Charles must have some resentment toward him, toward Seth's whole side of the family, at all they did to *not* acknowledge Charles and each ancestor who led to Charles and his family's very existence. It's this suspicion of resentment that keeps Seth on edge, he thinks, unable to relax and be himself, keeps him in the detached mode of "historian" when he wants, or should want, to settle in and simply know this decent man who is his cousin.

"Let me go and get some of my files," Charles says finally. "I should have brought them out already."

Seth waits, looking through the large living room window and admiring the line of longleaf pines that grow beyond Charles's yard. This part of the state had once been covered by a huge forest of longleaf, and he remembers now that Annie Mae Posey worked in this forest, harvesting turpentine and passing as Black to avoid Removal. This had been her life before coming to Riverfield, and he wonders if she regretted leaving it, leaving her daughter behind with a white couple as Charles had once related to him. What had that done to Elizabeth, to Annie Mae, to the both of them? The answer was probably lost to time just as so many longleafs had been lost to crosscut saws.

Charles re-enters the room and sits back down with folders in his hands. He opens the top one. "I want to show you this. It's a photograph I found online and printed about a year ago."

Seth reaches for it, holds the photograph by its edges, and sees an old man in stark black and white with a fierce expression and a moderately long beard. He is sitting, and a short, squat woman with her hair pulled away from her face and tied in a bun at the back of her head stands beside him, a hand on his shoulder. The photograph was clearly taken in the 1800s against a white backdrop, probably in some photographer's studio.

"Those are Rafe Anderson's parents," Charles says. "His name was also Rafe. That's how I found it. First thought I'd come across what I was looking for. Then realized my mistake. Searching for my great-grandfather I discovered my great-great. Taken in Durham in the 1870s. Her name was Lula." He hands Seth a sheet of paper. "And here's a second page where their children are listed with their birth and death dates. Notice what's missing beside the youngest son's name."

Seth looks down the list until he sees the name Rafe and finds the word *Unknown* in place of a death date. "Because he ran away," Seth says. "Whoever recorded this history had to have been a family member, and they couldn't have known what happened to him."

"But we know, don't we? And look at the father's expression again."

Seth does and then looks up at Charles, realizing they are probably thinking the same thing. "No wonder he hid down in a well. What fifteen-year-old boy would have wanted to face that? I don't think I've ever seen such fierceness."

"Maybe that explains something about who his son became."

"Maybe. We can't know," Seth says, and then considers what he knows about Rafe, the level of violence he was capable of, what Charles probably doesn't know—just how far it could reach. "So you've had this picture for a year?"

"Yes."

"You haven't mentioned it on the phone."

Charles reaches for the photograph with a claiming hand, looks at Seth while he waits to receive it, and says, "No. I wanted to wait and show it to you, wanted to see if you would come here."

Seth relinquishes the photograph. "Well, I'm here." There is a silence between them, and Seth wonders how Charles interprets those three simple words while also wondering what he means by them, an affirmation of their kinship or his being resigned to making this trip to get the information he wants?

He asks Charles now for the exact dates of birth for the two children Rafe and Elizabeth had, and then for the birth dates of the children Virginia Henry bore him. Seth has brought with him a list of all of Rafe and Melinda's children, and he sees with a quick glance how the birth dates of Rafe's outside children are staggered through the birth dates of his children with Melinda—the ones who lived, the ones who died young, and the ones who were never named. He has, of course, known for many years how poor a husband his great-great grandfather was, but seeing the list he's just made of Rafe's other children beside his "real" children—and at the moment he can't help feeling this way, making this hard distinction even though he knows it's wrong—reminds him in such a visceral way just how terrible a husband and man Rafe was, though fathering children outside his marriage is only a footnote in the history of his greater sins.

Seth scans his list of children a second time. He sees again the two notated by the simple word "unnamed" and wonders exactly how they died, knows how Charles *thinks* they died, and, maybe because some part of him wants to get into this subject, asks what might sound like a harmless enough question but realizes how much lies behind it, but he still can't stop himself. "I wonder what their names would have been?"

"Whose?" Charles asks, clearly not understanding.

Seth is turned away from him; he is looking out at the longleaf pines beyond the window, at their height and sentinel-like presence, as if they bear witness to the greater loss that took place around them. "The two unnamed children of Rafe and Melinda," he says and still doesn't look at Charles. Finally, it's Charles's long silence that makes Seth face him, a silence that surprises Seth and seems to promise something.

Charles remains quiet another moment, then speaks. "The last one was named Jacob," he says.

Seth knows he is wide-eyed. "How do you know?"

Charles leans forward. "Through Annie Mae. Remember, she delivered the child." He goes silent again, and Seth knows he must want to add, "And she helped cover up its death, for Melinda." Now Charles says, "She heard Melinda speak it, but Melinda didn't want the name known."

"Why? From what you told me, the child lived several days. Why wouldn't she have given him a name and already have written it in the Bible, if it lived that long?"

"Because of a Choctaw custom."

"What?"

"Annie Mae had told her of a custom she learned through her mother that forbade the name of a child who died to ever be spoken again."

"Why would that have anything to do with Melinda?"

"Maybe Melinda followed the custom just to spite Rafe. That's the story that came down through the family. She told Rafe she wouldn't name the child until the naming ceremony, another old custom of Annie Mae's. It was always done a few days after the birth. But Melinda of course had already…" Charles stops himself, though Seth knows again what he wants to say, that Melinda had already planned to kill the child. But that begs the question, Seth realizes. Why would Melinda ever have even quietly named a child she planned to kill? It doesn't follow, and Seth wants to say this now, but he holds himself back.

"What about the other unnamed child?" he asks.

"That one I don't know," Charles says.

"But you think Melinda killed them both?"

Charles nods his head. "She did." From what Seth can tell, he takes no pleasure in his answer, but there's a level of conviction in his voice that maybe suggests a pride of knowledge. "I do know one other thing I could tell you," Charles adds.

"What?" he asks, feeling himself growing anxious.

"Rafe went to a conjure woman after that second death."

"Why did he do that? What could he possibly have wanted? From what we know of him, that doesn't sound like something he'd do."

Charles seems to study Seth for a minute, as if he wants to interpret his tone and expression. "Maybe I've said too much. You might not be ready to hear this."

"Now I really want to know."

Charles takes a breath and slowly releases it. "You're going to have to forgive me. And anyway, it's not as if those conjure women had any real power. Nothing happened."

"So you won't tell me?"

"Maybe some other time. There's plenty other history we can talk about."

"True enough," Seth says, but he's more than annoyed and knows he has to hide it, but it grows worse when he considers the charges of infanticide Charles has made against Melinda. Easy enough to blame the deaths on the white mother, he thinks, whose blood you don't carry. "I may have some history for you that you aren't aware of."

"Really?" Charles says and seems surprised. "Something you've learned lately?"

Seth shakes his head. "Known since I was a boy."

"I'm listening. Want to know all I can, too."

Maybe not, Seth thinks. He's not sure where to begin but does. "During Reconstruction, about 1870, there was what my grandfather always referred to as an uprising." Seth pauses, remembers the sound of his grandfather's voice, his matter-of-fact, casual tone, and the term he actually used, "nigger uprising." "Former slaves, most of them in the Freedman's Bureau I would imagine, got tired of bad treatment and could see the old order coming back to power. I don't know the particulars of their reasons, but whatever they were, a large group of Black men banded together near where the steam plant is now on the Black Fork River, planned to march on Riverfield and kill white people. I don't know if they had white men in mind, or certain white men, or all white people."

He sees that Charles is listening most intently, his head turned at an angle so that he's not looking directly at Seth. It's as if Charles wants only to hear the words and not see any gesture or expression that might distort the essentials of what he's taking in. Maybe he's imagining those men, wondering if he would have been among them or if his white blood might have made a difference in the balance of his choices.

"But they never had a chance to begin," Seth says. "Rafe Anderson got word of it."

Charles's expression turns grave. "How?" he asks.

"Through March Whitney." Seth doesn't have to explain who this is. He and Charles found some time ago they both knew of the relationship between Rafe and March, both knew Whitney was buried somewhere in the white graveyard beneath a natural stone without markings. But Charles never made mention of how Whitney died; he did not ask, and Seth never brought up the subject. He does now, though. "He was killed for trying to get the warning out, and his wife was the one who finally made her way to Rafe. His wife, Rebecca, was the sister of Virginia Henry."

"That I didn't know," Charles says, "or that March was killed. I never thought about how he died."

Seth nods, wondering if his own knowledge makes him appear self-satisfied. "So Rafe gathered men," he says, "and led them against the group down near the river who were planning on the uprising." He pauses, maybe for dramatic effect, maybe because he wants Charles to have to ask what happened, or maybe he regrets he began this story now that he's so close to the bloody truth. The fact of it is a burden, really, if one believes at all in the sins of the father, and Seth knows he's about to place this burden on Charles, and that for Charles the burden will have to be greater because he carries the blood of both sides in him.

Charles doesn't ask but merely waits, as if he refuses to participate in what Seth is doing.

"There was a gun battle," Seth says finally. "Two or three white men were killed." He pauses again, this time because he does regret what he chose to do. But unlike Charles, who changed his mind and withheld the story he began, Seth makes himself say the words. "All the Black men were killed."

Charles remains quiet at first. He is looking down at the floor and then peers out of the large window. Finally he looks back at Seth. "Why did you tell me this?"

"I guess all families have their truths, and if we care about history we have to know them, even when it's a shameful history."

Charles nods slowly. He looks as if he's waiting for Seth to say more, as if he knows Seth hasn't answered the question fully, is not being completely honest, even with all of his talk about truth. Seth holds Charles's gaze and won't allow himself to look away. "Odd," Charles says, "that Rafe took part in such killing of Black people and then had children with women of color. Hard to reconcile."

"I suppose it is. Those men down on the river did plan slaughter, though, if there's truth in the story. It had to be stopped. And it was March who tried to warn Rafe. Virginia Henry must have had some understanding of that. After all, it was her sister who ended up getting word to him. Elizabeth didn't arrive until years after the thing happened. She might not ever have known about it or didn't know until she and Rafe were already together. Besides, the world doesn't live by any perfect moral code. People are full of contradictions in the ways they think and act. When people look at racial history, they want to dismiss the paradoxes, or don't even see them. But maybe it's in those paradoxes where truth really lies."

"Now you really sound like an historian. Are you lecturing me?" Charles asks but doesn't wait for an answer. "Funny how when the word 'truth' gets thrown around it can start to sound hollow."

Seth looks away a moment, hoping not to show his irritation, but he knows Charles is right. "Forgive me for getting too far into the abstract. I know we're talking about people who really lived and breathed and whose blood we carry."

"So your grandfather told you about this?"

"And father. I may be one of only a few people who know it happened. All the older people who knew are dead now. My cousin Andrew, Bunyan's son, who didn't have children and who died several years ago, he knew. Said when the foundations for the steam plant were dug back in the late 1950s, they unearthed the bones of a mass grave. There was a newspaper article about it that speculated about who the bones belonged to, but no answers. Cousin Andrew said, 'Hell, I knew who them bones belonged to.'"

Charles is quiet again, for some time, then seems to have decided something. "All right, I'll tell you," he says.

"Tell me what?"

"Why Rafe went to a conjure woman. You know, since we're telling everything and not holding back."

"All right. I said I wanted to know, and I do." He feels anxious again, realizes why Charles will tell him now, figures whatever it is, Charles intends on making it sound as bad as possible. They are using history against each other.

"After Rafe found out Melinda killed his children, he had a curse placed on her that was supposed to bring on early death. And he asked the woman to place protection around their other children."

"Protection from who?"

"From Melinda," Charles says.

"You're telling me he thought she would kill her older children, some who were almost grown?"

"I don't know. Maybe he just wanted to protect them from any kind of harm, wanted to guard against the loss of more of them. But like I said, it's not like there was anything real about hoodoo. It was all based on fear and superstition. Melinda *didn't* get sick and die. What Rafe did was move out of the house and into Betsy's cabin."

"He did? How do you know that?"

"It's all come down through the family."

"Just like that story about Melinda untying the umbilical cords?"

Charles nods. "That's right."

Seth hesitates for a moment. He tells himself he should let go of this argument they are pretending not to have. But he can't and wonders what he hopes to gain. "After you told me what she did," he begins, "I spent a lot of time thinking about it and hated to think she could have murdered her own children."

"Guess we don't want to know our own blood kin are capable of such things. But like you said, all families have their…"

Seth realizes he is sitting on the front edge of his chair, that his posture must appear unbending. "I ended up talking to a midwife about it, a woman my wife happens to know. Midwives are still around. They have to be licensed now. She told me the blood coagulates fairly quickly where the umbilical cord is tied, that untying it after a day or two wouldn't cause any bleeding. No child would bleed to death from that. There wouldn't be any blood."

Charles studies him again. "So what's your point?"

Seth knows he has to be careful here, doesn't want to offend or anger, and he *doesn't* want to create an ugly scene. He is a guest in Charles's house and still plans to spend the night. "It's just that what she told me seems to mean the death of the children couldn't have happened the way you described it."

Charles looks as if he's considering what he's heard. "Maybe your great-great grandmother untied their cords as soon as she was alone with them."

"Or maybe what you describe didn't happen at all. It could be Melinda didn't murder her children."

Charles appears as if he's about to stand. "Would be nice for you to think so, wouldn't it?"

"The fact that they couldn't have died days later from having their cords untied makes me question the story, but not you. If you understand what I mean. You must be able to see why I would question it."

"Oh, I think I can see. But those children were killed."

"If they were," Seth says, "how do we know Melinda did it? Maybe it was Annie Mae."

"So you want to blame it on the help? Why would Annie Mae have done it? Betsy was their wet nurse. Maybe *she* did it," Charles says in a tone that Seth knows is meant to mock his speculation, but Charles quickly goes silent; he seems to consider what he's just heard himself say, and all speech has left him for the moment, leaving him with the same thoughts probably that have come to Seth.

"You never told me she was their wet nurse," Seth says. "Hard to imagine Melinda would have allowed that. If she nursed them, the children must have lived a *few* days. But there's only the two days' dates for each of them in the old Bible, the days they were born and died, less than twenty-four hours."

"I guess we can't know," Charles says.

Or don't want to know, Seth thinks, but says, simply enough, "So Elizabeth would have had access to them. If she was their wet nurse."

"So you want to blame Betsy?"

Seth knows he can't back away from what was obviously his meaning. "She would have had motive," he says, and then adds, "at the very least."

"Yes, at the very least," Charles repeats.

Seth decides he's made his point and that backing away from it will be the polite thing to do, but he knows, too, that a feigned politeness will only underscore his point. "Or maybe it was SIDS," he says.

Charles looks directly at him again. "You want to think it was Betsy."

Seth hoped it wasn't so obvious, but Charles is right. He does want to blame her and realizes all the motives he might have for doing so, even if he doesn't want to contemplate them all and what they might say about him. "We can't know," he manages and realizes how weak the words sound.

"But you can write it any way you want, can't you?"

"This isn't something I'd write. Besides, I don't write fiction, I write history."

"And I imagine history can pretty easily become facts arranged as lies, of omission and even commission. You're bound to have read enough history to know that white historians have been guilty of that, wanting to hide all those uncomfortable sins of the past, or at least explain them in a way that makes them more palatable. You say you don't want to write 'this.' Which 'this' do you mean, the uprising or the acts of infanticide? And by *not* writing either one, aren't you lying?"

"Do you want me to write them? Either one?"

"You'll just write them your way."

"And my way would be lies?" Seth asks.

Charles looks away, as if he can't bear the conversation any longer. He doesn't answer with words. Seth sees the hardness leave Charles's face, and what replaces it is a clear and deep sadness that Seth begins to feel now also, one born out of his own faults and failures that Charles must be recognizing, and beyond them perhaps the failures inherent within the generations before both Charles and him that have brought the two of them to this point with an inevitability that is silencing.

EIGHTEEN

Earlier that morning Annie Mae had made the short walk to the kitchen from her daughter's cabin where she'd spent a restless night. It wasn't having to lie on a different mattress that had made sleep difficult, but despite the fact that she'd been in her daughter's bed—heard her breath, abided her movements, felt warmth from her body and all the closeness that would be a comfort to most mothers, even with a grown child—she felt she was lying next to someone whose blood was not born of her blood, whose speech was not hers, whose lighter skin had allowed her daughter to pass into a realm where Annie Mae could not follow. And also to know that where she was lying was the place where a white man, a buckra, often lay made her ill at ease, as if she were trespassing. And yet in her wakefulness she'd been grateful for the chance to reach toward her daughter in spirit if not in body—though their limbs did sometimes touch. She'd also found solace in knowing the two children were there, close and safe within the cabin walls, even while she remembered that the outside of those walls had once been stained with a color meant to mark harmful intent.

So the night had been difficult, and this morning there'd been work. Annie Mae had fed all of Melinda's children their breakfasts before they left for school, but she had not seen Melinda herself. Now she heard the dogtrot door open, felt a tightening within her stomach and chest that had become all too familiar to her, and when she finally prepared herself to turn toward the open kitchen door, she saw not Melinda but Rafe, and one look at him made her feel a deeper tightness in her chest, something akin to pleurisy.

"Miss Melinda hasn't been up yet," she said, hoping to somehow avert his attention away from herself and toward a concern for Melinda, but she knew Rafe could never be diverted by concern for anyone, certainly not once he was filled with his own concerns, as he appeared to be now. She stood with her back against a tall cabinet. He still had on his Inverness, the great coat looking worn with use. He hadn't taken the time to remove it upon entering, and she wondered how big a hurry he'd been in, if maybe he hadn't even put Wheeler in the barn yet, the horse still tied out front.

"I've just come from seeing Virginia in town. I know I don't have to explain to you who that is," he said, "since you've already gone and made her acquaintance, improperly enough, I have to add."

"I did," she said quickly and with some force behind her simple words, a way of inserting herself, making a firm place inside his harangue, which she knew was coming.

"My business is not your concern," he said. "And Virginia Henry is my business, not yours, though I know why you might think otherwise. But you are not to speak to her again. I'll contend with her. And right now, you've got to contend with me. You understand?" He paused a moment, apparently to consider how he might best proceed, and Annie Mae feared what was next, felt she knew. The known could be just as frightening as the unknown, if a terrible truth lay at the heart of it. "I'm coming to you first. I want to hear your answer. And here's my question. Do you think Miss Melinda killed that child, and the one before it?"

She felt caught. She understood exactly why he'd asked the question this way, though it wasn't the real question and they both knew it. He was going to shut one door after another on her. No matter what she might feel toward Melinda right now, she could not accuse her of something she knew Melinda hadn't done. He was counting on this, her inability to tell a complete lie. "No, I don't think she would ever do such as that. She love her children." Then she risked her own question. "What make you think both them children was killed?"

He shook his head as if in disgust. "You already know the answer to that. It's why you made your trip to town. Don't talk to me like I'm a fool."

"I ain't. I know better," she said.

"You *know* plenty." He looked at her as if he were more than certain of this, as if he knew exactly what she knew, what she had done, but she couldn't help but try to keep him from shutting another door.

"Sometimes new babies die. I been bringing them into the world a long time, and I seen them leave it quick. Ain't nobody's fault."

He neared the stove, opened his coat, perhaps wanting the heat for some deeper part of himself. "All these babies you delivered, ever had a woman, white or Black, ask you to get rid of one, a woman that maybe already had ten or twelve children and couldn't take care of another one, knew another might drive her to madness?"

Now she lied, said *no* without hesitating. Her instinct to protect every nameless, desperate woman she'd ever known—who'd ever confided in her though pain and blood and tears from so deep the salt in them must have burned their own faces—was too strong to go against.

"I don't believe you," he said, "but my real question is have you ever done it?"

"No, sir. I never done such a thing, and wouldn't never," she said. She simply couldn't lie and say she had, though she knew he'd shut another door on her, shut it just as firmly as the cabinet door she was pinned against.

"So Miss Melinda didn't do it, and you didn't do it." He nodded his head slowly, as if he were working through and confirming his own complex logic, was trying to see where it would take him next if only he had the wisdom to see. "When you had babies die on you, what did you do? I mean besides that Choctaw foolishness of telling their mothers not to say their names?"

"Don't know what you mean, What I do?"

"With their bodies."

She understood now, felt yet another door closing but had to give the answer she knew was true because it was the only answer. "I cleaned them up, swaddled them in whatever I could that was clean. Couldn't have no child buried in dirty rags."

"So did you clean up Miss Melinda's last two children?"

"Yes, sir." She realized how quietly she spoke. "'Course I did."

"And did you see anything wrong with either of them? Because if something was wrong, you *would* have seen it."

There was no time to hesitate. She made herself think only of the first one, who'd also been a boy, and she let her answer for him be the answer for both children. "No, sir. There wasn't nothing wrong." It was a half-truth, and she made herself believe the half of it hard enough to widen it, without stint, to cover Betsy, her grown child now swaddled in half a truth; but Annie Mae knew half could never be enough.

She watched Rafe take in her answer and study her. She knew he could see the unanswered half and would not let it pass for the whole. "Tell me," he said, "did you ever bring Betsy into this house? I mean before the other child died." The question did not surprise her, nothing he asked now would, but she still had the presence of mind to tell as much of the truth as she could.

"I let her in the kitchen sometime, when she might have something to tell me, so she knock."

"That ain't what I asked. Did you ever bring her in? Maybe to help you with some chore? After that maybe she started thinking she could come in when she wanted."

He waited now. She shifted her weight, looked down at the floor, then back up at him, and the very weight of his delay, the biding of his time, was heavy on her. "Sometime, like you say, when the work be too much."

He sighed, as if this chore of questioning her was becoming as tiresome as her answers. "I've never seen any work that was too much for you. I've seen you dig a grave, remember, when the top of the ground was frozen."

"Yes, sir," she said. "But I've brung her in. You know she was in this kitchen when you heard her and Miss Melinda argue, or you saw Miss Melinda right after they did." Then she added, because she felt she had to: "And I brung her in to nurse the last child 'cause Miss Melinda so tired." She hesitated a moment. "I watched her nurse." She hated to tell the lie at the end.

"I know that. Did you bring Betsy *back* in, or did she come back on her own, maybe slip in?"

"No, sir. She didn't want to come in at all. Never want to if she think Miss Melinda home, not ever."

He paused again, seeming to consider this and to see truth in it. But he shook his head, rejecting her logic, it appeared, because he knew, as she knew, that no one always did what made sense, least of all a woman who knew she could never completely unseat a wife, not when the wife was white and did not have to pass as white. And Annie Mae could not say to him, I *made* her come in the house that last time, pushed her into the room where Melinda lay asleep and the baby hungry. And so how much of the blame was her own? Annie Mae wondered again. What if she hadn't made Betsy come in, would the baby be alive now?

"No," he said aloud. Maybe he was repeating her *no*, agreeing with her, but he shook his head again finally, his disagreement all too clear.

"Why come to me?" she asked him, perhaps to simply keep him from asking his next question and realized as she spoke what she was really saying was, Why not go straight to Betsy? So here she stood, pointing him toward her daughter while all the while she'd been telling herself that was what she was trying *not* to do but failing with every answer, and now she was failing with a question.

"Because I want to know as much as I can before I go to her. So she'll *have* to answer and not put on that mask of hers."

"And so you can shut doors on her," Annie Mae said before she could stop herself, but did manage to keep from saying *Like you're doing to me*, though from what she could see of his expression he heard that too, as loudly as she heard it within herself, and understood what she meant on both counts.

Neither of them spoke for a moment, and then Annie Mae heard not a voice but a sound she didn't want to hear: the opening and closing of a door and footsteps across the floorboards, footsteps too heavy to be Philip's. She would have to face them at the same time now. Would they come together against her, or would Melinda stand apart from him, only here for herself, level her own charges and not care what her husband said or did? She noticed Melinda wore a dark blue dress she'd never seen before, one that fit her in such a way as to make her body appear shaped differently. Her hair was up, her eyes with their own light in them, not heavy with sleep, and Melinda looked from one to the other of them, seeing clearly that she'd walked into a tangled moment. "What is it?" she said. "Has Annie Mae told you?"

Rafe, already aware of her presence, turned toward her. "Told me what?"

Annie Mae saw Melinda hesitate, but only for a moment. "That she's moved out of her room and into the cabin with her daughter."

"No," he said, "I was not aware. When?"

"Two days ago," Melinda said with what sounded like some small surprise that he hadn't found this out yet on his own.

Annie Mae watched Rafe, expected him to ask why, but he didn't, maybe deciding, as best she could reason, that he already knew why, figuring Melinda had become bold enough to put an obstacle in his way, and he would wait to take this up with her when Annie Mae wasn't there to witness it. Or would he simply throw her out of the cabin, leaving her no place to live? The both of them looked at her, and she felt as if the answer to her earlier question of their uniting was coming clear, yet Melinda didn't move near him but continued to stand separate.

Rafe stepped away from the stove, having gathered more than enough of its heat, it seemed, and turned again to Melinda. "Have you ever seen her alone in this house?" he asked, as if Betsy's name had already been spoken. "See her maybe a second time that night she nursed the last child?"

Melinda remained motionless, unreadable, and Annie Mae shut her eyes, caught a brief moment of darkness within them, and hoped in the dark of that night from months before that Melinda's eyes had been closed into sleep, had not actually seen Betsy in her room again, had only reasoned out her suspicions and hadn't beheld what she might tell Rafe now. Melinda moved closer to the stove, or maybe a step closer to Annie Mae, who met her eyes and would not let herself look away. She would face what came.

Melinda pulled at the sleeves of her dress, as if the material felt unfamiliar to her. "I thought maybe I heard her one night, years ago, after she first came here, but I don't know. And I only saw her the one time that night, when Annie Mae brought her in to nurse."

Annie Mae watched Rafe study Melinda, weighing her words, it seemed, against her expression and the way she held her body. Melinda remained silent, immovable, even impenetrable. Then Melinda looked toward her, and Annie Mae saw no favor there. Yet with only a few words she could have condemned Betsy beyond doubt, whether she spoke words of lies or truth. Each could have led to the same end, whatever end Melinda wanted.

Rafe slowly nodded, as if he understood all, or all he needed, or merely wanted. "I have Wheeler tied out front. I may or may not come back inside. Neither one of you are to leave this house until I either enter it again or you see my horse gone. Do you understand?"

"Yes, sir," Annie Mae said, a sickness rising up inside her within the breath it took to speak the words, and within the thought of what he might do next, now that he was done with the two of them. She watched Melinda acknowledge the command without need of speaking.

"Annie Mae, I don't care where you sleep tonight," Rafe said, then moved toward the back door and went out it.

Annie Mae heard his boots cross the porch and descend the steps. She turned and looked out the back window, and he appeared within its frame, walking toward Betsy's cabin, where she knew he was headed without knowing exactly his intentions. If she had to, she would follow him there, despite her answer to him. It depended on what she might see from the window, and if she saw nothing, she would take that as a hopeful sign that he wouldn't throw Betsy out, that he wouldn't do her harm. She did not want, tried not to allow herself, to think what no sight of them outside the cabin could mean—that Rafe might act with a swift and terrible mercy. There were two children inside, after all. Surely... And Melinda had confirmed nothing for him.

Annie Mae turned to her and saw Melinda looking not out the window but directly at her, as if she expected a question from Annie Mae. Instead, Annie Mae simply spoke what was true. "You could have told him anything you wanted."

"Yes, I could have," Melinda said. "And I could have told him the truth."

"What would that have been, if you'd told it?"

Melinda looked at her as if from the other side of a wide road that was guarded by riders and could not be crossed, but the two of them could still see each other's features clearly across the distance. No shadows fell over them, only a yielding light on their faces. "I saw Elizabeth twice that night in my room, saw her with the child, and I did *nothing* either time. Nothing at all. Do you hear me? If I had only told her to get out, as I should have." Now the light went from her face, and she cast her eyes downward, as if she were looking for herself and saw that she lay across the ground and was sullied so badly by the earth she could not bear to see herself.

Annie Mae felt their kinship, the blood between them, a child's blood. If only she had not brought Betsy in and Melinda had thrown her out soon enough. It was their own sense of guilt that had not stopped bleeding its way out of them, that could never clot, the wound never to be cauterized. And they could not minister to each other, not any longer.

"Why didn't you tell him?" Annie Mae asked. "You know the truth."

"Because he'd have blamed me for not putting her out. And he'll do whatever he's already decided to do. Nothing I said would've made any difference at all, not months ago, not now."

"Was you quiet for me too? Lied for my sake? 'Cause she my daughter, and that all you could do?" Melinda looked away, her lips closed against any words. Annie Mae knew asking again would not help, and so she didn't. "I cleaned the child up," she said. "There was some blood. That what took me so long while you waited in my room. But there wasn't enough for him to have bled to death."

Annie Mae saw that Melinda showed no surprise, as if she already knew what she was being told. "Where did the blood come from? How?"

"She must of pulled the cord stump, tore it a little down at the belly where the skin real tender, thin. It'll break easy-like there, but not bleed all out."

Melinda was silent, but Annie Mae could see there was another question coming, and she knew what it was. "On purpose?"

She looked out the window a moment and saw no sign of Rafe; he must have entered the cabin. "I don't know. Maybe not." This was all she could make herself say. How close it was to a lie or to the truth she didn't want to think about. And she could not know for certain if her daughter had then taken the child's breath, smothering him. She hid inside this uncertainty, at least for the moment, from herself and now from Melinda, who looked at her with what might be pity but not forgiveness.

Once she was alone in the kitchen, Annie Mae stood at the window and kept close watch, but no one emerged from the cabin. The clock in the living room soon struck the hour and time seemed to stretch itself. Her mother had told her long ago there were no hours, that they were a white man's invention. For a Choctaw time was lines in the dirt, drawn so they did not cross, and how long something might take could be measured by how close or far the lines were drawn and how long it took a shadow to reach that second line. In her mind now there was only the first line in the dirt, the second one undrawn and clock time had become meaningless. Finally she became too restless for the kitchen to contain her and her heated worry. Despite what Rafe had said, she walked out the back door and down the steps, and each of her own steps came more quickly as she moved through the backyard and toward the cabin. When she neared it, little George came running out, aiming himself at her.

"What?" she said when he grabbed and hugged her legs.

"Mama, she on the floor, crying." He could not catch his breath now, though it couldn't have been from his running. He hadn't run that far. It was fear, she knew, and a confusion he could not outrun. Then she made out the words "Papa, he standing over her." There were more words after that, but she could not understand them.

She turned and saw Philip standing near them, hands deep in his empty pockets, as if he needed to fill them with something and his small fists were all he had.

"You go on in the house," Annie Mae said. "Go see your mama."

She left him behind her, George too, but she knew George might follow, and she couldn't take the time to stop him.

The only crying she heard when she entered the cabin was Lakeview's, who lay on a blanket on the bed, her round face tightened into her sobs, which came without her knowing why, only that something was happening that wasn't right, which any infant could feel and hear in the midst of a loud, puzzling commotion. Then she spotted her daughter in the corner, her back against the joints of the logs, with Rafe standing above her. Annie Mae's vision was quickly drawn to the flash of the long-blade knife in his hand, not held at Betsy's throat but at the side of her head, and Anne Mae screamed, no words, only a sound that filled the cabin and drowned out Lakeview's crying.

Rafe turned toward her, only now aware of her, his free hand still holding the shock of Betsy's long, braided hair. "Hush your screaming. I'm not going to kill her. Or cut her, not where she'll bleed."

Annie Mae wanted to rush him, but if she did, what would he do? A buckra's words meant nothing, his promise even less. "Leave her be," she said.

"She will not answer me, and she'll have to pay for that, and for so much more." He turned away from Anne Mae then as if she no longer existed, tightened his grip on Betsy's hair and pulled so hard it bent her neck. He cut downward with the bright, steel blade, and as sharp as it must be, he still had to saw through the thick braid where it protruded from her scalp. Then he held it in his hand.

Anne Mae understood all that was now shorn from her daughter, felt the pain of it, heard Betsy crying, the rawness in the sound, and knew the ordeal still wasn't over. He grabbed the other braid, twisted her neck, then wrenched it farther with another jerking of his hand, began to cut and saw down through the second braid.

George came running past Annie Mae, too fast for her to grab him, and she watched as he began to pound on his father's legs and backside with his fists, his own courage shaming her. Rafe pulled the braid free, dropped it on the floor with the other, and stepped away from Betsy and his son. He looked at Anne Mae, hard-faced and silent at first, holding the knife turned upward so that the length of the blade lay against the inside of his forearm, maybe to show its honed edge held no more danger. "I told you I wouldn't hurt her," he said. Annie Mae merely shook her head, felt helpless and at a loss before him. Then to George he said, "I'm sorry, son, but sometimes a man has to do a hard but necessary thing. One day you'll understand that if you grow into the man I hope you'll be." He walked past George, did not try to touch him, and once at the door turned back toward the room he was about to take leave of.

"Do not spend another night in this cabin, Betsy," he said. "Be gone from it, but send me word of where you are. I will see my children. They are mine. I do not let go of what belongs to me."

Annie Mae heard a whimper from her daughter, and then watched Rafe walk through the open door and slowly close it behind him, as if with the gentle closing of the door he'd offered a polite final gesture.

Betsy slumped forward now, from what had to be both exhaustion and despair. Annie Mae saw the jagged remains at the sides of her daughter's head, her pale, thin neck exposed, as if Rafe had wanted, at least in part, to prove her as vulnerable as an infant, and Annie Mae felt at the moment she could see the child she'd once known, had given birth to. The vision was a small gift, though it was delivered through meanness. Then Betsy raised her head and Annie Mae was not certain who she saw. She beheld a young woman who might be anyone, capable of anything. Her daughter then seemed to search the floor, found what she sought, and carefully picked up each severed braid of hair.

Annie Mae went to Betsy, kneeled down to her, and took the lengths of hair into her own hands, tugging at them lightly until Betsy reluctantly let go. Then Betsy placed her hands over her head, as if she could not bear the ugliness she imagined. Anne Mae studied her daughter's face as best she could through her raised arms. She saw no marks or swelling on Betsy's face, but a body could take punishment, and blood didn't always have to show itself to mean there wasn't bleeding. Sometimes the worst injuries didn't show. Blood could leak on the inside, where all pain lived.

"What all did he say before I come in?" Annie Mae asked, and what she meant was, What did he accuse you of? But they both knew the real question, and the answer. What she wanted was to see how much her daughter would tell her, if maybe this time she would finally tell it all.

"He kept saying, 'If not for these children here. If not for these children here.'" Betsy spoke through her hands and arms, hiding herself still, hiding all she could. "And I said, 'Send them out then, so they won't see. Then do what you want.'"

"He hit you?" Annie Mae asked.

Betsy shook her head. "He kept talking real quiet. Like I'd never heard him sound before."

Annie Mae looked over her shoulder. George stood just behind her, where she'd expected to see him. "Your mama gon' be all right," she said. "You don't have to worry none. I'm here. So you go on outside, let me see to things." George didn't speak or move. "Come here to me," she said, and he came, letting himself fall into her arms. Still on her knees, she was able to look him directly in his face as she wiped tears from beneath his large brown eyes. While she knew whose white blood ran through him, she knew hers did too; she knew this sweet boy was not his father's son, that who his father was did not matter, no matter that he carried the same end name as the man. She kept holding him tight, breathing in the scent of him. "You hear me now? I said it gon' be all right." He nodded his head and his tears had stopped. Lakeview had also stopped crying. "You go on outside now. Let me take care of your mama."

She let him go, and he went out the door but not before looking back at her one last time, needing to know again that his mother would be all right. Annie Mae nodded her head, slowly, offering assurance to him that she knew the shape of things to come even as she could see within her vision the bent shape of her daughter, the tangle of arms and hands she kept over her face and head.

"Were you thinking," she said now to Betsy, "that he was going to kill you?"

Her daughter moved her hands away from her face and looked at her mother. "At first."

Annie Mae wanted the question she was about to ask to shock her daughter, maybe jolt her into the truth. So she asked it: "Would you of deserved it?" She saw her daughter's eyes fill with tears that would not shed but remained caught in a thin layer, like curved glass that distorted not her daughter's vision but the sight of her eyes and what they held within them.

"Would you have wanted that?" Betsy said. "For me to be killed, and to deserve it?"

"Of course not. How could I *ever* want that?"

"Then why ask?"

"'Cause I want to know, want to hear you say it. Did you hurt them babies?" She stared at her daughter, at her cropped hair and the way it had re-shaped her face.

"You want to believe that, think that of me?"

"That no answer. And tell me, why wouldn't you give Rafe an answer?"

Betsy's arms were at her sides now. She was making no effort to cover herself. "Why answer something he thinks he already knows, especially when what he thinks comes from a woman he trusts more than me?"

"All you doing is answering me with questions. You mean that Virginia Henry."

Betsy merely nodded at first. "Why would he trust a woman who hates me for taking him from her?"

"I went to see her too," Annie Mae said and looked at Betsy with what she knew some might see as coldness, but she could not help herself, couldn't help the distance she felt toward her daughter, even after what her daughter had just been through.

Betsy's face showed surprise. "And so you believe her too? That's why you went to her. So you could let her prove to you I did what she said."

Annie Mae didn't look at Betsy but instead took up again one of the lengths of her daughter's hair that she'd earlier placed aside. She held one end tight in her right hand and ran the braid through the loosely closed fingers of her left, as if in doing so she might touch some lost part of her daughter, or find some trace of her that might be within her still, some goodness, maybe. "I went to protect you. To stop her from talking," she said finally.

Betsy looked at her as if *she'd* been the one shorn and who now sat exposed. "That's just what you *want* to believe."

Annie Mae stilled her hands but could still feel the smooth rope of Betsy's hair, and she decided that at some point every mother must hear from a daughter a truth she can't admit to, not even know it was a truth until she heard it spoken. "I shouldn't of made you go in Melinda's room that night, shouldn't of made you nurse that child." It was all she knew to say.

"No, you shouldn't have, but not for the reason you think. You shouldn't have done that to me, asked that of me. Of course, you didn't really ask. You pushed me in there, made me. Melinda was more important to you than I was."

Anne Mae dropped the length of hair back onto the floor, the braid loosening at the thicker end. "So you punished me by what you done. Punished all of us."

"I told you, I *didn't* kill that child."

Betsy continued to look at her as if she were as puzzled by her mother as Annie Mae was by her. She saw then that her daughter's tears were gone and not because they had been shed. They seemed to have simply evaporated, and all Annie Mae saw in her daughter's eyes now was a dry hardness that was maybe brought on by a mother who doubted and an absence of trust between the two of them, or maybe it was something more frightening that not even a mother could continue to forgive, though the act of punishment was beyond Annie Mae. She was unable to think what she might do.

But she could talk to her daughter, she decided, could say the words she'd once heard from her own mother, pass them down, and if Betsy heard them as a judgment maybe that would be its own punishment.

"Your grandmother had a brother," she began, "had many brothers, but only one she never spoke of by name. Do you know what that means?" Betsy nodded slowly, giving only the barest confirmation that she was listening. "He let hisself be killed." Annie Mae waited for Betsy to ask why, but her daughter wouldn't speak. "It was the custom, the way things had to be done. If not, it brought too much shame." She paused, letting the last word stand alone for a moment. Still no word from Betsy, only stillness and silence. "He killed somebody else in the tribe. With a knife. I don't know why." Annie Mae spoke quietly, just as her mother had the one time she told this story. "He went home, told what happened, and sat down by a fire. He never stood up again. Sat there all night and into the next day. Said they could come for him when they was ready. He didn't have to do that, didn't have to wait for death. But when the time came, he let it come." Annie Mae stopped for a moment, wanted to remember the sound and sorrow in her mother's voice. Then she began again, wanting to explain carefully. "If a murder was done, it had to be answered with a death. If it wasn't, if the killer ran, then the family of the one what had done the killing was shamed. And the other family," she said, "the family of the one what was killed, could revenge the death by killing anyone else in the family of the killer."

Betsy was not ignoring her now. She was staring. "I know of the custom," she said. She paused, felt at her jagged hair as if what was missing was a limb or some more basic piece of herself. "What would you have me do?" Betsy said. "Be killed? Is that why you let Rafe come to me and were so slow to follow him?"

"No, never. But maybe it's why I asked if you would of deserved it."

Annie Mae saw Betsy reach for the two braids of her hair and tighten her fists around them; yet it was Annie Mae who felt caught in a desperate grip that was no touch at all, only Betsy's own punishment, which she accepted with silence, the reckoning between a mother and daughter an old story that did not need words to be passed down.

NINETEEN

In the back room of the hotel that night, he lost hundreds of dollars and did not care. As soon as he realized his ability for concentration was shot, he knew he would continue losing but played on to keep himself occupied. He missed a straight by one card, a flush by another, but bluffed both times and was called. When jokes were made about a black queen never showing up when you needed her, how she would always do you wrong, it took him more than a moment to realize he was not the butt of the joke, and the man who'd first made the attempt at humor, a narrow-eyed drummer he hadn't seen before, didn't realize how close he'd come to having both eyes blackened and swollen shut to the point of blindness.

Rafe drank more than he usually did but still had enough presence of mind to realize it hurt his playing even further. He finally quit both, first the drinking, then the game, and laid down what he owed.

"You retiring?" asked one man wearing spectacles that had slipped down to the end of his nose, revealing weak eyes that no one, not even the man himself, could ever trust.

Rafe realized, perhaps because of his drunkenness, how pronounced everyone's eyes had become in his vision of them, as if all were watching him, and his awareness of the fact finally made him able to concentrate so greatly he felt his perceptions were enlarged.

"If you're retiring," the drummer said and held up a card, "maybe you'd like to take her with you."

Rafe looked, saw the queen of spades.

"Even I can see," the spectacles-wearing man said, "that she's probably too dark for his taste."

"But it's those lighter ones you really can't trust," the drummer said, his eyes even narrower slits that did not seem to hold meanness but had most likely engendered it in others due to his strange appearance.

Rafe put his hand against the door frame, steadying himself. "It's a good thing we don't know each other," he said. "If we did, I'd kill you right now. So I'll take your comment as a poor joke and not an insult."

Both men, these two strangers to Rafe, looked at each other, unsure, it appeared, which of them was being addressed. Rafe let them wonder, turned, and left the room.

He had no intention this night of sending for or seeing Virginia; she had said all he needed to hear last time. The children, though, Fannie and Walter. He wanted to see them, but not in his present state. Tomorrow evening he could take them gifts, something nice, something that might even meet with Virginia's approval. He owed her that for her courage to insist on what he hadn't wanted to believe. Never mind that Betsy wouldn't admit it, not even after what had felt like hours of his berating her, threatening her to a point not many men he'd known had been able to stand. He'd finally pulled the knife on her, and when even that hadn't persuaded her to speak, he could not simply put it away in a coward's empty gesture. He'd *had* to do something, and his anger led him, showed him what to do before his brain fully registered the thought. He'd grabbed her hair on one side and because he couldn't cut straight through it, despite the sharpness of the blade, he'd sawed through while Annie Mae looked on, leaving a jagged swath across the side of her head, and what remained did not look like hair at all but some dark growth rising out of her visible scalp. Then he'd done the same to the other side of her head, and as he worked the blade, he'd felt punches in his back, the sides of small fists reaching up to hit him. He had not pushed the boy away, hadn't cursed him. He knew if he were the boy he would have done the same, or worse. So he took the small beating, then said what he had to, and left.

Rafe hadn't awakened with a headache the next morning; he had not drunk so much the night before that he had to answer for it, though he did refrain from breakfast so as to avoid any possibility of repercussion. By noon he was dressed and had eaten in the dining room, and then had himself shaved by the hotel barber, an old man whose thin fingers looked skeletal but whose hands with a razor in them were as steady as a grandfather clock's.

That afternoon he had so much time on his own hands he felt in possession of it and could do with it as he pleased. He walked the stores on the Square, choosing a white porcelain doll for Fannie and a bone-handled pocketknife for Walter. He considered several items for Virginia, including a silver comb, but then thought better of it, knowing he couldn't count on any desired reaction and deciding he would give it to Kate instead. Then he bought perfume for Bunyan. It was much later, while going to check on Wheeler at the stable, that he realized he might have chosen something for Melinda. Perhaps he would remedy that later.

After one drink and supper at a saloon, and then going back by the hotel where the desk clerk had his wrapped presents waiting for him, he walked out to the stable again and had Wheeler saddled. When he rode the horse out onto the street, Wheeler turned in the right direction without being told, as if being ridden in town at this time of the evening was command enough. And somehow Wheeler's movements seemed to suggest this was the direction he preferred himself. "Glad we're in agreement," Rafe whispered to him.

Soon he was on the porch, Wheeler tied at his stob, the presents in Rafe's hands. He heard the children's excited voices and so waited for the door to open without knocking. When it didn't he decided to wait her out. It took some time, but finally Virginia was at the door, allowing him inside.

"See you brung something with you," she said. "Look like more than broke marbles this time."

"They weren't broken when I brought them."

"But they didn't last no time," she said, closing the door.

He ignored her and could see Fannie and Walter beside the stove, where they'd obviously been told to remain, but once he squatted down and placed the wrapped presents on the floor, they couldn't contain themselves. Fannie burst forth first to hug him, which caught him a little by surprise, sure as he was that she'd grab the larger present first and hope it was hers. Instead she'd stepped so quickly over them. Then Walter was at him, both the boy's hands on Rafe's knee, almost knocking him off balance. "What you brung us, Papa?" he said, the smaller present in hand already.

"Yes, what?" Fannie said and picked up hers after releasing him from her tight, strong arms that smelled like fresh milk.

He stood and glanced at Virginia, who did not seem displeased, at least with the smiles on her children's faces. "Open them up," he said.

Fannie tore into hers, reached into the box, and pulled the doll out, stared at its perfect porcelain face and blue eyes in disbelief, as if this manufactured child, with skin beyond any white she'd ever seen, could not be real or even an illusion, but something in between and unnamable. She looked up at Rafe as though he were something new also, incomprehensible to anything in her small experience. "Papa?" she asked in growing disbelief, as if questioning both the gift and the giver's very personage.

Walter opened his more slowly, soon holding the small knife in his palm and admiring the bone handle before finally opening the blade. He then looked up at Rafe as if there were some question in his mind, too.

"Yes, it's yours," Rafe said.

"He too young for that," he heard. Virginia was beside him now.

He did not turn toward her, merely stated what was obvious. "Every boy needs a pocketknife."

"If you got it, I know how sharp it be. He cut himself."

Rafe looked at her, holding her gaze. "If he does, he does. It won't kill him. He will have this knife, and he will have it now." Rafe saw Walter take a step toward him, away from his mother, and grip the knife tight in his closed fingers, as if the boy had made a choice of his own. Rafe was glad they were in agreement.

He reached then into an inside coat pocket and handed Virginia an envelope. "I assume you'll accept this."

She took it without a word, which said clearly enough it was her due, that she wanted nothing more, nor less.

He sat down in a chair near the hearth, and the children sat close to his feet, Fannie cradling her white child with what looked like love or maybe concern, as if she questioned not whether it was hers any longer, already believing in her imagination that it was born of her, but if she had the ability to care for it, to be a good mother. Walter kept opening and closing the single blade, placing a fingertip against its point each time, perhaps the little bit of pressure pain enough to tell him it was real, and his own to keep.

Virginia sat down across from him and waited, it seemed, for whatever it was he wanted to tell her. The longer he remained silent the stronger he could read the certainty in her face that he would finally speak and tell her what she already knew by looking at him, knowing him the way she did.

"I put her out," he said, and Virginia nodded with what was surely satisfaction, though she tried to hide it. Their knowing each other as they did was not a one-sided, feminine-only knowledge, though when he could read her, he felt some entry into a side of himself he would acknowledge to no man. Admitting you understood a woman to any degree was feminine itself, a letting go of the masculine, and so a weakness.

"Is that all you done?" she said finally.

Her voice was so flat he could not tell if there was worry in it or hopefulness for something worse. "I caused her no physical pain," he said, "but if you lay eyes on her, you'll see the seriousness of my questioning of her. She answered nothing, though."

Virginia waited a moment. "Did you think she would?" It was all she asked, pretending she did not need to know, was not curious, about what he had done.

He hesitated to answer the one question at first. Then, "Yes, I did think she would."

Now Virginia was quiet again, seemed to be waiting for some other word from him, and he realized she wanted acknowledgment for what she'd helped him see. But if she couldn't see that the presents he'd brought *were* acknowledgment, he wouldn't state it for her.

"Your fire's getting low," he said, slightly annoyed as he always was when someone didn't attend to their fire. She looked and nodded absentmindedly, as though it was of little consequence, which was a further irritation to him. He rose, walked past the children's play, and stepped out onto the porch. He took his time, smelled in the cool air the smoke from other houses and heard a quiet greeting from Wheeler, one suggestive of impatience. He picked up three sticks of wood, brought them in, and noticed Virginia had left the room. He stepped between Walter and Fannie and placed the logs on the fire, and as he did what he'd just seen of the children registered in his mind, the oddness of it perhaps throwing him for the moment. He looked again and saw it was Walter who held the doll, cradling it in his arms as he'd seen his sister do, and just as Rafe was about to say that boys did *not* play with dolls, Fannie, who held the knife with two fingers as far away from the blade as she could manage, looked toward her borrowed child and cried out in a short, high screech, then again, only this time both louder and longer. Virginia appeared suddenly in the room, the envelope no longer in her hand, and her curse came just as Rafe saw Walter's bleeding hand and his bright blood smeared across the face of the porcelain child, its eyes obscured, its blue, make-believe vision of the world marred.

Virginia quickly kneeled to the floor and took her son's hands in her own, turning them one way, then another. "Take the knife from her," she said. And he reached for it but Fannie had already dropped it, and he picked it up, wiped the blade on his pants leg, and folded it closed. "I reckon it just follow you around, don't it?" she said and almost spat.

"'Course, you lead the way, so how could it not? And don't be asking what I mean."

He let go of the knife; it hit the floor with a dull thud and one small bounce, then was still, its bone handle intact, unbroken. Virginia could do what she wanted with it, but if Walter was any son of his, he'd want his knife back. One cut and a little blood was nothing but a boy beginning his way into the world, his own masculine birth that no woman could lay claim to.

Rafe watched Walter pull a hand free from his mother and reach for the knife, and he decided then that there was nothing else he needed to do. The boy was capable of struggling with his mother, which was good to know. Rafe heard Wheeler's impatience again, as if the horse was answering what Rafe felt within himself, and Rafe decided neither he nor Wheeler need wait any longer to walk their way into the dark and away from a white, bloodied child who could be cleaned and made new, unlike those of his own who lay buried with, and without, names.

He was half dressed the next morning when he heard knocking at his room door. It was not Virginia, the sound too heavy and solid for her, and he was relieved once he realized it. When he opened the door he saw Richard, whom he would never have expected.

"Is something wrong?" he asked, trying to read the boy's face. "Is it Bunyan?" he said, making the quickest connection he could.

"No, sir. Nothing bad wrong."

"Well, what then?" Rafe asked, and when he saw hesitancy on the boy's part, he said, "Wait. Come in first. No need to stand in the hall." He stepped back, let Richard in, and closed the door. Still the boy seemed uncomfortable, and Rafe finished putting on his shirt and buttoned it. The boy seemed better able to look at him then.

"My father sent me. Brantley came down from the Lassiter Place. Said he heard from a woman up there that Samuel's still around."

"Where?" Rafe took in the news quickly, just as he'd learned to do early in the war when the enemy appeared where they weren't expected and in numbers greater than might have been foreseen.

"Daddy said at a little shack, in a clearing near the Black Fork. Said you'd know the one. But there's more to it than just where."

"Well, tell it, then," Rafe said, and some instinct had begun to work in his mind, a thought forming.

"That woman named Betsy is with him."

"And her children?" Rafe asked, though he could guess the answer.

"They're with them, if what Brantley says is right."

"If he said it, it's right. Same as if your father said it."

Rafe saw the boy took pride in the compliment of his father, which said there was something good about him, that he might amount to something yet. Rafe spoke his daughter's name again, "Bunyan," and looked at the boy to judge his reaction.

"Yes, sir?" he said finally.

"It might be all right with me if you start calling on her again."

Richard shifted his weight, remained silent.

"How old are you now?" Rafe asked.

"Seventeen."

"That's how old I was when I came to Riverfield." Richard looked somewhat puzzled. "Maybe it's just a little too late for you to still be a boy. So be a man. And if you do call on her, you best be a gentleman."

He looked away a moment, then back at Rafe. "Yes, sir," he said, held Rafe's eye, and slowly nodded as if he'd heard all Rafe intended.

"Give your father my thanks for sending you, and tell him to pass along my thanks to Brantley if he sees him before I do."

"Yes, sir."

He handed the boy a dollar. "Eat here in town before you go back. Take your time. I'll be traveling alone."

"Thank you," he said and walked toward the door, then slowed as if he might say something else, but didn't. Then he was gone down the hall.

By early afternoon Rafe was mounted on Wheeler and soon crossed over the Black Fork. He kept two extra revolvers in his hotel room because one could never have too many weapons available. In fact, after that day of blood and fire, Rafe had ordered dozens of rifled carbines, proper weapons should the need ever arise again, and kept them loaded and stored in the boys' side of the loft. But he carried only one Navy Colt on him now, having decided the one would be enough, and that he might not even need it. He'd take on Samuel any way Samuel seemed to want, if they were still in the shack. Rafe felt they would be, that this time Samuel had something running around in his mind other than enough alcohol to render a man stupid, easily beaten, and soaked in his own urine. He imagined they'd had a few nights together, Samuel and Betsy, and that what both joined them and lay between them was himself, each of them bent together by their own desire, not for the other so much as to seek a different kind of satisfaction aimed outwardly at him and that must have been full of enough violence to leave them feeling half dead after the final rush of their joined bodies.

Coming from town he was closer to his destination than if he'd been riding from home. And traveling a different route to it didn't increase or lessen the odd feeling that he was returning again, so soon, to a place he did not care to see despite the number of years that had elapsed since the event. Unpleasant business had to be dealt with, though. He knew what he'd promised Samuel and would have to make good.

The road he was traveling didn't follow the curves of the Black Fork but made a straighter cut toward the clearing and the shack at its edge. It seemed to him that the ground there should have been grown up in bramble and brush and scrub oaks by now, but he'd seen just weeks ago that was not the case. It was as if the fires set there over a dozen years before had scorched the ground so deeply nothing would grow, despite the fact that burned ground was supposed to create renewal. Perhaps the purpose of the blazes had their own bearing upon things, and malevolence nourished nothing at all except more of itself.

He dismounted and tied Wheeler, wondering for a moment about a horse's memory, if this place and the smell of the nearby Black Fork made him recall sound and smoke. Rafe approached the clearing's edge, looked toward the shack, and saw a thin, broken stream of smoke coming out of the chimney. He stood very still, watched, and neither saw nor heard anything more. He could have waited, bided time, as before, had planned to, but he was through with caution, and his disgust for it sent him out into the clearing walking steadily, not hurrying, exposed but calm, right hand resting on the grip of his holstered pistol. He then let go of that, let his arms hang limp, swinging slightly, naturally, with each forward step. Whoever wished him harm, let him or her come in whatever shape they chose: gathered fists, pointed as a blade, or a projectile rifling toward him with sound exploding just behind molded, spinning lead he would never see, though his eyes might end up as widened as March's had been, and maybe he would finally envision whatever March had in that stopped moment where all eventually arrive.

He drew closer, yet still heard no sound, witnessed no movement, and knew then, beyond whatever desire had possessed him as he walked across open ground, that Samuel was not in the shack, though *someone* was, and the notion came, briefly, that it was some old spirit, some haint made as thin with the passage of time as the escaping smoke rising above the brick chimney. It was but a fleeting thought, and what replaced it was a dark body that came flying out of the door and off the porch, so fast it seemed to lack shape but was its own being filled with an energy that bespoke either an outward danger or an inward desperation. Rafe drew his pistol in a reflex that bore no thought, only movement. He stood with feet planted apart, both hands steadying the raised pistol, the hammer cocked, first finger on the trigger, his aim a deadly focus on the small approaching body. And that's what stopped him, the smallness of what he saw finally registering, making him lower the pistol and ease the hammer down. In another moment the boy was on him, crying, his arms grasping Rafe's legs, hugging him in desperation, and then he felt the boy's fists again, slamming into him.

Rafe holstered the pistol, squatted, and let one knee down onto bare dirt. He put his arms around the boy, absorbed what was left of his fury, and knew it as a common trait between them, part of what made the boy his, and knew there was something deeper dwelling inside it.

Rafe finally placed his hands on the boy's shoulders, pushed him away just enough so he could see George's face, and the boy see his. Tear streaks lightened his skin, trailed down his face, and disappeared. Rafe knew how desperate the boy was to come to him this way after what he'd seen happen between Rafe and this mother. "Tell me what happened, son."

The boy choked out one word, "Mama," and that was all. He could not finish, could not even really begin.

"Is she inside?"

He nodded his head.

"Samuel, he here?" Rafe asked. "Or was he?"

Again the boy nodded, and his tears came harder, but why would he cry at the sound of Samuel's name? And Rafe couldn't be sure if he was saying *Yes, he's here* or *No, he's not here now*. He saw that George was beyond sense, that he might understand so little he *couldn't* make sense of anything, as if he were one of those children from years ago who saw the carnage and were left dumbfounded, truly speechless.

"Your mother? Is she alive? Tell me." Rafe found he dreaded the answer he might hear, if there was an answer to be had from the boy.

"'Live," George managed to say. Then he took further hold of himself somehow and took one of Rafe's hands in both of his own and pulled at him, tried to make him stand, and so Rafe did. The boy strained at him again, edging Rafe forward, staring up at him as he walked backward and continued with his pulling.

"Where?" Rafe said.

By way of an answer George turned from him, clearly wanting Rafe to follow, and he had to trust the boy enough to let him lead. At first he seemed to be headed toward the woods where the river lay beyond, and Rafe trailed just behind his son's form, wondering if they were headed toward the water's edge, something there past describing in the words of a boy, could only be shown, and that's when Rafe felt he'd begun to arrive at the very edge of knowing. But he saw quickly enough that they were headed to the shack where he scanned the familiar porch again, saw the small stack of firewood at one end. Even though they walked across level ground filled with sunlight, he had the strange sensation they were descending a narrow path into shadows formed by banked earth. George turned back to him a moment and then continued, though not toward the steps, but instead to the end of the porch with the dwindling stack of wood. He walked to its edge, stopped, and stared. Then Rafe came up behind him, placed a hand on the boy's shoulder and saw the spread white blanket, one he recognized from Betsy's cabin, and saw the mound beneath it. He feared he knew already what the mound might be but had to see with completeness the body that held his blood and now something deeper even, something that might be called a burden, both to lift and to carry within. He reached over the boy, pulled the blanket upward, and a breeze caught it, made it billow, and Rafe saw the small, dark head turned at a twisted angle, Lakeview lying on her back inside a stillness and surrounded by an absence of sound that Rafe was not aware of, not missing what he could not hear. He slipped past the boy and touched his daughter's body with his spread fingers and open palm, feeling the warmth of her, but not knowing if the warmth still came from within, some last remnant of her short life, or only from the sun's heat that angled in upon her. With his other hand he kept the blanket raised, found he could not yet cover her again, could not obscure her face, needed to *see* her, perhaps in a way he never had, needed not to see any part of himself but only her, this child who'd had her life waiting for her, however troubled it might have become. And within the soundlessness of his mind he heard her knowledge of him, of all he had ever done, some large part of it spread across the open field behind him and buried in the earth nearby, as she would now have to be buried, a part of the carnage of his life, a carnage that was ultimately too large to be buried, too much of it living within him, and so much more now, some degree of burden that he did not want to consider but belonged to him nonetheless. He lowered the blanket then, let it slowly fall over her as the breeze made it billow one last time, then settle. He took the boy's shoulders in both hands, turned him toward the open space, and looked out across it with him. He saw for a moment the movement of horses and men, women and children looking down at all that had been lost to them, heard them, then heard the sounds nearest him, the boy trying to stop his crying, the wind easing its way through the woods and toward the river where he imagined the surface lay rippled in the sun, and he became aware he'd dwelled within a soundless moment that had now ended.

"How long she been here?" he said. "Who covered her?" He waited for answers and when none came, he did not ask again. Someone else would have to answer.

As soon as he entered the shack, he saw her lying on the bed, a wool blanket over her. She stared at the ceiling and would not look his way, though she had to know it was him, if not by instinct and simple reason then by the sound of his steps. He stood and stared at her, waiting to see if she would speak, and saw it was to no avail. The fact that she lay there calmly suggested to him more than one possibility for what had happened. The guilty always knew the truth, knew their own hand in things, and so had no reason for anger, or in the case of a woman, hysterics. But what he witnessed in her now did not negate Samuel, what Samuel was capable of doing, his myriad reasons for leaving the child for Rafe to find, just as he'd left the bloodied mule.

"I have to know," he said. "Start talking."

She remained quiet for some time, then finally said, "Why? You won't believe." She spoke quietly, haltingly, as if her ability to speak was a dying thing itself. "Won't believe anything I say." She still did not look at him, only at the ceiling, as though it offered her an escape beyond its dark clouds of smoke stains, an escape that she longed for.

He walked near the bed, stood over her, and looked down at her ragged hair. "Tell me what happened."

Still she remained silent. Then, after some time, said, finally, "I didn't know what was in his mind." He noticed she didn't use Samuel's name, as if to name him was too great an effort. "Didn't see or hear him get up." She turned and looked at him for one moment, not with defiance but surrender.

"Go on."

"I was asleep." She looked toward the boy then. "But George saw him pick her up, take her out onto the porch."

"Don't you bring that boy there into this." He looked back at George too, who sat still at the table and seemed to be both looking at the two of them and beyond them into his memory. But what did he really see there, Samuel carrying the child or his mother? Maybe Samuel had abandoned them already after having what he wanted of Betsy, his use of her revenge enough, a coward's revenge. He couldn't know for sure. "Don't make this boy lie for you or have to be your savior. Even what might be true is too heavy for a child to carry." He paused a moment, pictured again how the blanket had settled over Lakeview. "She's covered in white. You going to tell me Samuel did that too?"

"She's always been covered in white."

He felt he understood the remark and let it pass. "And so you just left her there, crawled back into bed?"

She nodded, finally said, "Yes, that's what I did, after I covered her." He shook his head. "All you're hearing is lies," she said.

He knew this was no admission, only judgment of him, or a pretend judgment. "Maybe all words are lies, and the bigger the words the bigger the lies."

"I'm not using big words. It was Samuel's hate that was bigger than anything else, bigger than me and bigger than our child lying out there. You kill a man's daddy and then beat him and urinate all over him, that's enough to make him do anything."

Rafe sat down at the foot of her bed. "I did not urinate on him, and I don't know if I killed his father or not."

"That's not what he said."

"Then he lied."

"Doesn't matter if he lied or not. Only question now is which of us are you going to kill?" She asked the question calmly, as if his answer didn't matter, either because she was well past any concern for herself, even with George sitting there, needing her. What was one to make of that? He again looked back at the boy whose expression showed nothing, as if he'd already taken in too much and there was room for no more. "I'm not going to kill you," he said. "If I was, I would have done it already."

"You know it wasn't me." She whispered the words in such a quiet voice it was as if she were saying them only to herself, and then she added, perhaps only for herself, in a voice that was even quieter, "Why would I kill my child?"

He bent toward her, speaking quietly himself, though he wasn't sure why. Maybe sometimes words were weighted by their own gravity. "Maybe you had to take what was mine."

She slowly shook her head back and forth on the thin pillow beneath her, and the effort of it seemed to exhaust her. "It wasn't even really Samuel who did it," she said, and he would not have been able to hear or understand her if he had not watched her lips form the words.

"Then who?" he asked. "Who?"

She merely stared at him and kept staring, would not turn her dark eyes away from him, until he heard her answer within himself because it was the answer that was already dwelling there, had been at least since the cold afternoon when Melinda had spoken to him beside the small grave Annie Mae had dug through the frozen ground in the horse pasture. Maybe the answer had lain within him even before that, frozen inside him as hard as the ground where they all gathered around a dead and nameless child.

TWENTY

Annie Mae saw him on horseback when she walked out of the store with a bag of flour in her arms and looked down the road toward the old inn, which meant he had passed the store windows without her seeing. She'd heard a plaintive kind of grunt from Mr. Alfred at the counter, and she'd wondered why he'd made such a sound. There was George on the back of Wheeler, his arms around his father's waist, which struck her as not something quite believable, not something she wanted to see, or understand, not after all that had happened, and yet there was the knowing in sight for anyone who might be watching, beyond only family, a sight Annie Mae found somehow gratifying. She saw, too, what looked like a white sack draped across Wheeler's neck, a sack maybe no larger than the one she carried and now put down on the floor of the porch without thinking about why, let it drop and found herself walking down the steps as Rafe turned Wheeler beside the Teclaw house. She walked faster, pulled forward by what she saw and by what she didn't see, who she didn't see. But Betsy would not be with him, no way she could be. So where was Lakeview? Why were she and George not together, and what of that white cloth sack?

She moved faster, not quite running but a little closer to it. By the time she made the Teclaw house and turned, her breath was coming harder but not enough to slow her. When she reached the front yard Rafe was even with the porch, about to ride past the house to the barn. Henry and Philip were walking out of the dogtrot, surely come to see what their father carried, and why George rode the back of Wheeler, which they had never been allowed to do. She called George's name, and the boy turned toward her with such great need for her in his face. Rafe stopped, circled Wheeler, and faced her, his hand upon the white cloth, steadying it, keeping it balanced across the horse's neck. The two boys stood at the end of the porch now, with William approaching them from behind, his curiosity probably as strong as that of his brothers. All Annie Mae felt at this point was fear made larger by the grave expression Rafe wore and that made her look again at the cloth sack that she recognized now as not a sack but Lakeview's white blanket.

In a moment she was close enough to touch it, and did, taking a loose end of the still clean, worn cloth in her hand.

"Don't," Rafe said. "You don't need to see. Just leave her be."

"See what?" Henry said.

His words made her aware of the children again, these brothers. She watched William place a hand on Henry's shoulder and Henry actually quieted. And yet as close as they stood at the end of the porch, they all three seemed at a great distance from her, removed by loss, by the unfathomable that only their father could begin to explain, though no words ever really would, especially from a white man, even if his blood did flow in the boy behind and now lay quiet, she knew, in the girl before him.

Ignoring his words, Annie Mae pulled open the wrapped cloth until she could see the child's head at its twisted, heartbreaking angle and then her face, see the closed eyes, which she knew had been closed for her by someone, so that Lakeview looked like a child caught in dreams she would not awaken from, perhaps dreams of both heaven and horror, no matter how brief the latter.

She smelled Wheeler, the sheen of sweat on him, and heard Henry say, "She's dead," the smell and the curious sound of the boy's small voice weighted with the two heavy words taking over her senses, and only the feel of her grandchild's cheek enabled her to push away the sound and smell. When she tried to pull the blanket back farther, Rafe's hand stopped her with a force that was not unkind.

"So you've seen her now," he said and began to cover her again. "I can understand your need, but that's enough."

She let him cover the child, looking at the ground while he did so, away from all eyes, including each boy's and even Wheeler's, and into a private moment of quiet within herself but unable to remain there surrounded as she was by all these male presences. She lifted her arms up to George, unable to let herself forget his need of her. He let go of his father, leaned toward her, and let himself slide off Wheeler's back and into her hands and arms that had caught so many children, just-born infants, black and white and shades in between, from all manner of human union. His arms were around her neck, and she could feel his body shaking now, her touch allowing him to release whatever he'd been holding inside. And what was that exactly? What had he seen?

She looked back up at Rafe who sat Wheeler patiently. "How? Tell me," she asked over George's shoulder. "What happened?"

Rafe continued looking downward at her, then finally away at his boys, or maybe beyond them, studying on some answer he might give. "You'll have to ask your daughter that," he said. "If you go to her. I'd rather you didn't. She will not, cannot, come here. Know that. She does."

"Why do I have to ask her?" she said. "Why can't you tell me?" She knew the question was a bold one, but the presence of the dead child allowed it.

"Because I don't know. I found this child of mine under her blanket, already gone out of the world, and your daughter just about asleep in bed, weighted down with either grief or guilt. I don't know which, and don't imagine I ever will. If I knew for sure it was Samuel, and if I could find him, which is doubtful, I'd kill him. May kill him anyway if I ever come across him."

"What Samuel got to do with it?" she asked, and her confusion told her where her thoughts already lay, and with whom.

"Ask Betsy. See what you can believe. Samuel had been there. Maybe the child in your arms can tell you something. Take him to the cabin now. He's yours to raise, and protect. Mine too. I have never not claimed him."

She lowered George to the ground, keeping a hand on his shoulder as he stood next to her. "The baby," she said. "I'll take her now."

"No. She's clean. Doesn't need tending to." Wheeler stamped one of his front hooves; he knew food and water were near, she guessed, the small bundle he carried across his neck no concern to him, only the satisfaction of his wants, like all men. "We'll leave her wrapped in this blanket," Rafe said, "and I'll make sure it's neatly folded around her before I place her in the coffin."

"You gon' make it?"

"Yes," he said. "It will be well made. Trust that. I've had enough practice."

"What about the grave?" she asked. She felt outside herself, as if she weren't talking about the death of her own blood but that of some child she'd just delivered and who'd been unable to find his or her place in the world and so had left it quickly, seeing no point in prolonging a departure.

Rafe took a long breath, and she could see he was growing impatient. "I'll dig it, next to the nameless ones, and there will be a stone with clear lettering," he added.

She could picture a gray marker standing alone down in the horse pasture and wondered if Rafe intended it as a punishment of Melinda, her having to see the grave of a child not hers next to two unmarked graves of children who were. But the thought passed quickly enough. Melinda was not her concern now.

"I'll help you dig," she heard William say, reminding her of his presence again, this brother to George and Lakeview who cared enough to make such an offer. His father merely nodded, raising the hand in which he held the reins, ready to prod Wheeler forward.

"Take George into the cabin," he said. "I'm sure he needs seeing to, needs to eat."

She nodded, took him by his small hand, and began to lead the way. They were passed in a moment by Wheeler, the white cloth draping either side of his long mane, a garland that celebrated nothing.

She did not ask George once she closed the door to the cabin if he was hungry, feeling it best to simply prepare ham and peas and warm some biscuits and place them in front of him. He would most likely eat then, and would talk when he was ready. She wouldn't push and was glad to have a task at hand while the boy took a place at the table and sat quiet.

Her thoughts, though, still turned to the soft face and closed eyes she'd seen, and she'd needed to see them, see the undeniable fact of the child's death lest it feel as if Lakeview had been stolen by some unknown hand. But there had been someone's hand, a kind of thief, a thief by a different, darker name. But what was more important, the fact of the death or the cause? Knowing the who would change nothing, yet how could she not be filled by the question when the answer might lie within Annie Mae's blood, passed down to a thief of a daughter who'd stolen her own blood carried forward in the vessel of a child whose name held beauty in its vision.

As unfathomable as Betsy was, she had to try to understand what Betsy might have done after seeing a knife blade at her head and imagining what part of her body it might pierce or slice through down to bone or organ, and then feeling it cut and saw through her hair. What had she begun to think as she sat on the floor while Annie Mae looked down on her daughter's jagged hair and pale scalp? The story she'd told Betsy began to come back to her now. Maybe the old custom of punishment among the tribe, a killing answered with death, was something Betsy had taken and twisted to her own ends. She'd taken a life, maybe two lives, neither of her blood, and now had answered them, not with her own life but the life of her child, an infant, a replacement for her, who was more unknown to Betsy than her son who was already himself in many ways, while the daughter was not, not wholly aware and so the easier one to sacrifice, but she was no sacrifice, only an answer for what a buckra had done to a young woman who was a complex mix of Choctaw, white, and Black, a mixture of hurt and anger and impulses darker than her skin but as old as any tribe of people.

There was Samuel, though, who could not be denied, the fact of him and all that filled him, not blood but his hate and need that might have been greater than Annie Mae had known, a need to take from Rafe in the same manner Rafe had taken from him, no matter who else was injured in the doing of it. His need blinding him into as confused a state as that poor wretched Henry, who thought a simple animal that walked on four legs saw black as white and white as black.

She set the plate of food in front of George and took the chair across from him. He didn't speak, only stared at the food. "Go ahead and eat a little something," she said. "We don't let food go to waste."

He took the fork, ate a small bite of peas, and slowly kept eating, looking up at her from time to time for encouragement or maybe assurance, needing to know she was *there*.

"Don't worry about your mama. You'll see her. Just not in this house," she said, and then regretted the last words as soon as she spoke them. He stopped eating, put his fork down, and looked at what remained of his food as if it wasn't anything he could recognize any longer and so had given it up. "I promise you'll see her," she said, and she meant to keep the promise. "And I'll be with you when you do." He looked back up at her, seeming to search her face. "George, I need to ask you some things. All you got to do is answer real simple like. And if you don't know, just tell me you don't. All right?"

He didn't respond but kept looking her way, as if her gaze were something he could hold to.

"Tell me, where was y'all staying at?" she asked.

After a long moment he said, "House by the Black Fork," and she was glad to hear his voice, relieved to know he was still there within himself.

"Tell me now, did you see when Samuel left out?"

He nodded.

"Was it in the night, by hisself?"

George shook his head, seemed to be remembering the fuller answer she wanted. "'Bout daylight," he said.

"You saw him?"

He nodded again, slowly, as if he wanted to make sure he answered each question right. "Heard him first, moving 'round."

"Doing what?"

He seemed to think for a moment. "Putting some things in a sack. Him and Mama was talking ugly. Then she started to screaming-like at him."

"What she screaming?"

George's face tightened, his eyes squinted by a constriction of thought, it seemed. "Nothing that made no sense." He shrugged his shoulders, as if giving up his attempt at finding sense in what he'd heard or seen.

"Where was your sister at?"

He picked up his fork and pushed at the food on his plate as if he were playing in the dirt. "Didn't see her nowhere," he said. "She must of been out on the porch already."

Annie Mae reached across the table, took one of George's hands in her own, and held it gently, the skin on his fingers rougher than she would have thought. "So what happened then?"

"Samuel left out."

"What your mama do?"

"Run out on the porch."

Annie Mae tried to picture each moment, wanting to piece together what had happened. "How long she out there?"

"A long while."

"When she come back in, she crying, upset?"

"Crying hard. Then she got in the bed, got quiet, mostly. She be moving every once in a while, though."

She patted his hand then, took it in both hers. "What did you do?"

He was quiet again for a moment or two. "Went out on the porch, seen her blanket."

"Then you looked," she said, wanting to help him, realizing she was making him dwell on something he wanted to forget but knew he never would.

"Thought she asleep," he said, and there was still the sound of hope in his voice, as if he'd recaptured that moment, was again filled with it.

"But you couldn't wake her up." She spoke quietly, as if having to wake him from the dream of an exhausted child.

He shook his head, seemed unable to look at her any longer, and then his attention became focused on what neither of them could see but both heard, the first sharp strikes of a hammer coming from the barn.

"What then?" she finally asked when there was a lull in the rhythm of the hammer's pounding.

"Went sat in the woods," he said, with no hint of shame in his voice, as if that was what anyone would have done, gone and found a place inside God's own church where there was no balcony for darker-skinned people, the trunks of the trees like steeples beneath which anyone could sit where they wanted.

She asked no more questions of him, understood that his answers could not answer her larger question. She would have to choose what to believe, just as she'd already been choosing for months, each time going against her daughter, perhaps now to the point she could not do otherwise, was maybe damned by her disbelief, by something lacking in herself and *not* her daughter. "How innocent are you?" Betsy had once asked her. Maybe that was the largest question of all, another she could not answer, or did not want to. She had done nothing too terrible, or mostly not, but if she could believe the worst of her own child maybe that said something about the worst of herself.

The hammering began again, this time the rhythm unsteady, and she wondered if William was taking a turn; and if he was, Henry was bound to demand his turn too, not wanting to be left out, needing to prove he could do it just as well or better. She kept listening for a change in the sound. Strange what the mind could focus on at such a time.

Instead of a different rhythm in the pounding the next sound she heard was a knock at her door, and when she opened it she found Bunyan, whose face held sadness and also a sense of caution or wariness at how she might be greeted, and maybe there was some other concern there too that Annie Mae had guessed at already but could not know for certain.

Annie Mae nodded and motioned for her to come in, and when Bunyan did, she saw her looking around, taking things in, and realized the girl had never been inside the cabin, was seeing the inside of someone else's life, its domestic particulars so much lesser than her own.

"I'm sorry," Bunyan said, "about the baby. I'm really sorry."

Annie Mae decided that William must have gone into the house first and told what he'd seen before going to the barn. "George, let Miss Bunyan sit in your chair." When he stood, Annie Mae pulled the chair out a little and Bunyan sat. Then she took her own chair across from Bunyan. "You don't have nothing to be sorry for."

"I think maybe I do." Her eyes were so dark brown and serious, as they always had been, really, but all the more so now, as if her own hurts of late had deepened what she could feel for others, and Annie Mae felt she'd heard all that Bunyan meant.

"You don't have to feel sorry, child. And what you said just now, it enough."

The pounding stopped and started again, and this time there was no rhythm, only an uneven jarring that sounded like angry blows, so at odds with what Annie Mae felt at the moment toward Bunyan. But maybe the pounding echoed something that *was* in her and would find its way out, maybe when she saw her daughter, or if she ever laid eyes on Samuel.

"Mama wants to know if she can come down. I told her I was coming, told her to come with me, but she wouldn't. She said to tell you she wants your permission."

Annie Mae was surprised, knew Melinda didn't have to ask permission, but realized if Melinda had shown up at her door, she wouldn't have wanted to let her in; angry, she would have thought, *Who are you to come here to my house you once marked, pretended to curse?* But for Melinda to ask permission reminded her not of the distance grown between them but of the closeness there had been as friend, woman, midwife, one who'd caught Melinda's babies as they'd left her bloody, exposed, and spent. She'd known many women that way, some almost strangers, which in some ways was easier. Melinda was no stranger, not the first time she'd delivered for her and surely not the last.

"Tell her to come on. Just to knock and I open the door."

Bunyan nodded, was quiet a moment, then said, "So where is Betsy?" which was not a question Annie Mae had been expecting from her, and it felt like a trespass coming this suddenly.

"Child, I don't know," she said. And even though she did know, her answer felt like the truth, as if what Bunyan had really asked was, *Who is Betsy?* And her not knowing any better than she did felt like a failure. She did not want to fail anyone else.

Later, when the knock Annie Mae asked for came, it was Kate she saw first, her mother at her side, and which one had knocked Annie Mae couldn't be sure, though it had not sounded like Melinda. Kate walked through the doorway first, as if she wanted to make a pathway for her mother. She did not look around the cabin as Bunyan had done, seemed to simply accept it for what it was, someone else's home who had to live their life as they could, like everyone else in the world.

"I wanted to come too," Kate said, "to tell you how sorry I am..." She paused, seemed to not know how to continue, and looked down at the floor. "About what happened," she finally added, her words still sounding incomplete, and Annie Mae could not help her and didn't try, only thought to herself, *You mean about what happened to your sister. It your sister out in that barn, just like last time it was your brother, and the time before that.* Yes, she saw concern and caring in Kate's expression—Kate had that in her without a doubt, always had—but with no sense of loss for herself. It didn't matter that Lakeview was her father's child. Kate didn't seem to feel the kinship of blood, and Annie Mae realized Bunyan had not either. Maybe she shouldn't have expected them to. It was as if each of them had said aloud, "She was not our sister. We only came because she was your grandchild, your blood, not ours. That's the only reason." And at the moment it did not feel like reason enough. Or maybe Kate's deepest reason for coming was her mother, wanting to help her through the awkwardness and the discomfort. But that was not enough, either. Annie Mae felt then that Lakeview was more connected to her two dead, nameless brothers than she was to these two sisters, or she would be once her grave was dug and covered. She knew Bunyan and Kate would stand near her at the grave, and maybe she couldn't fault them for what they could not realize, could not feel. Maybe when they saw their own last name on Lakeview's stone, they would feel the pull and the loss of their own blood—if Rafe actually did put up a proper stone. She knew that all he'd done for March Whitney was to place a large red-colored rock at the head of his grave, though he was buried in the white graveyard, and she'd seen Rafe stand at that rock more than once.

Melinda still hadn't spoken, had let Kate speak first, but she'd moved toward George where he stood near the wall beside the neatly made bed, Betsy's bed. She placed a hand upon the boy's shoulder, leaned down toward him, and said something that Annie Mae could not make out, but the tone of her voice sounded gentle. Even so, Annie Mae felt herself wanting Melinda to move away from him.

Kate sat down at the table without asking, just as her father would have, but she did it simply, gracefully, in a way that was natural to her. There was no ownership of anything in her movements the way there would have been with her father.

Melinda finally walked away from George, away from the bed; she seemed not to want to look at it, and Annie Mae thought how hard it must have been for Melinda to enter this cabin, hard for more reason than one, probably not only because of her husband's visits here, but because of what she'd once done outside its walls. "I'm sorry too," Melinda said as she approached Kate and stood just behind her daughter. "I don't have grandchildren, yet." She placed a hand on each of Kate's shoulders, patted her, and Kate's color rose just slightly in her face. "But I know it must feel like losing your own child. It has to, especially in this way."

Annie Mae again thought what she wanted to say. *You mean because the child was killed?* But Melinda believed she knew what that felt like herself. There was nothing Annie Mae needed to explain. Maybe it was Betsy who most connected her with Melinda now, the two of them sharing the loss of a child, which was a kinship between all women, the fact or the fear of such a loss, but the loss the two of them shared might have been done by the very same hand, the violence deepening the kinship somehow. Yet there was such a repulsion in the thought of that violence, a repulsion that made Annie Mae want to draw apart. Here they were, though, having to confront each other in ways that couldn't be fully spoken, by either words or gestures. So the quiet that came over them now, this silent communion of grief, the body near but no blood this time, was the only way to share what lay between them.

Annie Mae heard a steadier hammering again, three blows, a pause, three more blows, a pause, the rhythm continuing. She knew who held the hammer again, knew he was sealing the small wooden box that would remain sealed until the earth rotted it away and the wood and the child became dust within a small hollow of ground that would finally sink.

The door swung open, this time without a knock first, and when Annie Mae turned, she saw Henry enter as if he'd been in the cabin many times, tugging Philip by the hand. It was as if he were leading a dog, but maybe Henry had love in him too, at least for Philip. Who was she to say there wasn't?

Philip pushed the door closed behind him without being told. Henry stood there, looking at each of them, understanding that they were all awaiting whatever pronouncement he was about to make. "What, Henry?" Melinda finally said.

"William's already digging. He won't let me. Papa says that's my sister. I thought I only had two sisters. I want to help bury my sister."

The room was quiet again, and even Henry remained silent as if he were waiting for some verdict to be pronounced on his having been done wrong. Annie Mae looked first at Kate who showed no surprise, only a hint of concern, perhaps, for her mother. Melinda was quiet for the moment, and Annie Mae waited, watching each member of this white family who had never before stepped inside this cabin but filled it now to the point where she saw George crowded into the same corner where his mother had sat after having been shorn of her hair. At least Henry had spoken it aloud among them all, maybe in some way caring more about his sister than anyone else or at least brave enough to say it. But she knew better, knew she could not use Henry to condemn the others. Henry's boldness was not born of love or blood, only from his own want to put himself in the middle of whatever he saw or sensed.

"It doesn't matter who does the digging," Melinda said, "as long as it isn't Annie Mae. Or George," she added and looked toward the boy in a way that was not without kindness.

"George, he's my brother. I knew that already."

"Yes," Melinda said. "He is."

There was no hesitancy in her voice, and Annie Mae watched George, saw that he didn't move, and wondered if George understood that he was a brother to Philip and Kate as well, and Bunyan. He was a smart boy, and now he shyly looked around the room, only his eyes moving as he took in each brother and the one sister. He knew, and always would, she decided. He was of them, but not one of them. He was hers too, though, maybe now more than before. Hers and Rafe's, a child in between, just as her own child was. What kind of man would he become? she wondered. And would anyone in this room care?

It was William who came and got them, and this time Annie Mae did not have to look up from a grave she'd just dug in top-frozen ground to see a part of the family approaching. She and George were among the family, William leading the way to the grave, the rest following her and George, who walked by her side. This was no formal procession, though. There was no crowd of mourners for them to walk through who could give witness to the kinship of a dead child who joined all of them, save one, by blood.

Rafe, she saw, stood at the small grave and mound of dirt, a shovel, not a Bible, in his hand. There would be no real funeral, but he would preside, his will be done.

And so it was when they gathered together around the opened ground.

That night, after she put George to bed and waited for him to fall asleep, she left the cabin, knowing she could make it back in less than two hours. Or maybe she wouldn't be gone that long if she was turned away.

The moon was bright enough to follow the road without difficulty, not unlike the night she'd walked to the Lassiter Place and back. It wasn't as cold this night. She'd passed the house before, knew where Leathy lived, and was relieved to find a light burning when she finally neared the front porch.

She had a silver coin with her, was willing to pay, and hoped it would be enough. But she was not coming for the same reason most came. While she might almost believe in some of the rituals she practiced as a midwife, the placing of scissors under the bed, the way to bury the afterbirth, she did these things more out of habit and custom than a deep belief, though she would never let on to any mother about to give birth. They needed all they could believe in, even the white ladies who would never admit it.

So she did not think Leathy held any special powers, only the power she had over the ones who did believe in her, which was strong enough. Annie Mae only had questions that Leathy might could answer, if she was willing, or might couldn't. Maybe this was a fool's errand, but it was one she had to make, one she felt the need of though she could not say fully why.

She knocked, and it took some time for the door to open, despite the lighted lantern in the front room that told her the woman was awake. Then Leathy stood before her, a candle in one hand, a heavy robe covering her body. She could see Leathy knew who she was when Leathy held the candle upward. "Thought I would of see'd you before now. Figured by this time you wasn't coming."

"Can I come in?" Annie Mae said, hoping she sounded polite enough. "I want to talk to you. I can pay."

Leathy turned with the candle, allowing her in, and Annie Mae saw the shelves surrounding the room, light and shadow giving vague shape to the items each shelf held, some she could name, the roots and plants, some she couldn't, either because she couldn't see them well enough or because she simply didn't know. What the jars held she could only guess. Taste or smell would have told her more.

They sat at the table where the lamp burned, and Leathy seemed to take a good look at her. "You got more copper in your skin than what she does. It a kind of metal, make you stronger than her."

Annie Mae didn't respond. Maybe she was stronger than Betsy, but it didn't have anything to do with the copper in her skin. "I know Miss Melinda come and seen you," she said. Leathy nodded slowly, as if she understood there was no need to deny. "I have to know, so I'm gon' ask now, did you believe what all she told you?"

Leathy kept studying her, it seemed, looking at her face, down to the lamp flame, then back at her face, as though somewhere in that light, between its source and its reflection in Annie Mae's skin, was something she needed to see and understand. "People what come to see me, they don't lie. I help people, just like you. A woman ever lie to you when she giving birth?" Annie Mae shook her head. "That 'cause people who be hurting, they don't think about lying. They can't. And the ones what come to me, they be hurting too." Leathy paused and looked past Annie Mae for a moment. "Sometimes what they think the truth, ain't though. They confused."

"Was Miss Melinda confused?"

Leathy looked again into that space between the flame and its reflection. "No more than you. And can't no woman make sense out the death of her child." Leathy touched the ends of her fingers together into an imperfect symmetrical shape. "Or her grandchild." Now she spread her hands apart, placed them on the table palms upward. "Word travels. I'm sorry for you."

Annie Mae nodded, decided how to proceed. "I know you come and talked to Mr. Rafe. About Samuel. How come you done that?"

Leathy appeared to grow weary now. "Ain't neither one a us got no love for Samuel. And you know how come already."

"You told him where Samuel was. You know where he at now?"

"If I knew, I'd tell you."

"How come you'd tell me? You think he done what I think he might of did, kill my grandchild?"

Leathy shook her head, not to say *no*, it seemed, but to acknowledge all in this world that couldn't be answered. "Who know with him? So much confusion in his head, so much pain. He dangerous. Even he don't know what he gon' do. Or if he done it already, he don't know why he done it. Just like you don't know why you come here." Leathy watched Annie Mae's eyes now, looking beyond the light and into her, it seemed. "You think you got some simple questions, these ones you been asking, and if I answer them the way you think you want me to, then *maybe* you can stop believing what you been believing—about your daughter, what you think she done. Maybe you could, maybe you couldn't. I got a notion which it is, but it ain't for me to say. What you *really* here for is to make me face you, 'cause a what I done to your daughter, or helped Miss Melinda do to her. That why you here. 'Cause I hurt your daughter. And you might like to hurt me some way or another. But you ain't no Samuel."

Annie Mae fingered the coin in her hand and knew what she'd just heard was not a lie. She'd wanted to hurt Virginia somehow too, when she'd gone to see her, but instead she had let Virginia convince her of what she'd wanted to believe, or that's how it had felt, at least. So maybe Betsy had been right about why she'd gone to Virginia—she *had* wanted to be convinced.

"Your wanting to hurt me—no matter what your daughter might or might not a done—maybe that the answer you been looking for, one that tell you the most 'bout yourself. A mother what love her child gon' side with her, protect her, even if she know the child wrong."

"But what she could of done was more than just wrong."

"Don't matter. Not to you. Not after all said and done."

"You said you thought I would of done come here already. What you think I was gon' do?"

Leathy seemed to think a moment. "Cuss me, maybe. Or maybe even slap me, 'cause you knew you couldn't cuss or slap Miss Melinda. So I thought you might have come to me. Didn't think it'd be no worse than that. Like I said, you ain't full of hate like Samuel."

"And I ain't like my daughter, either."

"How alike you think they are? That what you asking yourself, or if one worse than the other. But that ain't the question."

"What is?" Annie Mae asked, afraid of the answer but needing to know.

"Which one you want to blame, the one you love or the one you don't?"

"I want to know what my daughter done."

"You might not never know, not for sure."

"How I gon' live with that?"

Leathy did not answer but simply looked at her, as if answering were beyond all her powers, the ones she might truly possess, and even beyond the ones imagined by others who came to her seeking what was unknowable except by their very own flawed and uncertain faith.

Silence prevailed now. There were no other answers, so any question was meaningless. Annie Mae slowly reached her hand out and laid the coin in the middle of the table, the lamplight illuminating both its tarnished metal and its assigned value. Whether it was too much or too little she could not judge.

For the next two days she either kept George in the kitchen with her as she worked or kept watch on him through the kitchen window as he played in the backyard or in front of the cabin. Sometimes Philip sat or played with him, and when Henry returned from school, he would join them, lead them from one part of the yard to another or take them down into the horse pasture where the small mound of dirt awaited its promise of stone. She could not see the grave beyond the barn, but it was often in her vision, and the mound of earth, as small as it was, grew larger in her grief, grief for the loss of the child, and, she realized, for her daughter who was not dead but did not feel wholly alive to her. It was as if that mound, made by a white man, blocked a passageway both in and out of herself, and something larger felt closed off too, as though Nanih Waiya itself had been sealed and no kind of birth was possible any longer, all of creation stopped, was stillborn.

Kate and Bunyan were kind to her in small ways, helping with minor chores, and Melinda was mostly quiet around her, but only seemed uneasy with her in Rafe's presence, as if any show of the connection they'd once had must be guarded, its fact and its memory. Rafe remained close around the house, and twice he took George to the store with him, leaving the rest of the children at home. Maybe he felt the need to show that the boy was under his watchful eye. But Annie Mae could feel his deepening restlessness, the way he kept moving in and around the house, out to the barn, up to the store. He would soon be gone for days, and she found she was waiting for that, knew she could not ask him for what she wanted or allow him knowledge of it.

Finally, he was gone for a night, and she felt mostly sure that he would not soon return. Just beyond noon the next day, after she had fed George in the kitchen and Melinda and Philip had eaten at the table, she asked Melinda if she might borrow Ida. She knew she did not have to explain that where she was going would be too far, too hard a walk on foot, and that once she arrived she might have to search farther. Nor did she need to explain that she wanted to carry with her more items than her arms could hold.

"Will you return?" Melinda asked.

"I'll have to," she said. "If I take George, there wouldn't be no getting away from Mr. Rafe. And I can't just leave him. He need me."

Melinda remained seated at the dining table while Annie Mae stood, waiting for a clear answer. "When the other children get home from school," she said, "you can go then. I'll have Kate look after George. Then Bunyan can take a turn."

"Thank you. This something I got to do."

"You don't need to thank me. You're asking for a simple thing."

There was quiet then, from both of them, a balanced quiet, perhaps as each considered all that had been denied them, and what each had withheld from the other.

"You won't tell..." Annie Mae stopped and wouldn't let herself ask what she wanted.

"No, if he comes home before we expect, I'll tell him you took Ida to go tend to a birth."

Annie Mae nodded, then walked toward the kitchen, where work always awaited her.

By late afternoon she was astride Ida, who was loaded with clothes and food for Betsy. She realized she must be taking the same route as Rafe and all those armed white men had taken years before, but while she was headed to a place of violence, both old and new, she hoped she was now riding toward some kind of deliverance for herself and her daughter.

She managed Ida without difficulty, neither of their burdens slowing them. At various points she passed Black women she knew, who nodded and spoke her name, but seemed to have guessed at the errand she was on and let her pass without delay.

The lone cabin stood in the clearing, its rusting tin roof harshly lit by the late afternoon sun. No smoke rose from the chimney, and she grew afraid that Betsy was gone, disappeared to who knew where. Then the fear she felt enlarged but she wouldn't acknowledge its cause, only let it hasten her.

She quickly dismounted at the porch, tied the mule, and called out but heard no reply, and, hurrying through the door, found Betsy in bed, watching her silently.

All Annie Mae could think to do at first was ask her daughter a simple question. "How long since you ate?" Betsy didn't answer, seemingly so buried within herself that words couldn't find their way out. She sat down on the bed, touched her daughter's cheek, and stroked the shorn hair at the sides of her head. "You ain't ate at all, is you?" She leaned closer now. "You taken any water?"

Betsy blinked slowly, as if she were coming out of herself, rising to existence. "A little," she said quietly.

Annie Mae eased up from the bed, went to the bucket on the table, and filled the gourd dipper. She then carried it to her daughter and with her free hand helped Betsy rise farther and drink. After a moment, she placed the pillow against the headboard so Betsy could sit up more properly.

"Need to carry in what I brung," she said.

"Did you bring George? Is he outside?"

The question eased Annie Mae, telling her something of what she wanted to know about her daughter. "Not this time. Didn't know what kind of shape you was in. Didn't want…" She wasn't able to finish.

Betsy nodded her head to show she understood what her mother couldn't say. "Is he all right?"

"All right as he can be. Won't say what all he heard and seen, or don't know how."

"He seen enough."

She wanted to say, And what was that? but she didn't.

Betsy looked away, stared up at the underside of the tin roof, and for a moment seemed to disappear from herself. "Is she buried yet? she finally asked.

Annie Mae nodded. "She buried."

Betsy still looked upward, and Annie Mae wondered what vision she saw against the dull-colored tin whose outside rust was surely eating its way through. "Where is she buried?"

Annie Mae didn't want to answer but made herself. "Down in the horse pasture," she said, and then forced the next words out. "Beside the other two children."

Betsy turned to her, eyes opened wide, as if she wanted Annie Mae to see deep within her. "The two children I'm supposed to have killed."

Annie Mae shook her head, pursed her lips, and looked down at the floor, unable to meet Betsy's gaze, maybe finding, pooled on the floor beneath her feet, a vision of her own shame.

"Do you think I've now gone and killed my own child?"

Annie Mae remained silent at first. Then she slowly kneeled down beside the bed, her knees hard against the floor, and she reached for Betsy, embraced her, pulled her daughter toward her, and whispered the only answer a mother could give.

Twenty-One

The closing hymn was once again "O Worship the King." Melinda stood to sing with the hymnal open, but it was one she knew well enough without looking at the words, the voices of others carrying her past those moments where she might have faltered if forced to sing alone. Kate stood at her right, then William, who shared a hymnal with his sister. Beyond them were Henry, then Philip, a hymnal open in Henry's hands but clearly not to the proper page. His lips moved but she knew no sound emerged from them. Philip, though, looked up at his brother as if Henry were speaking a language only they knew.

Bunyan stood close to Melinda's left, their elbows touching, singing in a subdued voice that carried more of the melody than the words and the meaning. Perhaps it was Richard's presence beside her that made her hold back, knowing probably what she would never admit to him, that her voice was the better and stronger of the two. He had begun to call on her again weeks earlier, but Melinda had sensed things between them were not what they had once been. Maybe his mother had again conveyed to Richard her disapproval of his choice. Whatever the case, Melinda sensed some problem that was bound to reveal itself. She caught Richard's blue eyes in a glance, and he looked away in embarrassment, or maybe it was guilt, back to the verse that rang through the church and was echoed back down by the deeper voices in the balcony where Annie Mae sat with George.

After Reverend Lamar's benediction, the congregation slowly filed out the door to the right, the one not used by those in the balcony, and the reverend stood there shaking hands and speaking words of departure. When he took Melinda's hand, he said, in a confiding voice, "I hope you found the final hymn a blessing."

"I know it well," she said.

He nodded. "How is your husband?"

"Away on business."

"He's always welcome," he said, and his voice seemed to lack any tone of chastisement or mocking. The words he spoke were meant more for her than Rafe, she knew, and she took them as the offering she felt he intended.

Once in the churchyard she watched Bunyan and Richard walk away from her, out into the bright noon sun and into the shade of an oak whose limbs grew twisted and reached over the tin roof of the simple white structure. They faced one another in deep conversation, and Melinda waited for her other children to emerge for the familiar walk home that felt as much a part of the Sunday ritual as the responsive reading or the saying of the Lord's Prayer. Kate and William she soon found standing behind her; Henry and Philip then came through the opposite door, with Annie Mae and George, her sons' two small white figures among the darker bodies, the contrast tempered somehow in the line of former slaves by Annie Mae's copper, heightened by the sun's rays, and by George's lighter skin, all brought into relief under the hard light radiating down upon them.

Single men mounted horses, and families climbed into buggies and wagons. Melinda saw Alfred walking alone toward a buggy where his wife already sat, her hair pulled tightly back from her face, intently watching Bunyan and her son, who had his back to her. She hadn't acknowledged Melinda before or after the service, and she did not now, though Melinda sensed the boy's mother knew exactly where she stood. Then Alfred was in the buggy, taking up the reins, and their younger children crowded in. A brown gelding was tied to a back wheel. Alfred waited, holding the reins still, and when his wife Olive spoke to him he appeared to speak sharply in return, though his voice did not carry. Melinda saw Bunyan nod toward the buggy, and Richard finally turned, clearly troubled, and walked away from her and toward his family.

Annie Mae stood near her, and Melinda could see that she had watched the small drama play out also, not that it could mean a great deal to her considering all that she had lived through of late. Annie Mae had spent only one night away from her cabin and George. When she'd returned, Melinda hadn't asked if she'd seen Elizabeth, and Annie Mae had not volunteered a word about her daughter. Because of the briefness of her time away, Melinda was certain she must have found her, done for her daughter all she could and known it would never be enough. The silence between them after her return was confirmation enough for what Melinda hoped for Annie Mae. Yet she could hope nothing good for Elizabeth and wondered, not for the first time, if somehow the curse she'd placed on the girl, the curse she didn't believe in but had still felt some power from, had worked in a way Melinda could never have imagined.

Melinda began walking now, sure her children would slowly follow, as in any ritual, and both William and Kate came up alongside her. "When do you think Papa will get home?" Kate said. She knew better than to ask where he'd gone, knew Melinda could not usually answer such a question, though this time Melinda had an idea, one she wouldn't share.

"I don't know. Soon probably," she said. "It's been a week."

They walked quietly a few moments. Then William spoke. "Before Father left," he began, hesitantly, and Melinda thought maybe William had some knowledge of his father he'd been withholding and was about to offer up, but such was not the case. What came instead was part confession and partly an unmistakable measure of pride. "Before he left I saddled and rode Wheeler," he said, like a pronouncement he'd been wanting to make. "Just down into the horse pasture."

"Exactly when in the world did you do that?" Kate asked, and Melinda heard clear admiration, and yet distrust too, in her daughter's voice.

"After we covered the grave and Father had gone inside. I just wanted to."

"Was anybody around?" Kate asked, as if such an undertaking needed a witness and couldn't be possible, or at least believable, without one.

"Only George. He wanted me to pull him up behind me, but I didn't."

"Did Wheeler give you any trouble?" Melinda asked, suddenly concerned as if it were happening at this moment, her child riding the large beast, whose body rippled with muscle in a way that always seemed both casual and powerful.

"At first, but not much. He knew my voice."

They were passing the store now, its windows dark under the porch roof, their last name in well-defined blocked letters on the sign above, a name Melinda had taken as her own without full knowledge of all that it would mean. And this George behind them, what would it mean for him, how much of the name could he really possess? Enough to one day ride Wheeler on his own, or Wheeler's offspring?

"Does your father know what you did?" she asked, her mind moving quickly across time, backward from George's future to the recent, just revealed past, the balance of the two making what one might call the fleeting present that forever had to be made sense of. "Did your father find out?" Again concern filled her mind like the darkness behind the store windows.

"I told him," William said. "In his gun room."

"What did he say?" Kate asked, more curious than concerned, it seemed.

"He just looked up at me at first, like he didn't hear me or hear me right. Then he said, 'Very good' and wanted to know if I rode him well and took care of him afterward. I told him I had." He paused for a moment, and they drew nearer to the Teclaw house. "I want to run him next time," he said. "A hard mile, maybe."

Melinda heard these words that didn't sound like her son, and did not speak, her concern gaining ground once again. Then she hoped that Henry didn't know about his brother ever being atop Wheeler. George had been a witness, though, and was bound to tell in the way that all boys naturally would, boyhood being its own kind of brotherhood that was a bulkhead against all those who were older and wanted to hold sway over them, something Henry would fight, always.

Richard called that afternoon, arriving in his family's buggy. He spoke politely enough to Melinda in the parlor, but she heard a heaviness in his voice, which Bunyan seemed to hear also. There was no lightness in her movements in relation to his. But they left for a ride, as they'd done many times before and after their time apart, and Melinda hoped some time alone would restore them past any problem they were having and take them to a place where they could find their right selves again and each be what the other needed.

Well before dark, William sat in the parlor with her, and when they heard boot steps on the front porch, William said, "It's Father."

Rafe entered the house and then the parlor. Melinda looked up but remained seated. "William," he said. "Wheeler's out front. Go and take care of him for me."

"Yes, sir," he said and rose, his father making room for him to pass, no touch and no other greeting between them, and yet there was something held within their brief exchange, an animal's value acknowledged between them, a shared responsibility that maybe connected fathers and sons more deeply than words or touch.

They were alone then, she and Rafe, and he sat down beside her, close but also not touching, and she wondered what might fill that space. Maybe it depended on how much he would tell her. "I know you haven't been with her," she said. "So is it Samuel you were after? Or have you been with the other one?" She faced him, waited, and wondered which question gave him the most pause, the most surprise, and which one he might ignore.

He placed his right hand against his leg, moving it upward as if he were feeling for the holstered pistol he had already removed and put away in his gun room. "I decided I had to go after him, had to try."

"To kill him?" she said.

"If it came to that."

Why? she'd wanted to ask when it might not have been Samuel's doing, but after all their history of loss and living, suspicion and retaliation, their drawing apart yet still fitting together in the worn shape of their bed's ticking where children were conceived and born to live or to die, she understood him enough not to ask why.

"If I'd found him, I would have listened to what he could tell me, about what happened with," a pause, then, "George's mother," he said, "in that shack they were staying in. Could maybe better understand what was done to the child, by whose hand."

"Your child," she said. "Her name was Lakeview."

"Yes, my child. Samuel could have done it, would have had reason enough. It was his father who was behind the uprising."

She remembered March's death and the night his wife came to them with the warning; she remembered Rebecca's grief, the depth of it, and the grief for March that Rafe would not show, that might have poured out of him with each shot he'd fired that next day. "Where did you look for him?" she asked.

"I spent several days in Demarville," he said and did not seem to want to elaborate further.

"Why there? He could have headed off in any direction."

"Would have been easier to do from town. Could have got work on a riverboat, or gotten a train, headed to Meridian. That's where I ended up looking. Spent days there too."

"Why so long in Demarville?" She suspected the answer and, wanting to see if he would name it, decided to push. "If he went there, he couldn't have wanted to stay long."

"I wanted to be sure."

She took the fingers of each hand and entwined them, then tightened her fingers until she could feel the hurt in the bones there. It was as if she were trying to squeeze something out of herself. "I know you have others," she said.

"Other what?" He looked at her, did not turn away.

"Other children. Were you afraid for them, afraid he might go after one, do there what he might have done here?"

He nodded. "It crossed my mind."

"You were afraid for them. Didn't know how far he would go."

"Yes," he said, "I won't say different."

"You found him, didn't you? Killed him and walked away."

"No," he said, and his answer was quiet enough, simple enough, that she believed him, though she would never be sure. Maybe belief without some tiny portion of doubt at its edge was not really belief but blindness to the nature of truth and its vagaries.

"What are the names of these other children?" she said, surprising herself, and him, with the question.

He stared at her, shaking his head with his own portion of disbelief at her asking such a question, and he did not answer.

"If you had killed Samuel," she said finally, "you might have killed him for no good reason. Don't you think..." She found she could not say the name Elizabeth aloud. "Don't you think it had to be Annie Mae's daughter?"

"The very worst of what you can imagine about somebody is what's usually the most true. I know how others see me. They aren't wrong. And when I put out of my mind what certain people think of her, including you, of course, I can only see her with my own eyes, and my vision may be colored by too much of who I am. I want to think everyone's like me, capable of all that I know I'm capable of."

"But you would not kill a child."

"No, but maybe I've come close enough to it, in the war, to know others can. And I've buried the bodies."

"You would never kill your own child."

"No. I wouldn't." He paused now, looking at her again, and she felt as if he were seeing her not with the narrow vision that came out of his own darkness but maybe saw her illuminated by all she had suffered and lost. "You're bold enough to ask me the names of my other children," he said. "So tell me the names of our own that you've kept from me. Then maybe I'll answer you."

She did not look away from him, but she did not answer, and she knew her stillness and silence told him she never would, that after so much loss she had to keep something for herself. She also understood he would not ask her again, and that maybe he even respected her stubbornness.

The day was beginning to warm, the sun still at an angle less than noon, its brightness squinting the eyes, and as she approached the steps up to the store, two Black men came down off the porch into the open, with what looked like sun grins spreading across their faces. They each managed to nod and speak, and she nodded politely in return.

Usually when items from the store were needed, she sent Annie Mae for them, or Annie Mae saw on her own what was needed and went without being told, or asked. This time was different. Melinda had come for cloth and wanted to choose the color herself. Kate's birthday was approaching, and Melinda wanted to make her a new dress, something she hadn't done in some time, nor for Bunyan, either, who was in need of a new dress of her own. Maybe something pretty would lift her spirits. It was Melinda's mother who'd taught her to sew, and the learning of it had been difficult at her mother's hands, and finally incomplete with her mother's early death. So the pleasure in the act of making was lessened by memory, though a level of defiant pride always rose within her because she had finished the learning on her own.

Upon entering the store she saw Alfred behind the counter. He nodded at her politely, but she saw how unexpected her entrance was. Then a man turned toward her. It was Brantley, whom she had not seen in some time. "Morning, ma'am," he said. "A pleasure to see you."

"And you," she said, though she had never been comfortable around him. It wasn't as if he had ever been anything less than respectful toward her. Perhaps he and Rafe were too much alike, the one difference being that Brantley seemed less predictable and somehow more dangerous, or frightening, because of it. With Rafe she knew what to expect, and so her guess that Rafe had other children in town had not been vain, or new, speculation on her part, the confirmation one more wound, but it was as if the wound had already existed, and the pain she felt was simply a reminder of it.

Richard, whom she'd recognized from behind, turned to her now. "Morning, Mrs. Anderson," he said, and she sensed a hesitancy in him again, something that approached trepidation, which disappointed her in a way she couldn't explain and was all the more bothered by it because she couldn't. She had not seen him the evening before when he returned with Bunyan from their buggy ride. Bunyan hadn't seemed herself, and Melinda had begun to lose hope for the two of them.

"Good to see you again so soon," she said. And then, to Alfred, "I've come to look at cloth." With that, she stepped behind the counter where the bolts were kept on rollers against the wall. Usually customers weren't allowed behind the counter. Women simply had to point to the material they wanted, could not touch it, feel the weave, rough or smooth, between their fingers, were denied that tactile knowledge. But she moved with what she knew was a proprietary air, and it was not false but surely hard earned through the marriage she'd made to the man she had first met within these walls. Or perhaps he had still been a boy then, though at the time he had felt to her beyond boyhood, so much further into becoming who he was, or would become, or already was, that she could not comprehend it completely then, but would be forced to contend with him in ways unimaginable to her, as maybe he'd had to contend with himself and how others saw him, or wanted to see him.

She chose a cobalt blue, soft to the touch, but thick enough to be durable. Alfred cut it from the roll while Brantley and Richard looked on, waiting, she knew, for her to be gone so they could pick up with whatever conversation they had halted when she walked in. Sometimes it seemed to her, though, that the speech of men was so foreign that to understand it or care about it took more effort than she, or any other woman, really wanted to expend. It wasn't that she didn't have the ability to understand it, there just seemed no point in listening to something that ultimately was meaningless. The small mysteries of men weren't worth being solved when such larger mysteries of life and death existed, mysteries that were a woman's purview.

A Black woman from the other side of the store approached the counter. Melinda had noticed her already and now saw not only the washboard she meant to purchase but also the light-skinned children who followed her. They were both younger than ten and looked so much alike they clearly had the same father, and she wondered whose sons they were and, for a moment even, if they could be Rafe's.

The woman held back and would not ask to be waited on before a white woman. Melinda nodded to her. "Alfred, go ahead and tend to her. I'm in no hurry."

"Yes, ma'am," he said.

"Thank you," the woman said quietly while Alfred began to write down the charge. And then she turned to Melinda, meeting her eyes just for a moment before nodding downward. "And thank you, miss," she said. She finally moved toward the door, pulling one of her boys away from the candy counter.

Once the door closed behind the second child, Melinda asked, "Who is she? I don't remember seeing her before."

Both Alfred and Brantley looked at her with mild surprise, as if they understood the deeper question she was actually asking. "Lives down on McConnico Creek," Alfred said, then added, casually, "started showing up here about a year ago, I think, maybe more."

Brantley nodded agreement in an absent-minded manner, as though establishing the fact that the father of the two children could not be local was so automatic as to be second nature; or perhaps it was a collusion practiced so many times among men that it was done without conscious effort. Perhaps the two boys belonged to either Brantley or Alfred, even. Maybe Alfred had charged the washboard to himself while his son Richard looked on.

Alfred then handed her the blue cloth wrapped in brown paper and tied neatly in twine, a package now proffered so she could take her leave, the small, concealing efforts of politeness among them all at their end.

She worked on the dress in the parlor off and on for several days, Philip sometimes coming in to watch her with more interest than she would have expected, and more than Rafe would have wanted to see a son of his showing over such a feminine pursuit. But Rafe was out each day, whether at his store, in Demarville, or up at the Lassiter Place she didn't know. He returned home in the evenings but did not discuss his day's business.

Each night they slept together in their bed, though he didn't reach for her or make any demand. In time, he would, doubtless, wake her with his need.

After more than a week passed, she was indeed awakened, but not by Rafe, who continued sleeping beside her. It was Kate who stood over her in the dark. She first recognized her daughter's touch, gentle but forceful enough to call someone from sleep, and Kate's hand rested still against Melinda's shoulder, the continued touch maybe an apology for the wakening. Then Kate's voice confirmed for certain which child this was.

"Mama," she said, and already Melinda heard the concern, even the urgency, in her voice. "Bunny, she's sick."

Somehow the use of the old child's name for her sister was more worrisome than the word *sick*, as if by using the simple name Kate had spoken as a child could carry Bunyan back to a time when whatever was wrong now couldn't be happening. "What is it?" Melinda said and pulled the covers off herself carefully enough not to wake her husband.

"Just come," Kate said. "Quick. It's awful." She kept her voice lower than Melinda's and clearly felt the same desire as her mother not to wake the man who also occupied the room, as if his presence mattered to them only if he were awake and had to be contended with as all men demand during their every waking moment without being aware of their demand.

Kate led the way out of the bedroom and into the dogtrot, Melinda quietly closing the doors behind them. She followed her daughter up the stairs, and once they reached the top each crept soundlessly so as not to disturb the three sleeping boys on their side of the loft.

She saw that Kate had obviously lit the lamp between her and Bunyan's beds before she'd come downstairs, allowing Kate to see whatever it was she'd named as awful. The light burned low now, and Melinda could see that Bunyan lay flat on her back, her head against the pillow, her eyes open as she looked upward at the low, angled roof.

"She's covered herself again," Kate said. "She's going to have to show you. Bunny, are you still hurting?"

Melinda moved toward her quickly. "What's wrong? Tell me," she said, though her mother's instinct, and her own experience, was already moving her toward some suspicion of an answer, especially when she thought about how troubled Bunyan had seemed of late and how Richard had been acting.

Bunyan shook her head, not out of defiance, it seemed, but simply at a loss for what she might say.

"You're going to have to uncover her yourself, Mama. I did when she was twisted up with hurt."

Melinda reached for the top edge of the covers and began to pull at them, but her daughter held them tight. "Bunyan, let go," she said. "It's all right. I think I know. You have to let me, sweetheart. I'm your mama. It's all right."

Bunyan turned her head away, the light of the burning coal oil shining across the side of a face wet with sweat and tears, the edges of her hair darkened, absorbing what seeped out of her. Melinda tugged again at the quilt and the linens beneath it, and Bunyan finally relinquished her hold, allowed her mother to reveal her, her blood-soaked gown, and the stained white sheet under her curved woman's body. Melinda pushed the covers down toward the foot of the bed, and Kate was there and received them, pulling them over her sister's small, bare feet.

For a moment Melinda stopped, took a breath, and gathered herself. "Run get Annie Mae," she said. At no point had either of them spoken above a whisper. "I don't know what exactly she'll need. Just tell her to bring with her everything she takes on her calls."

Kate nodded, turned, and was gone, and if her steps down the stairs made any sound at all they were a vibration only a nocturnal animal attuned to the darkness might hear through an aptitude bred into it as far back maybe as the time its species began. The quiet would have to hold them all this night, and Annie Mae would understand that, she knew. What women had to do for each other in the middle of darkness was a world unto itself that sleeping men and boys could not fathom and did not need to.

Melinda placed a hand across Bunyan's forehead, gently rubbing the wetness into her daughter's hair. "Are you still hurting?"

"No," she said but kept her face turned away.

Melinda didn't speak for a moment, waiting for her daughter to truly feel her presence and to know they were alone. "You don't have to be ashamed. Not with me."

Bunyan looked at her now, and Melinda moved her hand away. "But if..."

"The only ones who'll know will be me, your sister, and Annie Mae." She saw that Bunyan was about to speak again, whether to protest or to question Melinda wasn't sure, but she knew how to answer. "You tell the boy you were wrong, that there was no child after all."

Bunyan closed, then opened her eyes, the lamp's reflection welling more deeply in them. "Why, Mama?"

"Why what?"

"Why don't I have to be ashamed with you?"

"Hold my hand," she said, and Bunyan reached for her, found her hand without looking, their ability to touch far from lost. Melinda could feel her daughter's warmth and the strength still in her fingers. "If you don't know yet, you will. A time will come, and you'll understand. What's happened is not uncommon. Babies get lost even before they are born."

Bunyan's look of puzzlement either turned to knowledge or simply abated from the preoccupation of her own shame, and the two of them remained quiet for some time and didn't try to force words that were not needed.

Finally, Kate slipped into the room again, and, just as quietly, Annie Mae came behind her. What Annie Mae saw did not seem to surprise her. Maybe Kate had already told her or her years of attending women in their beds had left her prepared for anything she might find once she entered their rooms and sat beside their half-naked swollen, or emptied, bodies.

She carried her worn leather bag and approached the same side of the bed where Melinda sat. "Let me see to her," she said.

Melinda leaned over and kissed her daughter's forehead, then stood, waiting for Annie Mae to take her place, but Annie Mae remained standing, seemed to be waiting herself. Then Melinda felt she understood. "You want Kate to step out?"

Annie Mae didn't speak, waiting still. Then Melinda fully understood.

"You want us both to leave."

Annie Mae nodded. "You know I'll take care of your child. That why you sent Kate to come get me. Let me see to her." Annie Mae paused again, and Melinda met her eyes, her own shadow cast against them by the light from the coal-oil lamp, an oddity somehow that the dark of a shadow could not exist without light. "Like she my own daughter," Annie Mae said. "That how I'll treat her."

Melinda stood still and looked down at her daughter again, then back at Annie Mae. "All right," she said. It was not a difficult decision to ponder. "We'll be in the kitchen." She patted Bunyan's hand, and she saw relief in her daughter's features that she hadn't expected but understood. During her last birth, she hadn't let Bunyan in the room. Now she was leaving her daughter alone with Annie Mae, and she would be the one who had to wait.

Kate followed her out the door and down the steps, both as quiet as before. They eased across the dogtrot, through the door opposite the stairs, and past the dining table and into the kitchen, still without speaking. Melinda lit the lamp on the table, and they sat close to each other.

"If your father or one of the boys comes in, we'll tell them we couldn't sleep," Melinda said, "that I found you in here."

"We don't have to worry too much about that. They sleep sound, especially Henry. William can hardly get him awake in the morning." Kate paused and faced the lamp, and Melinda saw the worry in her show itself again. "Is it what I think, Mama, with Bunyan?"

Melinda nodded. "Yes. It's what you think."

"So she's a full-grown woman now? Will she be all right?"

The way Melinda heard the last question made her want to attempt two answers, but she didn't think Kate realized how large the questions she'd asked really were. "Annie Mae will make sure she's all right. You don't need to keep worrying. It wasn't as much blood as it might have looked like at first. And, yes, in a lot of ways, she is a woman now."

Melinda wondered if Kate could see or sense the worry in her, and not just the immediate worry she wouldn't admit to, but at the contemplation of what womanhood would hold for Bunyan. Was her entering into it with loss a harbinger of more and more ill to come, greater even than Melinda's own, or was loss the only passage in for any woman?

Melinda took Kate's hand now, holding it between her own hands. "You don't have to be fearful. I mean for yourself. You're still growing up. You don't have to hasten it. And what happened to Bunyan, it doesn't always happen. Just sometimes, and I don't mean only what happened tonight. I mean what made tonight happen. You have plenty of time. And there are good men in this world. Not that Richard isn't good. He's just young."

She could see Kate's contemplation of what she was hearing and imagined that her daughter was trying to picture her own life, all that was to come, but such was not the case. "Papa's not a very good man, is he?" she said.

Melinda knew the simple answer, which she could not give to her daughter, but how true could any simple answer ever be? What was true was always at least as complicated as any lie. "In some ways I think you're closer to him than any of us," she said. "He's always seemed to care what you think. So what do you think of him?"

Kate slowly pulled her hand away from Melinda's, as if answering such a question for herself meant she had to be herself only, not connected to any other but drawn inward. "I'm not sure," she said. "He's never been not good to me. He's never hurt me, not exactly." She seemed to move deeper into herself, but what came from her now suggested otherwise. "He's hurt you. I know that."

She would not deny it. To do so would be an absurdity that a daughter Kate's age could not tolerate, even if she remained silent. "Yes, he has." It was a simple response, and all she could give.

"Do you forgive him?" Kate asked in almost as quiet a voice as she'd used earlier so as not to wake anyone.

She knew how to answer this, just as she was afraid Kate and Bunyan both would one day learn how to answer, though she hoped not. "I live with it."

Kate remained still a moment, then leaned forward, as if she were about to speak but didn't, as if she realized she shouldn't, and Melinda was grateful to her daughter in a way she probably never had been.

The lamp dimmed, seemingly of its own accord, and then brightened and remained steady. During their long silence a thought came to Melinda. She wondered if Bunyan had begun to think of names for what she'd carried. Idle wondering, maybe, but important too, somehow.

Kate heard her first. "She's coming. Annie Mae."

They both turned toward the doorway, expectant. When Annie Mae entered, Melinda saw in her burnished face what she needed to see, and every contracted muscle within her relaxed, let go of the worry that had grown larger inside her than she'd realized.

"She all right," Annie Mae said, speaking just above a whisper, as if the time of night and the task she'd just completed dictated quietness even in the safe confines of the kitchen that was her world of work and, until recently, sleep. "The bleeding had done already about stopped. I got her cleaned up and changed. The bed too."

Kate rose, went to where Annie Mae stood, put her arms around Annie Mae, and said something in her ear that Melinda could not make out but understood nonetheless.

Melinda pushed herself up from the table, turned the lamp down, then blew it out. They remained still in darkness and waited while their eyes gathered what little light came through the windows, the moon large enough and low enough to provide what they needed.

Annie Mae led them through the house and out into the dogtrot. At the foot of the stairs she stopped Kate a moment. "You go on up. Your mama be right on."

Kate nodded and turned, her steps quick but light on the stairs.

Annie Mae drew close to Melinda. "I made sure. Got her cleaned out good. Was a little more along than what I thought."

It took Melinda a moment to understand. "You knew?"

"Suspected. That all."

"Why didn't I see it?"

"Not far enough along to spot easy. And you wasn't looking. Besides, our daughters ain't gon' show us everything. That what make them hard.

Think 'cause we they mamas we gon' know everything already. But we don't. Just do the best we can for them, no matter what."

Annie Mae was silent then but didn't move away from her. Melinda smelled the scent of something warm and rich in the air that she could not name and didn't try to speak because there was no question she had to answer, not for herself or for Annie Mae. They knew where they stood in relation to one another, in the middle of a familiar dogtrot with the moon's light at both ends.

Supper the night before with Charles and his wife was more pleasant than Seth had imagined it would be. Sandra had returned home from shopping and both Charles and Seth had helped bring groceries in from the car. Somehow such a mundane chore, Seth decided, had helped pull them out of the past and into the now. And perhaps when Sandra first walked into the living room, she'd felt the tension and knew what was needed. "If y'all want to eat," she said, "you best be gentlemen and carry in the groceries."

He and Charles ended up sitting at the kitchen table while Sandra began cooking. Charles had insisted on pouring them shots of local moonshine, and while Seth wasn't a whiskey drinker, the clear liquor was smoother than he might have imagined, and it warmed him inside to a point where Charles looked at him and smiled. "Looks like the moon is shining inside you." He laughed. "Me too."

Now it is the middle of the next morning, and he and Charles sit outside on the back porch. The air is crisp but not too cool, and the green of longleaf pines in the distance stands in bright relief against the blue sky.

"You said you never saw the inside of the old dogtrot house," Charles says. It is the first time either of them has brought up the past this morning, and Seth wonders where the conversation will lead them.

"No," Seth says. "And it was torn down when I was a senior in college. The people who'd bought the property a few years before leveled it and put up the brick house that's there now."

"Did you ever walk down into the pasture behind it?"

"No."

"Then you've never seen Lakeview's grave."

"No, I haven't. When did she die?"

"In 1884," he says. "According to the dates on the marker, she didn't even live a full year."

"How'd she die?"

"We're not sure," Charles says, but there is something in his voice that tells Seth that Charles has at least some idea of an answer he may be holding back, and that Charles intends for him to realize this. "She's buried next to the unnamed children," he says. "They don't have markers. Rafe wouldn't allow it. You can guess why."

"Because Melinda wouldn't tell him their names." Charles nods. "I wonder," Seth says, "why he didn't just go ahead and name them himself. I guess it was a battle of wills, and that's how he won it."

Charles now looks as if he's about to say something else, perhaps about Rafe or maybe to tell what more he knows about Lakeview. Then his body language quietens and he remains still, whether in contemplation of this moment in time between them—two men related by blood and name but whose skin tones differ as sharply as evergreen against solid blue—or in contemplation of a past and the mysteries of it that led the two of them to be joined here, Seth cannot say. Maybe there is no difference. Charles might simply be a grown-up George, his mind not full of facts and dates and family stories brought back to life through imagination but a mind full of memory shaped and reshaped by time and the bending of time. And while Seth has never seen a photograph of his great-great grandfather, and so can't know, maybe his own features, the build of his body, are a perfect reflection as seen against the clouded, silvered glass of time, and Seth is not here in search of a forbearer and his history, but he is that history and that man he cannot describe and yet can recognize within himself and recall, not imagine, climbing out of a dark well, born into who he is and was. Who can say how he comes to be who he is? Does everyone, man or woman, imagine themselves into being or recall themselves into being?

These are the thoughts Seth lets run through his mind, and he knows if he could articulate them aloud that Charles would not look at him strangely, or dismissively, but might state them more ably than Seth on this blue morning.

"There's something I should tell you," Charles says finally. "I suppose you could say I committed a lie of omission yesterday, and I'd like to correct that."

"What?" Seth asks, curious and made slightly tense with anticipation.

"I knew." Charles pauses, maybe for dramatic effect. "About the uprising, and Rafe's part in it."

Seth is surprised at first, then, after a moment, feels foolish for not realizing this was bound to be the case. "Why didn't you say anything?"

Charles looks out at the pines, studying them, it seems. "Not sure. Maybe I wanted to hear how you would tell it, see if you knew something I didn't."

"Did I?"

"Not really. And I didn't have much I could add. I knew that all the Black men were shot down."

Seth measures what Charles has just said, realizing how it is no more than what he told Charles yesterday, and he begins to wonder if Charles is telling him the truth, if he really did know about the uprising or if he can't admit he didn't and is only repeating what Seth told him. Maybe he spent a mostly sleepless night trying to absorb what he'd just learned about his grandfather's white father, about the two halves of who he is.

"Only thing I can add," Charles says, "is that the whites burned some houses afterward, sent the women and children off. If you think about it, how could I not have known of the uprising? It surprises me you'd think the story didn't live on among Black people. It's whites who would have kept quiet about it, wanted it to disappear, not Black people."

Seth realizes Charles is right. "How does it make you feel about Rafe?" he asks. "Or how did it make you feel when you first knew?"

Charles looks out again at what might be old-growth pines that are so much larger than others nearby. "My grandfather George didn't hate his father, didn't pass any hatred down. And the Black men who gathered did mean to do harm, maybe had their reasons. You know good and well they had to have had violence done to them. There's one thing I didn't know, that it was March Whitney and his wife who gave the warning. If I ever did know it may be I was told so young it didn't stay with me. I'm not sure how I feel about it, a Black man and his wife giving out the word that led to such slaughter of their own people." Charles pauses and nods his head slightly forward, as if in contemplation and confirmation of some deeper, disturbing thought. "They were my people too, all those Black men. I can't let myself forget that."

"No, I'm sure you can't."

"But if a warning hadn't come, there might have been a different slaughter. Maybe the blood of my own family spilled. Still, I can't reconcile what March did."

"It is something he died for."

"Yes," Charles says. "Can you imagine?"

"Not as well as you. I am sorry, though, that March was put in that position. Sorry for the suffering that took place. Sorry, too, that March was owned, or had been. Maybe once a man is owned, he's never free, not really."

Charles slowly shakes his head, less in answer to Seth, it seems, than in answer to his own doubt. "Sometimes I feel like I lose the connection, maybe because I want to, don't want to think of the horrors that took place. Maybe I want to think these are all just stories that may not be even half true, and I know I probably want to romanticize some of them. I want to think of Rafe and Betsy as having had a great love, and maybe they did. But I know it didn't last." Charles pauses again and bites his lower lip for a moment. "Not if what I've been told really happened."

Seth waits in the silence Charles now lets settle between them. He knows Charles wants him to ask, but Seth remains quiet.

Finally, Charles begins. "There was a young Black man named Samuel. He worked for Rafe and went after Betsy's affections. Something happened. We don't know what. My grandfather was either too young to understand, couldn't remember, or would just never say. Maybe Rafe caught them together, or saw them together enough that he imagined Samuel had been in their bed. Whatever the case was, Rafe's jealousy turned ugly."

Charles stops, and this time it doesn't feel as if it's for any dramatic effect but true hesitancy on Charles's part to have to tell the rest.

"What happened?" Seth asks, not out of morbid curiosity but something more generous, he hopes.

"Rafe ran Samuel off. Told him he'd kill him if he didn't leave."

"I think I'm surprised he didn't go ahead and kill him anyway," Seth says.

"I don't think he did. But that wasn't the end of it." Charles looks down at the cement patio, then back up toward the treetops and blue sky, as if he's trying to orient himself between two distant points, and then looks at Seth. "He went after Betsy with a knife, cut her hair off with it, two long braids, which is how she sometimes wore it, kept the two of them pinned up. She thought he might kill her. But what he did to her was painful enough, scarred her so much she never wore it long again."

"What happened after that?" Seth asks.

"He threw her out. Annie Mae lived in the cabin, took care of George. But Betsy stayed close, never left her child. She may have felt like her mother had abandoned her when she was small. She wasn't going to do that to her child. Though that's really just speculation on my part."

Seth takes all this in and considers the lives he's hearing about. Annie Mae and Betsy are not, were not, his blood kin, but George was, just as Charles is. He can imagine these people who are now gone, but they don't live in his blood and memory the way his own side of the family does. Their existence, though, their hardships, cannot be denied, and he tries to imagine them, wants to bring them more fully to life than ever before, those lives shaped so strongly, violently, by a man whose blood and name are Seth's own.

"Why didn't the three of them just leave?" Seth asks.

"And go where? Besides, Rafe wasn't going to lose another child. Remember, he did *claim* George. He wasn't going to let them take his son from him. Least I don't think he would have."

Charles's words seem explanation enough. But Seth can see from the way he now leans forward that Charles has more he wants to say, as if some final summation is needed. "Doesn't the fact that Betsy stayed as near her child as possible tell you something? That she loved her children, wasn't what you want to imagine she was. Wasn't capable of hurting a child. She was just a young woman trying to live as best she could."

Seth wants to see her this way, but if he does, how must he see, or imagine, or even recall out of his own blood memory his great-great grandmother and the death of those unnamed children? Maybe there's no way to judge our private history, he thinks, if we can't completely know it. And another's private history, once shared, is still shaped out of their experience and need. Memories passed along become stories, yet even if they become part, or mostly, fiction, or enlarge into myth full of the fantastic, we still need them, he knows, need to believe them or we become lost to who we are, if we care at all to think back to a time before our own narrow existence.

In this moment, even after all the talk of two days, Seth understands what Charles means about losing the connection. It feels as if the struggle to know and understand and reconcile their shared history, the complexity of it, the unknowable parts of it, has only distanced them from that history.

They both sit in the quiet, within their own separate thoughts. "I have them," Charles says now, and Seth, perhaps too caught up in his own thoughts, doesn't know what Charles is referring to.

"What?" he asks.

"Wait here," Charles says. "I won't be long."

The sun is higher now, warmer. Crows sound in the distance. Seth tries to imagine the longleaf pines that once covered this land in a forest that reached clear into Georgia, the kind of woods where Annie Mae worked collecting sap for turpentine as a young woman with a child who did not look like her and who could pass, and did pass, into a different life from the one Annie Mae had known.

Seth hears the back door open again and hears Charles approaching from behind. Then Charles stands before him. His cousin is holding two long braids of dark brown hair, both secured at each end. He doesn't speak but simply holds one of them out to Seth, watching him.

The braid is tightly bound, and it shines like life, which is disquieting in a way Seth doesn't fully understand. A part of him does not want to touch it, but he reaches out slowly, strokes it gingerly, so smooth to his touch. He slips his fingers around the braid, then has to grip it suddenly, feeling it may slide away from his grasp. He takes a breath and glances up at Charles, whose eyes show little, only a kind of curiosity, maybe even amusement. Seth holds the thicker end that may have been weaved and held fast by Annie Mae after it was rent from Betsy's head. He imagines Annie Mae doing this for her daughter, needing to preserve some beautiful, perfect and wounded part of her life. He understands as he holds it how brutally this braid, and then the other, must have been torn loose in the moment by the man of his own blood—holding the struggling woman down, cursing her as he worked the knife between Betsy's hair and scalp, driven by rage and his own righteousness.

Seth feels the weight in his hand, the dead weight of shame—for dead children, for murdered Black men who wanted freedom more than just in name, for a woman who loved and suffered the death of her child, then lost the last vestige of her native pride, her long, glossy dark hair, a woman who had no real place in the world. It is all in his hand, every sin, not to be studied or written about but to be absorbed into who he is, and he sees a dark space opening around him, as if he has at last entered that log house, is walking its rooms where children, and guns, and death abide. It holds him fast, even as he peers out its windows at some future he will navigate his way through only if he confronts the past in the way that his cousin Charles always has, and always *had* to, because maybe that's what it means to be a man, or woman, or child, of color, tracing your way back into and out of every sin committed against you and against every member of your family, sometimes even by your own kin.

Seth looks up again at Charles, who meets his eyes, takes the smaller end of the braid into his opened palm, and closes his fingers around it. For a moment neither of them lets go, and neither attempts to pull away from the other.

ACKNOWLEDGMENTS

I offer my great thanks to Jaynie Royal and Regal House for believing in this novel and seeing it published with such great care. I'm forever grateful to Susan Starr Richards, a fine writer who put much thoughtful and tireless energy into reading the manuscript and who made such invaluable and countless suggestions about how to make it a stronger work. Her husband Dick was also helpful with his own suggestions. Their contribution can't be overestimated. The support and encouragement of the late writer Charles F. Price and his wife Ruth were much needed and appreciated more than I can say. The students and faculty in the Converse College Low-Residency MFA Program heard me read early drafts of many of these chapters. Their response and good will meant a great deal, and I'm especially grateful to Leslie Pietrzyk, Bob Olmstead, Richard Tillinghast, Susan Tekulve, and program director Rick Mulkey. Kirk Curnutt's friendship and support was also sustaining during the writing of this novel. And the response of Jeanie Thompson to the completed work was heartening in a way that can't be measured, as was Allen Wier's. I'm indebted to my cousin Blakely C. Barton for sharing so much family history with me and for his generous response to the manuscript. This was a difficult book to write for many reasons, and without my wife Rhonda's continuous support and unwavering faith, I don't know that I could have finished it. To say thank you to her just doesn't seem enough.

The following books were helpful, some more directly than others, in the writing of this novel: *Listen to Me Good: The Life Story of an Alabama Midwife* by Margaret Charles Smith and Linda Janet Holmes (Columbus: Ohio State University Press, 1996), *Where the Wild Animals Is Plentiful: Diary of an Alabama Fur Trader's Daughter, 1912-1914* by May Jordan, edited by Elisa Moore Baldwin (Tuscaloosa and London: University of Alabama Press, 1999), *They Say the Wind Is Red: The Alabama Choctaw—Lost in Their Own Land* by Jacqueline Anderson Matte (Montgomery: NewSouth Books, 2002), *The Rise and Fall of the Choctaw Republic* by Angie Debo (Norman: University of Oklahoma Press, 1934, 1961), *Source Material for the Social and Ceremonial Life of the Choctaw Indians* by John R.

Swanton (Tuscaloosa and London: University of Alabama Press, 2001), *Sex and Race* by A.J. Rogers (St. Petersburg: Helga M. Rogers, 1942, 1970), *Pickett's History of Alabama* by Albert James Pickett (Montgomery: River City Publishing, 2003), *The Life of Johnny Reb: The Common Soldier of the Confederacy* by Bell Irvin Wiley (Baton Rouge: Louisiana State University Press, 2008), *The Writer's Guide to Everyday Life in the 1800s* by Marc McCutcheon (Cincinnati: Writer's Digest Books, 1993), *The Expansion of Everyday Life, 1860-1876* by Daniel E. Sutherland (Fayetteville: University of Arkansas Press, 1989), *Coffin Point: The Strange Cases of Ed McTeer, Witchdoctor Sheriff* by Baynard Woods (Montgomery: River City Publishing, 2010), and *Southern Crossing: A History of the American South, 1877-1906* by Edward L. Ayers (New York and Oxford: Oxford University Press, 1998).

Grateful acknowledgment is given to *Carolina Mountains Literary Festival Anthology: A Celebration of Ten Festivals*, edited by Diana M. Donovan, for publishing the first chapter of this novel.